"Brandon's insider information makes for a realistic and chilling look at the 'system,' which sometimes works and sometimes doesn't . . . a finely plotted and written account."

—*Orlando Sentinel*

"In the tradition of Scott Turow's *Presumed Innocent*, a category that is full of pretenders to the throne, this one is a true prince."

—*San Jose Mercury News*

"A good look inside the workings of justice in San Antonio . . . Brandon's account is both accurate and interesting."

—*San Antonio Express News*

"A dramatic, well-written account of a bizarre crime. If you pick this book up and get very far into it, plan on neglecting some chores to finish it. It's that compelling."

—*Muncie Star*

"It is a novel which brings crime and legal maneuvering into your own living room. One you will enjoy deeply. One that will make you think far beyond the present to what legal brambles lie ahead of any ordinary modern family. Perhaps including your own."

—*The Macon Beacon*

(more . . .)

"The courtroom scenes are handled well and the reader is kept guessing. This one may make it to the big screen."

—*El Paso Times*

"I enjoyed this book . . . the whole thing proceeds with a good air of authenticity."

—*Greenwich Time*

"Fast-paced and authentic."

—*Pasadena Star-News*

"His characters are so human, so three-dimensional, that the reader knows and tastes real fear, real loathing, real love and real passion. The pacing of *FADE THE HEAT* is so intense it gives rise a new genre. This is not a courtroom drama, but a courtroom thriller."

—*Mostly Murder*

"One of the hottest reads of the year, and once you pick it up, prepare for a roller-coaster ride of exciting twists and turns that will keep you entranced until the very end."

—*Orange Coast Magazine*

Books by Jay Brandon

Deadbolt
Tripwire
Predator's Waltz
Fade the Heat*

*Published by POCKET BOOKS

FADE THE HEAT

JAY BRANDON

POCKET STAR BOOKS

New York   London   Toronto   Sydney   Tokyo   Singapore

A Pocket Star Book published by
POCKET BOOKS, a division of Simon & Schuster Inc.
1230 Avenue of the Americas, New York, NY 10020

Copyright © 1990 by Jay Brandon

ISBN: 0-671-70261-0

First Pocket Books paperback printing November 1991

10 9 8 7 6 5 4 3 2 1

POCKET STAR BOOKS and colophon are registered trademarks of Simon & Schuster Inc.

Printed in the U.S.A.

For Yolanda and Elena
my darlings

PART

I

Of relative justice law may know something;
of expediency it knows much; with absolute justice
it does not concern itself.

—Oliver Wendell Holmes, Sr.

CHAPTER

1

We deserve a celebration," I'd said with exquisitely poor timing.

We'd started out as a small group from the office, festive except for Linda. She was new to this side of a celebration, and didn't throw herself into the occasion. By the time drinks became dinner and more drinks, I had noticed her withdrawal. Gradually, the two of us began to pull away from the other five or six in our party. They went on toasting one another and reliving the moment of triumph while Linda and I at first exchanged wry looks, then began talking quietly at our end of the table.

"It's tradition," I told her. "It's for kids," she responded, and she was right.

"Well, they are kids." And not mine. Suddenly the years we'd spent together, Linda and I, seemed to surround us, to the exclusion of the kids. I reached for her hand, remembered where we were, and left my hand beside hers on the tabletop. She looked at the hands, at me, smiled a little. It was as festive as she'd gotten.

"You've never been very good at the celebrations," I said.

"No. I prefer the scheming ahead of time."

Remember . . . I almost said, but it seemed out of place. Suddenly I was ready to go. Then I realized we had left Linda's car behind, and her house was on the way to mine.

We didn't talk much in the car. It was a strange night for April in San Antonio. Last week the highs had been in the eighties. Tonight the wind was trying to blow the temperature down into the thirties. It made the interior of the car seem warm and isolated.

"Do they always take such delight in sending someone to prison for fifty years?" Linda asked.

I considered. No, prison didn't have much to do with it. "The number of years is just the way of keeping score. Prosecutors don't usually develop a grudge against the defendant himself. He doesn't much matter, in fact."

She shook her head. I wanted to change the subject and couldn't think of anything, so just fell silent. When we reached her house she didn't invite me in or say good-bye either; I just fell in step with her up the sidewalk. The wind blew us together, shoulders bumping. Inside we were out of the wind, but she hadn't left the heat on in the house that morning. It was cool and dark as a cave. "Cold," I said.

"Not so very." Linda turned on a lamp.

"You're colder than I am." I waved a hand at the evidence. Linda crossed her arms but didn't blush. Do brown people blush? Yes. I had seen her face flushed in the past. With anger, with breathlessness. From heat.

There was a clock ticking on the wall. I didn't look at it. "Should I make coffee?" she asked. Her tone was neutral as Switzerland.

"No." She had started to slip past me. I stopped her. She wasn't dressed for the cold either. Her blouse was thin and soft as a second skin. It slid smoothly beneath my hand.

"Mark," she began. It sounded like the announcement of an important decision, but she didn't continue. When I looked at her face to show I was listening I realized how close we were.

It was ever so short a bend to her mouth. We kissed tentatively. It could have been a brushing of lips for good-bye, could have ended in passion on the rug. Each of us seemed to be waiting for the other to take the lead. I pulled her closer. She put her arms around my neck. Her skin was still cool under the blouse, but wherever I touched it grew quickly warm.

"Linda." The air still seemed to lack decision. If she wouldn't make an announcement, I would. "Don't you think it's time I gave up the pretense?"

"Shh. Don't try to say something important so late at night."

"It's not late."

I jerked when the phone rang. It was right beside us on a stand by the door. I steeled myself to listen to it ring several more times, but Linda reached for it.

"Only a lawyer would answer the phone at a moment like this."

I was still holding her. "Hello?" she said, and almost at once turned away, putting a hand on my chest to free herself. "No—" She was interrupted. I waited impatiently while she did nothing but listen. "Just a moment," she finally said, and held the phone out. "It's Lois."

Why did you tell her I was here, I mouthed. Linda only pushed the phone toward me.

"Yes?" I said into it. "I'll be home in a minute, I was just—" Then like Linda I fell silent under Lois's rush of words.

"No, you stay there," I said a minute or two later. "Yes, Lois. You've got to stay with Dinah and he may try to call. I will. Don't worry."

I hung up. I stood stock still for a moment, thinking. When I looked at Linda again the room was bright with lights.

"David's been arrested."

"I know," Linda said. "She told me. Let me get a coat."

"No. I'll see you in the morning, Linda."

"Let me come, Mark. I can help."

"No." At that moment I wanted to be as far from her as possible. "It's okay, I can take care of it."

"Well—"

"It's okay," I said again, and hurried out into the cold.

My initial problem was who to owe my first favor. No, second; I'd owed one as soon as Lois had picked up the phone. A police detective had called, she'd said. Cops didn't extend that courtesy as a matter of course. It was one I owed him. Now I'd owe another. Favors are capital, not to be passed out lightly. In Texas lawyers can make bail bonds. Some criminal lawyers make more money getting people out of jail than they do defending them in court. But to do that you have to have property registered with the bail bond board to cover the bonds you make. Real estate is okay, certificates of deposit are favored. Register fifty thousand dollars in CDs and you can make a fifty-thousand-dollar bond. Charge your client ten percent of that amount for making the bond.

I didn't have any property registered with the bail bond board. I could call a defense lawyer who did and he could get David out with a signature. But then I'd owe a defense lawyer a favor.

I had the window cracked open as I drove and the wind cleared my head. The cold air was pleasant. Made you think summer wasn't looming so heavily. But it was. Heat was building behind this thin facade of cool April.

"Shit," I was saying under my breath. Shit, shit, shit. I wondered if Linda's was the first place Lois had called looking for me. Nobody would have been at the office this late to tell her a group of us had gone out. I'd called her from the restaurant. She must have tried there first. When they'd told her I was gone she must have thought I had never been there at all.

It wasn't being found out that worried me. It was that the night when Lois needed me, and David—how many times had either of them asked me for anything?—I wasn't home where I should have been. I was with Linda.

This wasn't like me, not anymore, late nights at the office. I'd been religious about not stealing time from my family. Shit. I pressed the accelerator harder and steadily pounded the seat beside me with my fist as I drove.

Settle down, settle down. There was plenty of time. I knew the routine. I'd done this a dozen times, more, been awakened or interrupted by a frantic call and rushed down to the jail to get someone out. It was curious how familiar the steps were, how easy it would have been to behave routinely. Then I'd be jolted anew by the thought it was David I was going to meet. Maybe I'd heard wrong, or Lois had. The detective had talked fast and said little, she'd said. Not even what David was charged with.

Linda would be gnawing her knuckles at home, feeling as guilty as I did. That was my fault too. At least I had something to keep me occupied. Linda would feel worse than Lois. It had been a long time since Lois had expected anything of me. In the future when I called to tell her I was working late she would say "Fine," disdaining explanation. If she were the kind to check up on me, it would be better; she would discover I was telling the truth. But Lois wouldn't check. All right, I just would never be home late again. But they would never need me again as they had tonight.

The detective had called Lois from the scene, but things must have speeded up after that. They beat me to the jail. I'd had to make a stop at the bondsmen's. But David wasn't in a cell. Thank God. I was in time.

Everyone still calls it the new jail, after two years. I remember taking a tour of it a few weeks before it opened. It was beautiful then, pristine and functional. The booking area looked like the bridge of the starship *Enterprise*, but bigger. It was a circular room with holding cells all around the outside edge. In the center was a smaller circle with administrative personnel inside. Desks held typewriters and computer terminals. There were prefabricated slots for every form. Along the outside edge of this inner circle were built-in chairs where arrestees sat to be fingerprinted and booked. Against the back wall was a photo area. The room was a model of design.

Funny, though, as soon as they put inmates and guards in it, the place turned into a jail. They brought that smell with them, for one thing: piss and sweat and vomit. Roughly half the people arrested in San Antonio for anything are drunk, and some percentage of the drunks tend to wet themselves when the lights scare them. It's a bad idea to yell at a drunk when he's sitting in a chair you have to work next to for the next eight hours. But try to explain that to a frustrated guard getting incoherent answers.

Plus they found once they'd moved in that the place wasn't quite as functional as it had looked empty. Those great built-in chairs, for example, didn't have any place to attach a handcuff. After the first time it took four guards to hold a belligerent speed freak in his chair, they'd bolted an extra bar to a few of the chairs. The bars looked like towel racks on the chair arms. They would have been out of place on the Enterprise.

And inmates stayed the same. Modern surroundings did nothing to improve them. When I walked in I saw a man on his knees in one of the holding cells along the far wall, throwing up noisily. At least he'd made it to the toilet. Two other men were standing near him, looking on and laughing, and a third stood with clenched fists, waiting. He turned to glare at the outside world.

David was wiping his hands with a brown paper towel. That would remove some of the fingerprint ink but not all of it. His face was white as salt. Sometimes people being booked weren't alert enough to be scared. He was. His suit was so rumpled it looked too big for him. He looked like a twelve-year-old caught wearing his father's clothes. He was looking at the men in the holding cell.

I deliberately crossed the path of his gaze and walked toward him on that line. When he focused on me his face took on a little color. His shoulders slumped as if he'd fall. He took a step forward. For maybe the first time in his life he was glad to be his father's son.

I put my arms around him. His forehead briefly touched my shoulder. "It's all right, son. Don't worry about it." He took a deep breath, swallowing a sob.

A guard nodded to me deferentially and led David back to the photo area. That was another idea that had failed in practice. The photo area was supposed to be just an open square with a camera, in view of the holding cells. But too many times catcalls and comments showered the photographee from the cells as he stood there. In the first few days of the jail's use they'd gotten too many pictures of the sides of heads, veins bulging, as the model yelled back. Now the area was surrounded by portable screens. David disappeared behind them.

When he emerged they didn't bring him back to me. The same guard led him along the back wall toward a door. David looked at me with panic. "It's all right," I told him. "They're just taking you to see a judge."

He relaxed. Judges held no terror for him. Not yet.

That was the other thing I could have done to get him released. Gone in with David to see the night magistrate, who would set the bond, and ask him to release David on a personal recognizance bond, or set the bond fairly low and let me post a ten percent cash bond. But if the night mag had done it—and he probably would have—it would have smacked of a deal. That wasn't necessary. Bail was one of the things I could play straight, so I had played it straight. I let David go in alone. The magistrate would inform him of his rights, tell him what he was charged with, and set the bond. I didn't know if Henry Gutierrez, the night mag, would recognize David as my son. It had been years since he'd seen him.

A deputy in the administrative circle was shuffling papers I took to be David's. I had to speak to make him look up. "What's the booking charge?"

"Agg sex assault," he said.

I stared into his bland, slightly hostile face. "Sexual? Aggravated *sexual* assault?"

"That's right."

Now I knew it was crazy. Stupidly, I suddenly hoped this could all be cleared up tonight, because the charge was ludicrous. "What makes it aggravated?" I asked.

The deputy leaned toward me and spoke with hostile sarcasm. "She's in the hospital, if you care."

"They all go to the hospital, Deputy. You take them to the hospital. There's nothing about a weapon?"

But our relationship was severed. He turned his back on me, taking the papers. This was how it would be. Some would help because of who I was and some would get their backs up, as if I were trying to intimidate them. I hoped the helpers would outnumber the hinderers.

There were two detectives hanging around the booking desk. I knew them by sight but hadn't approached them. When the deputy concluded our interview, though, one of the detectives came up to me. We shook hands.

"I wasn't sure he was yours, Mr. Blackwell. I didn't think you were old enough to have a boy that age."

It's a surprise to me too. Some days I feel hardly adult myself. "I appreciate you calling, Detective." Don't call a detective "officer"; you're demoting him. "Makes it a little less shocking for him for me to be here."

That wasn't the extent of the favor, as we both knew. There are any number of ways cops can tool you around if you have the bad luck to be arrested at night. The investigation can drag on for hours. The suspect can be hauled from the scene to the medical examiner's office to the police station with small or large hints being dropped along the way that the suspect could help himself out by admitting what he'd done. Many times in the small sleepless hours of the morning, with no apparent progress toward actual booking and release, the suspect does just that. Up until a couple of years ago the night mag would go off duty at three o'clock in the morning. If you got booked in after that, there was no one to set your bond until nine A.M., and you spent the night in jail even if you were rich enough to bail out everyone in the joint. A surprising number of arrestees, especially the loudmouthed, obnoxious ones, didn't reach the jail until just after that three o'clock deadline. Now we have magistrates on duty twenty-four hours a day, but I imagine veteran cops have dreamed up ways around that.

They hadn't subjected David to any of that delay. They had hustled him to the jail and through booking in record time, and the call had allowed me to be there to meet him. All on my account. And added to my account, another favor.

"Well, back to duty," the detective said. He shifted his weight. I didn't move to shake hands again. About the same time we both realized we were adversaries now. "You going to be tearing me apart on the stand over this?" he asked with fake joviality.

"Not me. But someone might."

He smiled innocently. "I don't know a thing about it. I just picked up the pieces afterwards."

"Thanks again," I said. He walked away, back to his partner, who was watching me. I nodded to him as well. I'd get their names off the offense report when I saw the file. As they went out the door back to the outside world I realized the detective and I hadn't said word one about the crime David was charged with. He'd never even named the offense. Out of politeness, I suppose; anyone who'd been on the police force long enough to make detective would be long past embarrassing. But I would have liked some details. The woman's name, whether she was hurt. It occurred to me that David might be on his way home before she was.

Who was she? I wished I could see a photograph, at least, of how she looked at that moment. I pictured her angry, screaming an accusation. I hoped she looked obviously like a woman who'd been spurned and made up a fake charge. It was not possible that David could do such a thing. As shaken as he'd looked when I'd first seen him, he looked more like a victim than a criminal. My son could not have raped someone. Held her down and threatened her, held a knife to her throat—no. That was a picture that would not take form. But how could he even have fallen victim to such an accusation? Where had it happened? Why was he out on the streets at night where someone could vilify him like this? He should have been safe at home.

A noise behind me attracted my attention. David was coming toward me. He had grown into his suit a little. The noise I'd heard was the bond form rustling in his hand. The same sheriff's deputy who had taken him was still following him but the deputy fell back and turned aside.

The night mag had set the bond at ten thousand dollars. "I told him you were out here," David said. "He said to say hello."

David sounded as if Henry Gutierrez had done him a favor, but ten thousand dollars was an average-size bond for a felony in San Antonio. The night mag had been given only a minute to make a decision and he had done what I would have done: treated David exactly like everyone else.

I had my own forms ready, already signed by the bail bondsman. It had been easy to decide to go that route rather than approach a defense lawyer or the magistrate. A bondsman was in the business of making bonds. It wouldn't look as if anyone had accommodated me particularly because of who I was. I had already decided to play the no-account parts perfectly cleanly, hoping that would make it easier to get away with whatever I needed to get away with to see David cleared.

The paperwork done, David appeared as free as I was. He embraced the illusion wholeheartedly. He began breathing more deeply as soon as we stepped into the night air. I knew this reaction. In a few minutes he would probably start growing very sleepy. When he hit the pillow this would all seem like a bad dream.

"Thanks, Dad." He gripped my arm very briefly. He was no longer insecure enough to need a hug.

We got in the car and I pulled out of the lot. David turned on the heater. For a minute its hum was the only sound. I began to think he wasn't going to speak. I'd wanted him to begin in his own way, but he wouldn't.

"What happened, David?"

For a moment I was back in time. David was in trouble and I had to both rescue him and decide what to do with him. He'd wrecked the car, he'd stayed out too late. But nothing like that had ever happened. This was my first rescue of him in his life.

"I don't understand it," he said. He was staring straight out the windshield, as if he saw something in the road far ahead but couldn't quite make it out.

I nodded. "Tell me."

He started talking as if he'd been confined for years and this was his first chance to tell the story. I listened for a minute or so, then pulled the car to the curb and stopped. He looked at me, surprised.

"David, listen. I'm representing you now. What you tell me can't go any further. Tell me everything now, while it's fresh. Everything. Don't be afraid, it can't hurt you."

"It's the truth," he said. "I was sitting at my desk. It was seven or so, I don't know, everybody else was gone. Tomorrow I'm suggesting to the president of the company that we contract out our training instead of having a full-time instructional division. Naturally, that's going to bring the trainers down on my neck so I wanted to make sure my figures were right before I made the report. I'd been over it a dozen times already."

That sounded right. David was twenty-three, but he'd never seemed young. He was the most serious young man I knew.

"I didn't even notice her until she was standing right in front of the desk. It scared me for a second until I saw who she was. One of the maids. I said, 'Hi, Mandy.'"

"You know her."

"Well, her name, just to say hello to. Mandy Jackson. She's black. But she didn't say anything. She had her cart with her, you know, with the canvas bag and the dustmop and everything. I thought maybe she wanted the trash can. I started feeling around under the desk for it."

"You were in your office?"

"No, in the outer office. I was using the secretary's word processor. But I mean, we're on the twelfth floor. Nobody else was even on that floor, I think."

"So she said—"

"Nothing. She just stood there in front of the desk, staring at me."

"Young woman?" I'd started driving again. Night turned the car's windows to dark screens. I tried to make this scene play on them.

"No," David said. "Thirty-five maybe. Thin, you know. Kind of—I don't know." *Pretty,* he probably stopped himself from saying. "I think I said something else, like yes? or can I help you? or something, and she reached up—she was wearing this sort of uniform, white blouse and black skirt— and she reached up with both hands and took the blouse and just pulled it open. The buttons just went every which way. And then she stroked one hand across her shoulder. The front, you know, like stroking herself, but then without making a sound she dug in her nails and just opened up the skin. There's these four streaks of blood across her arm and her shoulder and it didn't even look real because she didn't even—"

"Didn't you ever move?"

"I think I did then. I think that's when I stood up. And as soon as I did she started yelling."

"Yelling what?"

He didn't answer for a moment. " 'Rape,' " he finally said. "She started yelling, 'Help. Rape.' But like she knew no one else was around because she didn't even raise her voice much."

"She still hadn't said anything to you?"

"No." David was staring. He hadn't looked at me. The scene was playing for him. "But she was staring at me, just—glaring. Like I was the most hateful person in the world. Like she could kill me.

"I jumped up and I tried to grab her and stop her. When she jerked away from me I scratched her a little myself, not anything like what she'd already done, but when I did she screamed for real, like she finally really felt the pain. She pulled back from me . . ."

"Yes, what?"

His voice came very low. "This is the really unbelievable part."

"I don't think you've lied to me since you were six, David. Just tell me. I believe you." Even though the story was like nothing I'd ever heard before, even from the most pathological liars.

"She started tearing her clothes off," he said quietly. "Not being careful, just ripping them, like she wanted them to tear. She ripped one side of her bra loose so it was just hanging down on her other arm. Then she clawed herself again, across the—her chest. And she screamed again, for real. I was, I don't know, I was calling her name, trying to get her to say anything to me. But she was insane. She turned and ran into one of the inner offices, Mr. Tippett's office, that has a couch in it."

"And you followed her."

"I know, I was stupid, I should've gotten the hell out of there right then. But what good would it've done by then? And the way she was acting I thought she was going to throw herself out a window. So I went—I mean, I wasn't getting very close, I just went to the doorway. She was *scaring* me, you know? If she'd had a gun—"

"What did she do?"

David looked at me peculiarly. *I see*, I thought. *I'm* the one being tested now. I tried to mold my expression accordingly, but I didn't know the one for unquestioning faith. Do I let my mouth hang open slightly? Do I widen my eyes? David kept watching me for the rest of the story.

"She ripped open the zipper of her skirt and kicked it off. Then she put her hands in her panties and started to pull them too, but then she looked at me instead and said something like 'You want to help, boy? You just gonna stand there and watch?' And she came at me. I tried backing up but she came so fast I almost tripped over my feet. She clawed my face. Look." Yes, he had the scratches. "Her finger almost went in my eye. I thought she was going to try to claw my eyes and I swung at her, just trying to push her away, and I hit somewhere, her cheek, I guess."

"You knocked her away?"

"Or she just backed off. When I took my arm down from my eyes she had ripped her panties mostly off and she was down on the couch on her back, grinding and bouncing up and down. I know. I know how it sounds. It's the most—"

"Stop protesting, David. Whatever you say I believe you. Because it's so idiotic, if for no other reason. Maybe someone paid her."

"Paid her? Why?"

"I don't know. We'll figure it out later. Just tell me the rest."

"Well." David sounded very tired. And puzzled, as if my convincing him I believed him had made him hear how unbelievable the story was. "She was still screaming for help and I finally decided just to get the hell out of there. But finally the security guard—God knows where the fat so-and-so had been all this time—he was finally coming. I was back in the outer office by then. I said, 'Joe. Thank God.' He started to ask me what was wrong but then he looked past me. I turned around and looked too. You could see Mandy through the open door. She was slumped on the floor with her clothes just in rags and she was crying and she just said, 'He raped me. Help me.' Something like that. She just—she was the most pitiful-looking thing you've ever seen.

"And the next thing I know Joe Garcia's got his gun out, shaking like I'm gonna fight him for it, and he makes me sit across the room while he calls the police and won't let me say a word until they get there. Not that it would've mattered. If I'd told him, he would've just thought I was crazy on top of it. I mean, have you ever heard anything stranger?"

I probably had, but I'd have to search my memory. "Does she have a grudge against you?" I asked. "Have you done anything to make her mad?"

"I've hardly ever spoken to her."

"Has she gotten in any kind of trouble at work, something she could have blamed you for?"

"I don't keep up with the cleaning staff, Dad. If she's been in trouble, I wouldn't hear about it. I've certainly never complained about her. Anyway, don't you think this would be a little extreme as a reaction?"

"I'm just trying to understand."

A little silence ate up part of the dark road. "I'm sorry," David finally said. "I know it's unbelievable."

"No, I believe you." But I also heard the way the story sounded, the way it would sound to a judge or a jury. "We have to find out everything about her," I said. "Maybe she's crazy. Maybe she's done this before." I hope to God.

David nodded. He was beginning to look sleepy, as I'd expected. The world was turning dreamlike. Night, jail, crazy woman, the gentle waves from the car's heater, all lulling him into believing this hadn't happened, because it was too strange to happen.

Pulling into his driveway roused him. He blinked at the house. Finally he patted his pants pocket and drew reassurance from the jingle of keys. "Dad," he began, not looking at me. I nodded encouragement. He said, "I was terrified until I saw you there. Then it seemed okay. I can't thank you enough."

That was probably literally true. His language was turning formal, putting me at a distance. I pulled him close again before he could get away. "It'll be okay," I said, talking into his hair like when he was a boy.

"I know. I'm not worried." *He* was reassuring *me*. "They can't convict me of something I didn't do. After all, you're the district attorney."

How could I tell him? I had already realized that that was probably going to do him more harm than good.

CHAPTER

By the time I stepped out of the car in my own driveway the night had that feeling of lateness about it, as if not many people were left to share the crisp air. Before I took another step Lois was in the doorway.

"It's all right. He's home." I trudged past her. No homecoming kiss, no welcoming touch. Not that I deserved them. "Tell me," she said.

I hesitated a long moment, knowing how different the scene would be after I spoke.

"Let me peek in on Dinah."

I shed my jacket on the way. Passing through the dim living room and hall, my eyes grew used to the dark again, so when I reached her room I could see Dinah clearly, sleeping flat on her back, the way she'd been tucked in, arms out to the sides, absolutely secure. A hand touched my shoulder.

"David," Lois said.

I followed her into the kitchen. "He's not hurt," I said quickly. "He's out on bail. Nothing will happen for a while."

"He *was* arrested. It wasn't a mistake? What on earth for?"

"Lois, listen, it's crazy. Let me—"

"For what, Mark?"

"Rape."

I didn't expect her to faint like a Victorian mother, but the way she did react surprised me as much. She laughed.

"Well, I guess you *did* get him out. What did they have, an old case and someone saw his picture and thought he looked like the one?"

"It's not like that." I told her David's story, not blow for blow the way he'd told me, just the essentials: a woman at his office had faked a rape. Without details it didn't sound as bad. While I talked Lois started making coffee. Her movements were automatic; it might have been morning. Amusement had left her so quickly and completely it could not have been real. When I finished we stood with the gurgling and final hiss of the coffeemaker the only sounds. Lois didn't speak for a long minute. When she did there was urgency in her tone.

"The one thing you have to make sure of is that when the case gets dismissed it gets as much publicity as his arrest is going to get. You know? When you investigate it and find out why this woman, whoever she is, said this about him, and the case is over, the whole explanation has to come out. Everybody who sees tomorrow's stories in the papers has to see the last ones too."

She surprised me again. I thought she would at least understand the one basic fact, the one thing that had to happen. I interrupted to tell her that one hard truth. "But Lois, my office can't handle this case. Not even to investigate it, not even to present it to a grand jury."

"Your office?"

"The district attorney's office. You surely understand that. No one who works for me can touch it. What I have to figure out—"

"What do you mean?" Maybe the undertone of threat in her voice was only in my mind. But she sounded more than baffled. Aghast, at least.

"Lois. There's no way on earth the D.A.'s office can handle

this case, with me at the head of it. I'll have to disqualify myself."

She came toward me, one hand out and groping, the other holding her coffee cup. I thought she was going to throw it in my face. The groping hand found my shirt, twisted a handful of its fabric, and hung on with a death grip. "You can't back out of this. You mean to spare yourself the—the what, the—"

"Goddammit, Lois, are you insane? Do you think I'm saying I have a choice? I'm saying there's no way I can hang on to it. Come in here." I took her hand out of my shirt and pulled her into the den, sat her next to me. "Look, suppose I do it your way, accept the case, investigate it, announce why she lied, present the case to a grand jury, and get David no-billed. Suppose that. Forget the fact that nobody would buy it, that nobody would really believe he was innocent, which is what you were concerned about a minute ago. Think about everyone else involved—the reporters, the judges, the county commissioners, this woman herself—everyone who'd have some motive to scream cover-up and try to get some mileage out of it. Think of them. One of those groups would revive the case even if I killed it. Being no-billed once doesn't put a stop to a case. Some other grand jury could take it up again, and another one, and another. Maybe I could even stall it as long as I'm D.A., but that's four years and the statute of limitations on rape is ten. He couldn't breathe easy for another ten years.

"And look." The anger had faded from Lois's expression. She was starting to look scared instead. "When some other grand jury does start investigating it, they'll ask the judge who chose them to appoint a special prosecutor. The usual procedure is to ask the statewide District Attorneys Association to choose someone. And they'll pick someone from out of town, some prosecutor or criminal lawyer from another county. That's exactly what I can't have, someone trying this case who has no stake here, nothing I can influence him with. I have to make sure the special prosecutor is someone from San Antonio."

"But you can't pick someone. That would look as bad as you doing it yourself."

I was glad to hear her say that. She was starting to understand. Now the fear in her eyes was beginning to give way to another expression: calculation. I was relieved, but I knew she'd never make the next jump with me.

"That's right. But I can pick the person who picks the special prosecutors. And I can make it look strictly up-and-up."

"How? Who?"

I told her. The coffee almost came at me again. Lois grabbed my arm. "Are you crazy? He'd do his worst to hurt you. That means hurting David. He'd never help us."

"I don't expect him to, not on purpose. But his worst won't be bad enough. He'll think he's attacking me and so will everyone else. That's the beauty of it. No one will ever think cover-up after I announce it."

"No, but tell me why he can't hurt us," Lois said. I explained my theory. I listened to it myself, searching for holes.

Inexplicably, Lois began to look younger as the night and her worries deepened. I remembered long-gone bouts of infant illness when we'd be up in the middle of the night—short-handed, frantic, asking each other questions neither of us knew how to answer. Not like this, quietly desperate. But there was the same sense of encouraging each other through a crisis. After a while she was holding my hand instead of my arm. Her grip gradually loosened.

"When did you make all these plans?" she asked. "Just driving home, or have you thought about the idea for years? How did you think of all these things so fast?"

"Just thinking like a lawyer. I can't even help it anymore."

"It's horrible. I mean—David." I nodded. "If it wasn't David you could do what I said," she went on. "Couldn't you?"

I nodded again. "If it was anyone but a relative or an employee it would be no trouble at all."

Suddenly she hit me in the chest with her fist. Not hard enough to hurt, but not playfully either. "If you weren't D.A.—" she said.

"But if I wasn't I couldn't help either. Now I still can."

"Can you? Will it work?"

I pictured David inside that holding cell at the jail, the one we'd both been looking into when I arrived. The one he'd be in now if not for who I was. I jerked involuntarily, trying in imagination to pull him out, then realized I was still in the den with Lois. I'd frightened her again.

"It will," I said. "It will. Believe me, Lois. The one thing I know is how to work the system." I cleared my throat. I was tempted to let everything else slide, the crisis shoving it all aside like a glacier through gravel, but I felt I'd be sparing myself if I did, and I didn't want to spare myself.

"Two of my prosecutors won a big case this afternoon," I said. "We all went to celebrate after work."

"I know, you told me."

"Linda and I left before the others and she'd left her car at the courthouse so I gave her a ride. If you'd called two minutes later, I would've been on my way home already."

Lois had listened to this recital until she realized what I was explaining, then waved her hand, brushing trifles aside. "It doesn't matter, Mark."

That was the sad truth. It didn't.

I was in law school when David was born. Lois and I conventionally married the summer after college and I went right back to school. David was not exactly planned, though we did nothing to prevent him. We were very young and had more than our share of silly ideas. We thought we would let nature take its course. But we didn't expect nature's course to be such a fast track. David was born eleven months after our wedding.

Lois was supporting us working as a secretary. She had a fancier title than that, befitting her college degree, but when

you have to take a typing test to get the job, you're a secretary.
Those were great days, the sixties. A family could live on a
secretary's salary. We couldn't live without it, though. I got a
job clerking in a law office, which allowed Lois to stay home
with David for three months, but we couldn't live on what I
made as a clerk. We talked about my quitting school and
finding a job so Lois could stay with the baby longer. I had no
ambition other than being a lawyer, and pictured any other job
as a dead end or a delay. We decided I should stay in law
school, hurry through it, and then give Lois time with David
after I graduated. That was our next silly idea: that as if by
rushing I could move through time faster than the baby. He
would tread the timestream while I rowed frantically with it,
so that two years would pass for me without using up his
precious infancy.

We doted on David in the minutes we could spare. For me
that was the half hour between when I got home from the
office or the library and David's bedtime. I would carry him
that whole time, unless I had more studying to do. Sometimes
I held him while reading. I remember looking up once at a
touch on my shoulder. In the mirror I saw Lois standing over
both of us, smiling gently. I looked down and saw that David
had fallen asleep, the nipple of the bottle I was holding still in
his mouth. I pressed him against my chest, suffused with
family feeling.

Once in a while there was a holiday meal with my parents
or a weekend with Lois's parents in Dallas. For a year or two
David was the only grandchild on either side of the family,
and was held and cooed over unmercifully for these short
stretches of occasion. The attention unnerved him at first, but
by the end of the weekend he would be reveling in it.

These portrait opportunities were enough for me. Once a
day or once a week I had those attacks of feeling while I held
him, when it seemed that everything I wanted was encompassed there. During the day, though, I seldom thought about
him or Lois. As I sat at a library table or in class, mind full of

tort and compensation and treble damages, I might have been single still. Especially in the law office and my trips to the courthouse I saw another world opening.

Lois did quit working when I finished school and was hired at the D.A.'s office. My twelve thousand dollars a year made us feel rich. But I was wrong, of course, about having more free time. Some days I was late in trial or preparing for trial. Some days I went after work for a drink with other prosecutors. You had to do that if you wanted to get ahead. Saturdays I played basketball or softball with guys from the office. Once I make felony, I said. Once I make first chair . . .

David had become a child. You could have conversations with him. Once he started school he had his own interests. I found them boring, frankly. I listened politely as he explained soccer or the moral of the story he was reading. It didn't occur to me that he paid the same due to my courthouse stories. I assumed boys automatically found their fathers' worlds fascinating.

Lois went back to work, this time without a typing test. At first her earnings were spotty. We used her real estate commissions for savings and celebrations. Three out of four times our trips out of town were during the school year and David stayed at Grandma's. It was an adventure for him too.

When I went into private practice there were more late nights, but I had more control over my schedule too. I could be home at three o'clock in the afternoon if I wanted, or for a long weekend. I looked around for my family. But David was damned near a teenager by then. He belonged to more clubs and teams than I did. The only place I seemed to see him was in the car, and his hand was always on the door handle. To my surprise and slight annoyance he had found a world of his own instead of waiting for me to take him into mine.

Dinah was very much planned, but when she came it wasn't as if we were continuing our family, it was as if we were starting over. The results were altogether more satisfactory this time. Dinah got more of everything from us. And she hung on my stories when she got old enough. Comet David's orbit around the family grew increasingly long and elliptical. His childhood had an unhappy ending, as everyone's does: he grew up. Just as I was ready for him he went off to college. That was it. No more opportunity to correct the deficiencies of attention in his upbringing. He finished school and got a job. When I asked about law school his scorn was apparent, though he tried to hide it. He was a good boy; he wouldn't say what he thought of my profession.

Like most lawyers I know, I'm tired of being a lawyer. But I love the courthouse. The next morning was the first time in months the sight of the clunky old building didn't make me smile. It's a stolid rectangle composed of yard-square red stones, with a green roof of Spanish-style tiles overlapping one another so that they look like fish scales. The roof rises with a flurry of spires and turrets, as if the architect had decided at the last minute that he was building a cathedral or a castle instead of a courthouse. The first time I saw the building I thought it looked ridiculous. Now I think it looks charmingly ridiculous. It is a relic, a tribute to another century. The county is building a brand-new "justice center" next door, but I know I will never love it as much.

I've put in just over twenty years at this courthouse in various capacities. The building houses the county and district clerks' offices—property deeds, marriage licenses, birth certificates, criminal records—the nine county courts, where misdemeanors are prosecuted and smaller lawsuits resolved; the nineteen district courts, where felonies, divorces, and lawsuits over five thousand dollars are tried; and the Court of Appeals, where we all learn what blunders we made in the courts below. For any practicing lawyer the courthouse is inescapable. For criminal lawyers it is a daily fact of life.

The "courthouse" means something more than the building. It is a world of its own, a world where everyone knows one another, or thinks they do. It's like spending your life in high school. Always something going on, always a new scandal. The courthouse is Rumor Central. Gossip travels from the county courts in the basement to the Court of Appeals on the fifth floor faster than the elevators.

Unlike high school, though, there is a constant influx of fresh blood. As soon as you walk in you see them, the ones who've never been in the courthouse before and don't like being there now. They sit on benches anxiously or miserably waiting for their lawyers, stand in lines to get copies of birth certificates, find the information booth to ask where they go if they've been called for jury duty. On every floor there are more of them. For some reason they make me smile, too. They fuel us, they keep our controversies alive.

There is a side entrance to the courthouse that gives immediately onto an elevator that travels straight to the back entrance to the D.A.'s office on the third floor. I seldom use it. I like going in the main door and up the stairs, greeting those familiar faces and surreptitiously studying the unfamiliar ones. That's how I went in shortly after eight the morning after David's arrest, but of course that morning was going to be different from the start. A small throng of reporters was waiting for me. Maybe ten of them in all, counting photographers and cameramen. I know them all. For a moment I recognized individual faces and had the illusion I could communicate with them. There's not one who hasn't interviewed me formally a dozen times and swapped rumors with me dozens more. Today, though, they had melded into an unrecognizable mob. They jockeyed for position; they thrust microphones at me and overlapped each other with questions.

I made only one statement: "There'll be a press conference in my office at ten o'clock tomorrow. Anyone who bugs me now isn't invited."

They fell back at that. We know one another, these boys and girls, but they don't know me as district attorney. It's been only a few months, and we have all seen people change in office. Lawyers who used to leak secrets in the men's room turn into judges who try to impose gag orders. Maybe I'd turned mean. It was a mean occasion. They let me pass and the clot dissolved as they went to phone editors or find other interviews. They could tell I'd been thinking about them. A ten o'clock press conference is early enough for those of them with noon broadcasts or afternoon edition deadlines.

But they had reminded me how bad the day was going to be. I took the stairs two at a time, looking only at the stairs. I passed two or three people without looking up to see if I knew them. They in turn maintained respectful silence. On the third floor I emerged from the stairwell to confront the glass doors. Above them, in black letters a foot tall, is the legend CRIMINAL DISTRICT ATTORNEY, and above that, in letters the same size, MARK BLACKWELL. It's still a small shock to see my name in that space rather than one of my predecessors'.

I had become an assistant D.A. straight out of law school, and rose through the ranks at an average speed: a year and a half in misdemeanor, brief stint in appeals, then felony. I spent my last three years in the office as a first chair felony prosecutor. It was during my years as a prosecutor that I learned to love the courthouse. I had a place in the world, a position of responsibility and some power. People greeted me by name. They approached me for favors. The D.A. handed me the occasional important case—a capital murder or a high-profile defendant. I owned a piece of those halls. The courthouse was my home.

But you can't stay in the D.A.'s office forever. You'll never get rich at it, for one thing, and if anyone ever went to law school without at least a sneaking desire to get rich, he must have dropped out in the first year. After a while, too, you get tired of having bosses, layers of them. At least I did. I was growing dull from being part of what defense lawyers liked to call the biggest law firm in the city. Being awarded my five-year pin from the county scared me. I was a functionary, a lifetime employee. I made first chair about the same time, and that kept me hanging on for three more years, but it was time to quit. I spent my last year looking for the "right moment" before I realized any moment was okay. The change was scary, going into the outside world after eight cozy years in the courthouse. Prosecutors never have a shortage of clients. They don't pay secretaries or office rent, and all their supplies are free. The only improvement I could see in being a defense lawyer was being able to come and go as I pleased.

I spent ten years in private practice, made money, won my share of trials—which means, for a defense lawyer, maybe one a year if you're good. You learn to take a feeling of triumph from getting your client a lower sentence than the prosecutor had offered in plea bargaining. Outright victories are rare. Ninety-something percent of criminal trials end in convictions, and rightfully so. That statistic was on my mind the morning after David's arrest.

I did all right in private practice, but it was wearing thin after ten years. Hugh Reynolds made it wear thinner. He was elected district attorney four years ago out of nowhere. The day after he filed for the office, all of us in the courthouse were asking one another who he was. Turned out he was a civil lawyer, of the kind who don't even put in token appearances in the courthouse. Hugh had what's called an office practice, meaning you don't have to leave your office to do it. He wrote contracts, did taxes, advised corporate officers, that sort of thing. And harbored a secret, growing resentment of criminals and the criminal justice system, apparently. One story had it that his decision to run for D.A. stemmed from a speeding ticket he tried and failed to have fixed. Others said it sprang from having his home burglarized. Whatever, he put in his first known appearance in the courthouse to file for the D.A.'s race.

There was no scramble to oppose him. He was considered one of the usual joke candidates. The serious boys were chatting themselves up and starting campaign feelers. The old D.A., Eliot Quinn, the man I'd spent most of my eight years in the office working for, announced his disinclination to run again. That added candidates to the race. But while they scrambled for endorsements and backbit each other in the halls of the courthouse, Hugh Reynolds took his campaign directly to the public. He was a new-broom candidate. The good old boys had held the D.A.'s office too long; they were more interested in scratching one another's backs than in making the streets safe. I give him credit—he found the right nerve and struck it again and again. There was a lot of untapped anger out there. Hell, I'd been burglarized myself. If I'd been naive enough to think Hugh Reynolds, or any D.A., could do something about that, I'd have voted for him myself.

Enough people did. The second time Hugh entered the courthouse it was as the criminal district attorney of Bexar County. The walls almost trembled. An interloper had seized power.

He turned out to be every bit the terror everyone had feared. His first act was to fire half the lawyers in the office. Not the most junior lawyers either. Under the theory that corruption trickles down from above, Hugh fired the most experienced prosecutors on his staff. That might not have been a bad idea if he'd had any other experienced lawyers to replace them, but he didn't. He just thought he'd start over, with the most junior assistant D.A.s and new talent fresh out of law school. One week twenty-five-year-old prosecutors were trying drunken drivers and shoplifters and the next week they were trying murderers and rapists. And trying them, sometimes, against defense lawyers who had themselves been experienced felony prosecutors a week earlier. The conviction rate went to hell. Hugh's other innovations, such as a brief ban on plea bargaining, didn't help his cause either, with anyone. When you have a thousand new felony cases filed every month, you have to plea-bargain the vast majority of them. Hugh realized that after a couple of months, but he'd already made himself look like an oaf.

No one ever took the office with better intentions, and no one was ever a bigger disaster. As his four-year term ground toward an end, the local party machinery came to frenzied life, looking for an experienced prosecutor to oppose Hugh. I was one of the ones approached, and found almost to my surprise that I was interested. After ten years in private practice, being back in the D.A.'s office sounded pretty good—I missed being one of the good guys. And this was the only way I could ever go back.

Hugh Reynolds had learned in four years. His conviction rate was better, he wasn't the easy target he would have been after his first year. But I had the backing of damned near every criminal lawyer in town, even the secret support of many of Hugh's own staff. The public theme of my campaign was "Prosecution by Professionals." The private one was "Return of the Good Old Boys." As the election approached, Hugh had the disadvantage of incumbency. In the last few weeks of the campaign his hand-picked prosecutors lost a murder case that had received a lot of publicity. Another big case, one Hugh had tried himself, was reversed by the Court of Appeals. In his last days he began to look like a child lost in a fun house. I just had to walk up the courthouse steps carrying a briefcase and wearing a determined expression, and I looked like Abe Lincoln by comparison. When I was interviewed it was outside courtrooms; Hugh was interviewed inside his office. He began to look like a bunker king, and I began to pull ahead in the polls.

Hugh's response was to attack me personally—my record, my supporters, my history. "If you want the kind of corruption that used to be rampant in this office," he announced publicly, "Mark Blackwell's your man." I didn't mean to run that kind of campaign. But being insulted brings out the third-grader in me, the "Oh yeah?" Reporters ate it up. It became a game with them, to catch me in a hallway and pass on the Hugh quote that was going to appear the next day.

"Hey, Mark, Hugh Reynolds just told me the only reason you had a good record as a prosecutor was because you ducked the tough cases."

"Are you kidding? Listen, that would be insulting if it came from someone who had the vaguest idea what to do in a courtroom. That weenie. If he ever tried to prosecute a tough case, he couldn't keep his pants dry long enough to get to final argument." Before I knew it I would have said something like that for attribution. And the gleeful reporter would go scurrying back to my opponent for response. It was strange the way Hugh and I became bitter personal rivals without ever seeing each other—conducting these cat-scratch matches by proxy.

One day I decided to call him. I might've had a drink or two at lunch that day, I don't know. At any rate, I had one of those expansive moments when I thought I could cut through the bullshit with one bold stroke. "Hugh," I said, "I just called to say I think this thing has gotten out of hand."

"Why, what outrageous thing you said about me is going to appear in the paper tomorrow?"

I chuckled. "So far nothing. No one's waylaid me yet. But listen, I don't want it to be like this any more. I have nothing against you personally, Hugh, you know that. I like you. Aren't there enough professional differences between us we can run on without getting personal?"

"Professional differences like me being incompetent and you being a pro?" he said.

"Yeah, like that."

I thought he might laugh. He should've. Hugh wasn't such a bad guy, I started thinking.

Then he said, "What do you want, a deal?"

"What do you mean?"

"You must want something, why else would you call?"

"I've tried to tell everybody I'm not a politician, Hugh. I know, I shouldn't even have called you, I should've had my handler call your handler. But I'm not sure who your handler is, and I'm not so sure I trust mine."

He didn't recognize jokes. "What are you offering?" he said.

"Was that a click?"

"Just tell me what you want, Mark."

"Are you recording this, you son of a bitch?"

"Oh, Eliot Quinn taught you that much, did he? What else did you learn from him, the old sleazemaster? A lot, I'm—"

"Hey, Eliot Quinn knew how to try a case without losing or getting it reversed. Oh, what was that, another click? You didn't want to record that part, Hughie?"

"I'm sure whatever reporter you've got there with you has it all down," he riposted. Heady stuff. Too bad it wasn't recorded. It's good the conversation was by phone. If we'd been in the same room, our next moves would have been to start shoving each other's shoulders. My good intentions had worked as well as Hugh's when he'd first become D.A.

So we abandoned the high road. But I took to it again before Hugh. After his reversal and other setbacks I could afford to become statesmanlike. I won the election in a walk, leaving Hugh to slink back to civil law where he belonged, licking his wounds and loathing me.

I had taken office in January and made it all the way to April before this, my first scandal. Without a word those reporters downstairs had reminded me that this wasn't just a case. It was going to be a test of how I ran the office. What they didn't understand was how little I cared about the consequences. If I thought I could have taken the system by the throat and choked out a dismissal of David's case, I would have done it. Did any of them really think I had that power? I didn't. Besides, dismissal wouldn't have been good enough, as I'd explained to Lois.

Just inside the front doors of the D.A.'s office is a small waiting room. To the right is a window with a counter, where supplicants can talk to the receptionist. Beside this window is another glass door, this one locked. Before I touched its handle the lock buzzed and kept buzzing until I had it open. I fired a perfunctory "thank you" into the air, not even looking to see where it fell.

Jerry Fleming wasn't so easy to bypass. He was waiting for me just inside the door. Jerry had been chief of the felony section when I'd left the D.A.'s office ten years ago. Somehow he had held on to the post even through the Reynolds purge, and I'd kept him on. Big, bluff Jerry Fleming. I'd been surprised to discover, after I took office, what a kiss-ass he was.

"Hello, Blackie," he said. My name is Mark Blackwell. People who fancy themselves my intimates call me Blackie. My few friends know I dislike nicknames, especially that one.

Jerry's mien was solemn in deference to the night's news, but then he took my arm and went to business as he led me down the hall. "I could fade the heat from the press for you if you want, Blackie. No reason you have to talk to them yourself. I think it's the felony chief's position to discuss—"

"Thanks, Jerry, but I'll handle it myself. I couldn't hide from it if I wanted to."

He held up his hands in a backing-off gesture. Not trying to steal your spotlight, boss. He didn't even ask what I was going to do. But he stuck by my side as we maneuvered through the maze of offices toward mine in the back corner. People in the office would see that Jerry Fleming was the first person I consulted in this hour of crisis.

"Staff meeting in the conference room at nine, Jerry. You, me, Linda, two or three others."

"I'll be there." I know you will, Jerry.

Having guided me safely to harbor and been promised the high-level meeting in less than an hour, he didn't follow me into the administration offices. These are in the back corner of the D.A.'s hive, next to the back door. There is a large reception office with two secretaries' desks. Off this are two offices, the first assistant's and mine. When I walked in, the secretaries were at their desks but the door of the First Assistant's office was open and the room beyond was empty. I didn't even need to speak to Patty. Just hooked a thumb at my own closed door, and she nodded.

Linda Alaniz was sitting at my desk, consulting a printed

list of some kind and writing her own notes on it. When I walked in she came to her feet and around the desk as fast as she looked up at me. But when she got closer she slowed. I pushed the door closed with my foot and lifted my hands slightly. Linda came the last few feet and put her arms around me, her cheek against my shoulder. It wasn't a kindly little hug, it was a grip that pulled me back into myself, into my body. I felt as if I'd been diffusing into the atmosphere for the last twelve hours and Linda had suddenly condensed me back into myself, and made me whole. Then she let go, a little awkwardly, ending by touching my arm, backing away, and inclining her head as if helpless to speak.

"I called the jail later and they told me you'd gotten him out," she said. "I am so sorry, Mark. I'm sorry you—"

"Nothing about it was your fault. It was all mine. I must have given you a terrible night, too."

She shrugged. "How is David?"

"Okay. Home. Better than me, probably. He thinks the worst is over."

We looked at each other ruefully. Linda no longer holding me, I realized how tired I was. I felt grainy—my fingers, under my eyelids—as if too-long wakefulness had dried up my natural fluids. I opened the door again to say, "Patty? Could you get me a Coke, please?"

"Coke?" Linda said once I dropped into a chair.

"I'm coffeed out already. I've been up all night."

She drew up a chair close to mine. "What is your plan, then?" She leaned toward me, hands together, going to work.

Linda and I had been partners in private practice—and, some said, in private. Oftentimes two or three prosecutors leave the D.A.'s office at the same time and set up shop together. I hadn't wanted to do that. I wanted a partner already experienced in defense work. While I knew all the ins and outs of the courtroom and the courthouse, I had a lot to learn about representing clients. My other criteria in a partner were that he speak Spanish and be reliable—someone I could count on to back me up or take over for me, even in a difficult case.

He turned out to be she. Linda Alaniz was a dyed-in-the-wool defense lawyer. She would never have considered prosecuting, even for the experience. We had opposed each other on a few cases and respected each other. But it was only after I became her partner that I learned how intense she was, how driven by her work. Maybe that's why she was willing to take on a partner after a few years of solo practice. She was in some danger of burnout, the occupational hazard of defense lawyers, especially the committed ones.

Sometimes during our ten-year partnership, sometimes jokingly, she reminded me that I was not one of the committed ones. She thought I would rather prosecute than defend many of the people who walked into our office. I think she felt betrayed when I decided to run for D.A., but she had the next best thing to my loyalty: she had been proven right. My heart was in prosecution.

At first she wanted nothing to do with the campaign. She was drawn into it only gradually, mainly because of her dislike of the other candidates. But Linda is not someone who can take on a project halfheartedly. By the end we were almost running mates. Lois appeared with me at the important campaign functions, but Linda appeared at all of them. She had found something else to which she could commit herself. In San Antonio the speculation about our relationship probably did my campaign no harm. Probably helped, in fact. And Linda's uncle, Federico Ybarra—Uncle Fred—was a popular five-term city councilman. I sought his endorsement, but he gave it only at the last minute in political terms, a month before the election, maybe too late to be any help at all. He didn't want me to think he was endorsing anything else.

Much as she threw herself into my candidacy, Linda was surprised when I told her I wanted her to be my first assistant if I won. I had to talk her into the job. You could almost see her shudder at the thought of being a prosecutor. I told her the insight she would gain into how the office worked would be invaluable to her when she returned to private practice. She considered. She had been a defense lawyer for almost fifteen years by then and was tired, as all criminal lawyers get tired. The D.A.'s office was semi-retirement for her. Good salary, no hustling for business. She gave in.

Once, in a self-ennobling mood, I had thought maybe I decided to run for D.A. for Linda's sake as well as my own, to take the pressures of private practice off both of us for a while. In the last year or two of our partnership, Linda had been looking on the verge of middle age. She was only, what, thirty-eight, but too many days her once-delicate complexion looked dry and her voice rasped before the second cup of coffee. Only two or three years earlier she had looked like a kid. She still did, when zest fired her, when she found something to throw herself into. But her reserves of zest were growing depleted, and worthwhile causes were walking in the door more and more infrequently. We both needed a break.

This morning she looked young again. She must have been up very early, but there was no trace of it around her eyes. She was on the case. It was my son, it was a personal nightmare, but it was a case. Linda had already explored a world of possibilities this morning, I knew, and now she waited to hear mine.

I didn't have to outline as much of it for Linda as I had for Lois. But Linda was just as aghast when I told her my idea of whom to let pick the special prosecutors.

"Mark! Are you insane? He'll—"

"He'll what? That's the beauty part. He'll pick somebody good, sure, but it doesn't matter how good they are as long as they're San Antonians. That means it will be a local criminal defense lawyer—it's got to be a criminal lawyer, right? someone with experience?—so whoever it is will be under the same kind of pressure. He's not going to come after David full force, not the D.A.'s son. Say he's brilliant, say he gets a conviction and a big sentence. If he does, it'll be his last big case. Because once he's through he goes back to his private practice and finds out he can't get any decent plea offers from the D.A.'s office. Every case he gets he has to take to trial. He'll be run ragged. His defendants'll all end up doing time, even the ones who could get probation for a guilty plea. And forget ever getting a case dismissed, even if it deserves to be.

"After a while, you know, potential clients start hearing about that kind of thing. 'Don't hire Johnny, the D.A. hates him. He can't get you any kind of deal.' I don't think I'll have to spell all this out for the special prosecutor. He's not going to blow his whole career over one case. We'll be able to work with him. He'll find enough problems with the case to justify offering David probation, at least—dismissal, if we're real lucky. And it'll look perfectly legit.

"That's if we keep it all in town. If we go to the District Attorneys Association and they pick some out-of-towner, I won't have that kind of pull."

"And what if *he* picks an out-of-towner?"

"That's the risk. If he does, we'll just have to try to find some other kind of pressure. But I don't think he will. Look, this is an honor I'm giving him to hand out. Whoever's the special prosecutor, it's going to bring him some publicity. And the . . . the acclaim. It's a way of saying, For this job I had to find the best criminal lawyer in town, and here he is. It'll be a big plum. A favor. He won't hand that out to some out-of-towner."

"God, Mark."

Her physical mannerisms mirrored the narrowing down of her enthusiasm into concentration. She had started pacing while I talked, but now she was in the chair again. One hand went to her mouth and stayed there. Her other arm lay across her abdomen. Her shoulders narrowed. She stared at a point across the room. I stood beside her, watching her. This scene was familiar. I always had ideas quickly or not at all. It was up to Linda to slowly pick through them. It began to seem late at night.

"Tell me another plan, Linda. Please."

"I thought of one," she said immediately, "hanging on to it for a month, or two, or three, until it's the right judge's turn to pick a grand jury. Then let the judge pick a special prosecutor. That would make sense, it would be his grand jury the prosecutor would present the case to. And we might be able to influence the judge's selection if we wait for the right judge."

I looked at the ceiling for a minute, playing out that scenario. "Well, maybe, but it looks fishier because we stay involved in the case longer, and the result's the same. I feel like we have to move fast, Linda. If we're seen monkeying with the case any time at all, it's going to look like we pulled something. Then even if it works, where does that leave David? The boy whose father covered up his crime. He wouldn't be vindicated, he'd just have gotten away with something. It's not good enough. It would dog him for the rest of his life. He'd lose his job, probably his wife. . . . No. Better someone who looks totally independent investigates the case and announces there's nothing to it. Or gives him probation, or whatever."

Linda looked at me. "You said that before, probation. But will David even go for a plea bargain?"

Would he? Get up and say "guilty" to a judge rather than face the possibility of prison? "He didn't do it," I told Linda. "He says he didn't. When it gets down to the wire, maybe he'd change his story, but right now—God, Linda, his story . . ."

I told it to her. I wished I had David there to tell it himself. It sounded more sincere coming from him, it had that note of personal urgency. Linda rolled her eyes. She didn't pass judgment on it as truth, just as a defense. "I'd hate to have to sell that," she said.

"Tell me. That's why I don't want it to come to that."

"But your way is dangerous, Mark. Once it's out of our hands—"

"Tell me a better way, Linda. Believe me, I'm open to suggestion. I've been up all night. This is the only scheme I couldn't reject. Tell me a better one. Please."

She couldn't. Every other plan ended with someone taking the case away from us or David being haunted by it forever, or both. My scheme began to look better, but only by comparison.

"How will you communicate all this to the special prosecutor?" Linda asked.

"I'm hoping he'll realize it on his own. If not, I'll have to spell it out."

"If he should go to the press with that—"

"That's the one risk, but I'll take it."

"Maybe I should be the one. It would be nice if you could keep the job you worked so hard to get."

Momentarily I was mad at the world. "I had a job before this one. I could go back to it. I won't give up David to keep this one. I'm just afraid—tell me, Linda—I'm afraid I'm missing something. Lois thinks I have all this power, that somehow I could put a stop to it right now. Is that true?"

Standing made me feel shaky. Adrenaline had kept me up all night, gotten me as far as the courthouse, then dropped me off at the front door and gone home.

"Linda? Tell me if I'm wrong about this, Linda. I'm not sure of anything any more. I've been up all night, I'm not thinking any more, I'm just reacting. You know how I am, I come up with a plan and I get locked into it. Is there something terrible I'm missing?"

She looked at me with compassion, realizing, I think, that I wasn't just asking for her legal expertise. "No, Mark. It is a terrible situation. Any solution will seem equally terrible. But I cannot think of a better one. I don't think anyone could.

"But you should sleep on it," she added. "Speed is not so important that a day will matter. You need to be alert when you make the announcement."

I nodded. Good advice. "I still need to convince Lois, too, I think. You know what? When you hugged me just now it was the first one I'd had since David saw me in the jail. You'd think a family crisis—"

It was time to go home. When I got self-pitying, even displaying it only in front of Linda, I was losing myself. It was a mean thing to do. Linda started toward me again, then stopped, again with that awkwardness, and only looked at me sympathetically. When Patty knocked on the door with my Coke, Linda and I both started as if we'd been caught at something.

The rest of my senior staff didn't like the idea either, which encouraged me.

The grand jury chief took my arm as soon as I walked into the conference room. "Listen, boss," she said as confidentially as possible in that small room full of professional eavesdroppers, "I've been giving this some thought already this morning. First thing you do is wait for just the right grand jury to come along. You know some of them're as different as—then if I present it just right—I'm not saying we can get him no-billed, slim chance of that, but if I put it to them right, I think they'll come back with plain sexual assault instead of aggravated. From what I heard on the news, any injury wasn't—"

"Forget it, Helen. You're not going to be handling it."

She looked hurt. "*I'm* not? Then who—?"

"I might as well explain to everybody at once. Everyone here?"

Of course they were. I started talking and they started frowning. They had the same objection as Linda: it left us all out of it. They didn't phrase their complaints just that way, but it was clear.

The first time I paused, three of them spoke at once. Jerry Fleming held the floor by talking louder and more slowly. "I understand we need a special prosecutor, Blackie. Can't be any appearance of impropriety. But someone from our staff should sit second. You can't just set special prosecutors loose in the office without some supervision. I could second-chair the case and no one could say a thing about it. Hell, you didn't even appoint me to this position. I was here long before you."

And I'll be here after you're gone, he added in my imagination. I reflected briefly on what Jerry was saying. Was it really his ambition to prosecute the boss's son? Maybe send him to prison? Then I realized the possibilities the position would afford him. He could keep constant check on the progress of the case and report it to me. He could be my inside man. And maybe if there came a chance to do some damage to the state's case . . . I would be forever in his debt.

"No. There'll be two special prosecutors. No one from this office will be involved."

The clamor began anew. The suggestions were all of the bureaucrat's variety: *Stall. Maybe it will go away.* I gave Linda an ironic glance. The suggestions were the same courses we had mulled over and rejected. Linda didn't look back at me. She hadn't said a word since we'd come into the room and she wore a strange expression, as if she were surprised to discover herself in this den of prosecutors.

I overbore the discontent. "The special prosecutors are two of us as far as this case goes. Give them all the cooperation they need. Assign an investigator to act as liaison. Files, keys, whatever. And the defense will be treated just as we always treat the defense. Open file policy up to the day of trial. Treat this case exactly as you would any other, except for one thing: don't talk to me about it. And that's the last order any of you take from me in this matter. Questions? Good."

They just sat there. They couldn't believe they were so thoroughly out of it. No one spoke again, but they didn't realize they'd been dismissed either. So I left myself. I must've stayed awake long enough to drive home, but I don't remember it.

Finally, an appreciative audience. My press conference the next morning carried an even greater sense of anticipation due to its rescheduling. The reporters with their cameramen filled my office, and it was clear from the moment I entered that they loved me. They tried to look solemn but just couldn't pull it off. I had done the only thing they cared about: I was going to talk to them. No matter what I said, I would be a story.

The story they got fulfilled their fondest fantasies. Almost as soon as I started talking you could see they wanted to burst into applause. Oh, they loved me. You could see it in the way their pencils flew across their pads. I was such good copy, they almost hoped I'd weather this storm.

Just before I made the announcement I almost balked, almost stood up from my chair and left the room. I didn't want to say it. Once I told them, we would be embarked on the way I'd chosen, there would be no turning back. I was on the verge of avoiding that irrevocable course while it was still in my power. In my mind my face contorted with fear and outrage. I don't have to do this, I thought. They couldn't make me offer David up to them.

But there was no better way. I'd decided that in a long, sleepless night, and Linda had agreed. Part of the plan was speed, making the announcement right away, not looking as if we were stalling while planning something devious. I am as guileless as a child, this press conference said.

It seemed to me the pause had lasted minutes and that I had given everything away by my expression. But I looked at the crowd of reporters and saw it wasn't so. On one end of the front row, near the corner of my desk, sat Dick Heydrich, the regular courthouse reporter for one of the papers. We had known each other for ten years; it had been hard for him to take my candidacy seriously. Even in the last days of the campaign, when it was obvious I'd win, he and I would joke

about the race before I'd give him a quote. Now in my office he
sat literally on the edge of his chair, poised to take down
everything I said. He didn't smile when I glanced at him,
didn't give me a glimmer of recognition.

His expression gave me resolve. All right, I thought, you all
want a story. Hop on this one.

"Of course this case cries out for special prosecutors.
Special prosecutors will be chosen, but not by me. I don't see
how I could appoint someone, no matter how proper my
selections, without appearing to be trying to influence the
outcome of the prosecution. So I have asked Hugh Reynolds to
select two special prosecutors."

"Hugh Reynolds?" someone interrupted. The pencils had
stopped moving.

"My immediate predecessor in this office," I elaborated
unnecessarily. "He has graciously agreed to make the selection. That will be the extent of his involvement in the case."

"Unless he picks himself," someone muttered. But that
would be too good a story. They couldn't even dream of that.

"I think he'll want to pick a better trial lawyer than that," I
said dryly. When they laughed I relaxed. "Let's keep that
remark off the record, okay, at least until Hugh's done his best
to hurt me."

As easily as that I had them. There were smiles; they looked
at me as if they knew me.

Why are you all here? I thought irrationally. Why all this
attention to my personal family problems? When they asked
about David it sounded intrusive. "None of your business"
stayed on the tip of my tongue. But it didn't leave there. I had
to play this audience, not antagonize them. I found myself
falling into trial speech. My responses came in complete
sentences, measured and thoughtful, as if I could tell them
everything they wanted to know if only they could think of
what to ask. As a speaker I have one great advantage over
laymen: I have read myself in transcript. Early in my career,
after a year as a county court prosecutor, I spent a short stint in

the appeals section. One of the appeals I worked on was a case I had tried. When I read my questioning, reduced to implacable print, I was appalled. I sounded like an idiot. In trial I had been sure I was making brilliant sense, but in the trial record it looked as if I had been shoved into the trial at the last minute, with little idea of the issues or how to present them.

Other people's transcripts were seldom better. Trial lawyers fall into bad habits and never break them. Even before reading myself in transcript I had seen the most common mistake lawyers make. I vowed to eschew clichés and lawyerese, those time-honored slogans of which lawyers are so enamored and that mean jack shit to the jury. "Ladies and gentlemen of the jury, the prosecution has brought forward a prima facie case but not an irrebuttable one. It is hardly a laydown. If you will recall my cross of the complainant . . ." You can watch the eyes glaze. Jargon is inaudible to a jury. Too many lawyers in the courtroom communicate only with each other.

Early in my speech to the press conference I'd been talking like a politician: "Special prosecutors will be chosen." I consciously cut that off and started talking like a prosecutor again. I was taught better than that. I remembered old Eliot Quinn lecturing us baby prosecutors in our first indoctrination session: "Always active voice. Not 'a gun was displayed,' but 'He stuck a gun in the clerk's face.' And you stick it in theirs. Let 'em see it. Then turn around and look at him. This man right here, the defendant. He did it. He held the gun. *He* did it. He did it."

I learned. I learned to talk to the jury in complete sentences, with transitions. You sound thoughtful even if you're making it up as you go along. Spend enough years at it and you can fall into the pattern even when you're resenting every question you're asked; even when you're afraid you've just made the worst mistake of your life. I started turning the questioning into bantering. They fell into it easily.

"Has Hugh given you some idea who he'll choose?"

"If you think Hugh Reynolds would tell me anything, you

must've been out of town the past year." Laughs and nods again.

"Who's going to represent your son?" someone asked.

"I will hire the defense myself. I haven't yet."

"Which side will you be on?"

I gave the questioner a cool look, and he glanced at his pad. They all settled down momentarily. Where were the borderlines here? I was the chief prosecutor but I was also in the dock myself. My role kept shifting. Did they treat me with the deference due someone who could screw them out of future stories, or did they hammer me like any other hapless citizen thrust into the news?

"I am on David's side, of course. Prosecutors take an oath to see that justice is done." Well, there, I had fallen back on cliché. But it was a good cliché; it meant something. "In this case I see no conflict between those two positions. I have done what I've done, though, to avoid even the appearance of conflict. I have instructed my staff to have no contact with me about the case. None of my regular staff will be privy to any information about the case anyway. In effect, I am creating an independent satellite of the district attorney's office."

"Leaving you where?"

"Leaving me to go about my business of prosecuting criminals in Bexar County. As far as David's case goes, I will have no active participation at all."

They tried to get back on my good side. "You'll be in the audience, won't you?" Dick Heydrich asked.

"You bet, if it gets that far."

They went on yellow alert. "You think it might end in a dismissal?"

"If the special prosecutor knows what he's doing, it will."

"You think it's a weak case?"

"Hey, you don't see me trying it, do you? Hugh always said I ducked the tough cases. I think it was you he said that to, wasn't it, Dick? Well, this is the kind I'd duck: one witness, unbelievable story, no physical evidence to back it up. It sucks, I'm glad to say. I mean, he just attacks this woman, who knows him, in his own office? Come on. Even if you don't know David, that's a little hard to believe, isn't it?"

Jean Palmer was a small, almost frail-looking young woman who had been covering the courthouse only two years but turned up its supposed secrets with regularity. She not only seemed always to be standing by unobtrusively when something important happened, but she invariably asked the best questions. I had wondered before if she had some sort of legal background. She hadn't joined in the bantering today. Now into a small silence she inserted a small question:

"If there is no dismissal, might there be a plea bargain instead?"

The same question Linda had asked, the inevitable question. The real question it represented lurked behind it. I hesitated. I didn't want to cut off any options at the very beginning of the process. The pause lasted long enough to bring all their eyes to bear on me. My first sentence was just filler: "The special prosecutors will be empowered to make offers, of course." They were unsatisfied. Before the next question could come I continued. "But I doubt there will be any plea-bargain agreement. My son is innocent. I strongly doubt he'll be inclined to plead guilty." I saw the headline in their eyes: "D.A.: My Son Is Innocent." When their stories appeared they'd omit the jolly tone of the press conference, but their stories would be informed by what I'd given them: the idea the state's case was weak, and that I was doing the right thing because I was convinced of my son's innocence and eventual vindication. I glanced back at Jean Palmer, but she didn't return my look. She had faded back into her mousiness, and was writing slowly on her pad.

It was easy to wind it down after that. They had gorged on news. Time to vomit it out on paper or the airwaves. As soon as the door opened, Patty coming in in response to my signal, half of them broke through it. Two or three, including Jean Palmer, tried to linger behind, but Patty shooed them out. When they were all gone Linda came in.

"Pray for newer news," she said. "Something to shove this out of mind."

I shook my head. "It won't happen. This is too good. Too many angles to it. They're probably all on their way to Hugh Reynolds's office right now. Let him follow that act."

It was only eleven o'clock in the morning but it felt as if the day were over. I looked vaguely around my desk for something to do.

"Would you like to keep up with the business of the office?" Linda asked.

I blinked. "Have you been?"

She hadn't sat down. She leaned on her hands on the outer edge of my desk, leaning toward me. "I know, everything else should have ground to a halt, but it never does. For one thing, you have a court date tomorrow."

That startled me badly. For a moment I thought she meant *I* had a court date. Anything seemed possible this morning. What was I charged with?

"Clyde Malish, remember? You wanted to handle it yourself."

Oh yes. Clyde Malish. A prominent local crime leader no one had made a case on until now. But it was tricky and I'd decided to prosecute it myself. I had prosecuted another career criminal in February, almost as soon as I'd taken office, a laydown for the district attorney to get back in practice. This one would be much tougher and draw more publicity. I didn't need either.

"Blow that off," I said. "Get a reset, or better yet see if the regular prosecutors in that court are prepared to handle it. Frank should be; he was going to sit second with me."

"Don't you think it will look bad when you pull out of a big case right about now?"

"It might. Frankly, my dear . . ."

She nodded. "What else, then?"

I stood up. "Time to introduce David to his lawyer."

"I've been meaning to talk to you about that, Mark. One more suggestion. I resign from the office and represent David myself."

I closed my eyes and thought about that, not only about David but about Linda, and Lois. When I opened them, Linda was looking at me steadily, with a closed expression. I shook my head. "Looks funny."

"How? No one knows—"

"It would look like you went into the case with some kind of inside information, and maybe some hidden power. When you came back into the office afterwards—"

"I would not come back."

"People would think you would. So while you were in the case you'd look like a secret arm of the D.A.'s office, like I still had some control over the case. Like you'd had the power to force a dismissal. No. The defense doesn't make such a difference. We can afford—"

"That's nice to know, after ten years, that you think the choice of defense lawyer is insignificant."

"Linda, if it was me, I'd hire you. You know that. But there are others almost as good as you and I can hire one of them without looking suspicious. The things I can afford to look solid on I'm going to. Everything has to look clean. You know? Because if we play everything else absolutely straight, maybe we can get away with the one big cheat.

"That's what I'm counting on."

CHAPTER

David's was the first case in years I had discussed with my wife. This mainly consisted of my saying, "What can I do? What can I do?" Finally she looked up from the couch and said, "You could resign as D.A. and defend him yourself."

I stopped pacing and looked at her. The idea had never even crossed my mind, and she knew it. But she was wrong about the reason. I wouldn't give up power because it was the only way I could help David. Defense lawyers, as I'd tried gently to tell Linda, are damned near as helpless as their clients once the machine starts rolling. But what Lois saw was that I cared more about my position than about my son.

"If that would help, I would. You don't have any illusions that I'm the best defense lawyer in town, do you?" Lois only shrugged. She had made her point.

"Who's better, Daddy?" Dinah asked. She was sitting at the other end of the couch. Unlike her mother, who was doing needlepoint, Dinah wasn't occupying herself with something else while I talked. She was just sitting, watching me.

Dinah was the child of our last passion. She was ten years old. She was not close to David at all. He was more like an uncle to her, and not a particularly affectionate one. Dinah had been an embarrassment to David before she was born. Having his mother pregnant when he was thirteen and already in high school offended him. Everyone knew what caused babies. He couldn't stand to have Lois pick him up at school.

By the time Dinah was five David was gone, first to college then on his own. Dinah grew up an only child, as he had. She was a darling child, always. But she didn't draw Lois and me together as we must have expected she would. We had doted on David together. We doted on Dinah separately.

"I hired Henry Koehler," I said in answer to her question.

Dinah frowned in thought. She has her mother's mouth, lucky child, but my brow, and the rest of her face is a not-smooth-enough blend of both our features. Even I know she is only dazzling when she smiles.

"But isn't Henry Koehler a better book lawyer than a trial lawyer?" she asked.

"He used to be. Now he's good at both. Besides—"

"You want to preserve the errors."

"Yes." Dinah is an unusual child. From the time she was born I've discussed my cases with her. When she was tiny it was just a cute game, a way of organizing my thoughts aloud. But I kept it up after she was old enough to respond. She's never provided any keen insights, nothing like that, but she listens so intently I feel compelled to come up with answers myself. Realistically, I know Dinah is not particularly precocious, but she does have a fund of knowledge unusual for a ten-year-old. She understood immediately what I was saying about Henry. He would not only be good in trial, he would make the proper objections to preserve the record for appeal. That was one of the reasons I'd picked him. Too many of the better-known, old-style defense lawyers have too damn-the-torpedoes an attitude about appeal; it's win the trial or fuck it.

Dinah knew what I was saying: we would probably lose in the trial court, if it came to that. She nodded soberly.

"If I may intrude on this conversation," Lois said, smiling, "how *did* the meeting with the defense lawyer go?"

"Pretty well," I said automatically, then stopped to remember and to wonder what the real answer was.

David was already waiting in Henry's office when I came in. They didn't seem to be talking. David wasn't sitting in one of the client chairs in front of the desk, he was sitting on a couch against the back wall. Henry stood up from behind the desk to shake my hand. "This is flattering," he said, "considering the number of times you've beat up on me in court."

"All prosecutors beat up on all defense lawyers," I said modestly. "The odds are—" I realized how thoughtless that remark was under the circumstances.

"Not always," Henry said smoothly, also aware of David's presence.

"Congratulations on the Gonzalez case, by the way," I said. The Court of Appeals had come down with an opinion the week before reversing a DWI conviction on which Henry had done the appeal. (DWIs are the life's blood of defense lawyers in San Antonio. There probably aren't three criminal lawyers in town so rich and successful they don't have to handle them any more.) We were going to get the opinion reversed in a higher appeals court, I was sure, but I didn't say that in front of David.

"Thanks."

Many people were going to be surprised by my choosing Henry Koehler to represent David. But I had given it a lot of thought. Because David was accused of raping a black woman, I had considered hiring a minority defense lawyer and strongly considered hiring a woman. But hiring a black defense lawyer would have been too obvious and (since this isn't a political speech I can tell the truth) with Linda out of the picture there was no woman good enough. Well, there was one, but Hugh Reynolds had taken her away from me. I had also passed over the two or three criminal lawyers considered the old masters. Henry was young, under forty, but he was the one I would have hired if I'd been in trouble myself.

The first thing I often thought when I saw Henry Koehler (pronounced as if with a long *a*) was how unpopular he must have been in high school. Even now he looked something like a Chess Club nerd. He was almost slight, with small hands, and, of course, wore glasses. Not physically attractive; there was nothing about him to put people off. He dressed neither poorly nor well, favoring blue suits. You tended not to notice anything about him except his voice. The voice was not deep but very clear, and his diction was always precise. It carried without being domineering. When he spoke he sounded like a good actor working from a memorized script.

"Y'all've met?" I waved David up from his deep seat on the couch.

"Yes, but we haven't talked about the case yet. We were waiting for you." There was an odd edge in Henry's voice, but I didn't stop to think about it.

I laid a hand lightly on David's shoulder. He still hadn't spoken. I wondered suddenly if I should be there.

I explained the special-prosecutor arrangements to Henry. I would have nothing to do with the other side. "Needless to say, I won't be sitting with you at trial. But I want to be in on the preparations as much as possible. Think of me as co-counsel."

Henry nodded. He was looking steadily at David. Not threateningly; it was more a stare of appraisal and curiosity. He seemed to be willing David to speak. David still hadn't said a word since I'd walked in. He sat without fidgeting, apparently paying little attention to the conversation between me and his defense lawyer.

"Let's talk about plea bargaining for a minute," Henry said to David. "You understand plea bargaining? This is going to be tougher because of the publicity, but let's just talk about the bottom line for now. If they offer probation—"

"No," David said. "I'm not going to plead guilty to anything."

I looked at Henry sympathetically. He had the worst thing you could have: an innocent client. Or just as bad, one who won't admit his guilt. It limits your options as a defense lawyer so badly. And, if you believe your client's denial, puts such pressure on you.

Henry took it in stride. "Tell me what happened." He put a hand up to his mouth and stared at David over it.

David just sat there, not realizing for a moment that he was onstage. I pushed my chair back slightly so that I could see his profile, but he couldn't see my face without deliberately turning. From that position I could also watch Henry's face as he listened to David's version of what happened that cold April night in his office. Under other circumstances it would have been funny. The only evidence of emotion Henry showed as David spoke was to take his hand away from his mouth and lay it on his desk, but I knew what the lawyer was thinking: I'm supposed to sell this in court?

"Did you touch her?" he asked once.

"Only to try to stop her from hurting herself, and to protect myself when she came at me."

The story was an idiot's defense, the kind of horror lawyers swap in a bar years later. I had heard it once already, but today David was going into greater detail. After a while, Henry controlling himself so well he wasn't worth watching, I turned my attention to David. His voice was earnest, his expression almost unruffled. This seemed to be a chance he had waited for. He was leaning forward, his hands moving into postures of attack and defense and climbing out away from him to indicate astonishment. David seemed to have forgotten me. Then I looked away from both of them. I felt like apologizing to Henry.

"I was back in the outer office when the security guard

arrived, but you could see Mandy inside. She had almost all her clothes off by then. You can imagine what he thought."

"The police report says what he thought," Henry said tonelessly.

"Her whole manner changed as soon as other people arrived. She looked so pitiful I wanted to help her myself. Even after she said what she said—"

"—that you had raped her."

"—I thought it was just some horrible joke. I thought she would explain herself, or a psychiatrist would come in to say that she'd just broken away from intensive therapy. I didn't know what to think . . ."

It took another minute for David to wind down into silence, and then we all just sat there in it. David finally turned to look at me, as if for a clue to what should happen next. I kept my eyes on his lawyer; that was the clue. David took it, turning toward Henry himself.

When he had our attention, Henry said deliberately, "That is the worst defense I have ever heard."

He went on. "I have defended a man who was caught inside a house with jewelry in his pockets and he had a better story than that. I defended a child molester who took *pictures* and he had a better defense than your story."

"It's the truth," David said, instantly sullen.

"I'm not saying it isn't. I'm telling you how it sounds. Listen to it yourself." He held up a hand to forestall David's further protests. "Let's go into details. Maybe it will get better. How well did you know Mandy Jackson before this?"

"Hardly at all. She's the maid. Sometimes I'd be in the office when she'd come in to empty the trash cans. We'd say hello. You know . . ."

"All right, she's the maid. What are you? What does this company do?"

"Permacorp? We make software. Write the programs, sell them—"

"Computer games?" Henry asked.

David looked pained. "Business programs, generally. For example, our best seller is a program for small businesses that does the payroll. You just stick in the employees and their annual salaries and the program tells you what their weekly or bimonthly or whatever pay will be, with the deductions figured. I wrote that one," he added with measured pride, as if his audience wouldn't understand the achievement.

"So you're a computer programmer."

"Well, I started as the bookkeeper. Now I'm into a little of everything."

Henry uncovered his mouth. "So you're an important man with the company? Don't be modest."

"I'm probably more familiar with all the operations than anyone else. But we're hardly a giant corporation."

"Still, you're an executive, but you know the maid by name. How did you know Mandy?"

"I don't know, I guess I introduced myself the first time I saw her."

"To a maid?"

"Why not? It's just automatic, someone comes in, you—" David's face hardened slightly, but Henry peppered him with another question before his attitude had time to set.

"How long ago was that?"

"What?"

"That you met her. How long have you known her?"

"Since not long after I started with the company, I guess. Two years, year and a half. I don't really keep track—"

"Ever see her outside work?"

That would have been my next question, too. I pushed my chair even farther back, keeping out of it. David wasn't looking to me for answers, though. It was just the two of them.

"No," David said, but it was slower than his other answers, and he paused afterward.

"When did you?" Henry asked.

"I think I may have seen her at the mall once. She said hi to me, or I did. Was Victoria with me? I can't remember."

"So someone might have seen the two of you together outside the office?"

"Mandy and me? I guess, that once. Is that important?"

"Beats me. Let's get to the important question. Why does Mandy Jackson hate you?"

"Hate me? She doesn't hate me. What makes you—"

"Then why did she do this to you? She framed you for a crime that can send you to prison for life. That's the act of a horribly angry woman. What made her mad enough to do this to you?"

"I don't know." David looked unsure of himself for the first time. "I don't know. We hardly know each other."

It was obvious David had thought about the question. Either he hadn't been able to think of an answer or he knew and wouldn't tell us. Either way, his defense was crippled.

"Then it's impersonal," Henry said. I wondered if David could hear the irony in his voice. "Has she approached you for money?"

"Money?"

"Blackmail. Has she offered to drop the charges for a price?"

"She hasn't said a word to me."

"It was the security guard who came in and found you, wasn't it? Did *he* say anything?"

David looked fogbound. His voice emerged slowly from the scene he was surveying. He shook his head. "Joe Garcia. He just kept his gun on me the whole time. He looked scared to death."

"Which of you called the police?"

"Joe did. He made me sit across the room from him while he called."

"Right away?"

David nodded. "Within a minute after he got there. Thirty seconds. It was like he didn't want the responsibility."

Henry said, "Maybe the security guard wasn't in on it, he just blundered in at the wrong time. Maybe someone else was supposed to discover you. Someone who would have offered *not* to call the police, for a price. Or maybe it was Joe Garcia in on it but he chickened out at the last minute. Possibility at least. Let's hope somebody does contact you offering to drop the charges." Henry looked at me. "Have to hire an investigator." I nodded.

"Maybe since it's gone this far she'll be afraid to ask for money," David said. "That doesn't mean it's not true."

Henry gave him a brief scowl that made him look terribly ugly and authoritative. "Don't look so hopeful. The story sucks without some evidence. Let's go over it again."

Henry ran David through the story again like a hound running a convict down a jungle trail. This time he branched out into details that hadn't been covered the first time. Why was David working late that night? What did his wife think about that? Did he often work late? Why, did he dread going home? When David started getting mad, Henry cut it off by giving him a look that said that David's anger was itself probative. "You afraid of that question?" he said once. "It won't be the last time you're asked it."

There was nothing for me to do. I just sat there admiring Henry's technique. When I first became a defense lawyer I used to spend the first session with the client reassuring him that everything was going to be okay. That was moronic. Much better to show him how utterly bleak his future looked. Then if things worked out better than that he'd be grateful. If not, well, you didn't lie to him.

After an hour of it they both looked frustrated. Henry turned to me for the first time. I thought he was going to ask me a question. He did. "Mark, would you mind stepping outside for a minute? I'd like to talk to David alone."

I didn't mind showing my surprise. At the same time I was scrambling up from my chair as if I'd been caught listening at the keyhole.

"Just for a minute," Henry said apologetically. David didn't look up. I sat in the waiting room for another ten minutes, staring at the wall so I wouldn't have to make small talk with the secretary, wondering what they were saying. It must be about me, I thought.

"When they came out neither of them looked any happier," I told Lois that evening. I didn't tell her the aftermath, when I took David to lunch and asked him some of the same questions Henry had asked, but in what I thought a more conversational tone, until David put down his fork, glared at me, and said, "You don't believe me either, do you?"

He would probably get around to telling his mother that himself. I wondered if he had already called her this afternoon. Lois continued needlepointing. Dinah was looking at Lois as if she had the floor, but Dinah had a question she was burning to ask. After a brief wait she did.

"Daddy, why don't you just pick a real bad prosecutor to prosecute David? Couldn't you do that?"

The short answer was no. The worse answer was I didn't have any prosecutors on my staff bad enough to lose this case. I didn't give Dinah either of those. I picked her up and carried her to her bedroom, telling her about special prosecutors like a bedtime story. I left her to put on her pajamas and when I returned she was on her knees beside her bed. I hadn't seen her do that in years. She didn't pray aloud, and when she finished she didn't mention it.

When she was tucked in Lois came in too. We kissed Dinah good night from opposite sides of the bed. She put her arms around both our necks for a long, uncomfortable squeeze. "Don't worry about it, Dinahsaur," I whispered. Lois just hugged her back.

"Good night, darling," she said from the doorway a minute later.

We found ourselves back in the den at the back of the house. It seemed large and quiet. I waited to see if Lois had anything else to say to me. When she picked up her needlepoint again I went to the bar.

"David called me," she said as my back was turned. "I don't think he's happy with the lawyer you picked for him."

"I'm sure the lawyer returns the compliment. If he thinks he can find a defense lawyer who's going to fall down in gratitude at the chance to present that defense of his—"

"I told him it doesn't matter because the case will never come to trial."

I studied her for a minute. Lois is my age, forty-five, slender, still attractive in a businesslike sort of way. Sometimes—this was one of those moments—I wonder why we didn't get divorced several years ago. Then I remember Dinah. Our arrangement was not quite as old-fashioned as staying together for the sake of the child. It's just that neither of us wants to live apart from her. And there's no compelling reason for doing so. Lois and I are roommates, nearly always pleasant to each other. When we try to be more than that it makes us sad, remembering when we didn't have to try. Someday we undoubtedly will divorce; I can't see us growing old together, after Dinah's gone. That thought saddens me too.

While I pondered, Lois had put aside her needlepoint and was looking back at me. That's our usual method of communication these days, when we bother—studying each other for signs of interior life.

"Isn't that right?" she said.

"Yes. It'll never come to trial."

"Mark. Do you—I just wonder if it's crossed your mind that David might be lying."

"Of course I believe him."

"Don't snap at me. It's an important question. Because if you think he really did it, you might not be quite so aggressive about derailing the prosecution. Tell me—"

"No. Don't think that for a second. That doesn't even matter."

She turned away and changed topics. "I've been thinking maybe we're coming at this from the wrong end. Maybe before anything even happens you could approach this woman—"

"Can't find her."

"No?"

"No. She seems to be out of town. Haven't found anything to use against her either. She doesn't have a police record. Lives in a poor neighborhood, naturally, being a maid. Henry had a thought today." I told her about the blackmail notion. "If she is lying, she might be afraid to show up in court. If we get lucky with the judge and she misses two trial settings, it'd be dismissed. But I'm not counting on that. Maybe our investigator will turn up something."

"I'm glad you thought of that, too."

"You throw out every line you can, hoping something will hit one of them."

"One of them has to work, Mark. *Has* to. You say you'll do whatever it takes, but I would do anything. Anything, you understand? But I don't have the power. I don't have the position. You have them—"

Her hand was out toward me, fingers splayed, stretched taut, tendons standing out all along her forearm. "If you don't use them, I will—"

"Lois! Don't drive yourself crazy. I will do anything, too. I will."

"Even if you think he's guilty?"

"Lois, damn it."

Her shoulders slumped. She let her head loll back. For an instant I thought she'd had a stroke. "All right," she said quietly. "Anything. Whatever it takes. Promise me."

"I promise."

She raised her head and gave me a faint smile of approval. "That's all I wanted to hear."

CHAPTER

Linda had a suggestion early on, before I even met David at Henry Koehler's office the morning after his arrest.

"You've thought about this possibility, of course. Maybe it's political."

"Yes, but I couldn't make it make sense. Why embarrass me politically now, months after the election, years before the next one?" I had already been in office three and a half months. To try to discredit me now, through David, would be pointless. "What are you talking about, just some sick revenge? Using David against me?"

"Maybe it was mistimed," Linda insisted. She was selling herself on the idea, pacing in front of my desk and turning to point. "Maybe the actual players didn't know the significance of what they were doing. They didn't know it had to be done before the election. They screwed up."

"Linda—"

"It's possible, Mark. You're a politician now. You've never been one before. You have to start thinking in new terms."

She wasn't. Linda wasn't taking on a new role; she was

playing the one to which she was still committed: defense lawyer. Her face had gone cloudy as I'd recounted David's version of the facts. She stared across the room, unable to look at me, struggling to believe. Now her face was clear again, and she was leaning across the desk to drill me with her eyes. She had found a way to believe.

"What good does this theory do us?" I asked as if she'd convinced me, but she knew better.

"It gives us a way to go. If she's doing this just for money, she'll be susceptible to pressure. And there may be a connection we can find."

She stopped as that thought led her in a new direction, and for a moment I, too, considered the import of what she was saying. Only one person could profit from the scheme Linda was putting forward.

"And he's picking the special prosecutors," she said, reading my mind. "Maybe it's not just revenge. Who would be vindicated by this—not only David's arrest but your inevitable machinations behind the scenes to free him? The man who said you were trained in a corrupt administration and would be just as dirty a D.A. yourself. Which means he'll be watching, waiting for you to do something unethical."

No. It was silly. But Linda had found a way to make David's story believable. I turned it over in my mind, wondering if it could be used in court, true or not.

"I'll tell you something else you haven't thought about," Linda said. This was after I'd already held my press conference announcing my plan of letting Hugh pick the special prosecutors. She had a new objection. "Another way Hugh could screw you on this deal. Appoint two incompetents as special prosecutors."

"What good would—"

"Everyone would know you'd cut a deal with him. It would make you look devious and corrupt."

"And make him look just as corrupt."

"What does he care? He's already out of it. He'll never run

for office again. This is his last, best chance to discredit the man who beat him out of his job."

I literally waved away what she was saying. But I sat there thinking about it. Linda has an ingenious way of coming up with a ridiculous idea with a little barb buried in it, sticking it in your mind.

She saw me thinking about it. "You should be a lawyer," I said. "But Hugh wouldn't do that. And what if he does? Appoint Abbott and Costello to prosecute David? I could live with that."

He didn't. Hugh's press conference, held two days after mine, made mine look like an amateur show. His office somehow had more of the trappings of officialdom. There was even an American flag behind his desk. You would have thought he was still D.A. He managed to give the impression that he had initiated this whole business.

The conference was televised at noon. I sat in my office watching it. Hugh had grown white-haired and twenty pounds heavier in his four years in office. He appeared to me like the Ghost of Christmas Yet To Come.

He didn't shilly-shally, knowing he'd forfeit his live coverage if he dragged it out. In a few sentences he outlined why he'd been called on to make this choice, intimating that it was because of his reputation for integrity rather than our recent opposition. He referred to me by name rather than title and to David not at all. The camera pulled back as he announced his selections for special prosecutors. They were sitting at the right hand of power, behind the desk with Hugh.

I suppose the polite thing would have been to inform me ahead of time. If I had spent much time speculating, I could have guessed. When I saw them sitting there, they seemed the obvious choices. Hugh hadn't gone the route Linda had suggested of picking incompetents. He had picked the two best lawyers of his administration.

Javier Escalante was the *most* obvious selection, and I was glad to see him. He had been Hugh's first assistant. It was no surprise to see him sitting next to Hugh again.

"Yes," I said to the TV. "Yes, yes, yes." Javier was perfect. Completely respectable but a system man, a team player. Javier wouldn't have to have the situation explained to him.

Hugh's other choice was a surprise, though she shouldn't have been. Nora Brown had spent almost fifteen years in the D.A.'s office. She had started two or three years before I'd quit. We had even tried a couple of cases together when she was a third-chair felony prosecutor and I was a first. She had been rising through the ranks of the office at about twice the normal speed for an unusual reason: she was better than everyone else. Usually a rise like that was attributed to backstabbing or late-night backrubs of the felony chief, but Nora did it purely because of skill. She was the best I'd ever seen.

There was one case Nora and I did not try together. It was a murder case and it was unwinnable. I told her so. I regretted the necessity of the dismissal, but Nora refused even to recognize facts. "But we know he did it," she said like a petulant child. She was still fairly new to the felony section then. Maybe she'd risen too fast to understand reality.

"Knowing it isn't good enough. You have to prove it."

"But he did it."

"But we—can't—prove—it. We have the testimony of an accomplice witness and nothing else. The law says you have to have corroboration for an accomplice's testimony and we've got jack shit for corroboration."

"But the jury—"

I finally let her try it, as an object lesson. Nora was dazzling. But she didn't have to be half that dazzling. The jury was instructed on the accomplice-witness rule but refused to follow it, finding the defendant guilty. His lawyer was already shocked at that point. He'd been relying on his motion for instructed verdict of not guilty, but the judge denied it. The judge saw what everyone else in the courtroom saw and refused to do his job, refused to fade the heat he knew he'd take for letting an obviously guilty man go free. Let the Court of Appeals do it.

They did, a year later, reversing the case for insufficient evidence, meaning the defendant went free after all. You could say my judgment was vindicated by their opinion. But I'd already left the D.A.'s office by then and I didn't feel good about the reversal. Nora and I never mentioned it. She was the star of the office by that time, still with a reputation for suffering physical pain if she had to dismiss a case, even a weak one.

I was still trying to figure out why Nora had quit the office when I'd been elected. I would have made her felony chief if she'd stayed, a job she'd never held in spite of deserving it for at least the last five years of her tenure. She hadn't given me the chance. Her office was cleared out a month before I was sworn in.

She sat there placidly on camera as her former boss extolled her qualifications. Her dark hair was pulled back, making her eyes more prominent. I imagined she was looking through the screen straight at me. Nora had a message for me. I just couldn't read it. This was her chance to show me—what? something I couldn't make out.

It was a hell of a team Hugh was fielding against my son. Javier and Nora had combined for important cases before. There were two men on death row who had received their benediction, and a third who had already departed this vale of tears. They were that good: not only did they win convictions, which any first-year prosecutor can do, but their convictions stood up under almost endless appellate scrutiny.

I turned to Linda. "Think anyone's going to accuse Hugh of taking it easy on me?"

She didn't answer in words. She didn't have to. But looking at my own first assistant gave me something new to puzzle over. What was that momentary expression I'd surprised on Linda's face as she gazed at Nora Brown?

* * *

"Here's the report on Mandy Jackson," Henry's investigator said. "She's so clean you could eat off her."

I didn't know this guy, and I thought I knew everybody. I didn't like him either.

"This isn't a tryout for your stand-up act. Tell us what you know."

"Take it easy, papa. Truth hurts. This truth is, there's not a damned thing wrong with the gal who says your boy raped her.

"She won a perfect attendance award in third grade," he went on, glancing at his written report. I made a derisive noise. "This is significant," he went on, "because most of her peers had dropped out by that grade. She comes from a tough neighborhood, Mrs. Jackson."

"Mrs.?"

"Yeah, that's something else that distinguishes her from her crowd. She was married when she had her babies. The boy's twelve now, the girl six. Pretty good kids, too."

He was souring my stomach. "And the husband's gone?"

"The longest kind of gone. Three years ago somebody stabbed him in the alley behind a bar. Apparently he never was the mainstay of the family even when he was alive. I wouldn't be surprised but what they're all happier now."

"Are you saying she did it? Or hired it?"

"No, it looks like a simple retail exchange where the negotiations grew overheated. Your predecessor got a conviction out of it, but the guy only got twelve years. That's all anybody thought Mr. Jackson was worth. I think the guy's already out."

"Did Mandy Jackson—"

"Testify? No. Didn't put in an appearance in the courtroom from what I can tell. She'll be cherry when she comes to testify against your boy."

"Who is this guy, Henry, some slow-witted cousin you feel obliged to keep on the payroll?"

The investigator smiled placidly, as if being insulted were

just what he'd been angling for. Probably just as well for me he didn't take offense. He was somewhere in his thirties, balding, big arms and a bigger stomach. He looked like he'd been a college athlete and still ate like he had that nineteen-year-old's metabolism. Henry Koehler said, "How do they like her at the company?"

"They like her fine, cuz. She's been there three years, never been late without making it up. That's what she was doing that night, by the way. Usually she works a split shift, coming in very early, leaving before nine A.M., coming back in the early afternoon and she's gone by six. But that day she'd come in late and was running behind. Otherwise she wouldn't've been at the office that late." He gave me a funny, speculative look.

"Why such an odd shift?" I asked.

He smiled. He was hoping I'd ask. "Because she goes to school in the mornings. She's studying—wait for it— economics at, get this, Trinity. Gonna owe about five million dollars in student loans once she graduates. Good student, too. No dummy."

Student loans? Debts? And her husband died in a dope deal. It was a small tag. But how it could make a defense to rape I didn't know.

"What kind of criminal record does she have?" Henry asked.

"She was once five days late renewing her driver's license. Apparently managed to stay off the Most Wanted list for that. Other than that, zippo. Only times she's been inside the jail were to bail her husband out two or three times. The *first* two or three. After that she'd let him sit."

"And what was he in for?"

"Public intox, unpaid speeding tickets. Heinous stuff like that. Arrested once for possession but the search didn't stand up."

I didn't like his manner, but if this guy wasn't kidding around, he was good. That bit about being five days late renewing her driver's license, that wouldn't have appeared on any routine traffic record. He'd had to dig for that. He'd dug that far and all he'd struck was bedrock.

"I may have to come back and watch this trial," he was saying with that same grin. "I wanta see you impeach her with this stuff."

"I assume you're literate enough to have written all this down? Why don't you just leave the written report and skip the rest of the oral presentation? We can do the interpretation for ourselves."

Henry said, "Thanks, Damien. You brought a bill? Leave it with Eileen, would you?"

When he was gone I said, "Where'd you find that guy, Henry?"

"Houston."

I raised an eyebrow. "We're a big city now, Henry, we have investigators of our own."

Henry was standing up to move back behind his desk. Damien had delivered his report from the couch, where he could stretch out, and Henry and I had pulled the client chairs close to him.

"Maybe Linda's right," Henry said. "Maybe it is political. If it is, I don't know who to trust. This is a political town. Everybody's connected somehow. I wanted an investigator from outside."

"Well, I know at least one in town I trust. Let me have a copy of that report. I want to have it checked out myself."

Damien had left two copies. As Henry passed me one I said, "How soon do you want to see David again?"

"I'm seeing him this afternoon."

I looked at him and let three or four beats of silence pass. "Without me?"

Henry shrugged, too easily to be casual. "It's nothing you need to be here for. It's facts, not strategy. Background stuff, things you already know. Who we might call as character witnesses, that sort of thing."

I nodded, and lifted the papers in my hand. "Does this

include the medical examiner's report?" Henry nodded. "Well, that helps," I said. I'd seen the report. "No medical evidence to back up her story."

"That does help," Henry said. "But you know how Nora will come down on that. Half the time there isn't medical support for rape. It would be great if we had a motive for her to lie on top of that."

I indicated the report again. "Which we haven't so far."

Henry said, "It doesn't live up to my dreams, I'll tell you that. She's not the complainant I would have chosen if I'd had my pick."

"Just because she's never been arrested for anything before doesn't mean she couldn't have just started. There's some potential motive there. Hard life, big debts. She could be ambitious for her children. That takes money."

Henry suddenly looked tired. He smiled a little, unmirthfully. "You mean you buy that stupid blackmail idea of mine?"

I didn't smile back. "If I don't buy it, Henry, what am I left with?"

It was a week or so later when Patty said, "Am I a good secretary? Do you love me?"

"You're the best there is, that's why I tolerate you. What horrifying thing do you want me to do?"

"Call Gus Hollingsworth back. He's called fifteen times; he's starting to yell at me. He's as good as said he's going to make my life miserable until you return his call."

"So you in turn are going to make mine miserable?"

"I didn't run for anything. Why should I have to put up with him?"

"I will call him."

"Thank you," she said in a parody of perkiness, and left.

I sighed theatrically, which was wasted on my empty office. Gus Hollingsworth was a political adviser, one of the gang who had first approached me to run for D.A. I sighed again, picked up one of the dozen pink message slips Patty had laid on my desk, made the call. He, of course, kept me waiting. I had to be punished.

"Hello, Gus. Fine, fine—well, you know, under the circumstances."

"Thank you. I appreciate that. He's all right, he's bearing up . . .

"Well, Gus, I don't know what I can do about that. Once David got arrested there was only so much—"

I sat and listened. My silence was hostile, but he couldn't sense that. We were on his turf now, he thought.

"I know how hard it will be for you," he was saying, as if he actually understood human emotions, as if he ever gave thought to anything but politics, "but you have to stay completely out of it now. The temptation to meddle in the case will probably be overwhelming, but that won't do your son any good and it could kill you. If instead everyone sees you staying completely above reproach, showing your confidence in the system, this might actually do you some good. I hate to say that, but—"

I was trying to decide whether to hang up or just lay the phone down on my desk when I finally managed to break in on him. "Listen, Gus, you actually think I care about keeping this job? If I could have used this office to get David off, I would've done it so fast no one would've ever heard of the case. If I can figure out some way to do it still, I'm doing it. If it looks corrupt, tough. The political considerations are so far down on my list, I haven't even had time to think about them."

I grimaced at his response and at Linda, who had just walked in. "Look at it this way, Gus, be glad it happened so early in my term. This gives you plenty of time to groom someone to run against me."

I hung up and said to Linda, "Where did I get 'political advisers' anyway? I certainly didn't go looking for them. I guess they just grew on me, like barnacles on a ship."

"Or flies on shit," she said. Not even playfully.

"Did you just come in to insult me, or did you have something to discuss?"

She had just been fidgeting around, glancing at papers on my desk. When I asked the question she looked up in mock surprise. "You mean business? Something to do with being district attorney? You actually have some interest in that?"

Retorts jostled one another on my tongue, but I just looked at her instead. She looked back, no longer distracted. Her chin was up, ready to receive my reply. Linda Alaniz. I could go for days at a time without thinking about her ethnic origin. Then would come a moment like this, when she looked very Mexican. Her eyes looked darker than usual. Her brows were lowered as if to contain their heat.

When I said nothing she went on. "As a matter of fact, there is a hearing today in Clyde Malish's case. Since you once took a personal interest in the case, I thought you might want to watch. You did say once, I believe during a campaign speech, that you planned to drop into courtrooms occasionally to watch prosecutors in action."

I let another little silence pass. But I resented her resentment, and I couldn't resist replying somewhat in kind. "Has the pressure been too much for you, Linda, while my mind's been on other things? Are you having problems with anyone I should know about?"

"No, we in the lower echelons have been bearing up very well in your absence, thank you."

I was going to lose the staring contest. There was something behind hers. I knew well enough that she wouldn't tell me what it was. I had been leaving Linda in charge of the day-to-day running of the office lately. Probably she had run into a problem, but one she didn't want to report to me. It was strange being Linda's boss. Neither of us liked it.

"All right, let's go see Mr. Malish. I'm curious to see what the Moriarty of San Antonio looks like."

She fell into silent step beside me, and kept her head

lowered as we made our way through the maze of offices. I wondered if we looked to everyone else like a couple having a spat. Maybe, I hoped, we just looked deep in thought.

"Jack's report came back," I said in a conversational tone. "It confirmed everything Henry's investigator said."

"I know," she said. "I read it. I'm sorry."

"No political connections at all. Of course, that doesn't mean anything. They wouldn't have hired some campaign worker to do this. They would have hired someone who was already in place. Someone without a connection." Linda was silent. "Don't you believe in your political theory anymore?"

"Oh, I don't know." Her tone implied apology for her sarcasm of a few minutes earlier. I silently accepted. "It sounds silly, doesn't it? Like you said, it was pretty botched if it was aimed at you. Besides, Mrs. Jackson doesn't seem like the simple sort of fool who would do such a thing, does she? Maybe some idiot teenage girl—"

"Then what is her reason? Blackmail? She's certainly in a position to need money."

"Maybe she's just telling the truth."

We were out in the main hall now. There was no one close enough to see me glance sharply at her. It wasn't like Linda to give up on a case before it started. She was still walking with her head down, arms crossed now. Maybe, I thought, she was out of sorts and pessimistic because she wasn't actually involved in David's defense. I felt a little that way myself.

"Well, that's certainly not going to be the defensive theory. We need some angle, even if it's only to sell to the jury."

"I know." Linda raised her head. "It's just so . . . ."

I nodded. We walked on in a silence more companionable than the one in which we'd left my office.

On the third floor of the courthouse the main section of the district attorney's office occupies the south end, the 186th District Court anchors the north, and the district clerk's records office consumes most of the middle. It's not a very bustling floor—not like the first, where the district and county clerks transact most of their public business, or the second, which is lined with courtrooms and the central jury room. Unless a particularly well-publicized trial is going on in Judge Marroquin's 186th, the third floor is usually quiet. Today, with only a pretrial hearing being conducted in the 186th, the hall was almost empty. The lone figure sitting on a bench near the opposite end stood out as Linda and I walked in that direction. Our hands almost brushed each other. Almost but not quite. I could feel her skin pass mine. We had the warmth but not the contact.

"So you've been following Malish's case still?"

"A little. The motion today is silly, asking the judge not to let our witness testify because we may have made a deal with him."

"But that's something to impeach him with, not reason—"

"I told you it's silly. Of course, with Judge Marroquin, maybe anything is worth a try."

"Are Frank and Marilyn ready for it?"

"Yes. When you bowed out of the last setting they didn't even have to ask for a reset. Malish's attorney made a motion for continuance himself. We just didn't oppose it."

"Lucky," I said. "Linda, I've been hoping that one of these days after work . . ." Already I sounded like a schoolboy. I cleared my throat and tried to think of a better way to put it.

"When did you become so shy?" she asked.

There was no reason the black woman on the bench should look familiar. I was close enough now to see that I didn't know her. But something about her arrested my attention. She was better dressed than the average defendant, in a simple white cotton dress. She was sitting very straight on the bench, watching a door across the hall from her. The door of the grand jury room. Probably waiting to see if she was going to be indicted. Or a relative.

Linda had stopped talking, too. When we were almost abreast of this woman on the bench the woman turned to us, startled, as if we'd been sneaking up on her. There was a trace of alarm in her eyes as she looked at me. I made a reassuring motion, but by then she had already turned to look at Linda, and her face softened.

"Hello, Ms. Alaniz."

"Hello, Mrs. Jackson. Are you all right?"

"Yes, thank you. There's a lady with me . . ."

Of course. I had seen her picture in the newspaper, but those are always distorting. The woman on the bench was Mandy Jackson.

It was strange to see her so close after spending so many hours in speculation about her. I had pictured a temptress, a schemer. Even after the investigators had reported her stainless background my mental image had altered only to include great cunning. The woman before me didn't match at all. She looked like a Sunday school teacher in her white dress. Of course, Nora would have dressed her that way for the grand jury. But Mandy Jackson didn't look like a woman playing a part. She was somewhere in her mid-thirties—over a decade older than David—and somewhat harder used by time than most women that age. But there was something very sturdy about her too. Her straight posture was not rigid. It was natural, the way she had sat all her life. She looked uncomfortable in these surroundings, but she did not, unfortunately, look like a woman about to go in and perjure herself.

She and Linda exchanged a few sentences. I had walked on two or three steps past them and stopped. When Mrs. Jackson glanced at me I nodded, and she inclined her head slightly as well. I knew who she was, and I assumed she knew me. An introduction seemed inappropriate.

Linda must have thought so, too. She said good-bye to the lady on the bench without including me, and was moving to rejoin me when the door across the hall opened and Nora Brown emerged, saying, "We're ready for you now, Mrs. Jackson."

Somewhere halfway through this sentence Nora had taken in the tableau in the hall, but you couldn't have told it from her voice. She held out her hand and waited for Mrs. Jackson to cross the hall. Only after she did, and Nora had laid a hand on her arm, did Nora look directly at Linda and me. We all exchanged those formal nods, but no greetings. Nora ushered the woman who was in effect her client inside, and the door closed. Mandy Jackson was going in to testify to the grand jury. The state's attorney—that was Nora in this case—could present live witnesses to the grand jury if she chose. No one else had a right to be present, particularly the potential defendant or his attorney. No one else including the state's attorney was to be present while the grand jury decided whether to indict. That was the fiction, at any rate. In practice the state's attorney has countless opportunities to influence the grand jury's decisions—through the testimony he presents, the way he answers questions, the whole spin he puts on a case.

The grand jury could no-bill David, meaning there was not enough evidence even to bring him to trial, ask to hear more evidence, or—the usual event—decide what crime most fit the allegations they had heard and hand down an indictment charging that offense. That's what was happening now, behind that door I stared at.

Linda tugged at my sleeve. I walked on blindly toward the courtroom. But I was no longer remotely interested in what was going on inside it. I crossed instead to the windows on the opposite side of the hall. No one was nearby.

"When did you meet Mandy Jackson?" I asked. "I never could reach her."

"You didn't try soon enough. I went that first day. While you were taking David to Henry Koehler's office I went to find her."

"Why didn't you tell me?"

"Because I didn't find out anything good." Linda hesitated. She wasn't looking directly at me, but she wasn't embarrassed. She was troubled by what she knew. "She's not the right type, Mark. I thought I knew what she'd be like. I didn't figure she'd let me in the door once she knew my connection to you. But she seemed glad to see me—someone from the D.A.'s office. She'd been waiting to hear from us.

"She's scared, Mark. She knows who she's accused and she's afraid something will happen to her because of it."

"She said that?"

Linda shook her head. "But I could feel it. I found myself reassuring her. I told her we wanted her to hear about the special prosecutors from us before she saw it on the news. Something none of you career prosecutors thought of doing," she added sharply.

That was true. We had never thought of Mandy Jackson as a traditional victim. She wasn't the victim, David was.

"I sat there with my arm around her shoulders," Linda went on, "thinking about that damned staff meeting, all those section chiefs sworn to uphold the law, all putting their best efforts into torpedoing the case. Are there many meetings like that, Mark? I knew the D.A.'s office must be like this, I knew it. I have been on the other end of that kind of deal too often. Some prosecutor takes it into his head to get somebody and he goes after him like a holy war. But when it's one of your own—"

"You haven't been on the receiving end of treatment like that." We were speaking in fierce whispers. My voice was more controlled than hers. "Your clients maybe. But when has anyone ever been out to get you? You are not your clients, Linda. You never understood that. Everything's a crusade for you, too. You—"

"I *am* my clients. I am whoever I represent. That's something *you* never understood. For you it was just a job. If it was just a job for me, I would have gone into insurance defense. And now I—"

She made a disgusted sound. I said her name and reached for her arm. She turned and strode swiftly away down the hall. She did not want to be intercepted. When she reached the stairwell she disappeared down it. I wondered when I would see her again.

My own anger dissipated at once. I understood Linda's dilemma, and it was partly one of my making, one I shared. We could not be part of David's case. Linda had wanted to defend him, and I had brushed her offer aside. I thought she understood why. I wanted the case to end in a deal, but an honest-looking deal. If Linda left David's father's employ to defend him, the case would still be tainted by my touch. When it ended in a dismissal it would smell bad. I wanted everyone's hands off it. I had explained that to Linda. She couldn't think I'd doubted her competence, not after ten years. But lately I hadn't been much concerned with what she thought.

In the meantime, deprived of a client, Linda had found another cause. Mandy Jackson. For the first time in her life Linda had seen a victim from a prosecutor's viewpoint rather than from a defendant's. As a defense lawyer she'd always had a blind spot for victims. She was too committed to her clients. Everyone was out to get her guy, with only Linda to protect his rights. Even when she sympathized with the rape victim, the murdered man's family, the robbed, the assaulted, she thought they were being at least overly vindictive. She viewed their injured feelings dispassionately. It was a trait that had surprised me in so compassionate a woman. Her identification with the client was so complete, she had that cold spot in her heart for victims. Until now.

I was sure Linda had gone to see Mandy Jackson in aid of the defense, to learn what she could about her before our standing in the case was gone. But some time during the interview she had realized no one was representing Mrs. Jackson. That staff meeting would have put Linda off badly, as she'd said. It wasn't David against whom all the official powers were arrayed, it was Mrs. Jackson. And Linda was always drawn to the underdog.

But now she was out of it completely, which was the worst

thing that could happen to Linda. David wasn't her client and neither was Mrs. Jackson; she was Nora's. I was certain I understood Linda's feelings completely, but what advantage is there in being all-knowing? Her divided feelings scared me. If Mandy Jackson had gotten through to Linda, what would she look like to a jury? It must not go that far.

But with Nora for the prosecution, it could.

CHAPTER

The indictment was a surprise.

In 1983 the Texas legislature did away with the crime of rape. This was a feminist victory. As we all know now, rape is a crime of violence, not of lust. Feminists wanted the offense redesignated. The legislature complied. It was a happy case of appeasing an interest group without offending anyone else. So rape moved over a few pages in the Penal Code, out of the sexual offenses and into the assaultive ones.

The offense was renamed "sexual assault," but little else about it changed. There remained several ways of committing sexual assault. These all consist of the "actor" forcing the victim to submit to sexual conduct without the victim's consent. There are subtle ways the actor can overcome the victim's unwillingness, but the most common methods alleged are that the actor uses physical force or violence or threatens to use force or violence.

Few indictments for sexual assault are handed down by grand juries. Sexual assault is a second-degree felony punishable by two to twenty years in prison. Prosecutors always try

to find an element in the facts they have to work with to
elevate the crime to *aggravated* sexual assault, which carries a
maximum sentence of ninety-nine years or life. The most
common aggravating factors are that the person used a deadly
weapon during the sexual assault, that he caused serious
bodily injury to the victim, or that—this is the best—he
placed the victim in fear that death or serious bodily injury
would be imminently inflicted on her if she didn't submit.
When, I ask you, did anyone ever submit to rape without the
fear that she would be seriously injured or killed otherwise?

So it was no surprise that David was indicted for aggravated
sexual assault. Nora Brown would not have been so ineffectu-
al as to allow the grand jury to indict David for simple sexual
assault if she could squeeze a first-degree felony out of it
instead. The indictment alleged, of course, that Mandy Jackson had been placed in fear of serious bodily injury or death
during the course of the assault.

The surprise was the method of sexual assault. Two were
alleged, in separate paragraphs. The first was the standard,
claiming that David had caused the penetration of the female
sexual organ of Amanda Jackson, a person not his spouse,
without her consent. The second paragraph alleged that on the
April date in question "David L. Blackwell, hereinafter called
the defendant, did then and there cause the penetration of the
mouth of the complainant, Amanda Jackson, by the sexual
organ of the defendant, without the complainant's consent."

Even I felt a small worm of distaste crawl across my stomach
as I read that. That was the trick, and Nora hadn't missed it. A
trial begins by reading the indictment to the jury. I could
picture them turning to stare at David as this document was
read to them. He did what? He wasn't content with just raping
her, he had to stick it in her mouth, too? The judge would have
already instructed them by then that the indictment was only
a piece of paper, it was no evidence of guilt, but jurors who
could hear that accusation read without retaining at least a

small residue of disgust were more dispassionate than any I had ever known.

The beauty part, from a prosecutor's point of view, was that the state had to prove only one of those paragraphs. Either would sustain a conviction; you didn't have to prove both. So you could start out giving the jury that small extra nudge, yet not be forced to prove it.

The other killer for the defense was the aggravating element: that the defendant had "by acts or words placed the complainant in fear that death or serious bodily injury would be imminently inflicted." The state could prove that element, which added a potential seventy-nine years to the punishment, with one question to the victim. And how could the defense dispute her story? The fear is from her point of view. The defendant doesn't have to say anything. The acts that comprise the rape itself would put a reasonable woman in fear that the rapist will hurt her or kill her if he doesn't get his way. Or even if he does.

"Nora," I said to Henry as we read the indictment together. He just nodded.

"Judge Watlin," he added a moment later. I hadn't even gotten that far in my thoughts. A case isn't assigned to a particular court until the indictment comes down. David's was now in the 226th, Judge Watlin's court. It was hard to figure if that was good or bad. Watlin was pretty state's oriented—he tended to favor the prosecution in his rulings—both by inclination and because that's the best way to get reelected. He was a former prosecutor. We had been contemporaries in the office, in fact, but that was neither here nor there. It was hard to figure whose side the judge would be on because he would be so busily figuring himself. John Watlin would want to know how this case could hurt him. It was a criminal, so the public would expect a conviction, but it was the D.A.'s son. Could I hurt him? he'd be wondering. Too many angles.

"He doesn't like me," Henry said.

"Because you didn't contribute to his last campaign."

"Or to anyone else's."

"That cuts no ice with Judge Waddle. But he'll have bigger worries than a grudge against you. He has to figure out what this case will do to his *next* campaign."

"I don't like trying a case to a sweaty judge."

I looked at him in some surprise. "Why, Henry, I didn't think there were any judges that liked you."

He nodded. "And that's the way I like it. In the courtroom I want the jury to see every hand against me. I'm just afraid Judge Watlin will decide he should be on my side." He shook his head. "Don't let the jury think the judge is helping you out. They'll kill you for it."

I looked out the window. So much surmise. For a while we forgot the facts of the alleged crime. It had turned, for better or worse, from an event into a case.

Trial law is a young man's game. Or a young woman's, now. There are exceptions, but it is uncommon to see someone over fifty at counsel table. The prosecutors are nearly always young, because the D.A.'s office is where you start a career. Defense lawyers tend to be older and maybe more experienced, but it's a rare one who subjects himself to the courtroom long past his forties. Some say the stress and tension of trials burn lawyers out. My own theory is that not many want to keep placing their professional fates in the hands of twelve chowderheads who can do anything they want once they retire into the jury room—ignore the evidence, invent their own, base a verdict on the lawyer's tie. Anyone who's tried three jury trials has been burned at least once by that Hydra-headed monster. Trial lawyers start looking for an easier and more certain way of making a living. Civil lawyers become senior partners in their firms and send younger lawyers into court for them. Criminal lawyers become civil lawyers themselves, or judges, or get murdered by a client. Trial is battle, and takes as many casualties. There are about as many old trial lawyers as there are old Russian roulette players. These days when I put in an appearance in court I am usually, at forty-five, the oldest person in the room except the judge.

David's first docket call was the usual zoo. It was Monday morning, there were forty-five cases on the docket. Within an hour some of those would have pleaded guilty, some would be reset to other days, and some poor bastard who hadn't been able to scramble out in time would be saying, "Good morning, ladies and gentlemen. I want to congratulate you for your appearance here in court today. When so many people try to get out of jury duty, it's commendable of all of you . . ."

Henry didn't have to worry about that today. We were near the bottom of the docket, and no one would expect him to go to trial at his first setting. At most today the judge might rule on a few of the pretrial motions Henry had filed. It was an occasion to review the state's file and begin plea bargaining. I saw Henry sitting inside the bar with an open file on his lap.

Javier Escalante came up and shook my hand. I do not know anyone who dislikes Javier, even among the many who have lost trials to him. Someday he will run for a vacant bench and be elected. What he said to me that day was inconsequential, but merely speaking to me said what he wanted to say. It would not do for him to express regret at prosecuting my son, but his manner conveyed it. His tone was the same he would have used for words of comfort to the widow at a memorial service. Javier Escalante is a courtly gentleman of the old school, even though that school closed long before his time.

Nora Brown did not approach me. She turned once from her seat at the state's table, regarded me coolly, and turned back.

Around us was chaos. The state's counsel table was loaded with files. Lawyers picked through them, looking for their own defendant's name. Other lawyers waited in line to confer with one of the three prosecutors assigned to the court, or leaned on the jury box rail to talk to their clients.

There were twelve men in the jury box, wearing gray and handcuffed to their chairs. They were the few of the day's forty-five defendants who had been brought over from jail, where they were staying until their trials, having been unable to make bail. Most of them looked bored. Two thirds were probably courtroom veterans. Most of them were just waiting to plead guilty and be shipped off to the Texas Department of Corrections. The two or three who looked angry were not innocent men unjustly accused; they just didn't like the plea bargains they'd been offered.

The scattering of spectators were mostly relatives. They looked more anxious than the defendants themselves. The four or five reporters in attendance were there because of David. The print journalists carried notebooks. The TV people had left their cameramen out in the hall and looked a little naked. One of the newspapermen approached me as soon as Javier walked away.

"Comment?" he asked succinctly. Dan was a courthouse fixture. His suit had probably looked real spiffy in the early sixties.

"I don't know, Dan, do you think I should go with the confident-my-son-will-be-vindicated crap or the confident-our-system-of-justice-will-produce-a-just-result crap?"

He looked thoughtful. "I'd laud the system. After all, you're it."

"You may quote me."

He walked away, scribbling on his pad.

David was sitting on the first row of seats outside the bar. From the back I could see he was sitting so straight he seemed to be trying to see over the heads of those in front. Lois was beside him. I had tried to talk her out of coming today by telling her nothing would happen, but she'd have none of that. David's wife, Victoria, was not in evidence. David had given no hints of what this accusation had done to his home life.

He was turned out as if for a job interview. When I stood beside him I saw that his shoes were shined, his suit pressed.

He appeared well scrubbed. The effect was to make him look very young, a boy wearing his first men's clothes. When he looked up at me the expression on his face scared me. He looked calm.

"Hello, Dad," he said warmly, and returned to staring avidly at life inside the bar. He was studying the lawyers, prisoners, and clerks as if this were a fascinating opportunity for him to observe the law at work.

Lois was dressed appropriately for a funeral or high tea. She looked past David's back at me, mouth set. She had made her feelings clear to me when the indictment came down. "I know, I know," I'd told her. "It's harder now. It would've been nice if the grand jury had found her unbelievable, but obviously they didn't. But it'll be okay. Javier had to give Nora something, so he gave her an indictment. He'll take over when the plea bargaining starts."

"You keep saying it's not going to happen and it keeps edging closer," Lois had said bitterly. "When is it going to stop looking like an ordinary case? You know how ordinary cases end."

"Making it look ordinary is part of the plan." I had to take the sting out of the facts. Having Lois hysterical wouldn't help anyone. I couldn't tell her how much the indictment had scared me, too.

Now in the courtroom she just looked at me, angry to find herself sitting with her son in this dangerous place.

"Has Henry told you what will happen today?" I asked David.

"Yes. Very little, he said, but I had to be here anyway. Hello, Linda," he added.

I didn't remember her ever inviting him to call her Linda. Linda and I had been partners for ten years, but David had never taken much interest in my work. The last time I remembered him coming to our office he had been a teenager who called her Miz Alaniz.

I straightened up, making sure I wasn't standing too close to

Linda, that I didn't speak to her in a tone of professional intimacy or conspicuously ignore her.

"Hello, Linda," Lois said with more warmth than she'd shown me, that is, a trace. Linda responded, then nodded to me as I'd nodded to her. Occasionally at a campaign function I'd spotted Linda and Lois standing together talking quietly, which always made me stay on the other side of the room until they broke up. Afterward, Linda could never satisfactorily explain to me what they had to talk about.

"Will one of these go to trial today?" David asked. His eyes were still on the counsel tables and the jury box.

"All rise," said the bailiff. We all rose. David did so rather mockingly—his first chance to take part in the native rituals.

"The Two Hundred and Twenty-Sixth Judicial District Court of Texas is now in session, the Honorable John J. Watlin, Judge, presiding. Please be seated."

As the bailiff intoned the chant the judge was walking from the door of his chambers to his well-padded chair behind the high bench. He was called, inevitably, Judge Waddle, and had grown into the name in office. John was prematurely florid. The black robe only added to his bulk. Looking at him made me feel old. We were the same age, and Watlin already looked like a bejowled old fart.

He sat and looked at the docket sheet in front of him, apparently ignoring the fact that all eyes in the room were on him, yet confident they were. The room had grown still.

"The attorneys will please respond as I call the defendant's name. Jesse Stimmons?"

"Here, Your Honor. That will be a plea and an application. The defendant is requesting a P.S.I."

"Fine. We will take it up as soon as I finish calling the docket. Roy Benavides?"

Another lawyer stood to say, "We're conferring, Your Honor."

Judge Watlin looked at him over the top of his glasses. "This

is your"—he counted off the file jacket in front of him—
"eighth appearance on this case, Mr. Rawlings. It will be
disposed of today. State's announcement?"

"The state is ready, Your Honor," said the third-chair
prosecutor, who was standing by the witness box to the
judge's left. The prosecutor scribbled a note on his own copy
of the docket sheet. The judge continued down the list. Two or
three defendants announced ready for trial. Most announced
that they were still conferring with the state or would be
pleading guilty. I glanced at David. He was leaning back now,
arm up on the seatback.

I was afraid I understood. David was looking at the prisoners. They were so obviously lost souls, ferried into the
courtroom in bulk lots, predestined for prison. But David had
arrived on his own hook and would leave the same way. No
one would pick him out as a defendant. He was dressed like
one of the lawyers. The prisoners looked so guilty. They sat
stolidly, waiting to be transported. But he was here only by
mistake, a formality which formality would soon clear up.

Linda had sat down beside him, explaining docket call to
him. "Plea and application means the defendant will be
pleading guilty and applying to the judge for probation. P.S.I.
is a presentence investigation, a report the judge can order
from the probation department to determine whether the
defendant is a good candidate for probation. The ones who say
they are conferring are—"

"I understand." He turned to her just long enough to give
her a condescending smile. "My attorney explained everything."

"Did he explain that if you act like an arrogant little shit in
front of a jury they will hammer you just to see your face turn
gray?" These words were out of Linda's mouth so fast they
seemed a solid block. As soon as she finished she murmured
"sorry" in Lois's direction, rose swiftly to her feet, and stalked
away, already shaking her head at her own intemperance.

Lois was glaring at me as if I'd said it. She didn't like that one word: jury. David only shrugged, almost smiling. I did not return it. I had seen this happen with other first-time defendants who had money or otherwise thought themselves immune. Pretrial cockiness. Linda was dead right about the effect it would have on a jury.

Lois took my arm and led me out into the aisle. "Your partner seems to think this will go to trial. Isn't she in on the scheme?"

"She just got carried away. You know how L— She has a quick temper."

"Mark, you have to tell me how things really stand. Don't gloss them over. If what you're doing isn't going to work, I'll have to do something on my own."

I wondered what that might be as I responded automatically. "Lois, this is only the first setting. There has to be a first setting. It won't go much further. Watch."

"I am watching."

She returned to David. As I walked toward the back of the courtroom I heard his name called by the judge. Inside the bar Henry rose to his feet and said, "Please mark us conferring, Your Honor."

Watlin decided to give him a hard time. "For how long?" he asked.

Henry shrugged. "I suppose until we reach an impasse, Judge."

Judge Watlin looked at Nora Brown's set expression and said, "I'll give you two minutes."

It was a small joke applauded by small laughter. Judges' jokes are always funny. Even David chuckled. Lois did not. She looked at me.

Watlin was not far wrong, as it turned out. Henry closed the file and took it to Nora. She sat there at the table and made him come to her. Javier joined them and they retired to a quiet corner. Judge Watlin, having called the docket, returned to his chambers until the guilty pleas were ready to be taken. I watched the trio of prosecutors and defense lawyer arguing over David's fate. The course of the negotiation was apparent. Nora wouldn't make the first offer. She would say, "What do you think it's worth?" When Henry spoke she laughed soundlessly. That would be her response to the suggestion of probation. Henry grew more emphatic, leaning closer to her. Nora said a short sentence. Henry turned away, throwing up his hands. She had just offered, probably, fifty years.

Javier touched Henry's arm and drew him back. He spoke to Nora as well. Javier was the moderator. When he was in the D.A.'s office Javier was known for offering good deals. Though a good trial lawyer, he had never been the most hard-core of prosecutors. He had a soft spot his friends could tap. I was counting on that soft spot prevailing, even in a case as public as this one.

I stopped trying to follow every nuance. The bustle of the courtroom had died down. Business was being done. Lawyers' conferences with their clients remained quiet but had grown more emphatic. Some were filling out the papers for guilty pleas. Others talked to prosecutors. Two or three of these conferences would be growing less fanciful as the threat of immediate trial hovered over them. The gap of years between the parties narrowed.

Linda was back with Lois and David. A minute later she joined me, standing close enough that I could hear her low voice but no closer, facing away from me. "I told Lois again I am sorry," she said. "He got the better of me. I hated clients like that, so cocksure of themselves they made the judge and jury want to slap them."

"You were right. Someone needed to say that to him."

I don't know if she heard me. She was already walking away. A reporter approached her but she only shook her head. Crossing her arms and leaning against a back wall of the room, she seemed deliberately to have cast herself out. Like me, she watched the conferring group. It was impossible to tell, but I thought her eyes were particularly on Nora Brown.

As expected, nothing was resolved that day. The judge gave them a setting for pretrial motions and a July trial date. That did not mean the end of plea-bargain negotiations. It only meant they would not be carried on in the courtroom anymore. They would continue because plea bargaining is, if nothing else, a way to judge the strength of the opposing party's case.

Judge Watlin looked at me before leaving the bench for the last time. I thought I saw small surprise in his eyes—surprise that I had not approached him about the case? I turned over that possibility. Would Watlin short-circuit the whole proceedings if I asked him? Had he thought of a way to do just that while protecting his political career?

I spoke to all the participants before they left. Nora found me standing in her path. Ten feet away she lit up in a sunny smile. Nora is half a foot shorter than I am, and thin as a rake. Food doesn't interest her. I don't know what does, besides prosecution. She looked rather formidable in her suit and heels. The smile did not diminish that effect.

"Mr. Blackwell. And shadow," she added, looking past me to where Linda had suddenly reappeared. "How are you both?" Offstage there is a lilt to Nora's voice that is southern, gracious, and satirical all at once.

"Hello, Nora. I'm sorry this is going to be your last prosecution. I'd offer you your job back, but of course that's not possible now."

"No, quite im—" she said. "Even if I would consider working under someone who could switch sides at the drop of a paycheck. I had a certain devotion to prosecution, you know. I could never go from telling a jury to convict one day and the next telling them to acquit."

She had that same bright smile, but it wasn't aimed at me; it was aimed past me.

"But you'll have to," I said. "If you can't prosecute—"

"Oh, I could never be a defense lawyer. I'm a civil lawyer now. That is, I will be after this prosecution."

"You should be happy in civil," Linda said. "Something that requires no commitment to anything except money."

"At least—" Nora began.

Javier appeared and murmured politely a blessing that covered us all. "We need to talk," he said to Nora, and took her away.

Henry was about to pass me. I took him aside. "She offered fifty?"

Henry was flushed. He nodded. "Javier brought it down to thirty. But this case is not going to end in a plea bargain."

"David, you mean?"

Henry nodded again. "Any more secret meetings scheduled with him?" I asked.

Henry looked weary. It was much too early in the case for that. "Mark, there was no intention—"

"I know that. You wanted to ask him again what happened without his father the district attorney sitting beside him."

After a pause Henry said quietly, "Yes."

"And?"

"Same story." That accounted for the weariness.

"Do you think it's because of me that he won't confess?"

A look of slight pain crossed Henry's homely face. He would have liked to blame it on that, yes. But he just said, "I think it's because of him."

"Well," I said, trying to think of a bright spot. When I couldn't I manufactured one. "Maybe persistence means innocence."

"What if it does?" Henry said.

"Mr. Koehler? I'm Lois Blackwell. We should have met long before this, I think."

The weariness fell away from Henry as he made a point of looking bright and confident. "Yes, we should have. Would you like—?"

"To discuss the case? Yes, I would."

Dutifully, I joined the group as they started out. Lois turned and looked surprised to see me. "You needn't come, Mark. I'm sure it would all be repetitious for you."

Her eyes were more emphatic than the cordial words. I let them leave me behind. Linda was the one I wanted to talk to. She was no longer near me. I had to catch up to her. "What's with you and Nora?" I asked.

Linda's nose wrinkled. "She and I—"

"—are too much alike," I finished. "Just on opposite sides."

"No." She sounded even more disgusted. "Ms. Brown could never work under a woman, I think. Or a Mexican, I'm not sure which. Certainly not a Mexican woman."

"Nora? I never thought that about her. Anyway, listen, Linda—"

"I cannot waste all day here," she said, and abruptly hurried away. What had I done to offend her?

Nothing happened, and nothing happened, and nothing happened. That was the usual course of a case, but when this case started acting usual I got scared. Without consulting Linda or anyone else, I called Javier Escalante. He was very cordial. He agreed at once to meet me, without being dim enough to ask the subject. His choice of meeting places demonstrated his understanding.

"I'm meeting a client at ten," he said. "Why don't you come an hour earlier than that and we'll have time to talk."

I don't know who his client was, but the meeting place was a school, which struck me as odd, then when I'd parked in the lot behind the school to which Javier's directions had led me, it struck me as perfect. School was out for the summer. At nine o'clock on this June day there didn't even seem to be janitors there.

I was leaning back against the hood of my car when Javier's Eldorado slid to a stop beside me. Javier's greeting was so casual and pleasant, we might have been surrounded by people. I wondered if Javier's smooth manner was his natural personality or a front for something more raw. I thought I might find out in a few minutes.

"How does it feel to be a prosecutor again?"

"In this instance, distasteful," he answered with that same regretful tone.

"I'm glad to hear it. Why, then, does the case seem to be progressing toward trial?"

He only looked at me, surprised at my bluntness. "I don't—"

"Henry tells me you haven't come down from your initial thirty-year offer. You can imagine my surprise. I expected the usual diminishing of the state's expectations, ending in a dismissal."

He smiled gently at me. I was being treated like a client. "If only a parent's hopes could dictate the course of a case. Unfortunately, this one—"

"What's unfortunate about this one, Javier? I paved the way for you perfectly. I've been telling the press for weeks what a shitty case it is. No one would've blinked an eye if you agreed and dismissed it."

"Mark." He reached toward me, becoming a little more candid in manner. "If there had been any way to pronounce this witness unbelievable, I would have taken it. Believe me. But there was not. I'm sure you are familiar with her background by now. It is impeccable. And her story of the . . . the crime is a very common one. There are no flaws in it. The grand jury thought so as well."

"I knew there'd be no dealing with Nora," I said. "They could bring John Kennedy and Martin Luther King back from the dead and tell her to prosecute them for arranging their own murders and Nora would go for their throats. But I thought you at least would understand how things are. I thought you'd realize that this wasn't just a case. It's your livelihood. You're still in the criminal defense business, aren't you, Javier? That's what pays for your car and your office and your kids' schools and your nice suits. That business could get awfully tough after this case. Next time you walk into court with a DWI defendant, the state's offer is going to be ninety-nine years. And go up from there. I wouldn't condone retaliation, Javier. But you know how assistant D.A.s are. If you win a big case like this, against what seems to them the D.A. himself, they'll all want to try their hands against you. Nobody will ever offer you a good deal again. I hate to think what will happen to your business once clients start thinking you can't get a case dismissed anymore, you can't even get a decent plea bargain. There's plenty of other lawyers they can go to. And they will. Hasn't that occurred to you?"

Javier looked at me as if debating whether to tell me I was on the brink of committing a crime. Otherwise my speech had not made him the least bit nervous. He was just trying to decide whether to tell me—something. Suddenly I felt cold, in the shade in June.

"That—will probably not be a consideration for me much longer," he said.

"Jesus, Javier, you didn't just inherit a fortune, did you?"

"No," he said slowly. "Nothing so—so extraordinary."

"Oh my God, Javier. What did Hugh promise you?"

"Nothing, Mark. What is there he could offer me? Only his support."

"His support?" I had realized what it was, what it must be, but I continued acting ignorant, as if not understanding could make it not so. The governor and Hugh belonged to one political party and I belonged to the other. Though he'd lost the election to me, Hugh still carried certain power within his own party. He hadn't been stupid, he'd doled out lots of favors in his four years in office. He was owed. These thoughts were crossing my mind, but I still demanded it be spelled out. "What do you need his support for?"

Javier coughed. "As you know, Judge Vasquez is retiring before the end of his term. His health . . ."

"Oh my God. Hugh promised you the bench."

"Not in so many words." Javier found distasteful the way I was saying everything aloud. There were understandings between gentlemen.

"In the same conversation in which he told you he was going to appoint you special prosecutor against David."

"Yes, as a matter of fact. But there was no quid pro quo implied, no trade-off. We simply—"

"No, of course not, Javier. But now you don't dare dismiss the case because it might look scandalous and the governor doesn't appoint scandalous lawyers to vacant benches. Oh Jesus, if I'd known Hugh had something like this in his pocket—"

"It means nothing," Javier said. "One has nothing to do with the other. The case will go to trial, as it should. If the state's case is as weak as you say, David will be acquitted."

"You mean they'd still give you the bench even if you didn't manage to put my son in prison?"

"Mark."

"God damn it, Javier, I've got nothing to promise you in return. Isn't there anything? Maybe in a couple of years *I'll* have the stroke with somebody to get you something. Maybe—"

"Mark." His voice was compassionate. "Don't try to skewer the system. It works. Let David tell his story at trial. The truth will out. There's never been a better mechanism invented for getting at the truth than—"

"Don't give me that crap. What do you think I am, some fucking law student? Don't give me your civics lecture. I know what trials are. They're sausage machines. They're for grinding up defendants."

"People are found not guilty every week."

"Once a month maybe. In misdemeanor cases, where there

really is a presumption of innocence, because the offense doesn't amount to much. Not in district court. When jurors walk into a felony court, they look at the poor, hapless bastard sitting there and the first thing they think is—I wonder what he did? They look at him like he's the man from Mars. They don't afford him a presumption of innocence; they don't even think he's part of the human race. My God, Javier, how can you—"

I bent over as suddenly as if he'd punched me in the stomach. For a few seconds I thought I was going to throw up. He patted my back.

"Don't take on like this," I realized he was saying. "It does work, I believe the system does work. Juries have ways of ferreting out the truth."

I straightened up. "You think so, don't you, Javier. But would you trust your son to it?"

He started edging away. "I have my meeting inside. If there is anything I can do, Mark, to make your mind easier . . ." He backed away, trailing words.

Another rumble of nausea gripped my stomach. Javier was lost, Nora was unapproachable. Who else is there? I thought. And despaired. A trial. My God. A trial.

I entered the courtroom wearing full regalia: suit, tie, briefcase, polished black shoes. David followed sheepishly. He was in costume as well. I stopped to turn on the lights. When the first bank was on I liked the look of the courtroom—dim and empty. But then I kept flipping switches until it blazed like noon, like an interrogation room.

"These benches will probably be full of people," I said. "Maybe not, but probably, a case like this. I think you'll be surprised how easy it is to ignore them. There won't be many people in the room as far as you're concerned. Your lawyer, the prosecutors, the jurors. In this courtroom the jurors are practically at your elbow. They'll be closer than anyone else.

It's all right to look at them. I see witnesses all the time staring straight ahead, looking out of the corners of their eyes, like it's a crime to look straight at the jury. Look at them. They're your audience. Take your seat."

He climbed delicately the one step to the witness stand and sat as if the chair were resting on a trapdoor. He shifted around, looked at the imaginary jury, got embarrassed.

"Comfortable?"

"No."

"No. You won't be. For God's sake, don't look at ease when you're sitting there for real. Nothing puts a jury off like arrogance."

I put my briefcase on the prosecution table and took a file, legal pad, and pens from it. Spread them around.

"While Henry is questioning you the prosecutors will be writing notes. Lots and lots of notes. Don't let them worry you. Sometimes they hear you and start writing furiously and you think you said something wrong and start trying to backtrack and fill. Don't do it. Ignore them. Sometimes they do that just to fluster you."

David shook his head.

"I am the prosecutor. Look at me. Henry has just finished questioning you and passed the witness. To me. You're mine now. Look at me. Don't look comfortable, it's okay to be nervous. But you've got nothing to hide. Concentrate on the questions. Don't answer something they haven't asked. Trust your lawyer. If they ask you something damaging and it needs more explanation, trust Henry to let you explain when he gets you back on redirect. And don't blurt out your answers. Give him time to object if he needs to."

"I don't have anything to hide, but be grudging with my answers," David said. "Don't give them anything but what they ask for."

"Yes. I know it's contradictory. Don't—whatever you do—get belligerent. This is a crime of passion—"

"That I didn't do."

"—they want the jury to see you mad. It's like enacting the crime for them. Don't—whatever you do—get mad.

"Now. We begin. You have just told your story. You feel good about it because you've finally gotten to tell your side. Don't slump. It's not over. It's far from over. I sit here. I am Nora Brown. I look at you like something a sick dog left on my rug. You might've sold everyone else in the room, but you haven't sold me. I am your worst enemy. Be civil to me."

"Dad—"

"Good morning, Mr. Blackwell. My name is Nora Brown. I represent the State of Texas. I have a few questions for you too, if you don't mind."

"I don't—"

"Shut up. Don't be sarcastic back to her. Let her be the jerk. If you both look like jerks, she's won, because you're on trial and she's not. She hasn't asked a question yet, so you don't say anything. What time did Mandy Jackson come on duty that night, Mr. Blackwell?"

"I don't know."

"You're not familiar with her schedule?"

"No."

"Was this the first time you had worked that late?"

"No."

"You often did?"

"Once in a while."

"Had Mandy come in to clean before when you were the only one left in the office?"

"I'm sure she had."

"You're sure, or she had?"

"Yes, she had."

"So you knew she worked nights."

"I knew she did sometimes. I didn't know if it was her regular shift."

"Did you notice her when she came in?"

"Not really, not until she walked up to my desk."

"You were so engrossed in your work you didn't realize another human being had entered the room?"

"Of course I saw a maid had come in. I don't think I even realized which one it was until she walked up to me."

"Did you notice what she was wearing?"

"She was wearing the regular maid's outfit, dark skirt, white blouse."

"Mr. Blackwell. Please listen to my question. I am not asking what you remember now. I am asking what you noticed that night. Did you notice what she was wearing?"

"I didn't pay particular attention—"

"Mr. Blackwell."

"Yes! I noticed."

"Thank you. Her white blouse, was it buttoned all the way to the top or was it open?"

David looked over my head for a moment. "It was open."

"All the way open, as soon as she walked up to you?"

"No. I thought you— No, just open, the way a shirt has an open neck."

"Just open at the neck, then. One button, two buttons, three buttons? How many buttons were open?"

"Two, I think."

I wrote a note. "Did you notice her shoes? Tennis shoes, heels—"

"No."

I nodded as if he'd done well. David relaxed a moment. "What about her skirt? Was it tight or loose?"

"Not very loose."

"Tight, then."

"Well, fairly, I guess." David was leaning toward me. He didn't want to get any more answers wrong.

"Did it have a button or a zipper or both?"

"Button or . . ." he said slowly. "I'm not sure."

"Think of it this way. When you put your hand inside the

waistband of her skirt and pulled, did a button pop off or did a zipper tear?"

"Neither." He flushed.

"Neither? The skirt had no way of opening?"

"I didn't tear it open."

"All right, then. When *she* opened it," I said derisively. "Buttons or zipper?"

"I don't know. I wasn't paying attention to her clothes."

"Well, to be accurate, you weren't paying attention to her *feet*, Mr. Blackwell. Yet you remember exactly how many buttons of her blouse she had undone, don't you?"

"No!"

"No? But you just told me you did. Were you lying?"

"Where's my lawyer during this?" David asked, twisting in the chair. "Why isn't he saying anything?"

"Because I haven't asked anything objectionable. Let me ask you this, Mr. Blackwell, was this an unusual event in your life?"

"When?"

"Let me remind you of what you testified to on direct examination. Objection, Your Honor. Sidebar. Sustained. When this woman walked up to you and started tearing off her clothes, was that an extraordinary event?"

"Yes."

"Not the kind of thing that happened every week?"

"No."

"Even every month?"

"No."

"Or ever, in fact?"

"No."

"Why are you smiling, Mr. Blackwell?"

"Well, the idea of something like this happening once a week."

"Yes, unbelievable, isn't it? How did you feel when it happened? Objection, Your Honor. My client's feelings aren't relevant." I stood up. "They most certainly are, Your Honor. The state has the burden of proving this defendant's mental state at the time, among other facts. Objection be overruled." David was sitting up. He appeared eager for this mock exchange to be over so he could answer the question.

"I was appalled."

"Frightened? Horrified? I'm not sure what that word 'appalled' means."

"Yes, both those things."

"Did you go up and assist her in removing her clothes?"

"Not on your life. I stayed back."

"Behind the desk?"

"Yes."

"It didn't occur to you, Gee, here's an attractive woman— you did find her attractive, didn't you?—ripping her clothes off in front of me, something I've dreamed about since I was fourteen years old, let me run over and help?"

"No. I backed even farther away, I think."

"How far?"

"Ten feet. Fifteen, I'm not sure."

I made a note. "Did she ever slap you, Mr. Blackwell?"

"Slap? No." He looked confused by the transitionless question.

"Maybe slap is the wrong word. Strike you with her hand in some way?"

"I don't think so. Dad? Did I tell you—"

"You remember medical testimony, Mr. Blackwell, that traces of your skin were found under Mandy Jackson's fingernails?"

"Oh. Yes. Well, she scratched me once."

"Why? Objection, your honor, that calls for speculation. Put it this way, then, Mr. Blackwell. *How* could she scratch you? What occasion did she have, when you were fifteen feet away?"

"Well, at one point I went up closer."

"How close? Two feet from her? One foot? How long is her arm? How close did you get to this woman who frightened you so, Mr. Blackwell?"

"Two—I don't know, I went up and took her arm—"

"No!" I was on my feet. *"No! Don't* let her back you off your story! See what she does? Backs you into taking a position because you're trying to answer the question the way you think it should be answered, then two minutes later you have to say something else the other way and all of a sudden she's moved you fifteen feet across the room and you're a *liar!* Well, which is it? What you told us five minutes ago or what you're telling us now? Which was the lie, Mr. Blackwell?"

"But I had to change, once she—"

"Yes, once you gave her the answer she wanted to begin with. That's why you have to get it right the first time. Don't try to say the answer you think sounds good, say the *right* answer."

"Is that what we're doing now, concocting the best story?"

"Yes. That's what we're doing. Because no one remembers things perfectly—"

"Especially if he's lying, right Dad?"

"—but if you don't, she'll say why don't you remember, Mr. Blackwell? Wasn't this an extraordinary occasion, Mr. Blackwell? Didn't the details imprint themselves on your memory, Mr. Blackwell? Why not, Mr. Blackwell? You were confused? Or was it some other emotion that clouded your perception, Mr. Blackwell? Lust, maybe? Lust for subjugation?"

"Dad—"

"I am *not* your father, I am the goddamned prosecutor, I won't be able to say a fucking *word* when she's asking you ever so sweetly, when she's steering you into traps, I'll be out there, God damn it, with all the other geeks in the gallery! That's why you have to have this *down,* David, because I can't be signaling you the answers when the time comes. I will be out of it. I will be—"

I was out of breath. I leaned on the table. David came off the stand. He'd picked up a little of my technique. He asked a question that was completely unexpected to me.

"Why do we have to do this, Dad? Is this some sort of object lesson? You said there'd never be a trial."

"I didn't say that. Your mother probably said that. And I did everything I could to see there wouldn't be, and I failed. *That's* why we have to do this, because now it's up to you, David."

He waited until I finished speaking, then pretended I hadn't. "Is this supposed to pique my interest in the law? You think I'll go to law school after this?"

I straightened and looked at him. "Law school? I never wanted you to go to law school. There are too damn many lawyers as it is. I didn't care what you did."

"No, you didn't, did you? I could've been a janitor or a nuclear physicist or an anarchist, couldn't I? Because by then you already had a child coming along who was exactly what you wanted."

"I'm sorry, David, I said that badly. I didn't mean I didn't care, I meant I left it up to you. I wanted—"

"Why'd you say it that way, then? Were you lying then or are you lying now?"

I would never have believed David could twist my words on me. I realized I didn't really know how smart David was. He was always so unobtrusive. Standing there, I wished I could live twenty years over again in an instant, live them differently so David would be a different person and so would I, so we'd be standing somewhere other than where we were, having a witty conversation and laughing and clapping each other on the shoulder. "Son," I began helplessly.

He spurted air between his lips and twisted away. "Don't. Don't start appeasing me. I just—" Standing ten feet away from me, or maybe fifteen, he started crying. "I just wanted— You know, I think this is the most time you've ever spent with me, and it had to be for this."

"I know. I wish I could—"

"You know how good I am at my job, Dad? You know I got a

promotion the week before this happened? Did I tell you that? They love me there, Dad. They think—thought they had to pay me more money or I might leave and start my own company. You know that?"

"You still can, David. After this is all over. I've always been proud of you, David. I never—"

"Don't." He turned away. "Don't start now." He pushed through the gate and started up the aisle of the courtroom. I called him.

"David, we have to get this down. It's not for me, David, it's for you."

I was talking to myself. He was out the door, closing it quietly, a polite boy, as always.

I followed him slowly, turning out the lights, hearing again the silence of the building. Instead of taking the stairs down I went up, out into another dark and empty hall, through the door under my name in foot-tall letters. I couldn't think where else to go. Not home. David might be on his way there now. He needed Lois, without me competing for her attention.

Surprisingly, the office of the district attorney—my office— has no windows. It's a spacious office, but buried deep in the warren of other offices, surrounded by interior walls. Day or night means nothing in there. But as I sat at my desk I could feel the emptiness extending around me. Patty and the other secretaries had gone home three hours earlier. Diligent prosecutors might have stayed until five-thirty or six preparing for the next day. But it was eight o'clock now. You could fire a cannon down any hallway of the courthouse and do no human damage. The sheriff's department used to be in the courthouse, so there were deputies on duty at all hours, but their administrative offices had moved out to the new jail a year before. Now the building grew hollow at night. The silence pressed on me like a silent crowd jostling to get a peek at me through my open office door. I had no inclination to go anywhere.

The terrible thought blossomed, and this time I didn't stop it. Maybe David was guilty. He wouldn't be the first guilty man I had seen persist in denial all the way through his trial and beyond. His bland assumption that I would get him off made me wonder if he had counted on my position from the beginning. Had he thought he could do whatever he wanted because his father was the district attorney? If someone had put this to me as a hypothetical two months ago—do you think David could do such a thing as this?—I would have laughed it off. Now I realized how little I knew my son.

If it had been a different crime he was accused of, I would never have doubted him. Thieves and robbers we understand: they want money. And we have all felt rage strong enough to make us assault or kill. But rapists are the most twisted, unknowable criminals. What they want is something intangible; not sex but domination. They lust after that subjugation so powerfully they risk prison and disgrace to have it. Their thoughts are so alien to the rest of us, we have no way of spotting the clues to what they are. When uncovered, they may turn out to be the most respectable of men in their daily lives. Was David one of those alien beings? I had kept the thought down but it would not stay submerged. After all, Mandy Jackson and her story were without flaws, while David's was ridiculous. Still no one had come up with a convincing reason why his story could be true.

I didn't hear footsteps. The administrative offices are carpeted. I don't know how long she'd been there before I noticed her, just standing two or three feet inside my office, staring at me.

"Jesus, Linda, make a noise when you do that. I was just sitting here thinking I was the last soul in the building."

I might have been still. She didn't move or speak. Even her eyes were motionless. I began to think she was an illusion. Why do you haunt me?

"Linda?"

"This is not working," she said suddenly, the puppet of a bad ventriloquist. I still hadn't seen her move.

"You heard that scene with David? I don't know what to say to him. He's so—"

"I am not talking about David. I am talking about the first assistant district attorney."

For an instant I had to think who that was. She said the title as if it were the name of a person she had come to complain about. As she said the words she took two steps toward my desk, then, apparently, remembered her vow of nonmovement and stopped, rigid again.

"This is not working, my being your assistant."

"I don't think of you as my assistant, Linda, I think of you as—"

She made a disgusted noise I cannot reproduce. It stopped me dead, as intended.

"Don't treat me like a secretary asking for a raise. I didn't come to talk about titles. This is my resignation, Mark."

I didn't say anything. Maybe it was silence that released her from the spell. She moved across the room, gesturing.

"I have no function here. Everyone sees it. They tolerate me when I come into their offices, into courtrooms. 'Be nice, it's the D.A.'s girlfriend.'"

"No one thinks that, Linda. Everyone knows you're qualified."

"To do what? I never had these stupid worries when we were partners. I knew what to do then. I was respected as a defense lawyer. Good offers were made to my clients because they knew I wasn't afraid to go to trial and there was the chance I could beat them. Prosecutors didn't play stupid games with me. Now they do. They all do. They know I am not really one of them. And that is fine with me. But that leaves me nothing to do here, Mark. I didn't come here to retire."

She had talked about nothing but her job, but these were

things for a memo. What she said didn't account for the emotion in her voice, her slashing gestures. She had come to burn my office down. I said, "I don't have anything to do either, Linda. I know the sidelines are a terrible place—"

"Yes. You do. You are the district attorney, Mark. Be the district attorney. Don't ask me to do it. I've tried supervising prosecutors, and it is not for me. I would rather fight with them."

And with me, I thought. "All right. I know I've been neglecting the office. I won't slough so much off on you anymore."

"All right. And I will help prepare David's case."

"How? There's nothing for either of us—"

"There is always something to do for a case. You know that. Mock examination. Put him on the stand. Let Henry play the defense lawyer and me the prosecutor."

"There's casting."

Her eyes blazed. "Let me cross him and you'll see something."

I certainly would. I would see David hate us both, probably. After the scene we'd just had, further pretend cross-examination would make him certain I didn't believe him. "Maybe," I said.

She didn't let me explain. "Fine. While you think about it, I will be moving out of my office."

"Linda!" My voice stopped her. She was used to doing all the shouting, not having her serves returned. I was on my feet. "I need you here, Linda. *I* need you. Me. Not for the case or the office."

She made one of those sounds of hers, half laughs, all bitterness. "I believe you have someone for that."

"You know better."

"For that you have my phone number."

"What the hell is the matter with you?" I shouted. For a moment I scared myself. Trying to match angers with Linda was a suicidal business. But she did something worse than lash back at me. She changed tactics. Suddenly she had pulled away from me without moving.

"I understand why you chose to keep me out of this," she said sadly, making me wonder what she understood. "But that decision stripped me of my one area of expertise. I cannot help you as a lawyer and I don't know what to do for you as a friend. What kind of woman does that make me? One who— Mark. I could comfort Mandy Jackson because that was like handling a client. But I don't even know where to start comforting you.

"My staying here is a farce. Let me go. I am no prosecutor."

It was an exit line and she used it. Turning away was no dramatic gesture. She was out my door before I could stop her. I knew she did not want me to follow. She looked not on the verge of tears, but too sad for company. Linda was right. I should let her go. I dropped into my chair and tried to return to my thoughts of the case. But it was as if Linda hadn't left the room. I kept seeing her. The curl of her fingers as she made a sweeping gesture. Her body in profile as she turned to leave. Most of all, her amazingly mobile face, almost liquid in its ability to shift in an instant from one emotion to another. The fight we'd just had was the most passion we'd shown each other in a year. It recalled other emotions, her face in other moments.

She was in her own office, throwing books and papers into a box. Not angrily and not resignedly. She looked as if she had made a decision and was trying to avoid rethinking it. I hoped she'd been thinking the same things I had.

"All right, go," I said. "I'll help you pack."

She looked up, puzzled.

"If you can't stand this office, go back to private practice. But that's not the end of it because work isn't all we share. I won't let you go. I won't lose you, too."

She came around her desk. She was still angry, and sad, but

now I had almost amused her as well. "How can you stop me?" she asked.

"Camp on your doorstep. Tell you how beautiful you are. Handcuff you to me. Whine and be pitiful. I don't know. You tell me the best way."

She shook her head. "There is no way. You can't pursue me because you have an office to run."

"Fuck the office."

She did laugh at that. "You? No. It is your life."

"What's your life, Linda? Work, nothing else? Linda."

She didn't answer. I decided to tell her the one thing I'd been keeping from her. If she was leaving anyway, it didn't matter. "Do you know why I refused your offer to resign and defend David?"

"You told me the reason," she said.

"That wasn't all of it. Even back then, when I was confident I could head this thing off, I knew there was a possibility of it going to trial. And if that happened, the defense lawyer would have no better odds than defense lawyers ever have. I didn't want that to be you, Linda. I know how you are. If you had lost this case, you would never have forgiven yourself. That would have been the first thing you thought of every time you looked at me. It would have driven a wedge between us that eventually would have torn us apart. I couldn't stand that."

"At a time like that you thought of my feelings? That was wrong, Mark. You should have thought only of David."

"I know it was wrong. I knew it then. It was selfish of me, but I did it."

We were inches from each other. She was looking down as if for a graceful way out. I took her arm. Maybe I would have to handcuff her. The fingers of her other hand brushed my side. I pulled her closer and she let me. Her hands were on my back, under my shoulder blades. It felt like one of those brotherly sisterly good-bye hugs. But it didn't end. Suddenly I was gripping her as hard as I could, and she was pulling me even closer. That year's worth of unspent emotion held us both in place. I meant to stay like that forever if the alternative was losing her.

For a long moment we held each other fiercely, as if we would push inside each other's skins. Her hands were tight on my back. Then one of them slipped lower. I pulled her blouse free of her skirt, found the zipper, popped the button off. She freed a hand momentarily to help me, and the skirt slithered down her legs.

There was a couch in my office, and there were D.A.'s office legends about that couch. We didn't add to them that night. We never got further than the desk and the carpet. I leaned back against her desk, pulling Linda up so that she was stretched full-length against me, when I realized we were visible through her open door and the glass wall of the outer office. For a moment I thought someone was watching us. I picked her up, my hands under her thighs, and carried her into my office. When I set her on her feet she slipped her half slip off and reached for the buttons of my shirt as I pulled my tie off. I undid half the buttons on her blouse, then just pulled it off over her head.

It wasn't pretty and it wasn't sweet. I had forgotten how smooth her skin was. I had loved to run my hand down the long line of her side, from her breast to her thigh. But tonight we didn't take time to savor the details. If we had slowed down, we might have stopped. We were in a hurry, as if we expected to be caught. It was ourselves we feared. I was almost afraid to say her name, to remind her who we were. But I did say it—"Linda"—and touched her face as well as her breast and back. There were tears in her eyes. Soon I felt what my body remembered better than my mind: her hands clutching my back as if she would tear out handfuls of flesh. She jerked against me and cried out. A moment later I let my weight down on top of her.

For what seemed a long time we just lay there breathing. After a while our hands moved slightly on each other's bodies.

We looked at each other and kissed again. I thought of cute things to say like, I don't accept your resignation, but didn't say any of them. Linda didn't say anything either for a long while. When we did finally begin talking it was in low murmurs. I both felt and heard her voice. "Stay out of it if you want," I said. "I understand. I need you, not the case."

She laughed very lightly. "Try to keep me out."

The irony of my campaign had been that everyone had assumed that Linda and I were lovers and by that time we no longer were.

The idea of having a woman for a partner had been exciting when I'd first considered it, but that titillation had been lost in the daily flux of private practice. Linda was not a flirt, and I had a marriage I did not yet consider unsalvageable. Maybe there were rumors about us already, but they were not of our doing. In the office and the courtroom we were all business.

Paradoxically, it was in business that we built our intimacy, an intimacy that sprang from work rather than from sex. No one could have calculated our closeness; Linda and I were too different. But when we worked together we could almost read each other's minds. We raced each other to a conclusion, responding to objections before they were made. I was the idea man. I'd spin off ten in an hour. Linda seized on the good one and developed it. I can't remember the number of times we'd start talking about a case in the afternoon, in her office or mine, pacing, dropping into chairs, nodding and shouting and laughing, and look up to discover the coffee carafe was singed and the secretary had gone home hours before. After some of those late nights it made no sense that we left the office for separate homes, but we did. We weren't teenagers dating, we didn't kiss good night. There was seldom even an awkward pause after I'd walked her to her car.

We didn't drift into an affair, Linda and I. I've heard people use that expression and I don't know what it means. There are, after all, lines of demarcation. At some point you're taking off your clothes. Usually you've gone some place for that specific purpose. When Linda and I started, it wasn't like that later wild night in my D.A.'s office. We knew what we were doing. We had been partners for three years. I'd seen two or three boyfriends dissolve into nothingness. She'd heard the increasing difficulty with which I talked about Lois, or the way I didn't mention her at all when recounting family times. Lois had been cool to Linda at first and then inexplicably warmed up, as if she knew there was nothing sexual between my partner and me or no longer cared if there was. When Linda and I began, Linda knew the compromise I'd reached at home, that Lois and I might live together until we died but were no longer truly married.

During the years of our affair Linda never pressed me for anything more, never even hinted that she wanted more. Even when we were lovers it was peripheral to being partners. The affair never broke off, not in a big scene, but it had died out a few months before my decision to run for D.A. It seemed an inessential part of our lives for which we no longer had time. But we never lost our connection. When we needed each other, needed each other's thoughts, the connection was there.

Linda must have thought that bond was strained already when I became D.A., and broken irreparably when I fell into the mire of David's case. I left no line open to her. Maybe she even thought the family crisis was drawing me back into my family. I don't know; we didn't talk about what she had thought. But after that night in the office we were partners again. When I needed her help I had it. Even when I didn't want it I would have it.

CHAPTER

When Mandy Jackson took the stand my hopes lifted. She did not look nervous; far from it. She had, like many witnesses, overprepped herself. Nowhere is the presumption of innocence stronger than in a rape prosecution. Juries can't believe a woman could let that happen to herself without some willing participation. If she's telling the truth, she's describing something horrible, and she has to look horrified. If she doesn't cry they don't believe her. And many victims are too controlled to cry. By the time a case comes to trial they have fought hard for that control. Telling the story in front of strangers is bad enough; breaking down in front of them would make it even more intimate. Too many rape victims testify in an absolute monotone. They have removed themselves from the story, so it sounds made up. Mandy Jackson looked as if she would be one of those. She was absolutely rigid. She seemed blind to the jurors and the courtroom. I began to see some hope.

Then she took her seat and turned to look directly at David. She fixed him with a level stare.

And he squirmed in his seat and looked away.
And the jury was watching him.

Starting a trial, wondering what surprises are in store, is always nerve-racking. The day David's trial began was much worse. When I am trying a case I have the comfort of knowing that as soon as the trial starts I will know what I'm doing. You always settle down once the game begins. Today I didn't have that comfort. I was only a spectator. I found myself wondering why I had entrusted Henry with this.

I had struggled with the question of whether I should even observe. I had told Lois that I would do whatever I could to get this prosecution dismissed, but in fact I had distanced myself from it as much as possible—taken it out of my office entirely, put the prosecution in the hands of my worst enemy. There was good reason for that; in this case the appearance of propriety was essential. Even now that my scheme had failed, that appearance would serve us. With the case before a jury, any appearance that the system had been twisted in David's favor would hurt him with that jury. That was why I'd taken myself out of the case entirely. That was why I'd hired only one defense lawyer but specified two special prosecutors. Now that I had made David look as much an underdog as possible, I didn't want to jeopardize that appearance by hovering behind him at trial. I had gone over and over whether I should even be in the audience, but in the end there was no decision to be made. I was there because I couldn't stay away.

I would not, though, go inside the bar. I was at the back of the courtroom at nine-thirty the morning of David's trial. Judge Watlin's is one of the largest courtrooms, and it was packed. Trial vultures filled the seats not taken by the press. Quite a few of them were lawyers, both defense and prosecutors. No one wanted to miss Nora's last prosecution, and Henry had a following of his own. The trial purely as trial should be instructive. In this equation the defendant didn't figure at all.

The July trial date had fallen through. This was a special setting in the middle of August, which ensured maximum press coverage. August is traditionally a dead month in the courthouse. The heat drives some people out of town and incapacitates those who stay. Even this early in the morning many of the spectators looked heat-stained already from their treks in from the parking lots. Inside, though, it was remarkably cool, even in the large room with its sunny windows. It was Monday morning and the air-conditioning had been running in the empty building all weekend. By midafternoon the temperature outside would be soaring toward one hundred, which it had surpassed each of the past three days, and we would feel it even inside.

David was at the defense table. Henry was talking to him and David was nodding meekly. His attitude had changed remarkably. We had done as Linda suggested, held a second mock examination of David, with cross. He had done a little better than he had under my cross, and resented it less, but he was beginning to get a perspective on his own story. He was no longer dying to tell it in a crowded room. Now here he was, with a jury waiting to take their seats. He was scared to death.

He kept turning to look at his mother, sister, and wife, sitting in the first row of spectator seats directly behind him. Victoria was in evidence in the courtroom for the first time. She was beautiful, blond, cool in spite of the weather, well but discreetly made up. Henry had insisted on having her as lovingly close behind David's shoulder as possible. "We have that much going for us, a beautiful wife. Jurors will look at her and think, Why would he need to rape a maid? I just wish they had children. Little blond girl wondering if Daddy's going to prison—"

"Want me to rent one?" I'd asked. That was a month before trial, when jokes were still possible.

Instead, we had Dinah. She was wearing a frilly white dress and a hat appropriate for church, and looked younger than ten. She was sitting beside Lois, leaning forward to peer intently at everything in the courtroom, trying to apply all that she knew about trials.

Javier and Nora were at the state's counsel table. If this were a less-publicized and unusual case, all the lawyers probably would have been standing together joking until the judge appeared. The lawyers know they will still be working together long after whatever case of the moment is history. I've seen them in a hundred cases, the prosecutors and defense lawyers chatting and laughing while the defendant sits alone, wondering who's on his side. Henry, to his credit, didn't do that to clients. He wasn't hostile to prosecutors, but he kept his distance.

Javier said something to Nora. She shook her head. He spoke more urgently, until she shrugged. Javier leaned across the two-foot gap between the counsel tables and said something to Henry. I saw Henry give him a sharp look, then both hurried up to the court coordinator. The coordinator listened and left the room.

They had just told the coordinator to ask the judge not to come out yet. I knew what that meant: a last-minute plea-bargain offer. The jury wasn't in the box yet, so I couldn't hurt David in their eyes. I joined him and Henry.

"Javier's offered twenty," Henry said shortly. He was looking at David.

Shit. Why not probation? If they had offered probation, I would have tried to make David take it. How many times have I said, Even an innocent man would take that deal? That made me wonder again. Was David innocent?

"Sexual assault," I said. "Not aggravated." Javier was standing close enough to hear. He looked at me, solemn as a judge, nodded, then walked out of earshot.

Another aspect of the aggravated-offense charge was that if convicted of it, David would have to serve one-fourth of his sentence "flat" before he would be eligible for parole; that is, without his credit for good behavior in prison figured into the eligibility date. If convicted only of the lesser offense, he would be eligible for parole much sooner, I explained.

"With good-time credit you could probably do twenty years in three. Maybe even two. If you get convicted of the aggravated offense and get life, you'll have to do fifteen years before you're even eligible for parole. That's what you face."

David was paler than I've ever seen him. He looked as if he were about to throw up. I didn't blame him. It was a horrible decision to have thrust on him at the last minute. He might be able to picture doing two or three years. They would be terrible, but it was an envisionable sentence: less time than he'd spent in college. Fifteen years was impossible to imagine: almost his lifetime. I don't think he'd realized the horror of what he was facing until that moment.

Henry and I watched him without offering advice. David knew the chances as well as we did. And he knew one thing we didn't.

He took less than a minute. "No," he finally said. His voice squeaked. "I didn't do it. I'm not going to say I did."

I let out a long breath. Henry left us alone to give Javier the answer. I put my hands on David's shoulders. Some color returned to his cheeks. He even smiled a little. I would have been happier if he'd accepted the offer, but I was prouder of him for refusing, and sure again that I knew my son. I gripped him harder, as if he were sliding away.

A moment later we were taking our seats as the judge took his. I was sitting beside Lois. Again it seemed to me that Judge Watlin's eyes sought me out. I remembered the conference I'd had with him a month earlier. I'd gone looking for him and found him in his office. When I closed the door we were alone. It's known as an ex parte communication, when one side in a case talks to the judge without the other side being present. It's thoroughly improper and it happens every day.

"Judge, I just wanted to get your thoughts on this case."

To his credit he didn't ask what case and he didn't make

small talk. Watlin is a politician, and that means being able to project forthrightness. He was certainly selling it that day.

"You and I know Nora, Blackie. Hell, we helped train her. She'll never offer probation in a case like this. I see you're going to the jury for punishment. But in a case like this sometimes the defendant changes his mind at the last minute. Either pleads guilty without a recommendation or decides to go to the judge for punishment. I just want to tell you in advance. Don't do it. I'd have to hammer him. You know that, Blackie. A case like this could ruin a judicial career. You could be the finest judge in this town for twenty years, then one big case comes along where it looks like you rolled over for somebody and that's the one they remember at the next election. You see what I'm saying."

I nodded.

Watlin had been leaning across the desk, speaking in a low voice, the picture of a crooked judge making a deal. Now he leaned back and grew expansive.

"But I'll tell you, boy, I will hold their feet to the fire. If the state doesn't dot every *i* and cross every *t*, I'll grant an instructed verdict fast as you can ask for one."

I told him I appreciated that. I appreciated what it was worth: nothing. Nora wouldn't make mistakes.

This was the outcome of Watlin's dithering over what to do. Give the appearance of strictness but let me know he was on my side in private. Thanks for nothing, Judge.

As he took his seat at trial he caught my eye but refrained from nodding or winking. We're too subtle for that, right, Blackie? I wondered if I had enough pull to screw him the next time he ran for reelection.

"Both sides ready? Let's bring in the jury."

The uniformed bailiff, a sheriff's deputy, opened a door near the front of the courtroom and the jury came trooping in. Most of them looked startled to see so many faces. Last week when the jury was selected the courtroom had been almost empty. There are few trial fans so avid they will sit through the boring process of jury selection. The jurors took their seats awkwardly, embarrassed by the audience attention or trying unsuccessfully to pretend they didn't notice. There were seven men and five women, which represented a small triumph for Henry. The defense hinged on seeing what had happened from a man's point of view. Popular lawyers' theory holds that whichever gender is in the ascendant will dominate jury deliberation. If men are in the minority, they will be afraid to say that maybe she was asking for it, even if that's what they think. On the other hand, some prosecutors think women jurors hold women victims to a higher standard of behavior than men would. Jury selection is just voodoo. No one knows what jurors really think until it's too late. I watched them settle into their seats, trying to disguise their sense of importance.

I hated them. We put our trust in juries, but only because we have to. Jurors all lie. They take a solemn oath that they will base their verdict only on the evidence they hear in court and the law the judge gives them in his instructions, and they all violate that oath every time—casually, without a moment's hesitation. I have listened at jury room doors and heard them. Or they cheerfully tell me after the trial is over, "Well, we heard that one witness say he was in the left-hand-turn lane, but Mabel here has a cousin that drives that road ever' day and he told her they ain't no turn lane." "Then me and Ernie here come up with a idea none of you smart lawyers even thought of. We figgered whut really happened was they wasn't in the room all the witnesses said they was in, they was actually in this back room here . . ." Jurors all think they're fucking detectives. I hate them, and I am not alone. Every trial lawyer who mouths shibboleths about believing in the common juror is a liar. No one would ever try a case to a jury at all, except that judges are even less to be trusted.

My son's life was in their hands. I wanted to be in that box with them.

Lois slipped her hand into mine. Judge Waddle turned to Nora with grand impartiality and said, "Call your first witness."

She did, and I thought I saw Henry's back stiffen. "The state calls Joe Garcia."

In the vast majority of rape trials the only real evidence is the victim's testimony. If the victim is a poor witness, you put her on first, then bolster her testimony as much as possible with the cops and medical testimony. If she's good, you save her for last. So when the first witness the prosecution called was someone else, we knew that Nora thought she had a good witness in Mandy Jackson.

Joe Garcia wasn't much. He was a retired sheriff's deputy, fat, fifty, very dark in the face on this August day. A heart attack waiting to happen. Inarticulate as he was, Nora used him to good effect, setting that dramatic scene as the security guard had first come upon it: the naked black woman slumped on the floor sobbing quietly, scratches on her skin, her clothes in tatters. Nora cut it off there, no boring wrap-up, and turned the witness over to Henry.

Henry used Joe Garcia to plant one idea. The security guard had already identified David during Nora's examination. "How was David dressed that night?" Henry asked. Joe hesitated. A suit, he decided. White shirt.

"He was fully dressed when you came into the room?"

"Yes sir. Well, he didn't have his jacket on."

"Did he have on a tie?"

Joe didn't remember.

"Well, think about it. Picture him there afterwards, slumped over in a chair, looking dazed. Was he—"

Nora was on her feet. "Your Honor, I object to counsel testifying. None of that is in evidence."

Watlin said, "Just ask the question, Mr. Koehler."

"Was he wearing a tie?"

Joe had been thinking about it, peering off at a corner of the ceiling. "Yeah," he said now.

"Thank you. Now, when you first came in, was David in the same room with Ms. Jackson?"

"No, he was in the outer office. She was in the private office inside. I could see them both, though."

"What were the first words David said to you?"

Joe thought about it but couldn't remember. "He said my name," he offered.

"Weren't his first words, 'Joe, thank God you're here'?"

Nora interrupted, but not before everyone had heard. "Objection. He's already answered the question. And again I object to counsel testifying."

Before Henry could respond, Watlin said, "Overruled."

"That means you can answer the question, Mr. Garcia. Isn't that what David said to you?"

Joe nodded. "Something like that."

"That was pretty fast thinking, wasn't it, to get dressed like that and get out to the other room and pretend to be glad to see you, when he didn't even know you were coming?"

"Objection," Nora said disgustedly. "Calls for speculation."

"Sustained."

Henry didn't care. He'd said what he wanted. He passed the witness and Nora did a little mop-up, establishing that although David and Mandy Jackson had been in separate rooms, they were only a few feet apart. And she asked her own objectionable question, establishing that David could have heard the security guard's running footsteps coming down the hall.

Javier examined the next three witnesses, cops who had made the scene. Not much there one way or the other. Javier tried to reinforce the image of the shattered victim, beaten and violated, and Henry tried to paint a picture of a stunned suspect. When one detective mentioned the paper bags they'd placed over David's hands to preserve any possible evidence, Henry went over that again, incredulously, as if they'd been thumbscrews. But the jury was growing restive. They were tired of the opening acts and ready for the main event.

Between two of the cops Judge Waddle broke for his favorite phase of trial, lunch. The defense team had sandwiches in my office. We were a glum group, strangers who had been thrown together. Someone would say a sentence and everyone else would nod, but no one would respond. As there had been nothing surprising in the testimony thus far, there was nothing to hash over. David sat with us. Even he seemed like a veteran now. "Do you think they'll make another offer?" he asked once. "Only if their case starts falling apart, and then we wouldn't take it," Henry answered. I saw David thinking about that offer of twenty years, a small possible landing site that had swept by him and away, already receded out of view. So quickly passed, so long gone. It might loom large in his memory.

After the cops came the medical examiner, Robert Wyntlowski. Dr. Bob, as he was often called around the office, was a wonderful witness. He had testified in hundreds of trials and always made his testimony sound fresh. He wasn't a bored functionary reciting from a report; he made each case sound as if it had fascinated him. Consequently, juries thought they were hearing something important from him. But in this case, I knew, he had little to offer the state. I had seen his report, and the medical evidence was inconclusive. It usually is. But the jury wouldn't know that. We expected Dr. Bob to be more help to us than to the prosecution.

He started off that way. He had examined evidence taken from the alleged victim of the sexual assault. A vaginal swab had shown no semen present.

"Does that mean there was no penetration of the vagina?" Javier was asking these questions as if he were a doctor himself, leaving no room for tittering.

"No. It means there was no ejaculation."

Nor had the victim had vaginal tears. "Tears?" Javier said as if this were the first he'd heard of this. "You mean torn flesh inside the vagina?"

"Yes. That did not happen in this case."

"Is that unusual in rape cases?"

"Objection," Henry said from his feet. "What happens in other cases is no evidence in this case." He started to sit down again.

"I believe we are entitled to explain the evidence or lack of evidence," Javier said mildly.

Watlin stirred himself to overrule the objection.

Henry was still standing, an incredulous look on his face. "Your Honor, with all respect I must renew my objection. The state is attempting to bring in evidence from other cases that has nothing to do with this prosecution, to the extreme prejudice of my client. This is completely inadmissible, Your Honor."

"I have overruled your objection, Mr. Koehler," Watlin said mildly.

Henry sank slowly into his seat and shook his head. Silently I applauded him. He knew damned well that this kind of testimony always comes in in rape trials, and none has ever been reversed by an appellate court as a result. But the jury didn't know that. This was where Henry made it appear that the judge was in the state's pocket and David was being railroaded. At the state's table Nora was shaking her head.

"The question, Doctor," said Javier, "is whether it is common to find vaginal tears in rape victims?"

"It is common," said Dr. Bob. That's what makes him a great witness. He says things that make it sound as if he's not always on the state's side. But he always follows them up, as he did now: "It is also common not to find them."

"So their absence does not mean no sexual assault took place?"

"No. Not at all."

When Javier passed the witness, Henry just sat there for a minute as if trying to absorb what he had just heard. He didn't refer to the notes he had made. When he spoke he sounded both puzzled and faintly disgusted.

"You mean, Dr. Wyntlowski, that intercourse during a rape

can be as—I don't know what the word is I'm looking for—as gentle as during consensual intercourse?"

The medical examiner answered not as if he were being challenged, but as if he were speaking to a rather slow seminar student. "Consensual sex isn't necessarily gentle. Sometimes we do find tears in the vaginal wall after consensual sex."

"So the answer to my question is yes?"

"Yes."

"How can that be?" Henry asked, and I thought he'd stepped in it. He had violated the rule against asking a question to which you don't know the answer. He seemed to have forgotten the trial and was just asking for his own information.

Dr. Bob explained patiently. "There is a great variation in injury to rape victims. Most victims, in fact, don't fight back, out of fear or from being bound or threatened or whatever, and so suffer relatively few injuries."

"Thank you," Henry said. In passing the witness he sounded all business again.

Javier had saved something for his redirect. "Doctor, did you examine the defendant in this case?"

"Yes."

"That same night?"

"That same night. They got me out of bed."

"What did you find?"

"When the suspect was brought into the office he had paper bags over his hands the investigating officers had placed there to preserve any evidence. I took scrapings from under his fingernails."

"And what did those scrapings turn out to be?"

"Remains of human tissue and blood."

"Was there enough of a sample to compare with other similar samples of skin and blood?"

"Yes."

"Is that possible to do?"

"Oh yes." Dr. Bob launched into a long, boring explanation

of spectroscopic examination and points of comparison and types of blood. Javier would have liked to cut him short because he was losing the jury, but he had to lay the predicate or he couldn't get to the question he wanted. Which was, finally:

"Did you compare those samples taken from under the defendant's fingernails with known samples of skin and blood taken from the victim in this case, Mandy Jackson?"

Henry objected to characterizing her as a victim, which hadn't been established yet. Javier rephrased his question while Dr. Bob waited patiently. "Yes, I did," he said.

"And what was the result of that comparison?"

"The samples matched."

"So the skin and blood under the defendant's fingernails were Mandy Jackson's skin and blood?" Javier asked. I admired his phrasing.

"Yes."

Henry first said he had no more questions, then, "I'm sorry, I do have one. Did you examine Ms. Jackson's fingernails?"

"Her fingernails? No."

"So you don't know what might have been found under her nails. Thank you, Doctor."

And suddenly there were no more preliminaries. Nora announced that the state called Mandy Jackson. Someone went to get her. I don't know where she had been waiting. She hadn't been in the hall. There is one rule known as the Rule, and Henry had invoked it at the beginning of trial. It means that while a witness is testifying no other witness may be present. This is designed to prevent future witnesses from listening to the foregoing witnesses and tailoring their own testimony to fill any gaps or correct inconsistencies. The defendant, of course, is exempt. He can't be kept from his own trial.

So we all turned as the back door of the courtroom opened and we all watched Mandy Jackson come up the aisle. She was in a simple blue outfit, a well-worn dress worn well. She was oblivious to all of us. She stared only at the witness stand. Somehow she did not look like the woman I had seen in the hall weeks ago. The out-of-place look was gone. She might have been walking down an empty hall in her own home. Her head was high. She looked tall and thin and strong. I was glad of that strength. Mandy Jackson did not look like a victim.

The hands give it away. Ms. Jackson's were clenched, the only part of her that showed tension. I thought, she is going to stare this jury down. She is going to sit there and be haughty and rigid and strong as steel and they are not going to believe a word she says. I took an easy breath for the first time that day.

And Mandy took her seat and directed that accusatory stare at David. And David couldn't take it. He looked away, the picture of guilt. I saw what the jury couldn't, Henry squeeze his knee under the table. David turned back to her.

"Proceed," said Watlin, and Nora stopped what she was writing, laid down her pen, and smiled reassuringly at her witness. "State your name, please."

"Amanda Jackson."

"Do they call you Mandy?" That was a leading question. An idiot would have objected. Henry sat silent.

"Where do you live, Mandy?"

She gave her address. Nora established that it was in San Antonio. "Are you married?"

"No, ma'am. My husband is dead."

"Do you have any children?"

"Two. A boy and a girl. The older one's twelve." For the first time her voice betrayed some life. She sounded as if she wanted to say more but then steeled herself again and fell silent.

These preliminaries sound trivial but they are vital. When I was a third-chair prosecutor I had a first chair who said that your case is won or lost by the time your best witness finishes establishing her name and family situation. That's how long it takes the jury to decide whether they like her. And when they go in to vote on guilt, they're voting on who they like.

"Where do you work, Mandy?"

"The Grande Building, out on the Loop. There're about ten or twelve companies in the building."

"And what do you do at the Grande Building?"

"I'm a maid."

"Do you do anything else besides work and take care of your children?"

"I go to school. Trinity University. I have two more years to go."

I tried to read the jury's faces and couldn't. I don't know where they get the idea they have to look dead neutral during testimony, but they usually do.

"Were you working on April thirteenth of this year?"

"Yes, ma'am."

"What time?"

"Well, I'd been there that morning but then I went back late afternoon. So I was working at night that night. I don't usually do that. I try to be home for supper with my kids."

"Do you know someone named David Blackwell?"

"Yes." Very tight. She wasn't looking at David now, she was looking only at Nora, being guided. Her voice was as flat as I could have hoped.

"Does he work at the Grande Building, too?"

"Yes."

"Are you friends?"

The witness made a noise of disbelief. "I'm the maid. He's an executive."

I liked her resentment.

"Were you cleaning Mr. Blackwell's office that night?"

"Yes. It was almost the last one I had to do."

"What time was it when you got to that one?"

"Eight, maybe. Maybe later."

"Were there many people in the building that time of night?"

"Nobody, on that floor. I was surprised to see anybody."

"What floor was it?"

"I'm not sure. High up."

"Was it well lighted?"

"Yes."

"Bright as day?"

"Well, some of the offices were lit up. Others were dark. It changed from room to room."

"What about David Blackwell's? Describe his office for us, please."

Her eyes drifted upward as she pictured it. That was the only sign so far that she was testifying from personal memory rather than by rote.

"There's a big main office with filing cabinets and a couple of secretaries' desks. Behind that there's three smaller private offices with their own doors. That night there was a lamp on in the big office, so it was a little dim."

"What about the smaller offices?"

"Two of them had their doors closed. The other one was dark, but the door was open."

"The David Blackwell we're talking about, is he in the courtroom today?"

"Yes."

"Could you please point him out and identify something he's wearing so we'll know which one you mean?"

She pointed. "At that table, in the blue suit with a striped tie."

Nora asked Judge Watlin to let the record reflect that the witness had identified the defendant. He allowed it to do so. Some prosecutors would wait until the end of the victim's testimony to ask her to identify the defendant. Nora did it early, for a reason. She didn't want to refer to David as Mr. Blackwell any more.

"Where was the defendant when you came into the office?"

"I didn't see him at first. I went around behind the secretary's desk to get the trash can. As I was reaching for it I heard something behind me and I turned and I—I made a sound or something because he startled me. I didn't know anybody was there."

"Where was he?"

"In the doorway of the small office. It was dark behind him so I couldn't see his face."

"Did he say anything?"

"He said, 'It's all right, Mandy, it's only me.' Something like that."

"Did you recognize his voice?"

"Not exactly. But I figured out who it was from what office it was and what he looked like."

"What did he look like, Mandy? How was he dressed?"

"He'd been wearing a suit but he didn't have the jacket on. He looked a little—like it had been a long day."

"Did he say anything else?"

"He said something like he was glad to see me because he was tired of being the only one in the building."

"What did you say?"

"I said it was too late for people to be working, they should be home with their families."

"Was he still in the doorway?"

"Yes. Just leaning there. He sounded funny."

"Funny how?"

"Like he'd been drinking, or asleep."

"What happened next?"

"I bent down to pick up the trash can again and carried it over to my cart. And he said don't do that, why don't you take a break?"

Nora had not taken a note. She was leaning forward, interested, as if listening to a friend. She asked an oblique question, as friends sometimes do. "What were you wearing, Mandy?"

"Sort of a uniform they have us wear. Just a black skirt and white blouse."

Nora produced these items from a paper bag at her feet. She

took them to the court reporter and had identifying tags affixed to them. The jurors sat up straighter. Finally something for them to see, not just the drone of Mandy Jackson's testimony.

"These are marked state's exhibits eighteen and nineteen, Mandy. What are they?"

"The skirt and blouse I was wearing."

"Are they in the same condition now they were in when you went into that office?"

"No, ma'am. The blouse is missing some buttons and the zipper's broke on the skirt." She looked at David again. This time he managed not to look away.

"Your Honor, I offer these in evidence," Nora said. Henry was on his feet before she could hand them to him. "No objection."

"They're admitted." Watlin sounded bored. He thought that was part of a judge's duty.

Nora didn't hand the clothes to the jury yet. She let them sit there on the shelf in front of the judge's bench, looking crumpled. She resumed her seat.

"So the defendant asked you to take a break. What did you say?"

"I said I was too busy. Wanted to get finished."

"What did he do then?"

"I was at the cart, emptying the trash can, and he came up behind me. I hadn't even heard him move, so I jumped."

"Why did you jump? Did he touch you?"

"He took my arm. Right under the elbow. And I gasped again. He said, 'What are you scared of?'"

"Were you scared?"

"He was making me nervous, moving so fast and standing so close. But I wasn't really scared."

Mrs. Jackson had looked tense when she first took the stand. Nora had managed to relax her, undoubtedly more than the prosecutor wanted. She began building the tension again.

"Was he still touching you?"

"I'd jerked my arm away when he startled me but he put it on me again."

"Did you pull away again?"

"I stepped back, but he stepped with me. Still real close."

"Did he say anything else?"

"He said I should come sit with him for a while. He said I must be tired. I said I was, that's why I wanted to finish and go home. He said—I thought it was real strange, I didn't know what he meant—he said, 'Do you always go home at the end of the day?'"

Lois had been holding my hand. I hadn't noticed her grip tightening until she suddenly stood up beside me. I looked up at her, afraid for a moment she was going to make a scene. She wasn't even looking at me. She took Dinah by the hand and made her way out to the aisle. As they hurried out, Dinah was looking back, trying to hear more. Her hat had fallen askew.

Their departure left me sitting with Victoria. She didn't move over to close the gap between us and neither did I. I glanced at her profile. Beautiful girl, Victoria. David had been dating her since high school, but I'd never gotten to know her at all. I had no idea what was going on beneath that clear, taut skin. She was looking at the witness. The only expression I thought I could identify on her face was contempt, but that was so close to Victoria's normal expression in repose that I wasn't sure.

I had missed a couple of sentences of testimony. I saw David shaking his head slowly from side to side. Henry touched his leg again and he stopped.

"He was standing behind me and he had put his hands up on my shoulders by my neck. He was rubbing. He said he'd give me a massage. He said to come into his office, where there was a couch."

"By that time," Nora asked, "did you have some idea what was going on?"

While I was still trying to decide if that was objectionable Henry had already objected. "What she may have thought was happening is irrelevant."

Nora stood to contest it. "Of course it's relevant, Your Honor. She was there. Her impressions are the only ones we'll have to show the menace conveyed in small ways—"

"Impressions aren't evidence," Henry said.

"I sustain the objection," said the judge.

Both lawyers sat down. Mandy Jackson began. "I knew what he—"

Before Henry could stop her Nora had. "No, Mandy, the judge has ruled you can't answer that question. I'll ask you another one instead. Did you say anything in response to his offer of a massage?"

"I ducked out from his hands and around to the other side of the cart. I started backing it up. I told him I'd come back later to clean the office."

"Were you scared then?"

"Not scared to death. I just thought it would be better to leave."

"What did he do?"

"He laughed. He said, 'Oh, relax,' he wouldn't bother me anymore. And he walked away. I should've left then."

Henry was making a note. Nora anticipated him. "Why didn't you leave then, Mandy?"

"I figured it was all over. I thought he'd had his fun and would let me be. Besides, I needed to finish cleaning that office. I didn't want him or somebody else reporting me."

"So what did you do?"

"I emptied the trashes and I ran the vacuum cleaner. I didn't see Mr. Blackwell any more. I figured he'd gone back into his office. I cleaned the other two in a hurry and was trying to decide whether to go in his. Why court trouble? But then I saw he'd moved his trash can out from behind his desk so it was settin' right inside the door. I figured that was his way of making up, tellin' me I could just empty it and be gone. So I went in to get it."

She took a breath. Nora let her hang there, suspended for a moment, in case some jurors hadn't gotten it yet. When they were waiting for the question she asked it. "Where was the defendant?"

"He was right inside the door. As soon as I walked in he grabbed me. He said, 'Changed your mind, huh?'"

"How did he grab you?"

"The same way, from behind, hands up by my neck. I tried to twist away again, but he was holding me too hard. I reached up and tried to pry his hands away, but I couldn't do that either. He held me like that until I quit tryin' to get away, then he pushed up right behind me."

"Pressing his body against yours?"

"Yes. He put his arms around me from behind and he was breathing in my ear. I could feel him."

"Feel what?" Nora said. This was the breakpoint, the point where cases fell apart because the witness didn't. She had to replicate the emotion of the scene and she had to describe it in detail. She couldn't be general about it, she couldn't just say "He raped me." She had to give the details, break the act down into its component parts. So far Mandy Jackson wasn't getting the emotion. She was speaking a little faster but still tightly controlled. Her hands were clenched on the bar in front of her.

"His whole body, pressing against my back. And my—my behind."

"Did he say anything else?"

"He said, 'Wouldn't that backrub feel good?' And he stuck one hand down inside my skirt. I tried to pull his hand out and turn around at the same time. He jerked on the skirt, and that's when the zipper broke."

"Then?"

"He let me go. Just like that. I almost fell over backwards. I turned around so I was facing him and I was backing up, and I grabbed my skirt to keep it from falling down. He looked real concerned for a second, like he was scared at what he'd done, and he said, 'Here, let me help,' and when he reached for me I slapped his hand away."

"How did he react to that?"

"It was strange. He smiled. Like I'd given him an excuse. He said, 'No, I'll help,' and I backed into the wall, and he reached for me and he grabbed my blouse in both hands and pulled it open.

"I was screaming at him to stop, but that didn't do any good. I ducked under his arm and ran and he grabbed the back of my skirt and pulled and it came half off and I couldn't run and then he grabbed me and held me from behind again. He was trying to pull my bra off, and when I tried to stop him he clawed my chest. I yelled again, but he knew—"

"Your Honor, I object to the narrative form," Henry said. "Some of this is objectionable but I don't have the opportunity."

"Yes," Watlin said. "Question your witness, counsel," he said to Nora.

Mandy Jackson had come to a sudden stop, taking a deep breath but otherwise unmoving. I saw something in her I had never seen in a dozen rape cases I'd prosecuted. Always the victim either broke down completely or remained in such control that the jury found her unbelievable. Mrs. Jackson was one of the controlled ones, but in her I could see the strain of keeping control. She didn't cry and she didn't raise her voice, but every moment she seemed on the verge of flying out of her chair. The strain of suppressing her emotion was as powerful as the emotion would have been. I realized I was listening to her as if finally hearing the truth of what had happened that night. Her testimony came in such a rush of memory that doubt had not entered my mind while she talked.

Nora let her wait for a moment. Mandy Jackson blinked. She started to turn her face toward the jury but then stopped. I didn't think she saw the spectators either.

Nora asked the judge's permission to approach the witness and handed her a photograph. "You said he scratched you, Mandy. Can you identify state's exhibit twelve, which I've just handed you?"

"That's a picture of me that one of the police officers took at the hospital that night."

"What does the picture show?"

"Scratches on my chest."

"How did you get those scratches?"

"From his fingernails, when I tried to pull away from him."

"Him meaning the defendant?"

"Yes."

Nora resumed her seat without passing the photograph to the jurors. It, like almost twenty other items, had already been admitted in evidence, but Nora hadn't passed any of it to the jury for inspection yet.

"What happened then, Mandy?"

"He was holding me from behind. One arm was around my throat so I couldn't breathe. I was tugging on his arm, trying to pull it off, and while I did that he reached down and pulled my skirt the rest of the way off. Then he grabbed my panties and ripped them."

"Were you trying to stop him?"

"I just wanted to breathe. I think I was startin' to pass out. I tried to reach down but then his arm got tighter around my neck and I reached for that again."

"What happened next?"

"He let up the pressure a little so I could breathe. And I felt him movin' behind me. I heard his zipper, and some fumblin' around."

"Could you tell what he was doing?"

"Oh yes. Oh yes, I knew. He grabbed me and he picked me up off the ground and walked me forward. There was a couch in front of me and he just sort of dropped me down onto it but he was still holding my legs so I fell onto my hands and I tried to hold myself up. And then he pushed between my legs."

"What do you mean, he? What was between your legs? . . . I'm sorry, Mandy, you'll have to speak up, I don't think anyone heard that."

"His penis. He put his penis between my legs."

"Mandy. I'm sorry you have to do this, but you have to be more specific. Where did the defendant put his penis?"

Mandy was looking down at her hands. "In my vagina," she said softly.

"Did he penetrate your sexual organ with his?"

"Objection, Your Honor. Leading."

"Sustained."

Nora didn't go back to it. She'd certainly gotten enough for the jury already. "Didn't you try to stop him?" she asked instead.

"How?" Mandy Jackson said, looking up from her hands. "You tell me how. I've thought and thought. I was off the ground. When I tried to reach back I couldn't reach him and I fell forward onto my face. How could I have stopped him?"

"What were you doing?"

"I was crying. And I was saying something. 'Please,' probably. Please, please."

Nora looked across the tables at David. "Did the defendant say anything?"

"He was saying, 'Don't scream, don't scream. It'll be all right.' And once he said, 'I'll give you money.'"

Henry made a note. Nora let the jury think for a few seconds. "What happened next?" she asked then.

"He dropped me down and he must've been kneeling behind me, 'cause he kept on. He—"

"Kept on what?"

"Pushing. Into me. But it seemed like he couldn't—"

"I'll object to any speculation," Henry said. Watlin sustained him.

"Did he ejaculate?" Nora asked.

"No."

"What did he do next?"

"He pulled out and he turned me around so I was sittin' on the couch. And he said, 'Here.'"

"What did he mean by that? Was it obvious to you?" Nora added, anticipating Henry's objection.

"He wanted me to take it in my mouth."

"What do you mean by—"

"His penis," Mandy Jackson said. She sounded too weary to be angry. She was looking only at Nora. "He wanted to put his penis in my mouth."

"And did he?"

She looked down. There was no longer anyone she could stand to look at. "Yes."

"Why didn't you stop him?"

"I was scared."

"What were you scared of?"

"I thought he was going to kill me. I thought any second he was gonna start hittin' me. I thought if I did what he wanted maybe I could get away."

Nora nodded. So did one of the jurors, a woman. "How long did this part go on?" Nora asked.

"I don't know."

"A minute? Five minutes?"

"More like a minute. Then he heard something."

"Objection, Your Honor. Speculation."

"I heard something, then," Mandy said to Henry. He sat down. "I heard the elevator."

"How far away is the elevator from that office?" Nora asked.

The rest was quickly told. David hurriedly pulled himself together and was in the outer office when the security guard arrived. Mrs. Jackson just slumped onto the floor and tried to cover herself. Eventually police came and took her to the hospital. She described the tests, the clinical surfaces of the hospital. The crying at home. Her voice grew lower and lower and her head bowed until she looked the complete victim.

Nora passed the witness.

Before she did, though, she asked the judge's permission to "publish" the items admitted into evidence to the jury. Permission granted, Nora handed a bundle to the first juror: clothes, photos, a medical report. The first juror looked it all over and began passing it on. Others leaned forward to get their share.

Henry didn't fall into the trap of beginning his cross-examination while the jurors were thus distracted. He sat there writing until the last item had been passed to the last juror. Mandy Jackson looked around as if seeing the court-room for the first time. Her eyes passed over me without snagging. Finally Watlin told Henry, "Proceed."

Henry finished what he was writing, turned back a few pages in his legal pad, read a note, then sat looking at the witness until she raised her eyes to his.

"Mrs. Jackson, my name is Henry Koehler. I represent David Blackwell. I'm going to ask you a few questions now, all right?"

She nodded.

"This sounds rude, but I have to ask. How do you support two children and yourself and go to school with no child support on a maid's salary?"

This may have been an objectionable question, but Nora let him ask it because it made her complainant sound distressed and heroic. And because Mandy Jackson had an answer for it: "We get AFDC," she said.

"Aid to Families with Dependent Children?"

"Yes. And my mama lives with us and she gets some social security."

"Who was staying with your children that night, April thirteenth?"

"Mama."

"You had already arranged that, you knew you'd be working late?"

"Yes."

As she answered that question someone walked by me in the aisle. It was Linda. She had been sitting somewhere farther back. She was wearing a suit and looked very much an attorney. Jurors wouldn't know who she was, but other people would. Reporters, for example. Linda was obviously unconcerned about appearances. She passed through the gate in the railing and when Henry heard it creak he turned. Linda handed him a note and walked back out again. Did I say she was unconcerned with appearances? But she didn't look at me as I sat with my daughter-in-law.

Henry glanced at the note but then dropped it aside and appeared to resume his line of questioning. "Why were you working late that night?"

"I had a test at school that afternoon. I left work early to study for it and take it."

"What course was that in?"

"A European history class."

The jurors were looking at Henry, wondering what this had to do with anything, but Mandy Jackson was looking toward the back of the courtroom. I turned and saw Linda going out. When I turned back Mrs. Jackson was looking vaguely troubled. Linda didn't return. Henry glanced again at her note from time to time.

There are various strategies in cross-examination. Some lawyers try to befriend the witness, leading her on until they can drop a hammer on her. That seldom works. Few victims are prepared to make friends with the defense lawyer. Others start attacking the witness from the first question. Others sound puzzled. Most lawyers use no particular tactic, they just blunder back through the testimony, having the witness repeat everything, hoping for contradiction. Henry's tone was perfectly neutral. He sounded like a scientist.

"How long did you say you've known David Blackwell?" he asked.

"I guess about two years."

"Ever seen him outside the office?"

"No."

"Never ran into him at the mall or anything?"

"Oh. Maybe once or twice at the mall."

"Was his wife with him on that occasion?"

"I don't remember." That didn't matter. Henry had managed to mention that David was married, and at least a couple of jurors looked at Victoria sitting behind him, cool and faithful and beautiful.

"But you never intentionally met him away from work, for a drink or anything?"

"No." She sounded faintly disgusted by the suggestion.

Henry nodded and made a note.

"Would you say you were friends?"

"No. Not a bit."

"So even though you had known who he was for two years you didn't really know each other."

"No."

"How much do you know about David Blackwell? Do you know who his father is?"

"I remember people talking about that at work when he got elected."

I sat very still, aware people were looking at me. I wondered why Henry had brought this up and wished he'd get off it. He did.

"Let's talk about that night in the office. After that first business in the outer office with David rubbing your neck and everything, he suddenly left you alone and went into the inner office, out of sight?"

"Yes."

"But you didn't take that opportunity to leave?"

"No. I thought it was all over then, I thought he'd leave me alone."

"Why take the chance?"

"Like I said before, I had to finish the cleaning. I can't afford to lose that job, Mister. I've got kids."

"You don't think you could have told your supervisor if he or she asked why you didn't finish, Well, the man in there got a little too frisky and I left? You don't think they would have accepted that explanation?"

"I didn't want to risk it."

"Had you ever had that kind of trouble before?"

"A little. Nothing this bad."

"With this man, David Blackwell? Had he harassed you before?"

"Nothing like this," she said again.

"Anything? Loose talk, touching you?"

Mrs. Jackson hesitated, but she didn't look as if she were searching her memory, she looked as if she were deciding what would be the best answer. Of course that was my hopeful, subjective impression.

"Not that I remember."

"So it wouldn't have been surprising if your supervisor didn't believe you if this was the explanation you gave for not finishing cleaning that office?"

"Objection," Nora said. She was on her feet before Henry finished the question. "That calls for speculation."

Watlin sustained her, rightfully so, but I wondered if she should have objected. It left the question hanging without an answer.

"After you did the other offices you even went into his private office, isn't that correct?"

"To get the trash can, like I said."

"Did you think he was inside there?"

"I don't know, he could've gone out while I was in the others with the vacuum running."

"But chances were he was still in there, since someone had moved the trash can?"

"I suppose."

"Did you suppose that that night? Did you think he was in there?"

"Yeah, I imagine."

"But you went in there anyway. So you weren't afraid of him at that point, were you?"

"I was a little leery."

"But you went in for the trash anyway. So you weren't too afraid, were you?"

He had to ask her to speak up. "I guess not," she said again.

Henry nodded, wrote a note, flipped a page on his legal pad. Without looking up from it he said, "When you went into his office, how was David dressed?"

The witness paused again. She was growing more hesitant with every answer, though she spoke up boldly enough. "The same as I said before, a white shirt and the pants from a suit."

"Was he wearing a tie?"

"I think so. Wait— Yes, he was."

"Still, when you went into the inner office, he still had on the tie?"

"Yes. Pulled loose, but he had it on."

Henry looked surprised and made a note. Mandy, watching him, said, "I could be wrong about that," and looked down at her hands. Henry nodded again.

"How about shoes? Did he still have his shoes on?"

"I didn't look at his feet."

"Well, what was your impression?"

"Objection, Your Honor, that's been asked and answered."

Henry waited for the objection to be sustained and went right ahead. "Think about when you heard the sound of the elevator and he started getting dressed in a hurry. Did he have to put on his shoes and socks?"

She looked up, eyes moving back and forth across the ceiling. "No. He still had them on."

Henry gave the impression everything was going well. He nodded.

"Now. Remember when you were fighting with David?"

She nodded.

"Remember you said he scratched you. Did you scratch him?"

"I don't know."

"May I approach the witness, Your Honor?" Mandy watched him come toward her as if he were going to strike her himself. Henry handed the court reporter a photograph and had it marked on the back. "This is marked defendant's exhibit number one," he said to Mandy. "Do you recognize that person?"

"It's Mr.—the defendant."

"Is that how he looked that night, after the police came?"

"I guess." She wasn't going to give him anything.

"What do you see on his face?"

"Scratches, it looks like."

Henry took the picture from her and carried it back to his table. As he sat down he said, "So you did scratch him?"

"I guess I did. You want me to be sorry?"

"No," Henry said softly. "Any woman would." Nora rose half out of her chair, but I could see she didn't know how she could have been hurt by this sidebar remark. She sat down again.

"So you did fight him," Henry said.

"Yes. Much as I could."

"When he tore your clothes off you struggled?"

"Yes."

"When he picked you up from behind you fought to get away?"

"Yes. Of course I did."

Henry nodded. "And when he bent you forward over the couch did you keep struggling?"

"Yes," she said, but not as vehemently. She couldn't decide where this was leading, but she knew the answer had to be yes.

"And when he penetrated you, did you still fight to get away?"

"Yes, as much as I could move. There wasn't much room to go."

"But you fought?"

"Yes."

"Was this exciting for you in any way? Was it pleasurable?"

She looked at him as if he'd suggested she take her clothes off on the witness stand. "No."

"Were you sexually excited?"

"Your Honor!" Nora shouted over the murmuring from spectators. "This is badgering, this is harassment, this is irrelevant. This is outrageous! She doesn't have to defend her—"

"May we approach the bench?" Henry said, and they did. When Henry and Nora stood there before the judge they were maybe ten feet from the witness. Mrs. Jackson watched him come until he was about halfway, then she lowered her head and didn't look at anyone.

Henry leaned far forward over the bench, obviously keeping his voice low enough that the witness couldn't hear what he had to say. The shorter Nora was at a disadvantage, but Watlin leaned forward, too, the bench pressing into his stomach. There was some intense whispering for a minute, two minutes. Nora was still arguing when Watlin leaned back and motioned them away from him.

"The objection is overruled," he said aloud to renewed murmuring.

Henry was back in his seat. Nora stood for a moment between him and the witness, glaring at him. She moved slowly out of the way. "I'll repeat the question, Mrs. Jackson," Henry said. There was no lasciviousness in his voice. He still sounded the disinterested scientist. "Were you sexually excited when the defendant penetrated you? Let me be more specific. Were you lubricated?"

"Oh my God," Nora said by way of objection. Watlin waved her down. "Overruled."

Mrs. Jackson had the vilest taste of her life in her mouth. She spat it out. "Was I—was I wet? No! Are you—there was nothing fun about it. He hurt me! Excited? Next you'll want to know did I come. The answer is no. There wasn't—" She broke off with the trace of a sob in her voice for the first time.

"No," Henry said. "I wouldn't ask that. It wouldn't be relevant."

"Objection!" Nora said. I don't think she had ever sat down. "I object to these constant sidebar remarks by defense counsel."

"Don't make remarks, counsel," Watlin said mildly. From the reactions of the spectators they thought the judge had let the trial get completely away from him, but Watlin appeared unmoved. I imagine he thought he was projecting superior knowledge, but what he actually showed was indifference. He sat there as if just waiting for the next meal break.

Henry went on to something else, thank God. Background questions about the building, the layout of the offices, the security guard's rounds. Mandy Jackson calmed down. We all calmed down. I think boredom began to creep over the assembled crowd. The courtroom door opened and closed three or four times. Judge Waddle's eyes were at half mast. It was after four o'clock. Sun had been pouring through those big windows for two hours. Henry continued.

"Do you know David Blackwell's salary?" he asked.

"No."

"What would you guess he makes?"

"Objection. Calls for speculation."

Henry rose too. "No, it doesn't, Your Honor. May we approach the bench?"

"Not necessary. I overrule the objection."

"What would you imagine David makes?" Henry asked again.

Mandy wasn't giving. "More than me," she said.

Good enough. Henry didn't press her. "What do you make?" he asked instead.

"Five thirty-five an hour," she said before Nora could even get to her feet.

"What does that come to a week after deductions?"

"I object again," Nora said. "If this is relevant, I'd like to hear how."

"I am the one who gets to ask for explanations, counselor, and I understand the relevance. Your objection is overruled."

"It comes to one sixty-seven a week," said Mandy.

"What does one semester hour cost at Trinity University, where you're attending school?"

"I told you, I have a scholarship. And loans."

"Actually, I believe you just mentioned loans. But that doesn't answer my question. What does one semester hour cost?"

"I think it's about two hundred dollars."

"And how many hours are you taking this semester?"

"Fourteen."

Henry paused to write the figures on his pad, and to give the jurors time to do the simple math. I still couldn't read their expressions. But I thought Henry was going at her too long. Longer than I would have. Mandy had looked rather hard and calculating there for a while, but now she was starting to appear sympathetic again. How could she live on that salary, with two children? Live and go to school, too. I was impressed by her, if no one else was.

"Let me ask you about your children," Henry said, and he did, at some length. Names, ages, grade in school. Mrs. Jackson's voice softened. Henry's grew softer as well. If you glanced away, they became background drone. The room was now baking. The bailiffs had lowered and closed venetian blinds over the west windows, but that only made the sun's presence seem more threatening. The blinds glowed, as if the sun hung just behind them, waiting to blind the first person who peeked out. Judge Waddle nodded, caught himself, looked at his watch, shifted uncomfortably.

"I pass the witness," Henry said abruptly.

We all stirred as if a cool breeze had passed among us. Watlin looked happy, until he turned to Nora. "I suppose you have redirect?" he said discouragingly.

"Yes, Your Honor."

"And then you'll probably have recross," Watlin said in Henry's direction. "Well, we've passed beyond my attention span, if not the jury's. We'll resume tomorrow at nine o'clock. Remember the instructions I've given you about talking to people or letting them talk to you," he said to the jury, and they nodded as if paying attention. "Everyone remain seated until the jurors leave."

We did, then milled out into the aisles. The crowd lost its definition. No longer spectators, just hanging around an empty public room. Taking Victoria along, I joined Henry and David at the front. Nora had already hustled Mandy Jackson out, without a backward look. My group went out the same back door and up the back stairs to my office.

"Losing us all a little toward the end there, Henry," I said to him on the way up the stairs.

"I couldn't let her go," he said, and passed me Linda's note. It said, "Ask why she was working late, then keep her on the stand the rest of the day." Linda hadn't returned, or if she had she was keeping away from my family.

We found Lois and Dinah waiting in my office. Lois reached up to arrange David's hair. There was nothing wrong with his hair; it was just an opportunity to touch him.

"Can I come back in tomorrow?" Dinah asked. "How am I going to learn anything?"

I promised to fill her in that night. She sat quietly while we adults had our little conference, made plans as if the situation were evolving, though nothing had changed. David appeared a little more cheerful. "She's getting caught, isn't she?" he said hopefully.

"I thought it could have been less graphic" was the only thing I heard Victoria say.

After they left I didn't have to ask Henry to remain behind. He hadn't moved from where he was slumped in his chair, back of his neck resting against the top of the chair's back, staring upward. We sat in companionable silence for a moment before I said, "You're doing an excellent job, Henry."

His voice seemed to come from behind the chair. "I know. This is the best cross I've ever done. But I've got a lot to work with."

"You're using it all."

"To good effect?" he asked, sitting up. I just looked at him, raising my eyebrows questioningly. "Do you doubt her story?" he said.

I hedged. "There are contradictions."

"But do you believe that woman is lying? In the essential truth of it?" He took my silence for answer. "Do you know what I think?" he said just as I started asking, "You have a pet theory?" We had to wait a moment to sort out our voices and hear what we'd said, then Henry continued.

"I think she's telling the truth, except for one thing. It didn't happen when she says it did."

"Earlier that day? What do you mean?"

"I think it happened just the way she said it did, at the office, one night late. But not April thirteenth. And she didn't report it. Most of them don't, you know, I don't have to tell you that. She didn't report it because she was scared for her job and she thought maybe he'd accuse her of leading him on, or because she was ashamed, or whatever reason she had.

"And time passed and she saw him still sitting fat and sassy in the executive suite and her life still hard as a slave's and she got mad. Mad at him and mad at herself. You saw that look she gave him when she took the stand. She hates him. And finally she couldn't live with it any more and she set out to get him."

"So that cockamamie story David told us is true, too."

Henry nodded. "She just restaged it. This time with the security guard on his way and the police called in. And this time she's seeing it through."

I sat and thought about it. While I did, animation left Henry and he sank back into his seat again. While he'd talked the idea was vivid, but in the silence it became what I said a minute later: "Crazy idea, Henry."

He agreed. "And not worth shit even if I could prove it."

The indictment alleges a date, but it also says "on or about" that date, so the state isn't bound to prove that specific day. All the state has to prove is that it happened within the statute of limitations and before the indictment was handed down. I wouldn't want to take such a theory to a jury anyway. Try to win acquittal with that: "I didn't rape her when she says I did, I raped her before."

I didn't bother to tear Henry's theory apart. He had obviously already done that in his own mind. We were still sitting there when Linda arrived.

Henry and I looked like shipwreck survivors. Linda looked like our rescuer. She was exhilarated. Sweat glazed her forehead. She had some sort of document in her hand.

"I issued a defense subpoena for this," she said.

"With your name on it?" I asked, sitting up.

"Of course not. With Henry's name on it. Don't challenge the signature," she said to him.

She knelt beside Henry's chair and explained to him what she'd learned, speaking as rapidly as if there were a deadline to meet tonight. As she talked she touched his arm, looking intently at him to be sure he followed her. Henry leaned close to her. Neither of them glanced at me. A stranger watching wouldn't have guessed at any connection between Linda and me. If anything, she looked like Henry's girl, in one sense or another. I came from behind the desk to stand over them but they didn't look up from the document Linda had brought.

"It's not much," she said a few minutes later. "It's not going to turn the tide of the trial, but it's a curiosity. Something for the jury to wonder about."

"No, it's more than that," Henry said. "It suggests calculation on her part. You see? It's the first thing that does. This is great, Linda. This needs thinking about. I should've thought of something like this."

"That's what comes of not having a second chair. So how is the trial going? I missed most of it."

Henry sighed, sinking back again. Linda pulled him up from the chair. "You need a drink. Come on, come to dinner and tell me all about it. I am full of insight."

At the door Linda stopped. "Coming?" No special meaning in her voice or her face as she looked back at me. Henry had already started talking.

"Uh, no. I think I'd better go see David."

She nodded. Henry didn't even look at me. "See? She already knew," he was saying. I could hear their voices in the outer office until the door closed. Henry had regained his animation. I fought hope myself. Linda's knack. It was undiminished.

David's house looked unfamiliar to me. I was sure I had the right one but he had changed something since the last time I was there. I couldn't tell what. I sat in his driveway for a minute, hoping he'd hear me and come out. The house leaked a trickle of light but no sound. I wondered if David and Vicky had ever yelled at each other.

He had a wooden-slatted screen door, so that when the heavier inner door opened I couldn't see who was standing there. The pause made me think it was Victoria. But it was David who pushed open the screen door. "Dad," he said.

I slouched inside. Now that I was there I didn't know why I'd come. I had nothing to say.

David led me into his den, where a drink sat beside his recliner and the TV was on without sound. It was a nice house they had, but not very personalized. Like a model home. Just the right number of magazines fanned on the coffee table. Wedding pictures on the wall above the TV. I wondered suddenly how much David made. Was he over his head in debt? Henry probably knew.

"Vicky's gone to bed."

With a headache, no doubt. David waved me to a seat and offered a drink. I shook my head. "I should call your mother and tell her I'm here."

He didn't say anything to that. On the screen some sort of sporting event was being enacted, something fluid and unviolent. It could lull a person to sleep.

"You'll probably be on the stand tomorrow. I came over to make absolutely certain you'll be as nervous as possible."

He didn't laugh. "She can't trip me up," he said of Nora, "because I'm not going to lie. I know it's a crazy story, but at least I won't contradict myself. Mr. Koehler made Mandy look bad, didn't he?"

"Yes." Not bad enough, I thought. "David—"

"I'm not going to say it again."

For a moment I didn't know what he was saying. Then I realized he was denying his guilt again.

"I believe you, David. But it's gone way past that. I don't even care. I'd do anything I could to keep you out of—from being convicted of this, no matter what. Do you believe me?"

He didn't answer, but he looked at me instead of the TV screen and we developed a conversation of sorts. I gave him worthless tips about testifying that I'd already given him. This time he nodded and asked for more explanation and nodded again.

I never heard anyone stir in the back of the house. When I rose to leave, David followed me to the front door. I held him against me awkwardly, and he awkwardly responded. It went on a little too long. "Well," I said.

* * *

By the time I got my front door open Lois was standing in the dining room staring at me, fists on hips. "Where have you been?"

Lois doesn't curse when she gets mad. She eschews such adornment. Her sentences grow short.

"At David's."

Her mouth didn't loosen. What was the source of this anger? It couldn't have been jealousy. We know the foundation of jealousy, and Lois and I don't have that any more.

"Dinah's been asking for you. She won't go to sleep."

"All right." I left my jacket over the back of a dining room chair, my shoes in the hall, and tossed my tie toward our bedroom. Dinah was awake, lying on her back in the dark. "There you are," she said without recrimination.

She wanted to hear all about the first day of trial. We went over it very nearly line by line. I grew sleepy before my child did. "Daddy," came her voice in the dark after a pause. "If they find him guilty, what will you do next?"

I thought I'd taught her better than to say *if* a defendant was convicted. Hardheaded Dinah was becoming a fantasist like the rest of us. I mumbled something about appeal. She said impatiently, "No, but right away. Before—before they can—"

"I don't know, darling. I'll do something."

"Daddy?"

I lay next to her, holding her until she fell asleep. I was thinking, I'd never let it happen to you, baby. But I didn't say it aloud. Why should she have believed me? I was letting it happen to her brother.

CHAPTER

7

enry met me in my office the next morning before trial resumed; I had called him at six. He acted as if everything were normal, discussing the case with me in casual, professional tones, until he stood to leave and I moved in front of him.

"I need to get into this, Henry."

"Get into what?"

"Don't act dense. The trial. I'm going to take over the cross-examination."

Henry looked at me as if uneasy at having me between him and the door. "You can't get into it, Mark. The conflict is so clear Watlin wouldn't even wait for an objection. You know—"

I was shaking my head. "I'm taking a leave of absence. The letter's right there on my desk. If that's not good enough, I'll resign. I'm coming in, Henry."

"You're firing me, then? Because it's too late for me to take on co-counsel, especially in midwitness. The cross I'm developing leads straight into my final argument. If I let you or anyone else take over now . . ."

I could barely hear him over the rushing sound, the one that had kept waking me up all night. It was the sound of a trial terror such as I'd never felt as a participant. Yesterday I'd fallen outside the bounds of reality; I was surprised no one had seen it. One part of me could watch the trial as if it were any other, finely gauging the progress, trying to read the jury, following the course of questioning, and jumping ahead of it. But another part of me was screaming for it to stop. That part saw David and no one else. I'd always been so casual about the steps in the process. "If you get convicted, we'll appeal," I'd tell a client. But if David got convicted, he'd be in prison! It was never supposed to get so far. Four months ago, when he'd been arrested, trial had barely seemed a possibility. It had seemed so possible to head it off. But now the case had become a runaway train that couldn't be stopped without extraordinary intervention. Some time in the small hours of the night I'd decided I had to provide that intervention in the only way left to me.

"I can't just sit there and watch, Henry! How about if I do David on direct, then? And started choking up while I was questioning him, as if I believed in him so strongly I was terrified of them finding him guilty. I could do that, Henry, believe me, I could sell that."

Henry intended his voice to be soothing, I'm sure. He had no way of knowing it sounded to me like the skittering of insects against a very thin windowpane. "A, it wouldn't mean anything to the jury, Mark. You're his father. They'd expect you to believe in him, no matter what. Or B, it would look like you were crying over what he'd done. There's no way it can help. Let me do it my way. Be clinical, Mark. Think about it. Think like a lawyer."

I'd tried that; look where it had gotten me. Even while trying to manipulate the system I'd expected it to operate to clear David. I hadn't been devious enough.

But it was too late to correct it. I tried to let that clinical part of myself to which Henry was appealing take over. For a moment I could picture the unappealing spectacle my way

would present to the jury. It was witnesses who were supposed to break down under questioning, not the lawyer.

"All right, you're right. Just, Henry, for God's sake—"

"I know, I know."

"Sorry, as if you didn't feel enough pressure already. This
doesn't mean I don't have confidence in you."

"It's okay, Mark, I know how you feel."

A lie, a facile homily. But he did know his job. I let him
escape with enough time to go over his notes. He seemed to
take that detached part of me away with him. When the door
closed behind him, my whole body clenched as if I would
spasm my way into another dimension. I fell backward,
caromed off my desk, hammered my fists on it. All the papers
swept away before me; I couldn't see my hands spraying them.

I don't remember what else. I was in the chair, eyes clamped
tight against tears, when I came to myself. What brought me
back was the thought of that door opening again and David
walking in. He couldn't afford any more fright. I had to look
confident for him. Gradually, the shell recaptured me, as if I'd
been laminated. The mirror showed me a neatly dressed
lawyer, grave but sure. On my way out I asked Patty to get
someone to clean up the office before the first trial recess.

It is not only prisoners who can be rehabilitated. Witnesses
can be, too. That's what it's called when the other side has
beaten up on your witness on cross-examination and then you
get her back on redirect to clear up some of the inconsistencies or bad impressions. You are rehabilitating her. That's
what Nora did to Mandy Jackson the next morning.

And I had done my bit to reform David. From behind I could
see that he was sitting up straight in his chair and was looking
directly at his accuser. Not hostilely, if he was doing as I'd told
him, but steadily. With a trace of puzzlement in his expression.

Nora had been at Mandy overnight as well. The witness
huddled in the witness chair. It was the wall her back was

against. She would not look at David, and stole only sidelong glances at Henry. Yesterday Mrs. Jackson had been too assertive for the good of the state's case. Today she looked a victim again.

"Are you all right?" Lois said to me, leaning across Dinah.

"Yes, fine. Are you?"

"What Linda found, is it going to help?"

"Yes. But I don't know how much." I was past lying to Lois. "It's all up to Henry," I said.

Henry had a little show for the jury before testimony began again. Victoria was sitting at the defense table, talking earnestly to David. She was wearing a white dress and either wearing no makeup or it was so artfully applied that it looked like none. She stayed there until the jurors were seated in the box, then squeezed David's hand, gave him a sad smile of encouragement, and came out through the gate in the bar to take her seat. The jurors watched, of course. They were to think that David's wife, at least, didn't believe the charges. I thought Victoria looked a little awkward and let her face go blank again a little too soon, but who knows.

Nora ignored this playlet. She started her redirect of her most important witness by resetting the scene: the dimly lit offices, the dark inner one, the trash can sitting there innocently. Mandy looking at it and thinking about her job.

"You said you'd had some trouble before of this nature," Nora said, switching topics.

"A little. Nothing much. The usual thing, you know, man might be a little flirty. More from other maintenance men than from the men in the offices."

"Did this defendant ever do anything like that?"

"No."

"Nothing, never? Never touched you, or said anything that could have two meanings?"

"He certainly never touched me. I don't remember anything else like what you're saying."

"Is that why you thought you had nothing to fear when you went into his office the night of April thirteenth?"

That was Nora's reason for asking these questions, but I thought she had fallen into Henry's neatly laid trap. These things are always more obvious when you're looking at the trial lawyers' backs. Besides which, I had seen Henry's notes for his final argument.

"Yes. I couldn't believe it'd go any further than it already had."

Nora nodded. Without wasting time on transition she plunged into her next subject.

"You testified that there was no pleasure in the act for you when the defendant raped you. How did you feel?"

"It hurt. It was just such a shock when he—when he actually . . . I started crying." She was on the verge of crying now. Her shoulders hunched inward. She looked like a woman shaken by chills. "I was begging him to stop, but he— After that I just sort of gave up."

Henry made a note. Nora asked, "What were you thinking?"

"About my children."

"Your children? In what way?"

"Just glad they weren't there, that they were home safe. And I thought I'd seen them for the last time."

"Why?"

"I thought he'd kill me after he was done."

"The defendant? You thought he'd kill you? Why?"

"What else would he do? Just let me go? Any second I thought he'd start beating me. There was such a look in his eye—"

Nora nodded slowly. After a long count she leaned over toward Javier. He shook his head. "I pass the witness," Nora said.

Henry said immediately, "David had never flirted with you at all?"

From her slumped position in the chair Mandy said, "No," in a low voice.

"Did you ever flirt with him?"

"No," she said more forcefully.

"I don't mean anything obvious. I mean the little ways people have of communicating with each other. You never gave him any sidelong looks when you found yourselves in an office together?"

"No."

"Were you more conscious of your own body when the two of you were in a room together? Did you stand straighter or—"

"No."

"—throw your shoulders back? Did you move differently? That night, for example, you said you bent to pick up a trash can while he was in the outer office with you. While you were doing that did you look back over your shoulder and—"

"No! Wiggle my butt at him? No. Mister, you are crazy. By that time I had been on my feet for most of about fourteen hours. I wasn't interested in a little office quickie at the end of a day like that. I just wanted to get done and get home to my kids. I—"

She looked at Nora and realized she was being too forceful. Henry had roused her anger again. She fell abruptly silent but her eyes were blazing and she took deep breaths. I saw at least one juror, a man, turn from Mandy and look at Victoria, where she sat in my row. I discovered something in his expression. Victoria was not the asset to the defense we had hoped. She was beautiful, yes, but she looked like what she was: cold. The contrast between her and Mandy Jackson was vivid. There was passion in the maid. You could burn yourself on her skin. The jury could see why a man with a wife like that would go looking for a woman like this.

Henry wasn't looking at the witness. He opened a folder in front of him and removed a document, the one Linda had brought him yesterday afternoon. "I want to ask you about the test you took earlier that day," he said.

Mandy looked confused. You could see her shifting gears. Henry helped her:

"I believe you said it was in European history?"

"Yes."

"Your Honor?" said Nora. "Relevancy?"

"We discussed the relevance in chambers earlier this morning, as I'm sure you remember, counselor. Overruled."

Judge Watlin didn't look at me—pointedly, I thought. He was slipping the defense another break.

"What did you make on that test?"

Mandy looked completely baffled. She was beginning to appear victimized again. "I don't remember. Everything that happened later—"

Henry walked toward her and handed the document to the court reporter for marking. He identified it for the record and handed it to Mandy. She took it from him by the far edge. "Do you recognize that?"

Her puzzlement didn't decrease. "It's a list of my grades from Trinity?"

"Can you find that April thirteenth test on there?"

After a brief scan: "Yes."

"Does that refresh your memory?"

"Yes."

"What did you make on that test?"

"Fifty-three."

"A fifty-three. Is that an F?"

"Yes."

"Was that an average grade for you in that course?"

She hesitated. But she had the list in her hand. Henry knew the answer. She had to give it. "No."

Henry took the paper from her and walked back toward his seat. "In fact, your grade-point average is a solid B, isn't it?"

"Yes."

"Have you ever made another F?"

"I don't—" Henry raised both his eyebrows and the page in

his hand ever so slightly and she changed her answer in midstream. "No. That's my only one."

"Why did you do so badly on that test that day?"

She was looking down at her hands. "It wasn't a very good day for me. After what happened at the office I couldn't concentrate very—"

"But that happened later. If you mean the alleged rape. That hadn't happened yet when you were taking your test. How could that have made you nervous? Did you have a premonition that it was coming?"

"I don't see how—"

"In fact, you knew what was going to happen that night, didn't you? You had already planned what was going to happen, hadn't you? That's why you had trouble concentrating earlier in the day. Wasn't it?"

"Planned to be raped? No sir, I never planned that. I never—" She hid her eyes by lowering her face to her hand. "I can't help one bad grade," she said miserably.

Don't look triumphant, I begged David in my mind. *Look sympathetic, for God's sake.*

Henry gave her a few moments to regain her composure. "I have just one more topic to ask you about," he notified her. "You have testified that you were in fear for your life."

Mandy nodded.

"Meaning you thought David was going to kill you or seriously injure you, is that correct?"

"Yes," she said quietly.

"That's one of the elements of the offense, isn't it?"

Nora objected to the relevance of the question, and Watlin sustained this one.

"Did you really think he was going to kill you, right there in the office? Or beat you so badly you'd have to go to a hospital? How would he have explained that?"

"I was afraid he'd make trouble for me somehow."

"So what you were really afraid of was losing your job, not death or serious bodily injury."

"I was just scared, I didn't stop to think what of." Henry was happy with that answer, but she continued. "But I remember thinking, how can he do this to me and let me live to tell anybody?"

He couldn't shake her from that position, and so passed her back to Nora. Conventional wisdom has it that you always try to get in the last series of questions, but Nora has never been conventional. "I have no more questions," she said. "The state rests."

It seemed awfully abrupt. We all stirred and looked to the judge. It seemed to take Watlin a moment, too, to remember what came next. To Henry he said, "Are you ready to begin, Mr. Koehler?"

"First I have a motion to make, Your Honor. Then, assuming my motion is denied, I want to recall Officer Canales."

"Is he here?" Watlin asked Nora.

"He's on call, Your Honor. He told me he could be here in fifteen minutes if he was needed."

Watlin looked at his watch. It was only ten-thirty in the morning, but he made what must have been an easy decision for him. "All right, we'll release the jurors early for lunch while we take up the motion."

The jurors filed out. Henry made his motion for an instructed verdict, arguing that the state had failed to prove its case. It was not a vigorously urged motion. There had certainly been testimony which if believed would allow a conviction. Whether that testimony was believable was up to the jury. Watlin left it up to them. "That will be denied. I will see both sides here at twelve forty-five."

We spent the long lunch break mostly in my office. Lois and Dinah and Victoria didn't join us, so Linda did. "That test business shook her up a lot more than I expected," Henry told her.

Linda nodded. "She's hiding something."

Henry and I glanced at each other. He didn't raise his

theory in front of David. Instead, "You know what we have to decide," he said.

Everyone but David nodded. "What?" he said, looking around the circle. He looked so innocent. Naive, I mean.

"Whether you're going to testify," Henry told him.

"What do you mean? Why wouldn't I?"

"Because we might be better off without you testifying." I took over the explanation. "Henry's put some holes in the state's case. There may already be reasonable doubts in the jury's minds. But then if you testify and they decide you're lying, that will erase their doubts. Sometimes—maybe most times—it's best for the defendant just to sit there."

"You may not want to subject yourself to the cross-examination," Linda told him kindly.

"She can't do any worse to me than what you did in practice." I was proud of him when he had the grace to smile at Linda while saying it. He glanced sidelong at me. Maybe the smile was for me too.

"I wouldn't count on that."

"It's the hardest decision of the trial," Henry said. True, I thought. Well, after the decision to reject the plea-bargain offer. "I'm going to let you make it."

David looked around at us all again. His expression was like a high school quarterback's while being told he can't play in the big game.

The first defense witness was the first police officer on the scene that night, a patrolman. He had already testified and looked a little surprised to be back, especially as a defense witness. He looked at Nora as if he'd done something wrong. Henry just wanted to know one thing from him. Had he smelled alcohol that night?

"Alcohol? No."

"Was there anything to indicate to you that David—the defendant here—had been drinking?"

"No, nothing. He certainly wasn't drunk." The patrolman

looked at Nora for approval. He'd denied the defendant that defense. Nora didn't look up. She had no questions on cross.

Next Henry recalled the other police witnesses, and the security guard, to ask the same thing. The witnesses shuffled on and off the stand quickly, but time passed. There were going to be no surprise defense witnesses, no alibi, no explanation of why the rape couldn't possibly have happened. It would just be mano a mano. And Mandy Jackson, in spite of whatever doubts Henry might have raised about her testimony, had been a damned good witness. That was one reason the defense would not call the defendant as its first witness. Henry wanted to put as much distance as possible between the two main witnesses. Give the jury time to lose the emotional impact of the victim's testimony before they heard David's.

After the recalled witnesses Henry called reputation witnesses who testified that David had a good reputation for "truth and veracity." The law allows such testimony to be given only in a precise formula: "Do you know David Blackwell? Are you familiar with his reputation for truth and veracity? What is that reputation?" "It's good," says the witness. Exciting stuff. Henry kept them coming—co-workers of David's, old school friends, former teachers—until the state objected to the parade. "How many more?" Watlin asked Henry.

"Your Honor, I can keep witnesses to my client's good reputation—"

"I object, I object, I object. Can you please keep him—"

"—coming for the rest of the week," Henry finished over Nora's upraised voice.

"No doubt," said Watlin. "But do you think one more would suffice?"

"Very well." Henry scanned a list in front of him. I was on that list, but only as a remote possibility. I didn't think it would be wise to call me.

"I call Dinah Blackwell."

What? Dinah had *not* been on the list. She jumped up from beside me and was already in the aisle. I almost reached to stop her. I don't like stunts, and I had no idea what Henry had in mind.

It was Javier who stood. "Your honor, I'm afraid I must object. To allow this witness to testify would violate the Rule. She has been in the courtroom for the whole trial. Hello, Dinah."

"Your Honor," Henry responded, "I didn't know I was going to call this witness until she spoke to me during the last break. She is only a reputation witness, she's not going to refute any prior testimony."

"I'll allow it," Watlin said. He *did* like stunts. They got his name in the papers.

Dinah had been standing quietly by the defense table, her hand on David's shoulder, while the objection was ruled on. David was speaking softly to her. I had never seen them look so close. This was the dream of her short lifetime for Dinah. She responded to the oath in a voice that carried clearly and took her seat, folding her hands together.

"State your name, please."

"Dinah Blackwell."

"How old are you, Dinah?"

"Ten."

"Have you ever been in a trial before?"

"I've seen them, but I've never been a witness."

"Do you know what it means to take an oath?"

"It means you have to tell the truth. Theoretically," she added, looking at the state's counsel table. She got the laughter she was looking for. Even from Javier.

She declared that she would tell the truth, and when asked the formula question about David's reputation for truthfulness replied emphatically, "It's good." And she turned to be cross-examined.

Javier did it, gently. "How much older is your brother than you are, Dinah?"

"Thirteen years. He's twenty-three."

"So you were never in the same school together?"

"No, sir."

"Then you don't know what his classmates thought of his truthfulness. And of course you don't work with him?"

"No sir. I don't work, I go to school."

"Do you love your brother, Dinah?"

Dinah looked at David. "He's all right."

Javier joined the laughter again. "Thank you. I have no more—"

"But he *can't* lie," Dinah blurted out. She was leaning forward in her earnestness. Javier, flustered, had nothing to say for a moment. "You should see him try," Dinah hurried on. "He gets red in the face and he can't finish a sentence. He's so bad at it that he—"

"That's enough now. Objection."

"—he gave it up. He can't lie to me, and he told me he didn't do this. He didn't do—"

"Your Honor, I object!"

"Yes. Miss Blackwell, stop now. Miss—"

No one was laughing now. Dinah looked about to cry. She fell silent, still leaning forward almost out of her chair. She was looking at the jurors now. They were too embarrassed to return her stare.

I was looking at Lois, who in turn was watching Dinah intently, the way I'd seen her watch our daughter at school pageants, but without the little smile. Lois nodded slightly as she had on those occasions, when she had gone over Dinah's lines with her at home.

When Dinah was excused I met her at the gate. She sat beside me with her head lowered and I kept my arm around her for the next hour. "It's true," she muttered to me.

When I looked up again David was on the stand. I hated to see him there. I'd hoped he had changed his mind. He sat very straight in the chair, stiff as a corpse. He glanced at the jury, remembered that he was supposed to look them in the eyes,

tried that, looked away again. Shortly into his testimony he lost
his sterling posture and his voice began to drop. Watlin had to
tell him two or three times to speak up. I've seen the witness
stand do that to countless people. David was embarrassed to
be there, and his embarrassment looked like guilt. He began to
look the way Dinah had described him looking when he tried
to tell a lie. He hesitated, stammered, backed out of a sentence,
and tried to start again.

Once he was well launched into his version of the events of
April thirteenth, it didn't really matter how well he told it. An
awed silence fell across the whole courtroom. In that silence
David's voice was a tiny, fragile instrument, a dry whisper
across a prairie.

Henry tried to take the curse off the story by attacking it
himself. "She scratched herself?"

"Yes. She did."

"And she tore off her own clothes."

"Yes."

"How did her skin get under your fingernails?"

"I did scratch her once, when I tried to stop her and she
pulled away from me. She scratched me, too."

As the recital neared its end David grew more impassioned.
Maybe he began to sound believable. He did to me. For the
millionth time I thought about the implications of his story.
Why would it happen? What did it mean? In answer to
Henry's next question David turned to the jurors, leaning half
over the rail in front of him.

"David. Did you rape Mandy Jackson?"

"No. I did not. I would never do such a thing. I didn't."

Some of the jurors looked back at him, not all of them.
Through the course of the next few questions their eyes fell
away from him.

"Did you penetrate her sexual organ with yours?"

"No."

"Or her mouth?"

"No. No."

"Aside from that, from the question of rape, did you do anything to Mrs. Jackson to make her afraid that you were going to injure her or kill her?"

"No, nothing. I just stood there like a fool."

Henry nodded. He sat there as if his work were done. He didn't look down at his notes, just steadily at David. Then, as if he couldn't contain his own curiosity:

"David, I have to ask. Why would she do this?"

Nora pushed back her chair. Javier laid a hand on her arm and leaned close to her ear. She stayed where she was.

David on the stand looked thoughtful and slightly perplexed, as if this were the first time he'd been asked that question. "The only reason I can think of is money," he said slowly. "That it was some sort of blackmail scheme."

"How much money do you make a year, David?"

"Thirty-two thousand dollars."

"What do you wear to work?"

"Suits, ties."

"What kind of car do you drive?"

"Buick Regal. We bought it last summer."

"About the time you were arrested, in April, had there been any recent event that would make your name talked about at work?"

"My father had just become district attorney, if that's what you mean."

"Your family had become politically prominent?"

"Well, I didn't think of it that way, but I guess some people might."

"One other thing, David. Could Mandy Jackson's motive for this have been rejection?"

David looked so genuinely puzzled that I was sure Henry hadn't asked him this before. "I—I'm not sure what—"

"Had she ever propositioned you sexually?"

"Mandy? No, never."

"Well, flirted, then. Had she ever given you little hints that she might be interested?"

David looked as if he wanted to take Henry aside privately. He was almost scowling. "There was never anything like that. We were strictly businesslike."

"I pass the witness."

The words a prosecutor waits to hear, when a defendant is on the stand. I looked at Nora, not surprised she was waiting, savoring the moment. There are so many factors that prevent a defendant from testifying: that he may have prior convictions his lawyer doesn't want to come out, that his testimony isn't necessary and the lawyer doesn't want to subject him to cross-examination; or simply that he wouldn't make a good witness. In less than half of criminal trials does the prosecutor have the hapless defendant handed over for cross. To be handed one like this, with a defense such as David had just given, was a prosecutor's wet dream.

To my surprise it was Javier who did the cross-examination. I hadn't even been watching him. David told me later that he sat there with a puzzled expression on his face before he asked his first question.

"How much money did Mrs. Jackson ask you for?" Javier asked politely. His pen was poised as he waited to write down the answer. Watch out, I thought.

"She didn't ask me for any," David said.

"Oh." The puzzlement was back on Javier's face. I couldn't see it, but I heard it. "But I thought you said she was trying to blackmail you."

I saw Henry stir uneasily. Javier's questioning was like that. It made you think you should object, but you couldn't think what the objection should be. The only real objection would be, Your Honor, he's trying to make my client look like a liar. With which no one could argue.

"I said I thought that must be her reason," David explained. "Because I couldn't think of any other reason for her to do it."

"Ah. But she didn't ask you for money?"

"No."

"At least, that night she didn't?"

"No."

"This was in April?"

"Yes, sir."

Javier counted out fingers. "May, June, July, August. It's been four months? Has she asked you for money in the last four months since it happened?"

"No." David realized how that sounded. Javier let him explain. "Well, I guess after the police came and all, she thought she had to go through with the story."

Javier mused over that. "Do you know how many arrests actually come to trial?" he finally asked.

"Objection. Calls for speculation." Bravo. Henry had thought of the proper objection.

Javier addressed Watlin. "His father is the district attorney —which is in evidence. I assume he knows something about criminal law."

Watlin hesitated. He didn't want to look protective of the witness. "I'll let him answer if he knows."

David didn't pick up the broad hint. "I'm not sure, but I know not all of them."

"Cases are dismissed all the time. Have you ever heard or read about cases being dismissed before trial?"

"Yes, sir."

"Don't you imagine Mandy Jackson could have dismissed this one if she'd wanted, if you'd met her demand?"

Henry's objection was uselessly sustained this time. The jury had already heard the question. The judge solemnly instructed them to disregard it. Right.

"So she never said anything at all to you about money, is that right?"

"That's right."

"What did she say?"

"While she was tearing her clothes off she didn't say anything."

"Did she do anything, make any sounds?"

David searched his memory. "I don't remember any."

"Did you hear the security guard testify that she was crying when he came in?"

"Oh. Yes, she was crying then."

"Then? You mean she wasn't crying before?"

"I don't remember her crying."

"You mean she just started crying the instant someone else appeared in the room?"

"Well, that was the first time she made a sobbing sound. I guess maybe she'd been crying before, but I hadn't noticed."

When Javier got an answer he liked he wrote it down, laboriously, letting the words replay themselves. That was one he wrote down.

"Let me ask you about this flirting issue, although I'm really not sure of its relevance—"

Henry said, "Your Honor, I object to the sidebar remark. I'll explain the relevance when the time comes for argument."

"Now *I* have to object to *that* sidebar remark, Your—"

"Let's just both cut out the sidebars. And move on." Those west windows were growing hot again, and Watlin testy.

Resuming his seat, Javier said, "At any rate, there was never any flirting?"

"No, sir. None."

"Why not?"

"Why not?" David looked around the room for an answer, spotted Victoria. "I'm a married man, I don't flirt with other women." I could have thought of a better response than that.

"If you did flirt, would you maybe have flirted with Mandy Jackson?"

"Obj—" Henry began, and Javier said, "I'll rephrase. Do you find Mandy attractive?"

Dinah was right, David was a lousy liar. He couldn't do it worth a damn. "I don't know. I've never thought about it," he said.

"Well, think about it now. Is she?"

Henry felt obliged to bail David out. "Your Honor, what he

may think of her attractiveness now isn't relevant. If he didn't think about it before—"

"I guess not. Sustained."

Javier's voice was still gentle. "You mean you never considered her as a woman? She was just the maid?"

There were no blacks on the jury, but there were, of course, Mexican-Americans. We all waited with interest for David's answer. I turned my head slowly and saw Linda at the back of the room, staring at him with an absolutely dead expression. Was this another reason she had empathized with Mandy Jackson?

"No, I don't mean that," David said brightly.

"Then you did think about her as a woman. When she passed in or out of your office, did you ever think to yourself, There's a good-looking woman?"

David was looking down at his hands. He couldn't look at Victoria or the jurors or anyone else. "Probably," he mumbled.

"'Probably'? You mean you thought that about a lot of women, so you probably thought it about her, too?"

"Objection."

Many prosecutors would have withdrawn the question, but Javier waited politely for the objection to be ruled on, looking a little surprised when it was sustained. "I'm sorry, your honor, I'll try to phrase that better. David, did you think Mandy Jackson was good-looking?"

Henry's objection was overruled. "Yes," David mumbled.

"Sexy?"

"I don't know about that."

"Did you ever think about making love to her?"

David looked up, flushed. "No!" he said sharply. It was a completely automatic response.

"No?" Javier said. There was a faintly chiding tone to his voice. "Your mind doesn't drift from one thought to the other, from seeing a good-looking woman to thinking you'd like to make love to her?"

David wasn't quite so hasty. "Not—" He stammered a little. "Not automatically," he finally said, and looked down again.

Javier made a sound of disbelief or surprise, too faint to be objectionable. I knew the expression on his face. It was one as if he were examining his own conscience, wondering if *he* was the unusual one.

"I pass the witness."

Henry started with a thoroughly objectionable question. "David." He waited until David looked up. "You were offered a plea bargain in this case, weren't you?"

He let the objection to relevancy be sustained, then returned to the same topic. This is one advantage to being a defense lawyer. The prosecutor has to worry about reversible error, but the defendant's lawyer can ask any damned thing he wants. He doesn't care if the case gets reversed on appeal. That's one of his goals.

"Why didn't you take the offer, David?"

The objection was sustained again, then Henry nodded to his client and David said, "I wouldn't plead guilty because I'm not. No matter what they offered, I wouldn't say I did this."

It was the most sincere David had sounded all afternoon, but Henry must have known Judge Waddle would allow Javier's question on recross, because Henry had invited it. Javier asked David, "The plea-bargain offer was for prison time, wasn't it?"

"Yes."

The examination of the defendant dribbled away with fewer and fewer questions on each cycle. Javier's tone when he passed the witness for the last time implied there was no point in asking him anything further. The last words were David's repeated denial, still impassioned but now tired.

The defense rested.

Reporters posed like sprinters. One was standing at the back door and as soon as Watlin turned to the jurors and said, "I'm going to release you now," he was out the door. He was a TV reporter, it was almost five o'clock, and his cameraman was already set up down on the sidewalk in front of the courthouse. He had his lead-in.

After the jurors were gone Watlin said to the lawyers, "Let's talk about the charge," indicating with a tilt of his head the side door leading to his chambers. Henry paused long enough to ask me one question. "Ask for the lesser?"

"Of course," I said. The defense question is whether you want the jury to be allowed to convict of a lesser included offense, such as in this case sexual assault, or do you want to force them to go all or nothing. The way I felt now, I wanted to let them compromise.

Besides, if he asked for it, Watlin might deny it, and that would be reversible error. The evidence had certainly raised the possibility that David had sexually assaulted her but hadn't caused her to fear death or serious bodily injury. That's all a charge conference is usually good for, to try to lure the judge into error. I didn't try to force my way into it. The lawyers and judge gone, the courtroom emptied out quickly. David was still on the witness stand. His tension hadn't abated. I thought I knew what he felt. There must be something else he could have said, something that would have turned them wholeheartedly in his favor. He was trying to think what that was. He probably wanted to go home with the jurors and explain it again. "Listen," he'd say, unconstrained by questioning and rules of evidence, "I know it sounds crazy, but crazy things happen, you know? Sometimes there's no explaining." And if the juror was just a guy hunched over on the next bar stool, he'd nod reflectively.

"You did fine," I told him, taking his arm and leading him down. "You looked innocent, that's what counts. They'll like your looks."

"They have to believe me," he mumbled. "They have to."

We walked past the reporter Jean Palmer, still sitting in the front row. She was writing down what David had just said. He saw her and stopped. "I didn't do it," he said. "Put that in the paper. Maybe the jury will see it in the morning. I swear to God I didn't do it."

"The judge just instructed them not to read any stories about the trial," Ms. Palmer said. I laughed almost soundlessly.

When Henry emerged I was the only one waiting for him. "You surprised me calling Dinah," I said. "But it didn't surprise Lois. It was her idea, wasn't it?"

"Yes." Henry sounded perfectly neutral. Maybe he was providing fuel for me to quarrel with my wife, but not with him.

"What else did she tell you?"

"Not to call you as a witness." I started to protest. "Or her. She thought it would be useless. And she said to have David lie on the stand."

I sighed. "My wife hasn't much respect for my life's work. If she could—"

Henry was shaking his head. "No. She meant for the contrast. You saw him when he denied that he'd ever thought about whether Mandy was attractive. Most obvious liar you've ever seen. But when he told his own story . . ."

I saw Lois's point. "He sounded sincere."

"Let us hope," Henry said.

It was as August as it could be. The next morning when I stepped out of my car in the parking lot at eight o'clock it was eighty-two degrees. The strip of grass beside the sidewalk was as dry and yellow as broom straws. The courtroom already seemed burdened with the heat. The jurors looked sleepy with it.

Watlin opened the session by reading the court's charge, the instructions authorizing the jury to convict if they found certain claims to be true, ordering them to acquit otherwise.

The instructions went on for pages, including definitions, presumptions, the elements of the offense. There is a large body of "charge law," holding what must go into such a charge and what must not, or what may be if certain evidence has come up during trial. It is all useless. Watlin read the charge with thespianic fervor, as if he had written it himself. The jurors nodded along. We solemnly explain the law's premises. They solemnly pretend to listen. Then they go into that jury room and do exactly what they want.

"Is the state ready?" Judge Waddle concluded.

"Yes, Your Honor."

"You may proceed. Each side will have thirty minutes."

Javier opened for the state. That is the subordinate's position. Nora had taken charge of the case once more. Javier did his duty, outlining the elements of the offense, explaining that those were the only things the state had to prove. Not motive, not respective histories. Just this: Did this defendant, on this date, perform these acts, causing this response in his victim? The state had proven that he did. Javier concluded:

"People tend to dissociate themselves from rape. They turn away from its brutality. They look for some way to blame the victim, because blaming the victim makes them safe from the same horrible crime. They say, This couldn't happen to me, to my wife, my daughter, because we wouldn't do what this woman did. She was in a bad place, or did a stupid thing. She wore the wrong thing or talked to the wrong man. She led him on until she was sorry.

"What was Mandy Jackson doing? She was working. She has no husband and she has two children to support the only way she can. On April thirteenth she was doing nothing but her job. She wasn't at a bar, she wasn't in a bikini at the beach. She was at her job and she had been there off and on since early that morning. That job, to her surprise, left her alone with this man in a dark office on a deserted floor of an office building and that was all it took. Was Mandy Jackson 'asking for it'? Is that what she wanted at the end of a long day, to have her clothes torn and her face scratched? To be humiliated? There is no way you can believe that.

"You have heard two stories in this trial. The only question you need to ask yourselves is, Whose story makes sense? The answer to that question is obvious, and it means your verdict must be guilty."

He hadn't raised his voice and he hadn't lectured them. He was their friend and he was making the decision easy for them. Jurors sat unmoving, but when I glanced back I saw spectators nodding.

Henry was brilliant. Personally, I think jurors have unshakeably made up their minds long before the evidence ends, but if argument can sway jurors, Henry swayed them. He began abruptly by responding to Javier's argument.

"The prosecutor has told you Mandy Jackson wanted no part of this rape she testified to, but did David want it? It was the end of a long day for him, too. He had been in that building more than twelve hours. Lying in wait for a woman he didn't even know was coming? And remember this: he had worked there for two years. David knew there was a security guard on duty at night. He knew he couldn't possibly get away with something like this. Why on earth would he try it? Why would he risk his good job, his marriage, his happiness?"

He paused to let them ponder the probabilities. When he looked up he had changed subjects and expressions. He was rueful as he walked close to the jury box rail. "The prosecutor has told you something else. He's told you to compare the stories. What do you get when you do that? What do you have on David Blackwell's side?" He shrugged. "A crazy story. Crazy. Woman comes in and starts tearing off her own clothes. Fakes her own rape. Why? Maybe for money, but she didn't get any money. Maybe she miscalculated, maybe the security guard wasn't supposed to come in when he did. Maybe somebody else was supposed to come in, with a camera. I guess we hear about things like that happening once in a while, but still— Crazy story. Not the kind of story you'd choose for a defense. You could make up a better story than that if you were making up a story, couldn't you?"

Nora was shaking her head, but she didn't object.

"Here's what I want to ask you," Henry went on. "What if it's true? What if that's what happened? I don't mean think it did, I mean think about what that means *if* David's story is true. What follows?

"Well, if there was no rape, there'd be no medical evidence of rape. There'd be no semen. And there wasn't. There'd be no physical sign that Mandy Jackson's sexual organ had been penetrated. And there wasn't. I asked Mrs. Jackson some very obnoxious questions. Now I can explain why. I asked if she was sexually excited. She vehemently denied it, and I believe her. I asked if she was lubricated during the sexual assault. She said no. No way. And she said she kept fighting during the assault.

"But what did the medical evidence show? No vaginal tears. No abrasions on the vaginal wall. But if it happened the way she said it did, when she was dry and force was used, there would have been tears. What did the medical examiner say? He said sometimes there aren't tears during a rape because the victim submits, she doesn't struggle. But Mandy Jackson told you she did struggle. Why wasn't she injured, then? Again, what if what David told you is true? Then the medical evidence would reveal exactly what it does reveal.

"This business about his tie. Maybe that's insignificant. But it certainly sounds funny to me. The security guard said David was fully dressed when he burst into the room. Even had his tie on. Mandy Jackson said he never took it off. Does a man keep his tie on during a rape? Does he? Does he remain so fully dressed that he can dress himself completely in the time it takes a security guard to run down a hallway? Or does this support what David said, that he never removed any of his clothes because he never committed rape?

"And if what he told you is true, what would he say to that

security guard when he came rushing in? Wouldn't he say something like 'Joe, thank God you're here. She's gone crazy'? Which is just what he did say, according to both of them."

He stopped to let them add it up. Henry was standing right in front of the jury. His head turned slowly as he looked at each of them.

"Look at all the evidence. You've heard more than two stories over the past two days, you've heard a wealth of evidence. Here's what it adds up to: If what David has told you is true, everything else falls into place. But if what Mandy Jackson told you is what happened, nothing else makes sense. There is no support for her story anywhere."

I couldn't read the jury. Henry made sense to me, but those faces were stone. Words left no impression on them. I would have to ask him later if he saw something up close that eluded me in the audience. I doubted it.

"What the evidence suggests is another explanation. What it suggests is a woman who has a very hard life. She is a maid. She has two children to support and doesn't make much money to do it with. She is an ambitious woman. She is not content to stay where she is, and that's commendable. At first she tries a commendable way of bettering herself. She's going to college. But college is time-consuming; it's going to take another two years, and that's assuming she gets a good job with her degree when lots of college graduates are going unemployed. And there's something else wrong with college. It's expensive. Very. She's getting deeper and deeper in debt to pay for it. What's she done for herself and her children so far? Nothing but make her life even harder.

"In the meantime as she goes about her job every day she sees people whose lives look much easier than hers. The men wear suits and ties to work, they drive nice cars, they pull down a lot more money than she's ever seen. They must seem rich to her.

"And one of them is suddenly not only rich, he's part of a

prominent family. A political family. A family that couldn't afford scandal. David Blackwell's family.

"Mandy was at work that morning. She testified to that. She overheard someone say that David would be working late that night. And a plan started to form. Maybe it's a plan she'd already had, but now it starts to get specific. She leaves work to go to school but she can't leave the plan behind. It stays on her mind. She can't concentrate on the test she's taking, so she makes the worst grade she's ever made. Maybe she enlists some help. Maybe it was already all set up and this was the opportunity.

"When she goes back to work that night she waits until David is alone in his office. And she goes in and without a word starts tearing off her own clothes.

"And that, ladies and gentlemen, is a version of events that the evidence does support."

I thought that was an exit line, but Henry had one more thing to say. "The flirting," he said.

"That is, the question of flirting. There wasn't any. Both of them testified to that. They denied that emphatically, and I believe them. There were never any sly looks that passed between them. Never a change in Mrs. Jackson's posture or walk to give David Blackwell the idea she might not reject any advances he might be inclined to make. She did nothing— nothing—to hint that she might be interested in him sexually. And he did nothing to pass her the same kind of hint."

Henry had walked over until he was standing behind David. The jury couldn't help but look at him, my twenty-three-year-old son, in the most public seat in the room. I couldn't see David's face, but I knew his face. Rigid and responsible beyond his years, it was still inescapably boyish.

"Mrs. Jackson said he acted as if he might be drunk, but all the other witnesses without exception said there was no sign David had had anything to drink. He hadn't given himself some false courage with liquor.

"So that night, with nothing to lead him on, he attacked her physically. This wasn't a failed seduction, if you believe her story. It was premeditated rape. It wasn't a flirtation that went too far, it was an all-out physical assault. You saw Mrs. Jackson. She is a formidable woman. Not to be trifled with. And you see David Blackwell now. Do you believe it? Can you even picture her version? He's never even made an off-color remark to her and suddenly he's raping her?"

He was shaking his head. "No. No. Look at the evidence, look at the participants, and you *must* have a reasonable doubt about the state's case. Forget belief, talk about doubt. Can you believe her story, without doubt, when no evidence supports it, none at all? How could you? And the judge's instructions tell you that if you harbor such a doubt, your verdict must be not guilty."

I knew this moment. He couldn't stand to let them go. Like David, he thought there was one more thing he could say to them that would ensure their verdict. Henry stood behind his client for a long moment's staring. But there was nothing left for him to do except thank them and sit down.

No one moved for another long moment. A couple of jurors thought it was all over and shifted restlessly in their seats. Nora sat there with her eyes on the page in front of her. When she sensed the jury's escaping attention she looked up. No one moved after that.

She pushed the single sheet of legal paper out to the edge of the table, where she could see it once she was in front of the jury, and she rose slowly to her feet. She looked hesitant, unsure of herself. I tensed.

The first person she looked at was Henry. "I congratulate defense counsel," she said, "on the novelty of his defense."

"Objection, Your Honor. She is attacking the defendant over the shoulders of counsel."

"Overruled."

"He had to say something," Nora went on as if there had been no interruption. "And what he found to say—" She drew a deep breath. "Well. Pieced together out of rags and snatches of testimony, he has found a theory that exonerates the defendant. And it almost works. Almost."

She shook her head bemusedly. "To use the coincidence of a bad grade against Mandy Jackson. That was a bad piece of luck for her, wasn't it, to make her worst test score on the same day she was later going to be brutally assaulted? It wasn't a good day for Mandy, no one can deny that. Maybe that day in the classroom she had a premonition of what was going to happen when she returned to work that night. We've all felt those, haven't we, those tugs of—"

"Your Honor, I must object to this. This is completely outside the record."

"So was much of your argument, counsel," Watlin responded with quiet satisfaction. "I believe this is proper response to your argument. Overruled."

"Maybe, as defense counsel suggested, something happened at work earlier that day to make Mandy uneasy. Maybe an encounter with the defendant himself. Maybe that was what planted the seed in his mind, the completely mistaken idea that she was taken with his charms."

She made the word *charms* obscene.

"This wasn't a failed seduction, defense counsel has argued to you, but wasn't it? What does he call the suggestive, taunting remarks Mandy testified this man made to her? The offers of a massage? The touches on her arms, and her neck? No, it wasn't seduction from Mandy's point of view. She found his touch creepy. But in this man's twisted mind he was seducing her."

She pointed. Eliot Quinn, the D.A. who'd transformed me from a law student to a prosecutor, lived in both of us, Nora and me. She pointed at David and for an instant she pinned him with a look.

"Why wasn't he concerned about the security guard? Why would he try this when he knew someone else was in the building? Because he was charming her. Because she was going to fall for his subtle wiles and cooperate. Those doors had locks. The office had a couch. He didn't need to worry about the guard.

"And by the time it was clear she wasn't taken with him, by the time Mandy Jackson made clear she wanted no part of this defendant's plans, he wasn't thinking about guards. He wasn't thinking of other people, he was thinking only of her. And how he was going to have her no matter what. Defense counsel would have you believe that the defendant thought of consequences at a time like that, or of niceties like removing his tie. Rapists don't think of things like that, my friends. Rapists think of having what they want no matter who gets in the way or who gets hurt. No matter how his victim struggles and begs and cries. You heard it from his own lips. 'Well, I guess I didn't notice that she was crying.' No. He didn't notice much. She wasn't even a person to him, she was an object."

Nora crossed back close to the defense table, then stopped as if afraid of contagion. She turned back to the jury.

"And now he'd have you acquit this man because his victim wasn't hurt enough. Because she didn't sustain vaginal tears. But you're not going to be fooled by that. The medical examiner explained that. Many rape victims don't have vaginal tears, he testified. They don't fight back and so they don't sustain that kind of injury. Mandy did fight back, as he's told you, but you remember her whole testimony. Once the actual rape began, once this man penetrated her, she stopped struggling. She gave up in despair. She thought about her children and she lay there helplessly, begging him to stop, thinking he was going to kill her.

"Now he wants to use her despair against her. She quit fighting too soon, so she didn't get hurt enough, so this man isn't guilty." She shook her head in disbelief. While she said her next sentence she crossed to the shelf where the evidence sat.

"No, there wasn't much medical evidence of the rape.

There usually isn't, the doctor told you. But there was this."
She held up a photograph. "And there was this. And this. Look
at these. These are in evidence. You'll take these into the jury
room with you. Look at them. Does a woman do this to
herself? Does she claw her own body? Does she beat herself?
Even if you could entertain such a ludicrous idea for a minute,
you couldn't answer this: How did her skin get under his
fingernails if she did all this to herself?"

"Objection, Your Honor." There was a note of anger
in Henry's voice. He'd have no opportunity to rebut this
argument except through this objection. "That's a mis-
characterization of the evidence. What he testified was
that—"

Watlin said to the jurors, "You will remember the testimony
as you remember it, not as either of the lawyers remembers for
you."

"Yes, the evidence supports Mandy's testimony," Nora went
on. "Or at worst the evidence is inconclusive either way.
There's certainly nothing to support his speculations that
Mandy knew the defendant was going to be working late that
night or that she had some unknown confederate waiting to
help spring the blackmail. So that leaves you with the two
stories themselves. There is Mandy's that is consistent, that is
horrifying, that describes the kind of brutal crime that happens every day. It is horrible but unfortunately there is
nothing out of the ordinary about it.

"And then there's the defendant's story." She pointed again.
She walked closer to him. "His own lawyer has characterized
it for you. A crazy story, he called it. To say the least. And he
implied that if the defendant was going to make up a story,
he'd make up a better one than that.

"But what would he make up? He was caught dead to rights.
The security guard came in and saw it. He saw Mandy Jackson
lying on the floor, her clothes shredded, her skin torn and
bruised, tears running down her face. What kind of story is

the rapist going to come up with to explain that? A lousy story. The best he could think of on the spur of the moment. But don't make the mistake of thinking that because the story is lousy it must be true. The truth is only one believable story explains what the security guard saw, and the rapist had to come up with something other than that explanation.

"Let's pass on from the stories and look at motives. You remember during jury selection I told you that was one way of judging who was telling the truth. Look at their reasons for saying what they did. What is David Blackwell's motivation for lying? The most obvious one in the world. He is charged with a crime. He is on trial here. He faces conviction and humiliation and prison for what he did. If you can think of a better motive than that for lying, I'd like to hear it.

"Then there's Mandy Jackson. What did she get for telling her story? Money? Where's her money? How is she better off today than she was before this happened? All she's gained is the notoriety of being humiliated in public, the shame of having to tell what happened to her in front of a room full of strangers, reported in the papers and on television, being made a totally public victim. Letting her children hear from strangers the degrading details of what happened to their mother. How has Mandy Jackson benefited from that? What food has it put in her children's mouths?

"Well, he says, she was probably going to ask him for money. Then why didn't she? She's had four months. She's had lots of time to go to him for money and she could drop the charges in exchange. Do you think we could have dragged her onto the stand if she said she wasn't going to? If she'd gotten what she wanted out of it and didn't want this man prosecuted any more?"

"Objection, Your Honor. The state has subpoena power, they could have forced her to testify."

"Subpoenas can be dodged. And do you think we'd let our case hinge on an unwilling witness? Cases are dismissed all the time. He knows that." She was pointing at David. "He's no novice to the criminal justice system. He knows just how to work it. His father knows how to work it."

"Objection! That's completely outside the record."

"Sustained," said Watlin. "Ladies and gentlemen, disregard that last remark of the prosecutor's."

"He knows—I'm talking about *David* Blackwell now—he knows that even a ludicrous story might save him. He knows that the burden of proof is on his side. The state has to prove its case beyond a reasonable doubt. If he can plant that doubt in just one of your minds he's won. He does what he can. Deny, deny, deny. Admit nothing. Obscure the issue. Someone might begin to doubt.

"But there is no doubt. There can't be."

She had moved until she was beyond David from the jury's viewpoint. They couldn't look at her without taking him in as well. Nora moved closer to him. Her voice lowered.

"Mr. Koehler has asked you to look at his client and told you that he couldn't do what he's accused of. Well, do look at him. He looks harmless enough. Here in this public arena. How else would he look? He is no fool. He is not going to sit here in front of you looking like a drooling, twisted beast. Yes, you can look. And you can see the carefully coached appearance he presents in public."

She held up the photo of Mandy Jackson again. I hadn't seen her palm it. It was the one showing the scratches on her chest. David glanced up at it and looked away.

"But one person knows what this man is like in private."

She walked slowly toward them, holding the picture aloft like a torch. The jurors stared up at it. Nora lowered it as she approached them, until she laid it on the rail in front of them.

"He is the man who did this. He is the man who did everything Mandy described to you. Who brutalized her and penetrated her and made her fear for her life.

"Only you can make him pay for it."

No one moved for a long, still moment. How could such a large room full of people be so quiet? I became aware for the

first time in minutes of the people around me. I turned and
Lois met my eyes. I reached for her hand as she was reaching
for mine. Dinah was between us. She shouldn't have heard
this. She had lost her avid, trial-hungry expression. She looked
scared. I could feel her trembling. Lois's hand found mine in
front of Dinah's chest. We held her in place. Otherwise I think
she might have bolted up from her seat and shouted something. She touched our joined hands. "Daddy," she whispered.

The bailiff was leading the jury out. They kept their heads
down, embarrassed again by the attention. Or maybe solem-
nized by their task. The door closed behind them before
anyone in the room moved.

Only amateurs wait in the courtroom for the jury to come
back. Even a fast jury will take an hour. This one asked for
sandwiches to be sent in after an hour. I went to see Watlin.
Linda was with me. "Mark" was all she said the first time she
saw me after the jury went out. I nodded. Linda wouldn't
touch me with my wife and children in the building. She was
stiff with not touching me. We put everything we could into
nodding. She followed me into the back hallway of Watlin's
courtroom. It was empty.

Nora rounded the corner ahead of us. When she saw me she
gave her parody of a polite smile. I stopped in her path. Nora
stopped, too, unafraid of confrontation.

"You did your usual excellent job, Nora. Why did I feel
David wasn't the one you wanted to prosecute?"

There was such equanimity in her expression. I had never
seen Nora look doubtful. "I try the one I have," she said.

"I still wish you were using those skills for the D.A.'s office.
I hated to lose you."

Nora's smile flickered with puzzlement. "Didn't she tell you
why? I told her."

She was looking at Linda. I looked at her, too. On her brown
cheeks were high red circles. She stared back at Nora.

Nora said, "I told her I didn't like what a woman has to do to get ahead in your administration."

Having reduced us both to hot silence, Nora strolled away, leaving Linda and me alone in the dim corridor.

The jury was out for four cruel hours. Cruel because they raised our hopes. This was the kind of thing in which a defense lawyer took a measure of triumph. "I kept them out for four hours." But that wouldn't be good enough for this case. Henry looked nothing but miserable. We sat around my office engaging in useless speculation. The common wisdom is that the longer a jury stays out, the more likely is a verdict of not guilty. If they can't agree, that means someone has doubts. But they were staying out long enough to resolve those doubts. What I kept thinking was that Henry had offered them a picture of David: very young, frightened, incapable of doing such a terrible thing. But it was a mental image. And they had taken into the jury room with them tangible images of Mandy Jackson's battered body.

Four hours. I will never understand juries. How can people discuss something for four hours? They must have had disagreements or they would have been back with a verdict by lunchtime. If they were talking for four hours, it meant some of them were swaying. They believed one thing but allowed themselves to be talked into believing something else. During jury selection one of the usual questions is whether the person will stick to his guns if he finds himself the only person on the jury voting one way. You want people who will say yes. But in reality they back down in the face of hostile majority.

Four hours is a long time for twelve people to be stuck in a room together, and a long time for others to wait for them. After two hours of glancing at one another and away, at the walls and the ceiling and the newspaper my group spread out. Henry and Linda claimed work. David just wanted out of the little room. I wondered if he was thinking about running. No. I knew he was thinking about running. About three-thirty the door opened and Lois came in, then stopped, apparently surprised to find only me.

"Where's David?"

"He took Dinah to the basement to get a Coke, but that was an hour ago. Probably just walking the halls."

Lois dropped her purse on a chair. She unbuttoned her jacket, pulled it off, laid it carefully on the back of a chair, smoothed it, put her hands on her hair, walked to my wall as if looking for a mirror, instead studied my certificates and pictures, turned back to me. Her movements were deliberate. She didn't look nervous but she couldn't find anything worth doing for more than a minute.

"How did Henry talk you out of getting into it?" she asked.

"Told me the truth. That it wouldn't do any good. Might hurt."

"He's done a good job. Three hours."

Yes. It had been long enough that I'd begun to have hope again. For a hung jury if not acquittal. If they hung up, it would mean a second trial. In the face of one jury that couldn't decide whether David was guilty the prosecutors should lower their offer the second time around. They should offer probation. David would take it. After this experience he'd jump at it.

"Is three hours a long time?" Lois asked.

"It seems like it, doesn't it?"

"God." She finally let her hands capture each other.

"It's been harder for you, not being able to do anything in the case."

She closed her eyes. For a moment her face fell in on itself, exposing wrinkles around her eyes, her nose, her mouth. Her voice was choked. "If anyone had told me three months ago it would last this long, I wouldn't've thought I could stand it."

She was only a few feet from me. I just had to lean forward, pushing myself off the desk, and she was against me. I put my arms around her and she clutched me. Her eyes were still closed. I thought she'd start crying. I was speaking so softly it was little more than a hum, a wordless crooning of comfort. Lois held me as tightly as ever in our lives. A long time. The office door behind her was ajar. After a while it was pushed open and Linda came in. She stopped just as Lois had. I should have said something to make the moment less awkward for her, but I couldn't think of anything, so I just stood silent. Equally silent, a few seconds later Linda withdrew, pulling the door closed behind her.

No one's loyalties are clean, I thought. They are all alloys.

Lois didn't seem to have noticed. She drew back from me a little, hands still on my arms. She drew a deep breath but hadn't cried. "If this works, it will have been the best way," she said. "Public exoneration like this. You were right about that. Better than something underhanded."

"If it works. But it's not what I intended."

She nodded. "How do you stand the waiting like this?"

"You know how. It never mattered before. Sometimes I thought it did, but now . . ."

She squeezed my arm a last time. We walked around the office. Henry returned later, and Linda. No one talked. Afternoon turned into later afternoon. I couldn't imagine what there was left for the jury to decide, or what avenue they could take to decision.

But they found a way. There was one compromise they could make and they made it.

I had noticed something about Judge Waddle over the years. The bailiff would bring him the jury's verdict and he would look at it before having it conveyed back for the foreman to read aloud. When the verdict was one he approved he would say, "Read the verdict," participating in it. It came from his court, so it was partly his. When he didn't like the jury's decision he would say, "Read your verdict," disassociating himself from it. Lawyers who knew the system had those few moments of notice. But to read Watlin's reaction you had to know how he felt about the case.

When Watlin received this verdict he grunted slightly. His almost sour expression soured a little more. He didn't look at me and he didn't say a word, just returned the verdict form to the bailiff. When it was once more in the foreman's hands Watlin nodded. The foreman read it in a voice that squeaked on the first couple of words and then steadied.

Decorum was lost. The courtroom erupted. David was on his feet to hear the verdict. I saw him sway and somehow in the next moment I was there. I must have vaulted the railing. I caught him as he fell.

CHAPTER

he rhetoric was more subdued during the punishment
phase. Often the only real issue in a trial is the amount
of punishment. The case has to be tried only because the
state and the defense haven't reached agreement. The first
phase of trial is a chip shot for the state and then the real trial
begins. In this case, though, the plea bargaining had been
negligible. The issue was guilt or innocence. And neither side
was satisfied with the jury's decision on that issue.

The jury had reached a decision by finding in David's favor
on the one issue that had barely been contested. They had
found him guilty of the lesser offense of sexual assault. They
found, in other words, that he had raped Mandy Jackson but
that she had not been placed in fear of death or serious bodily
injury during it.

What it really meant was that someone on the jury had
caved in. Someone, maybe more than one, had voted not
guilty, probably several times during the afternoon, until
finally someone had suggested the compromise of finding him
guilty of the lesser offense. Someone had believed him not
guilty but had voted guilty with the others. I hate juries. I

searched their faces for one displaying the sour but submissive look of having given in but couldn't find it. They all looked like someone who had just found a man guilty.

The verdict put a cap of twenty years on the possible punishment. The state's pretrial offer was now the best they could get. I was sure Nora hated that jury as much as I did. Convincing them that David had committed the crime as brutally as possible had been her only hope of getting a high sentence. They had no punishment evidence. Apparently they hadn't even been able to find witnesses to say David had a bad reputation as a law-abiding citizen. The state rested without offering any new evidence.

David was in shock. The night that had passed since the verdict must have been terrible for him. He lay across his chair like a towel someone had flung there to dry. Henry couldn't have called him as a witness today even if he'd wanted.

He had plenty of others. The same people who'd testified during guilt-innocence that David had a good reputation for truth returned to testify that he'd be a good candidate for probation. The one other thing that Henry had to establish was that David was eligible for probation. He called Lois for that. Like me, she'd changed her stance on participating in the trial. She sat on the stand holding her purse and looking older than she'd looked yesterday. When Henry asked her if David had ever been convicted of a felony, she said, "He's never been convicted of anything. He had never been arrested. He was never in any kind of trouble." She sat up straighter and looked at the state's table, daring them to refute what she'd said.

Nora launched into her cross with "Now, Mrs. Blackwell, you've testified that your son has never been in any kind of trouble with the police."

"That's correct."

"But David doesn't live with you, does he?"

"No."

"He hasn't for some years."

"No."

"It's possible, then, isn't it—"

Javier stirred himself and leaned close to her. He put his hand on her arm. When Nora whispered back to him, his hand tightened. You could see his knuckles growing white. Nora shook him off, frowning, but said, "No more questions."

The only issue would be what this particular crime was worth. The jury could give probation if they sentenced him to no more than ten years. I was afraid they'd go for the maximum. I've seen it happen a thousand times. The jury convicts somebody of the lesser, then gets mad when they find out they can give him only twenty years for it. So that's what they give him: twenty.

During a recess I went inside the bar and laid a hand on David's shoulder. It was the first time that morning I'd been within speaking distance of him. He raised his deadened face to me and it grew an expression for the first time since the verdict. He glared at me.

"Why did you put me through this?" he said.

I was literally taken aback. My hand was no longer on him. "There was no way to stop it," I said, but he wasn't looking at me. He had that outer-space look again.

I resumed my seat to watch the punishment arguments. Javier went first for the state. He seemed to share David's daze. Javier had been his usual excellent self during the guilt phase. On cross he had made David's story look ridiculous, and his argument had been good. Now, though, he seemed to have lost his drive. He looked forgetful. As if he had emerged from the spell of trial and realized what he had done. His closing was not forceful at all. Rather perfunctorily he asked for the maximum punishment of twenty years in prison.

"The maximum?" Henry said. He was on his feet at once, stunned by the state's temerity. "The maximum? Who do we reserve the maximum punishment for? For repeaters. For people who've shown they can't reform. For people we just want to put away for as long as possible."

He stopped in front of the state's table. The argument was

more against them than it was for David. "Have they brought you any evidence to show you he can't reform?" he asked. "Have they told you any reason not to grant probation in this case?

"Do you know what happens too many times in trials? The jury votes someone guilty even though they have lingering doubts about his story, then during the punishment phase they find out he has three prior convictions for the same thing. They—"

"Objection," Nora said. "He's arguing outside the evidence in this case."

"Sustained. Stay within the record."

Henry changed his tack ever so slightly. "Why do we have a separate phase of trial for punishment? So that the state can put on new evidence showing you why you should give someone a high sentence."

"Objection. Outside the record again."

"Overruled. This is argument." That is a judge's favorite sort of trial remark: explaining his ruling by stating the irrelevant obvious.

"This was their chance," Henry continued. "They couldn't do it during the first phase of trial, but during this one they could bring in everything bad about my client. They could prove any past convictions for other crimes. They could prove that he has a bad reputation as a law-abiding citizen. Have they done that? Have they shown you anything? No. This is a case that cries out for probation . . ."

He rehashed his own punishment evidence, demonstrating that if David actually had committed this crime, it was a complete aberration from his past life. He didn't deserve to be sent to prison with hardened criminals. And Henry slyly hinted at the length of time this same jury had taken to reach a verdict on guilt. They must have some lingering doubts. With those doubts about his guilt would they send David to prison? How could they?

He convinced me. I thought he'd convinced them. Until

Nora began to speak. Slowly she stood, as if under a heavy burden. But it was not a burden of arguing something she didn't believe. It was the burden of convincing the jury of what they *had* to do. She spoke slowly, but gathering steam.

"This case was basically a swearing match. Mandy came in here and told you this man raped her. He clawed her skin, he bruised her face, he tore her clothes off, and forced himself on her. Into her. She mustered up her courage and came in here and told you that he had done to her the worst thing a man can do to a woman. And then this man, this good citizen, beloved son, valued employee—this defendant took the stand and told you he didn't do it, that she was just making up a crazy story.

"Well, you decided between them. By your verdict you said, We believe you, Mandy. We believe he raped you. We believe you were beaten and horrified and shamed and violated.

"Now, what are you going to tell her by your verdict at this stage of trial? Are you going to tell her, We believe he did this thing to you and we think it's worth probation? We think for his crime he should have to report to a probation officer once a month, pay a little fine, and commit no more crimes, something we all have to refrain from already? Are you going to tell her, Your pain and humiliation that you're going to live with for the rest of your life is worth just a few years' inconvenience to him? Are you going to tell her, We think he did it to you, Mandy, but we're going to let him buy his way out of it with a fine and a monthly fee, like an overdue library book? . . ."

Then she asked them for something specific. She couldn't tell them why, she said, but she asked them to sentence David to no less than fifteen years and one day. She couldn't explain the significance of the day, but it had significance. Then she asked for what she really wanted: the max. Twenty years in prison.

The significance of the fifteen plus was that a person who receives a sentence of fifteen years or less is entitled to remain free on bond while his appeal is pending. Nora couldn't explain that to the jury, but she was asking them to see that he went straight to prison while a higher court decided whether he had had a fair trial. I wanted to cry out across the room, No . . . Give him this one little thing, more temporary freedom. Don't take him yet.

The jury did not take so long to decide this time. An hour and a half. They gave Nora what she wanted. They gave David sixteen years to serve in prison.

Lois came to see me that night. I was in the den, but that's how her visit felt, as if she didn't have an appointment and thought I might not see her. I was sitting in the deepest chair in the room. My glass was empty and I wished I could fill it without moving. Everywhere I looked I saw David's last expression, the one he turned toward us as the bailiff was taking him into custody. I thought he would lunge for the window, but the bailiff was already tightening the handcuffs just outside the cuffs of David's blue suit. David looked terrified. His eyes were globes. He was looking to me to make it stop. His eyes. His eyes were everywhere now.

"What will you do now?" Lois said.

"File a motion for new trial."

"Will the judge grant it?"

"No."

She came to stand directly in front of me. "What will you do that's worth doing, then?"

I didn't need this, an amateur relying on me for a miraculous delivery. She sounded like too many mothers of clients I'd had to tell it was all over.

"Lois, there is nothing else to do. A jury has found him guilty and sentenced him to prison. I cannot overturn that. Maybe on appeal, although I didn't see any reversible—"

"I'm not talking about appeal."

There was a long pause, though she didn't move. I wasn't looking up at her.

"What would you do if you thought he was innocent?" she finally said.

There was a glimmer in her face of a woman I'd once known. She reminded me of someone. It took a moment for me to realize it was Lois herself, twenty years ago, when she was a young mother. The crust had cooled over that face.

"I don't think he's guilty," I said wearily. "But it doesn't—"

"But you don't *know* he's innocent. Mark, think about David. His whole life. His first date. Remember when he started saying he had a fever and couldn't go? He married the first girl he ever dated because he's afraid of girls. He didn't do this."

I didn't think I'd ever have to give this speech to my own wife, after all the stories I'd told her about dealing with hysterical clients. None of it had stuck, apparently. "Lois, you know how many times I hear this? Every single day someone says, 'He couldn't have done this, he's always been a good boy.'"

She almost shrieked. "Don't talk to me about that Goddamned courthouse! This is not a case, this is your *son!* Think, Mark, damn it, think. Tear yourself away from what always happens. This is a boy you know. Think about him! He—could—not—have—done—*this.* Don't you know that?

"Why do I have to explain to you what David is like?" she went on after a pause that made her quieter but no less intense. "I know it must cross your mind that he did this, but how can you let the idea take root? Believe me if you don't believe him. I *know* he's not guilty. Dinah knows. As surely as if we'd been there."

We stared at each other. There was no point saying anything. The house seemed deathly quiet after the skittering heights of her voice died away. I stood up. She didn't back away so I had to edge around her to get to the liquor cabinet. She followed close behind me. When she spoke she sounded like herself again.

"Let's go back to my question. What would you do if you were sure he didn't do it?"

"There's nothing to do either way. Anything we could—"

"I'm not talking about legally." She came around to face me. "What if the state joined the motion for new trial?"

"They'd never agree to that."

"Not 'they,' Mark, you. You're the state. You hired two outsiders, but it's your office that prosecuted him. What if you joined the motion?"

I gave some thought to that. Nora would protest that it was still her case, but she was gone now, she had no standing. I could fire her, like Nixon fired Archibald Cox. It would do for me what it had done for Nixon, but who cared about that? Would it work?

I finally shook my head. "Watlin wouldn't go for it. He'd think it would look like he was in on the scheme, too."

"Could you make him do it? Do you have any leverage on him?"

I looked at Lois with a certain fascination. I hadn't understood in what absolute contempt she held the system in which I'd spent my life. "Next you'll be asking me to forge his signature," I said.

"Yes. Yes, I will." She was gripping my arm. "Remember when I asked you if you'd do anything to get him off? Lie, cheat, break the rules? You said yes. I hold you to that. That was a vow. I do not release you from it. Be convinced, Mark. If you can't be convinced, act convinced. Do what you'd do if you knew for a certainty David isn't guilty. You wouldn't let him go like this, would you? You wouldn't let them take him."

Three weeks later the sheriff called me. You couldn't say the sheriff and I were friends, but I had always gotten along with him in private practice and he hadn't liked my predecessor, which made us friendly by comparison. We exchanged favors in a businesslike way. "It's about your boy," he said after the preliminaries. "He's scheduled to go on the next chain to TDC."

The Texas Department of Corrections. State prison. The initials had a horror for me they'd never had before.

"He don't have to go, far as I'm concerned. I'll keep him here for his whole sentence if you want."

"That's a kind offer, Sheriff."

"Cause a stink when the press finds out, but I don't care about that. I think the press'd find nobody else cares either."

"Well—"

"But the thing is, it might be better from his point of view."

"To go to Huntsville? Might be better?"

"Well, you know he's gonna get good time credit on his sentence. The way they're lettin' 'em out early down there he could be out in two years, with the credit. But you know they don't get that credit while they're here in the county."

"I know."

He cleared his throat. "So really the quicker he goes the quicker he gets out. It's not doin' him no favor keepin' him here."

I paused longer than I realized, I guess, thinking about David in TDC. The sheriff took my silence for argument.

"If it's safety you're concerned about, well, I hate to say it, but you know we've had two killings in the jail this year. Compared to, I don't know, six or seven in TDC, but they've got twenty times as many prisoners as we've got. Not that anything like that'd happen to your boy. But really, his odds're better—I mean . . ."

He cleared his throat again. "Here's another thing. I've been keepin' him pretty isolated, but you know we're overcrowded ourselves, and he's gotta rub elbows sometimes. I think some people're hittin' on him for favors. Nothing rough, you know, just pesterin'. 'Cause they know who he is and they think he might be able to help 'em out. I don't know why they'd think that, with him in the same spot—well. But they do bother him. In TDC he'd be more anonymous, with guys from all over the state."

I almost said what I was thinking. You don't want him in your jail anymore, do you, Sheriff? But what he said made sense. David would never become eligible for parole in the county jail. You had to go to TDC for that. If I kept him close to home, I'd be doubling the time he had to serve, or more. If he went now, he might be free in two years. Two years. Around the courthouse two years was nothing. Prosecutors said it in disgust. Two years.

"When does the chain leave?" I asked.

I was there to see him off. Lois wasn't. I'd had to lie to her to keep her away. It wouldn't do David any good for his fellow inmates to witness David's mother kissing him good-bye.

There were twenty of them on the chain. At first, as I looked down the row, I skipped past David's face. He didn't look so different from the other men in gray now. A little frailer, younger than most, but there were others as young and thin as he was. He had that gray look, the expression that doesn't ask for anything. He no longer looked stunned. His face was closed, unexpressive. I hoped he had grown harder in almost a month in jail.

The sheriff was there, too. He had the deputies remove David from the chain, and they started shuffling the others aboard the bus while I talked to David around the other side. There wasn't much to say. I wanted to hug him but I wouldn't, not in sight of those other prisoners. They'd make his life even harder.

"I'll get you back here when we have the hearing on the motion for new trial." That was the kindest thing I could think to say to him. For state prisoners, I knew, court appearances back in the hometown were vacations to anticipate.

"If you get a choice, ask to work in the print shop. It's not bad at all, you'll see. They even do their own writing. They've got computers. That's the assignment I'd want."

He gave me one sharp look and looked back down at the ground. That was the best thing. I was about to start crying. He couldn't afford to, not with that bus waiting.

"Mr. Blackwell," one of the deputies said respectfully. The bus was loaded except for David. I stepped back. When the deputy touched his arm he started moving. He had that ankle-chain shuffle.

The bus belched into life. It was an old school bus, saggy on its springs. The windows were rolled up, of course. It looked steamy inside. I couldn't see David among the heads at the windows. Most of them weren't looking out.

The sheriff came to stand beside me. "He'll be okay. I sent word to a couple of the wardens, buddies of mine, to keep an eye on him. They'll put him on a first-timers' unit. It won't be bad."

The bus started moving. Its motion almost wrenched me off my feet, as if it were towing me. As it passed through the gate and turned onto the street I was running for my car. It was parked almost half a block away, but I had no trouble catching the bus. It was a lumbering old thing. I stayed close behind it, hardly more than ten feet. Two or three of the inmates were looking back curiously. So was the deputy driving the bus. I could see him watching me in the big outside mirror. The two other deputies in the accompanying squad car kept their eyes on me, too, all the way to Huntsville.

CHAPTER

9

It's over two hundred miles from San Antonio to Huntsville. At the bus's slow pace that was four hours for me to consider what I was doing. But I didn't think ahead, I thought back, over David's whole life. Nothing he'd ever done could have prepared me for this. Now it seemed as if he'd been *too* trouble-free; as if he'd been saving up for this or as if he'd finally grown desperately tired of restraint. After seeing Mandy Jackson on the stand it was harder for me to believe in a conspiracy against David. But the timing of his arrest, so early in my term, still seemed too coincidental. The thought crossed my mind that it had been David's timing. I'd thought of David as grown for years, but maybe, because he'd grown up too fast, he had retained the child in him. Could he have done something as childish as groping for my attention the only way he could get it?

No. Again I thrust away the idea David could be guilty. But there are a great many thoughts in more than two hundred miles of highway. Blame settled heavily on me, filled the otherwise empty car. I couldn't escape the feeling that David was paying now for the love he hadn't had as a child.

When the bus lumbered through a Cyclone fence gate with barbed wire spiraled across the top, I turned off for the administrative offices of the Texas Department of Corrections. David would be a while in the diagnostic center, I knew. Maybe a week. They test them, review their records, find a unit for them. The very rare inmate stays right there, typing, pruning hedges, even working outside the walls at wardens' homes. Murderers make the best houseboys, a warden told me once. Your average murderer probably killed his wife or his brother or his best friend, a once-in-a-lifetime occurrence, and was no threat to anyone not close to him. "Most of 'em are pretty easygoing old boys, too, once they got that out of their system. Plus they usually got long sentences, so you don't have to go training new ones ever' couple of years. Take a thief, now. You couldn't have a thief workin' for you. A thief'll lie to his own lawyer. And he'll always steal again. Cain't have 'im in your home." I wanted David to be as privileged as those easygoing murderers.

Lewis Thurman was the third director the Texas Department of Corrections had had in four years. His predecessor had been recruited from out of state and never enjoyed the support of his staff. But Thurman was an up-from-the-ranks kind of guy. I expected him to be someone I could work with.

I took it as a good sign that he didn't keep me waiting long in his outer office. I had only paced once across the room and back when he appeared at the door, waving me in with a grin and a tight, hard handshake.

"Mr. Blackwell. Surprise, surprise. Hope you're not here for a parole hearing. They hold those up in Austin, you know. But you know that. Congratulations on your election, by the way. You got promoted about the time I did, I remember. Beautiful town, San Antone. Go there every year."

This flood of good fellowship took us all the way into his

office, to opposite sides of the desk. The visitor's chair was hard and narrow, not designed to encourage a long stay. His desk was massive, it must have been thirty square feet. It was made of some dark wood and the top was covered by a sheet of glass. Papers and files were stacked at various locations that might have been strategic. It made me think of a battle map stretched between us. His chair looked a lot more comfortable than mine. Its padded back rose a foot above Lewis Thurman's head.

He was a lean man who looked like he came from a line of West Texas ranchers. He had that dry range and far horizon look. Instead of a uniform he wore a white shirt and black tie. His suit jacket hung on a coatrack behind his shoulder, on a hanger. I suspected he'd waited his whole life to move out of uniform into that white shirt.

"How can we accommodate you? Pretty as Huntsville is, it isn't much of a tourist center. People usually come here with a purpose, especially law enforcement people."

I hadn't expected the good old boy salutations to die out quite so soon. I wanted to ease into my subject, not lay it out as the answer to a direct question. As the silence lengthened, the director's eyes grew more piercing. He had lifted his arms and put his hands behind his head, and as I hesitated he froze in that position, like a man on the ground who hears a dry rustle off to his left.

"Should've come up to meet you before this," I said, hoping to revive the friendly banter. "But you know what it's like when you start a new position, there's too much to do to get out of town. Being on opposite ends of the pipeline, so to speak, I should've written to you before now to introduce myself. So far you and I only seem to've communicated by chain letter." That's a joke, son. The skin around his eyes and mouth crinkled in acknowledgment. It looked like the expression pained him.

"But this isn't just social. I wish it was. Fact is, this may be the worst day of my life." You'd think that would call for response. There was none. Thurman waited. "I just brought my son in."

He lowered his arms to the desk. "Your son?" He looked past me as if the office door would open again. "Where is he? Somewhere in the building? Why didn't you—"

"No. He's not with me. Actually, it's sheriff's deputies that brought him in. He's—he was convicted in San Antonio. He's at the diagnostic center right now."

Thurman was on his feet. "San Antonio," he said. "That's right. Somebody said something about this, but I thought he was joking. I saw it in the paper, but I thought you'd keep him in Bexar County his whole sentence."

"I would've, except for the—well, good time, parole, all that. He had to come here sooner or later. I came to see you because— He doesn't belong here, Mr. Thurman. He's not one of those boys who was always in trouble because his father was in law enforcement. There's never been anything like this. He's married, had a good job. He doesn't belong here. I'm working on it from my end, but even a reversal will take a year, maybe. He may even have to stay here until he's eligible for parole. I want to make it as easy on him as possible."

"They all do," Thurman said. "The parents that come, the ones that have parents that still give a damn. Put money in the commissary for 'em, that's what I tell all of 'em. And come to see 'em on visitors' day. That helps a lot."

I was nodding as if I found this advice helpful. When he stopped talking I took a breath and held it until it was stale. "I want more than that. I want him to make trustee from the first day. He'll deserve it, believe me. He can do any job you set him to do. He's worked with computers, he can— But something outside the walls'd be best. I know some of the wardens have houseboys. That would be perfect for David. You wouldn't have to worry—"

"Wouldn't have to worry about having a rapist home with my wife and kids while I'm here every day? Yeah, I read about the case. You'd be out of luck anyway, though. There ain't any more houseboys. Don't they know that? I cut out that little scam first week I was here."

They who? I thought. Thurman still seemed to be looking over my shoulder. He was affixed to the corner of his desk, standing stock still.

"You think you rate some special treatment because you're a district attorney? Well, screw that. Half the D.A.s in the state're threatening to sue me 'cause I don't take prisoners off their hands fast enough. While we're burstin' at the seams and got that crazy federal judge breathin' down our necks if we go one con over capacity. Now you want me to take one by the hand and let him sleep in my house and drive my kids to the movies while he does his time? How stupid do you think I am? You go back and tell 'em it didn't work. Lewis Thurman don't do favors. Lewis Thurman does everything by the book. You tell 'em—"

"Snap out of it," I almost shouted. "Look at me. I'm not wired. This isn't a fucking test of your integrity. This is my son. Look. Listen. If I was trying to get you to do anything wrong, it'd be entrapment anyway. 'Cause it was my idea. I suggested it. You're not on any hook."

"No, and I'm not gonna be. How dumb do all of you think I am? I'll tell you exactly what I'll do for your son. Nothing. Just what I'd do for any of 'em. He'll get just what he's got comin'. Just what any rapist has comin'. Now, you get the hell out of my office, and if you look back over your shoulder before you're out of here, I'll have you in a cell. You're just lucky you didn't mention money. I'd have you facing charges so fast—"

"Listen to me. It's not a crime I'm asking for. It's simple consideration, one law enforcement—"

He punched a button on his intercom. "Cindy, get two guards in here fast. They got an arrest to make."

"All right, all right." I was backing away. "Just forget it, forget I was here. I'm out, I'm gone."

That's what I was still wishing an hour later, that Thurman would forget I had even come. I hoped he didn't bother to look David up. I had just made things worse.

Through a call to Sheriff Marrs in San Antonio I managed to find one of the wardens he'd talked to about David, one he'd said was a friend of his. The warden, Ed Preston, was of the same mold as the sheriff, looked typecast to a T but spoke with the force of long thought behind his sentences. It takes a brain to do that good old boy act just right, to turn the colorful phrases instead of relying on clichés.

"Thurman's heard the cry of the loon, all right," Warden Preston said. "We all knew he was cracked when he was just a warden, but unfortunately nobody consulted us. Nobody took him seriously then and now he makes sure everybody has to. He's down to his last bunker now, though. Got the wagons circled in his office. By Thanksgiving he'll be as cooked as the other turkeys. Meantime, though, you're right, you didn't do your boy any favors goin' to see 'im. Wish you'd talked to Jack first and come to see me instead. I'll do what I can. Cain't let Thurman catch me takin' a hand in the case, though, or it'd be as bad for the boy as what you done. No offense. Try not to worry. I'll keep an eye out. And buy Jack Marrs a beer for me."

Try not to worry. If I'd had any laughter in me, that would have drawn it. I thanked him, sober as a judge. And wondered what kind of twisted response director Thurman would think appropriate.

The next time I saw David was through glass and mesh, a week later. It was his first visitors' day on his permanent unit. It was no soft unit, either, for first time offenders. It was Ellis, one of the toughest. Thurman's hand was apparent. Ed Preston had already told me he might be able to arrange a transfer later, but not now.

Ellis, like most of them, was a field unit. Inmates worked in the fields during the day, planting and tending and picking. Cotton, mostly. David's fingernails were black. There was etched dirt in his knuckles and blisters on the once-soft pads of his hands. I hadn't asked him yet about the black eye.

The thin veneer of toughness he'd developed in the Bexar County jail was gone. I hoped that was just in my presence. He was on the verge of crying. At first he glanced furtively side to side at the other inmates, but once he saw that they were engrossed in their own conversations he forgot them. There were only the two of us and his horrible story.

"The first time I fought him off. The second time he came back with friends. I thought if I fought and yelled long enough, somebody would come, but nobody came. Two of them were from San Antonio. They knew who I was. They made jokes while they were doing it, about you. The D.A. had stuck it to them, now . . ."

"Do you know their names? Find out their names. I'll have them charged. Maybe after—"

David laughed. "They've all got life sentences. What do they care about one more? You don't understand. Nobody's afraid of law in here. The law's already done all it can to them. It's like hell. Nowhere else to fall.

"The days aren't bad," he said. "In the field it's hard and it's hot and you have stretches of being alone. The sun just burns away thinking. It's when it starts to go down that I—think of it, dreading to go home. 'Home.'" He shuddered. "It's like living with a . . . a—I don't know. But there's no rest. That's what's killing me, the constantly being on guard." He was crying now. "You want to just pass out from the fatigue, but you can't. Why aren't *they* tired? Maybe you get used to it. God. Get used to this."

A guard was coming around telling people time. David saw him from the corner of his eye and went stiff. He wiped away his tears with the palms of his hands and tried to regain that dead expression, but it wasn't there for him. "You must," he said. "Something must happen. Nobody could do twenty years of this." His shoulders shook again.

"Tell Mom—I don't know. Tell her it's not as bad as I

expected." He managed to smile at me. "Don't tell her it's worse."

"She'll be here next week. I'll see the warden as soon as I leave here. Find out those names. David, we can do something about it. There're still laws."

He laughed again. The guard touched his shoulder and he nodded. He sniffed and tried to straighten his face. Maybe he thought he'd achieved the look again. He looked scared to death. I looked at the other men rising to their feet around him. David was right, something had to happen to them. They looked like what I expected of prisoners, calm, resigned— men going back to the barracks or the factory line. One of them glanced at David and then at me. I wondered who I could bribe or who I could have killed.

"I'll do what I can, David. You'll be coming back for the new trial hearing soon. We'll keep you there longer this time."

"Good-bye, Dad."

"We'll write, son. David—"

He didn't look back.

Every night at home was a late night, thinking of David, wondering if he was safe yet. Midnight, one—they must sleep, with the hard days they had ahead. Not until I was sure he was asleep could I sleep myself. While I sat I thought. I thought of the many men I'd sent to prison, both as a prosecutor and a defense lawyer; of the times I'd said, "Twenty years is a good deal for a case like this. I'd take it." While giving no thought to the reality of prison time. I'd taken one tour of the state prison, fifteen years before, when I was a young prosecutor. They showed us the Walls Unit, the oldest unit in the system, and the one that housed the oldest prisoners. I saw almost no inmate below middle age. This was in the days when people really served good chunks of the years they'd been assessed. They all looked fairly placid, men cupping cigarettes, standing around a courtyard that looked like a school playground. A warden showed us the cafeteria and a row of empty cells—concrete walls with pictures torn from magazines taped beside the metal bunks. As a defense lawyer I'd been in the prison waiting room two or three times, getting information for a writ someone wanted filed. But of day to day, night to night life in TDC I had little idea, and had never given it much thought. Now I found I had no details on which to base my speculations about David. Only imagination and David's face as he'd told me his story.

I sat in my den and drank and stared and rolled with the night across the two hundred miles to Huntsville.

"Mark?"

He couldn't survive. I had known it would be bad, but I hadn't realized it would be unendurable. Maybe there was a fundamental difference in lifelong criminals that allowed them to shut down systems and survive conditions that would kill someone like David.

"It's your decision, Mark. I can't make this one."

If I brought him back he'd be safer, but he wouldn't get credit for his good time and he wouldn't be eligible for parole. Maybe I could bring him back just until his appeal was done. But there'd been no reversible error in his trial. None I'd seen. The judges on the Court of Appeals sat in three-judge panels to decide cases. That meant I'd have to get to two of them to have a majority. But the state—

"Are you listening to me? Mark, you have to pay attention to this. Judge Marroquin—"

I got up from my desk, brushing by Linda. I couldn't concentrate in the office. Linda was still saying something, but it didn't break down into words for me. It was just background drone as I walked out. The fastest way out of the courthouse was down the back stairs, so that's probably how I went. I didn't see people, at any rate. I don't think I did.

Jury verdicts have a strange effect on me. Much as I despise juries, sure as I am that they violate all our carefully devised rules to reach their decisions, once that decision's made it slowly sets in concrete in my mind. Maybe they're right to ignore our rules. Their common sense cuts through the crap. They decide guilt or innocence the way we all decide whether to buy tires or which college to send the kid to. Once a jury's reached a decision I start coming round to their point of view. There are so many of them. If twelve people all agree on something, a thousand would probably have the same opinion. When I've lost a case as a prosecutor, I start thinking maybe that cop witness of mine *was* lying. I'd had my doubts myself the first time I'd heard him, hadn't I? As a losing defense lawyer, I start thinking no, that alibi didn't make any sense, did it? After all, they were his family, they'd lie for him. I come around to believing that the jury objectively saw something in a case I'd missed from my participant's perspective.

That was the only consolation I'd been able to find in the first days after David's trial. Maybe he was guilty. If he was, justice had been served. He'd gotten no worse than any guilty defendant, and a lot better than many. As a prosecutor I wouldn't have been satisfied with a mere twenty years for a brutal rapist. If he was guilty, he'd gotten no worse than he deserved. Prosecutors had a standard line about rapists: He'll like it in prison.

Hundreds of thousands of men had graduated from the prison system. David could, too. That's the thought to which I'd clung. But seeing him there had disabused me of any frail notion that the punishment fit the crime. No matter what he'd done, he didn't deserve that. After a week he'd already paid for that a dozen times over. Justice was done. I had to get him out.

But I couldn't. Whatever power I'd had over the case was ended. I might as well have been any other despairing parent. I had no more recourse than they.

I found that I was on the Riverwalk. There were two or three entrances to it near the courthouse, steps winding down. I must have taken one. It was still late summer, the walk was tourist-ridden. Why people come to San Antonio in August is beyond me, but they do, in herds. They all end up on the Riverwalk eventually. When I was a boy, downtown San Antonio was a dark, dirty place. Now it is lively and loud. No one ever gets killed on the river any more either. It seems to me that when I was young, hardly a week would pass without a body being fished out of the river. Maybe there weren't so many. One multiplies the highlights of one's youth.

In the last few years they've expanded and extended the Riverwalk. It winds under most of downtown now, through or past the big hotels near the convention center. The walk varies from broad flagstones to pebbled concrete. Tourist barges navigate the river and cafés line it. The river itself is no great shakes as a waterway. I'd be surprised if it's more than three feet deep anywhere in the city. But water lends festivity. It also inspires contemplation.

The crowds did not. I found myself walking into a press of shouts and bare arms. I had walked into a group photo. In my dark suit I looked like the specter of death amid their shorts and bright shirts. Sunglassed eyes stared at me. "Excuse me," I muttered again and again as I blundered back in the direction I'd come from. I hurried through the strolling throngs, bumping and excusing again.

In the past year, city crews had extended the Riverwalk beyond the fringe of downtown toward the old armory and the Pioneer Flour Mill, into the King William area of fine old homes, some of them fallen to ruin and junkies. That part of the walk was uncrowded because no shops or bars lined it. There was only the river itself and glimpses of old houses high above the banks. It was much too sunny, because it was too new for shade trees. But I could stand sun better than I could crowds. I made my way to that part of the Riverwalk and was soon alone. A block ahead of me was another solitary walker, head down, hands in pockets. In a minute he turned off and climbed stairs to street level. I was the only person in sight.

I had given up legal and was turning over illegal ways of getting David out. I could get him back to San Antonio for his motion for new trial hearing and the sheriff would probably release him in my custody if I asked. After that . . . But there was a long life after that. Would I be doing David any favor? He would probably lunge for the first glimpse of freedom. But would he still be grateful when he was forty and still a fugitive, with a prison sentence still hanging over him, a sentence he would have long since discharged if not for my intervention? The two or three years in prison had to be weighed against the rest of David's life.

And what if he had no more life? What if he were killed in prison? It happens. There was something else to worry about, too. AIDS. A dozen inmates had died of AIDS in the past year. Soon it might become an epidemic. David might already be infected. He might—

I walked faster. My fists were balled in my pockets. Sweat poured down my back under the jacket. The sun off the sidewalk was blinding. A misstep would put me in the river. That seemed not a bad alternative.

Under the shade of a bridge I slowed. The bridge arched overhead. By angling left I reached the spot where the bridge was no taller than I. I leaned my forehead against its cool stones. My eyes closed.

Footsteps followed me, the sound of hard heels echoing under the bridge. I waited for them to pass. Instead, they slowed. The steps came up even with me, passed, and stopped.

The humorous thought occurred to me that it was a mugger. I probably looked like the best target on the river. If he had a gun, I would resist. Maybe they would let David out for my funeral. Then Lois could make the decision of what to do with him. I knew what Lois would do.

"Mr. Blackwell?"

Shit. I kept my eyes closed, hoping he would go away. I didn't recognize the voice, but I didn't want to talk to anyone who knew me. Reporter, defense lawyer, one of my assistants. I had already decided they were all useless to me.

"Mr. Blackwell, this—"

"Go to hell, will you?"

"This is for your benefit, not mine."

I gave him nothing but my back until he added, "And your son's benefit." I whirled, ready to swing. I was sure now he was a lawyer. Anyone who would try to get to me at a time like this had to be a brother professional.

His appearance stopped me. My accoster was a small man of about fifty. Everything about him was small: his white mustache, his well-polished shoes, his houndstooth jacket, his hat. He was wearing, for God's sake, a felt hat with a tiny feather in the band.

"If you want a favor from me, I am going to bang your head against the sidewalk and then hold it under that river until you choke and die."

I looked like such a bully, towering over him. I hoped he had the nerve to ask me anyway. I wanted to see if I'd really do it.

He was unperturbed. "Your son was framed," he said.

It was much more effective than punching me in the stomach. He waited for all the threat to drain out of me, then continued.

"The maid lied. She will recant her testimony under oath during a hearing on your motion for new trial, under one condition."

"Who are you?"

"I represent a client, Mr. Blackwell. You will never see me again after today. I would have contacted you sooner, but this is the first opportunity I've had to catch you alone. You are overstaffed, I might suggest."

"Who—"

"But that is neither here nor there. Please listen very carefully. This is the only notice you will receive. Here is what you have to do in return for your son's freedom. There is a case pending in your office against a man named Clyde Malish. Do I need to repeat that name?"

"No."

"You will see that the case disappears. Simple dismissal is insufficient. A dismissed case can always be indicted again, as, of course, you know. You must see that the case is dismissed with prejudice. Jeopardy considerations are suggested. But how you do it is up to you. You are the district attorney. You will undoubtedly find a way. Evidence is not indestructible." He made a gesture of dispensing with suggestions. "You had best move swiftly, because the time for urging your motion for new trial on the trial court is rapidly slipping away. If you want the maid's testimony . . ."

Neither of us had moved. He was well within arm's reach. I waited to hear everything he would say voluntarily, and I studied him as I waited. He was a dapper little man, but the cuffs of his white shirt were slightly frayed. I wondered if he had bought his clothes secondhand just for this role. I decided not; they looked too much a part of him. My next thought was who had written his speech.

"You understand? It is very simple. Do this and the maid will appear and testify. Your son's conviction will be vacated. Don't do it, and he stays where he is. It is automatic. No exchange of ransom, nothing to go wrong. You do not have to give me your approval now. We will know by your actions if you agree. Understood? I am not authorized to answer questions, but if you didn't hear something clearly, I can repeat."

"What proof do you have of this scheme? Why should I do this favor for Clyde Malish without being sure what I'll get in exchange?"

The little man cocked his head back. "You mean you're not ready to grasp at straws? What kind of father are you?"

I wondered if I should take him back to the office or find a spot farther along the river. Maybe an abandoned house in

King William. He had obviously said everything he had to say without persuasion. I realized how happy I felt. Maybe it was only comparative joy. Maybe it was purely physical. I was breathing more deeply, my muscles were expanding with blood. The chance to do something was a release almost orgasmic.

"There's just this," I said earnestly, taking my hands out of my pockets. "I wonder if—"

"Well," the dapper little man said regretfully, and his own hand came out of his jacket pocket. He wasn't a San Antonian, I was suddenly sure. Bexar County buckaroos favor .357 Magnums or .45's. The guns Clint Eastwood or Matt Dillon would carry. This was no more than a .32. Maybe even a .22. It would make neat small holes. The little man stepped back.

"Doesn't this seem silly?" he said. "Desperadoes under a bridge. You—" He stopped himself.

"Who are you?" I asked again, and he gave me the same answer:

"You will not see me again." He walked away, only half turning away from me, keeping the dapper little pistol low but steady.

When he was ten feet away I followed. The gun was only a mild deterrent. I didn't think he would shoot, I wasn't sure he could hit me if he did, and I strongly doubted the shot would kill me. He wasn't fast enough to get out of my sight and there was no getaway on the river. When he walked faster I did, too. He looked back at me annoyedly and waved the gun. I stopped.

Searching the ground at my feet, I found a fist-sized rock at the edge of the walk and picked it up. It had a good heft, like a baseball. I used to pitch a little in high school.

The little man had seen me. He had taken the opportunity to increase his lead, which bothered me even less than the gun. I loped toward him.

The top of the bridge we had been under was a street

crossing the river. At the side of the bridge was a spiral staircase rising to that street level. The little man started up it. I reached the bottom before he was halfway up. The winding stairs gave me no clear shot at him, but he had the same problem. I was running up the steps. I hoped he would run, too, when he reached the top, not wait and try to pick me off. If he moved away, I was confident of stopping him. At this range, fifteen feet or so, my rock would be about as accurate as his gun. The way I felt, lungs pumping and blood racing, I thought I could even take a hit or two and still bring him down.

He did move away at the top of the stairs. I slowed a little as I reached the top myself, waiting to see if he'd taken cover elsewhere or just turned and waited to shoot.

He was looking at me regretfully again. I had disappointed him with my childishness. Maybe worse, I had made him rumple his clothes. He stood beside the open door of the car and shook his head once mournfully as he looked back at me. The car was already moving as he jumped inside. I ran full out, almost close enough to catch its bumper before it outpaced me. Stumbling, I pulled up and threw the rock. It bounced off the back window. Only the little man looked back. The driver was an anonymous back of a head.

"I want to see him and I want to see him now."

"Mr. Blackwell, this isn't the way to go about it. Thurman gets wind of this 'n' there'll be no holdin' 'im back. Why don't you just let me—"

"I don't care who hears about it, and there won't be time for your crazy director to exact any petty revenge. My son is innocent."

Ed Preston looked embarrassed. "Well, excuse me, Mr. Blackwell, but that's something that don't make a whole world of difference in here. Why, most of the men you talk to—"

"I mean I have proof. Don't humor me. David isn't going to be here much longer. And I am going to see him now."

The warden studied my face for a long minute. I looked as ludicrous trying to bully him as I had towering over the dapper little man, but for a different reason. Preston was two inches taller than I am and outweighed me by at least fifty pounds. And there was a heavy length of oak hanging from his belt, just beside his hand.

After the long minute of study he took his eyes off me just long enough to glance at a guard and nod.

"Your funeral," the warden said. "Mine, too, come to think of it."

The black eye was fading. I didn't see any new marks on David, but he looked like an entirely different person. A month ago there'd been a boyish suggestion of plumpness in his face. Now his cheeks were hollow. There was darkness under his eyes. When he put his head down you couldn't see his eyes. His hands were no longer his own either. They looked hard and permanently highlighted with ground-in dirt. They were the hands of a much older man, competent but unsupple.

What an actress Mandy Jackson had been. Where had they ever found her?

David looked like a man wasting away from disease—not as if he were being beaten or harried to death but dying from the inside outward. What scared me most was that he now looked like a man who could survive prison.

"Has anything else happened, David? Are you okay?"

He shrugged. "I'm not going to keep telling you stories for the next twenty years. I'm getting by. The lucky thing is, there's always a fresh batch of new boys."

"Did you get the names of those men, the ones who—attacked you?"

He looked me hard in the eyes. "You think I want anyone to

know their names? You want Mom and Dinah to come watch *that* trial, too?"

I let his eyes bore into me. He had never looked at me so long in his life. His stare had a force it had never had before, but there was something crippled in it as well. I wished I could reach his hand.

"David, I have proof that the maid lied."

His breath came harshly through his nose. For the first time he looked fearful again. His hands searched across the bare counter for something to grip, and, finding nothing, closed into fists. "Mandy?"

"Yes."

"Don't tell me this. Don't try to do me a favor. Is it good proof?"

"It needs work, but it's good enough to start with. I'm going to get you out of here. Back to Bexar County. It'll be the jail, but it won't be—"

He stood up. "Today?"

"It can't be today. I don't have any authorization yet."

He turned his back on me.

"David, listen. I've decided exactly what you have to do. Beat someone up."

He looked back. He was looking at me over his shoulder.

"It doesn't matter who. The less provocation the better. One of the new fish or one of the—somebody you already know. Do it in front of guards. Make sure of that. Let a guard see you."

The first trace of liveliness had appeared in his eyes. "I'll get thrown in solitary," he said.

"Yes. And by the time you get out I'll have you out."

He considered it. He almost smiled. But then he sobered. "I'll lose all my good time."

"I already told you, that doesn't matter now."

"Easier to say from your side of the counter."

"I'll get you out, David, I swear I will. I'll pull every string I know. This time—"

Now it was me he was considering. "I thought you already did that."

I stood and put my hands on the glass. A guard who had been standing in the corner of the otherwise empty room came closer. "David." I couldn't let him go back through that inner door, into that world where I couldn't reach him, where I couldn't do a thing for him.

But there was no hesitation as he walked away from me. His step was lighter than when he'd entered the room. I stayed clinging to the glass long after the door closed.

It had happened exactly as David had said it happened. The ludicrous story was true. He was innocent and he was in prison. I kept trying to picture the scene the way it had happened. It had become a picture instead of mere words: a woman walking into his office and beginning to tear her clothes off, to scratch her own skin. On the flight back to San Antonio I thought about Mandy Jackson. Jack Pfister, one of my investigators, had already checked and found that her kids had been withdrawn from school and none of them was at home. The house was still furnished but empty of people. That was the only evidence I had that the little man had been telling me the truth. Of course, she could have decided to move, or at least take a vacation, after the trial. I didn't have any proof to support the story. I didn't need it, but Watlin would.

I still found it hard to believe she could have been so convincing a witness and so thorough a liar. Only David, Lois, and Dinah had never been fooled by her. I remembered the fire and horror of her testimony. And the hate in her eyes that couldn't be faked. I had thought it was David she hated, but it was someone else. The man who had put her in that witness stand. Clyde Malish. It was probably her children he had threatened. Nothing else could make a woman give a performance like that. I found it impossible to hate her. Mrs. Jackson was another victim of the same scheme. But she wasn't in prison. If I had to harass and bully her myself, I would, for David's sake.

If I could find her.

"There's hope," I told Lois. I had to invade the sanctity of her study to say it. I don't know what she was doing in there—possibly writing to her senator. Lois hadn't given up, I was sure of that, but she wasn't consulting me. Maybe she had hired a good lawyer.

"What do you mean?"

I told her about the dapper little man with the gun. I had debated whether to tell her, whether to give her, too, the false hope David had complained about. But I couldn't keep it from her. It would come out later, and my failure to tell Lois would appear to be a betrayal. So I told her, as simply as possible, leaving out details.

"Did you get the license number?" she asked at the end.

"Stolen, of course. I knew it would be when they let me see it." I changed the subject. "I've told David already. I tried to tell him not to worry."

Lois didn't show a trace of the elation I'd expected. She sat in her desk chair, shoulders hunched inward. You would have thought that at least the vindication of her son would have cheered her. "But there's nothing to be done," she said.

"Of course there are things to be done. Bring David back here, first of all. I'm getting him bench-warranted back for the hearing. By the time we have it, maybe I can find evidence that he was framed. Maybe Mandy Jackson will recant her testimony after I find her. There's plenty to be done."

I was fired up, standing in the doorway gesturing and almost twitching with energy. I seemed to have absorbed it all. Lois still sat slumped. She looked at me strangely, still without a trace of joy. She wouldn't let herself hope. I understood. Finally she nodded, dismissing me. I hurried away, vaguely disturbed but eager to get on with it. I wished Lois could take some comfort in the renewed crackle of events I felt pushing us onward again. She would see, though.

"What do you mean he won't sign it? What's wrong with it?"

"Nothing is wrong with it, Mark. It's a bench warrant, it's standard. I presented it to him and he said no."

"Where, in his chambers or the court? Was anyone else there?"

"Does that matter?" Linda asked.

"I don't know. You can't know with Waddle. There wasn't a reporter around, was there?"

"I don't remember. Not within earshot. I approached the bench. There was nothing wrong with the warrant, Mark. He started frowning as soon as he saw the name. He just shook his head and handed it back to me."

"Did he ask to see me?"

"No." Linda was frowning at me. I took a moment to think of her feelings. I'd sent her to perform a simple task, a clerk's errand, really, and she hadn't gotten it done. She knew its importance. I'd told Linda about the dapper little man, too. Before I told Lois, as a matter of fact.

"Don't worry about it, Linda. It's nothing you did wrong."

"I know."

"Waddle just has to think about the implications. Where's the warrant?"

"I'll come with you."

"No. The judge won't want witnesses. Besides, it'd look like you went and brought back your big brother to beat him up."

"I don't need—"

"I know. Thanks, Linda. I've got something else for you to do while I'm gone."

Judge Watlin was in his office. I wondered how long he'd been waiting there. I knew he was waiting for me because he didn't have anyone else with him, any of the toadies inevitably attached to his ass by suction. He still had on his robe, as if he'd just left the bench for a few minutes to peruse some law.

"Hello, Blackie. What can I do for you?"

Come to think of it, Watlin was the first person to start calling me that hated nickname. Fair enough, though. I think I'd been the first to call him Judge Waddle.

"I came for some continuing legal education, Judge. Obviously, you spotted some technical flaw in this bench warrant that eluded me. I came to share your learning."

Watlin's laugh was an unsudden thing, forthcoming only after he'd decided laughter was the appropriate response. He looked like a poor job of animation, his little flinty eyes unconnected to his laughing mouth. When the mirth subsided, he wiped his eye and said, "Blackie, you and I both know my legal learning wouldn't exhaust a minute of your time. There's nothing wrong with your bench warrant that I know of. Nothing legal."

"Then—"

"Its timing. Hell, what's he been gone, a week? And you want me to bring him back already?" He shook his head. "It's still a story right now. There's still reporters prowling around looking for an angle. But we've given 'em nothing so far, because everything's been done by the book. Just an ordinary case. Let it die down for a little while. Then we'll bring him back for a hearing."

"Judge, I think your concern—"

He picked up a document from the desk in front of him. "This amended motion for new trial you filed—which I'm not sure is timely, by the way, but forget that for now—this is pretty vague stuff, you know. You actually have new evidence? Something you can prove, or just some—"

"I can't prove it yet, John. I just got hold of it. But I'm not asking for a hearing today. Another week, maybe two—"

He nodded. And again tried to hand the bench warrant back to me. "That's what I thought. We'll bring the defendant back to Bexar County when we're ready to hold the hearing. Just like we'd do for any other convicted felon."

I didn't reach for the warrant he was stretching toward me. "He's not a felon," I said.

Watlin sighed. "Is every step of the way going to be like this, Blackie? I know what this must be like for you, but you've got to learn to let it go. Your control only extends so far. It's over now. You've got—"

"Listen," I interrupted. "It's not like that, John. I know David's innocent. I have proof."

He looked skeptical. "If you've got the proof, let's have the hearing. I'll be more than glad—"

"It's not good enough yet. Someone's blackmailing me. Since the trial I've been approached and told that Mandy Jackson will recant her testimony if I do someone a favor."

The judge chewed that over. He was not a slow man. He digested the information and found the flaw in it in less time than it took me to decide what to say next. "Just because she'll recant doesn't mean she was lying to begin with," he said.

"I know. That's one of the problems with my proof, that's why I'm not ready for the hearing yet. But I know David was telling the truth. Understand, John? I'm not talking legal proof. I know he's innocent and he's in prison. My son."

Watlin nodded. His pursed lips were moving slightly in and out, reflection of an inner dialogue. We don't have to think about prison much at our end. It's the bogeyman we use to scare erring probationers or the club we use to make them plead for probation in the first place. We relish or bemoan long sentences, but those are only numbers. Longtime defense lawyers see clients go away and return apparently unscathed and unrepentant. We have long given up on the power of the horror of prison to reform.

Judges are even further removed from it. They see men shuffle before them pleading true to their motions to revoke probation or guilty in exchange for sentences to serve, in effect saying they are ready for TDC. Judges' courtrooms are daily filled with prisoners who look indifferent to whether they will spend the night on the street or in a cell. Watlin had never even been a defense lawyer and talked to a client through wire mesh while smells and noises of the jail wafted into the airless enclosure.

Watlin's one marriage had been short-lived and produced no children, which further impaired his sympathy. I couldn't remember the last time he had seen David before the trial.

"Have you seen him there?" he asked.

"Yes. Already raped and beaten."

Watlin gave a slight shudder but didn't reply. He touched my arm in sympathy. Then his eyes moved and I could almost picture his thoughts shifting to the public perception of his doing me a favor. His lips pursed again.

"This is all going to come out one day soon, Judge. People are going to know David was sent to prison just because someone wanted to get at me."

I didn't have to spell it out any more than that. There would be heroes and villains, I was saying. Dupes and schemers. Watlin knew where a judge who'd had a chance to perform real justice and passed it by because of self-interest would fall in that crowd. He didn't respond, as if he hadn't heard me, as if he had already been about to sign the bench warrant out of nothing more than consideration for David. Maybe he would have. I didn't know which was stronger, his sympathy or his self-interest, but I did know it was best to have both on my side.

He didn't release the warrant as soon as my fingers closed on it. His eyes held me as well. "You know what I'm handing you here, don't you, Blackie? A little piece of my career. Maybe it's not something that could ruin me, but I don't take chances lightly. That's why I'm serving my third term. You wouldn't lie to me, would you?"

Yes. Lie, cajole, club you senseless. "I'd hoped you knew me better than to ask that, John," I said solemnly. We nodded, men who understood honor.

It took me about fifteen minutes to get the bench warrant to the sheriff and get two deputies dispatched to Huntsville with it. The sun was still high. They'd get there before dark. I felt pounds lighter as I walked back to the courthouse.

Then I set about doing what I'd been told to do: wreck the case against Clyde Malish.

CHAPTER

10

Uncoincidentally, his trial was set two days after my meeting with the dapper little man. They wanted me to have time only to act, not to plan. I dropped a hint to the trial prosecutors to push the case to trial, but they didn't have to do anything. Malish had had so many resets already that his case was at the top of the docket, and his lawyer announced ready.

I was in the courtroom to see that. Judge Marroquin looked at me approvingly. We were fellow politicians, the only overt ones in the room, even members of the same party. Besides, he knew Malish's was an important case, and seeing me there made him think it was more important. That meant press. Any elected official likes to see his name in the papers. Judge Marroquin was far from being an exception. He nodded at me courteously.

My eyes were for Clyde Malish. He was sitting in the front row of the spectator seats, flanked by lawyers. The one on the right was Myron Stahl, who worked for Malish exclusively. He wasn't a criminal lawyer and I didn't know him. One of those men who made me wonder why they had become lawyers in the first place, when they didn't want to try cases. The one on the other side was Joe White, a trial lawyer who'd been hired just for this case. Joe was an avuncular man in his early fifties who wouldn't be very well versed on the law that applied to the case but would rip your throat out if you gave him an opening in trial.

They were both talking to Clyde Malish at once. Bent as they were, he was a head taller than both of them. He was staring into space, apparently not listening. He didn't nod or speak. He looked like a champion racehorse being calmed by two grooms.

I knew of Malish. As Linda had pointed out, I'd once planned to prosecute this case myself. To outward appearances Clyde Malish was a small businessman with two appliance stores in run-down parts of town. Why, then, did he live in a five-thousand-square-foot house, with six cars, a ranch in the hill country, and house servants who bulged under their arms? He was a businessman all right, but there was nothing small about him. The biggest dope importer in South Texas, he never came within ten miles of a needle anymore. Malish had been more forward-looking and much smarter than your average pusher. He had realized he could make more than one score off his customers. Fish gotta swim, junkies gotta steal. Clyde Malish told them where and what to steal. It had been at least ten years since he had organized his customers into a burglars' army. He arranged their break-ins and paid them off in the dope he got cut-rate, so his take was even bigger than a usual fence's. The cash flow allowed him to branch out into other enterprises: hijacking, corporate espionage, undoubtedly a dozen suborganizations no police agency knew anything about. And no one had ever been able to put together one case against him even strong enough to get an indictment, until this one.

I stared at the side of his head, willing him to turn. I wanted to see his face. Did he even know what David looked like? I drifted closer to him, and I realized my hands were clenched. Myron Stahl did glance up at me, nervously. Clyde Malish did not.

He obviously knew the case would go to trial today. He had come dressed for it. Malish was wearing a new, cheap suit and clunky black shoes, polished for the occasion but worn in the heels. He looked like a farmer all got up for his son's high school graduation.

It took an hour to get the pleas out of the way and get a jury panel sent up. I stayed in sight all that time. If nothing else, I wanted Malish to know that I was responsible for what was about to happen. He didn't seem to notice. Before the panel was brought in he took his seat at counsel table and looked around as if still dazed to find himself there. Myron Stahl faded away before the jury selection began, and so did I.

"What do you want me to do?" Linda asked.

I shook my head. "I want to help," she insisted.

"Don't worry, there'll be plenty of major felonies to go around. You can be a party to the next one."

I wasn't at my desk, I was on the couch across the office, stretched out. She was standing over me, but I was treating her the way Clyde Malish had treated me. I wasn't looking at Linda, I was looking at a blank corner of the ceiling. "What will that be?" she asked.

"I haven't had the luxury of thinking that far ahead," I said.

"Bullshit. Mark, you always think you're two steps ahead of everybody else. Usually you are, so it works out okay. But now you're dealing with someone who's always been three steps ahead. And who will do *anything* to get what he wants. Anything."

"Then maybe I won't try to think ahead at all. Maybe he'll trip himself up with his own cleverness."

Linda blew a disgusted noise. She looked worried as hell, and I knew how I looked, stretched out on the couch. Linda was on my side. Maybe she even loved me. But she didn't trust me. And I couldn't explain to her how I felt. I hadn't realized it myself until I'd come back to my office from the courtroom. I was happy. Filled with ease and lightness. I'd been freed of the burden of wondering if David was guilty. That made everything else of no consequence. Clyde Malish would do anything? Well, so would I. And I knew more of the possibilities than he did.

I was back in the courtroom that afternoon to see the jury be sworn in. That was all I needed to know, but I stayed for the rest. The state called its first witness, the cop who had been first on the scene of a burglary of a house on the near north side. His testimony almost put me to sleep—broken window, no blood, no fingerprints, catalogue of items taken—but the jury seemed interested. I wondered how many of them had been burglarized. You can't pick a jury anymore that doesn't include crime victims.

That was the end of the trial day. Judge Marroquin is no fiend for work and he is usually a friend of the state. He knew the prosecutors would want to put on the meat of their case all in one day so the jurors wouldn't have time to forget the details overnight.

Again Clyde Malish seemed ignorant of my presence, but the trial lawyers knew I was there, my own employees especially. I'd be surprised if they enjoyed having the district attorney at their backs. Frank Mendiola might have, though; he was that kind of crazy man. I was sure he had questioned the officer at greater length knowing the boss was watching.

He feigned surprise when he saw me, though, said my name loudly and shook hands. Marilyn Ebbetts, his second chair, looked disgusted with him. We waited for the bad guys to file out past us before I said, "Good case?"

"Could be better," Frank said. "But we'll get him."

"Come to my office and tell me about it."

They were surprised, but they came, of course. Frank stayed at my elbow, chatting away. Frank was barely thirty years old, the youngest first chair in the office, an ambitious boy not as smart as he thought he was. Before today he had treated me with condescending deference. I had campaigned as a professional prosecutor, but Frank had known me only as a defense lawyer. He should have been grateful to me for letting him keep his job, and maybe he was, but he resented having to be grateful. *He* was the professional prosecutor. He had never been anything else.

Marilyn hung back a little in the hallway but stayed within earshot. In my office she turned her chair so that she was facing both of us. She knew Frank's reputation, that you didn't turn your back on him and you didn't leave him alone in a room with someone who could do him good and you damage.

I asked again if it was a good case. Frank was in the difficult position of wanting to express confidence in his abilities while letting me know that it would be due to his abilities that he would win—not just to the airtight nature of the case. "I've certainly tried easier ones," he said, "but we can pull it out."

"What's our evidence? I'm assuming Clyde Malish didn't go in through the window himself."

Frank smiled. "He was the organizer. The house was owned by a doctor Malish had once had some dealings with—investments of some kind. The actual burglars took some papers Malish would have wanted, besides the usual things. And he bought all the loot."

"Drugs?"

"Some drugs, yeah. Mostly electronic equipment, stereo, VCR, things like that."

I turned to Marilyn. "What ties Malish to it?"

She began answering slowly. Marilyn was more obviously curious about why they were being quizzed than Frank had been. She wasn't sure what answers I wanted. "The papers that were taken, of course. And the accomplice's testimony."

I raised my eyebrows. "The burglar himself?"

"Yes."

"Sounds good. Where is he?"

"In my office," Frank said. I knew he was. "We didn't know if we'd get to him today."

I nodded approvingly. "Bring him in. Let me get a preview."

They looked at each other. Marilyn stepped to the door and asked Patty to send an investigator for the witness. We waited in a minute of silence. They both looked uneasy now. Frank finally cleared his throat and said, "Are you still thinking of trying this case yourself?"

I waved the idea away. "I wouldn't step in now that the trial's started. I'm just curious about what kind of case I would have had. If you'd rather I not interfere between you and your witness—"

"Oh no, no."

"You've woodshedded him thoroughly, I assume."

"Of course," Frank said. "He's our case."

But he still looked uneasy when the burglar came shuffling into the room. Frank didn't gaze on him as a star pupil. The burglar was not a prepossessing young man. They should have had him dress better if they thought he might go on the stand. He wore painter's pants and a plaid shirt. He was a very thin young Mexican man with a lot of unruly hair, and eyes that slid across things rather than fastening on them.

"Sit down," I said, jovial-host–like. Frank moved a chair for him. "What's your name?"

"Jesse."

"Jesse. Good. I suppose if your last name becomes significant, I can find it out from someone. Well, they tell me you're our star witness, Jesse. Have you ever testified in court before?"

He nodded, looking into his lap. "Once."

"Really? This isn't the first time you've testified against someone?"

"No. For myself."

"For yourself? You mean you were tried for something?"

Frank Mendiola leaned forward. "We'll bring that up ourselves, of course, right up front. He's got two priors."

"Two? How old are you, Jesse?"

"Twenty-six." He still hadn't looked at me. His eyes had climbed as high as my desk, though. He might have been appraising the pen and pencil set.

"Those the only two crimes you ever committed?"

He shrugged. "I used to shoot the dope. Sometimes get caught. You do crazy things. But I don't do that no more."

"You've quit since this last burglary?"

"Yeah."

"And now you're going to testify against Clyde Malish in this burglary you committed. You did do it, didn't you, Jesse? Break into the doctor's house?"

He nodded, but he contradicted me. "Office."

"Office? I thought it was his home." I looked at my prosecutor.

"It's both," Frank explained. "Downstairs is his office, waiting room, all that, plus a kitchen. Upstairs is the living area and bedrooms. It's a big old house in Alamo Heights right on Broadway."

Jesse the burglar volunteered information again. "It was the office we wanted. For the drugs."

"Was that Mr. Malish's idea?"

"Well, the drug part was my idea. This was when I was still shooting the dope, you know, so, like—"

"Uh-huh. What part of it was Malish's idea?"

"He told us where to hit. And the papers, he wanted the papers."

"Yes, the papers. What were they, contracts? Deeds?"

"Papers, man, I don't know."

"Did you get them?"

"Yeah."

"Did you give them to Malish?"

"I guess."

"You guess you gave them to him?"

"I give them to his man."

"Carl Stengel," Frank Mendiola interjected. "He works for

Malish." I looked at him expressionlessly, then turned back to the burglar.

"Did you see Mr. Malish in court today?"

"Uh-uh. I don't wanna go near him till I have to."

"What does he look like, Jesse?"

"White dude. Kind of tall, got a little bit of a belly on him."

"How old is he?"

"Old. Fifty at least."

I turned to the prosecutors. "So far I don't know if he'll identify Clyde Malish or Joe White in court. Come to think of it, I'd better not be there myself. Don't want to make it too tough on him."

"He knows him," Frank said a little testily. To the burglar he said, "Tell him about when Malish told you to pull the job."

The witness grew a little livelier. He had finally realized he was performing now, or at least auditioning. "It was in this little restaurant on the south side. Just a joint. Mexican food takeout, maybe six tables in the place. We met there on a Wednesday morning when nobody else was around. We had breakfast tacos. Mr. Malish had potato and egg and I had chorizo. The guy with him—"

"He remembers food details," I said to the prosecutors.

"Yeah. Anyway, Mr. Malish sits across the room eating and the guy with him comes over and tells me about the job. He writes the address down on a napkin—"

"You still have the napkin?"

"No, man. Napkin? Get real. But he writes the address down and he tells me the papers Mr. Malish wants are in a desk in the office. We can break the lock. Then he told me the doctor was gonna be out of town Sunday so we wouldn't have any problem. Then we talk about the cut, haggle over that a little—"

"What's Malish doing all this time?"

"Just munching down tacos, pretending not to watch us. But at the end he comes by my table and says, 'Got it?' And I say, 'Sure, man. Whaddaya think, it's my first time?'"

"So you did the job Sunday?"

"Yeah, Sunday. Me and Ernie Valenciano."

"Another junkie?"

"Yeah, man, but he ain't reformed like me."

"Tell me this, Jesse. You're the one that actually did the burglary. What's going to happen to your case?"

He laughed. "Nothing good, I hope." He looked to Frank for support.

"The prosecutors promised you a good deal if you'd testify that Clyde Malish was behind it all?"

"Yeah. Well, nobody come right out and said it, you know, but I get the idea."

"You've got two priors, Jesse. That makes you a habitual if you get one more conviction. You know what the range of punishment is for that?"

"Nah," he said sarcastically. "Everybody knows what the bitch is worth. Twenty-five to life."

I nodded. "Twenty-five minimum. And you're how old, Jesse, twenty-six?"

He was nodding so hard he was almost bouncing in his chair. He looked happy. We'd gotten to the part he liked. "But they drop the habitual after I testify. I get something like maybe ten, maybe—"

"They told you that?"

Marilyn cut in angrily. "Say what we told you to say, Jesse."

Like she'd hit the back of a robot's head to jar a circuit into place, he said, "No deals. They haven't promised me nothin'."

"Right. How about the cops, Jesse? They promise you anything?"

He looked at Marilyn for help. She just stared at him. The burglar said slowly, "They said it would help my case, you know, if I wasn't a hardass about it. They said Mr. Malish was the one they really wanted. So if I wanted to do myself some good—"

"They brought up Malish's name first?"

He looked puzzled. "I think. I don't know, maybe I did."

Now he was just searching for the right thing to say. He looked at the trial prosecutors but Frank was looking at Marilyn and Marilyn was gazing south. "They knew about the papers, see, so they knew he had wanted them—"

"Right, good." The burglar cheered up at my enthusiasm. "We have these papers?" I asked the lawyers.

"We have the doctor's testimony that they were missing after the burglary," Marilyn said, not with any pride. "And he'll testify that they showed Malish's part ownership of a building that was being used as a chop shop. Malish didn't show up in the deeds, but this agreement the doctor had showed that Malish had put up the money. After the chop shop was raided Malish obviously wanted those documents. So . . ."

I just sat there, trying to look like a juror trying to absorb these convolutions. After a long, quiet minute I stirred myself and smiled at Jesse, the eager witness.

"Thank you, Jesse. You'd better hurry home now, or wherever you'll be safe tonight. You have a big day tomorrow."

He stood up, smiling, looking me in the face for the first time. He thought he'd done good. His face fell a little when Frank Mendiola told him, "Go back to my office. We've got more work to do."

The burglar eased out of the room, looking back for approval. I smiled, but his trial partners wouldn't look at him. When the door closed I said, "You've got *huevos*, Frank. I wouldn't want *my* career riding on this case."

You could almost see his stomach drop. "What do you mean?"

"I mean I wouldn't bet much on it. Gee, I sure am sorry the press of my duties didn't allow me to try this one. What have you got for corroboration?"

It's not just common sense; in Texas it's statutory law. When the state's case depends on accomplice testimony, that testimony must be corroborated by other evidence showing the defendant's involvement in the crime.

Frank ticked it off: "We've got the doctor about the papers. We've got the counterman at the restaurant who remembers Clyde Malish being there with Jesse that morning."

"I can't wait to see Joe White cross him. What else?"

"We've got, uh—"

"The best part," Marilyn reminded him. "Some of the property taken in the burglary was recovered in a building owned by Malish."

"Well, finally. That sounds more like it. What've you got proving his ownership of the building? Deed?"

"The deed's too messy with subsidiaries and DBAs. But we've got a lease agreement with Malish's signature on it."

I let my face fall. "He had the building rented to someone else?"

"Yes, but he had access. It's one of those self-storage places, and Malish had keys to some of the units."

I sat there as if absorbing it all. I let them watch me. "So what you've got is this," I finally said. I was no longer saying "we." "You've got Malish and Jesse the habitual but reformed junkie burglar who will probably say anything the cops suggest he say to keep out of prison for the third time in his short life—you've got them in the same restaurant one morning and Malish says two words to him on his way out. You've got the victim saying papers were missing that Malish wanted, but you don't have the papers themselves. You've got Jesse giving those papers—no, *some* papers, because he doesn't know *what* they were—to somebody other than Malish. And finally you've got some of the stolen property turning up in a building Malish maybe owned but had rented to someone else. Have I left anything out? Is this the state this case was in when I was supposed to try it? Have we lost a witness or something?"

"You know how it is, Mark," Frank said with the eagerness of a salesman letting a closing slip away. "He doesn't hack the day-to-day shit. This is probably the closest Clyde Malish has come to hands-on involvement in a street crime in ten years.

Of course he protects himself. The jury'll understand that. We know what we have to argue. If it's all just coincidence, there's too many for him to explain away."

"Maybe."

"Besides, we'll have Jesse better prepared for tomorrow. Joe White won't be able to trip him up like you just did. He's not as good at cross as you are."

"Don't kid yourself," I said. "Joe's not the best in the business, but he can see what's in front of him."

"Also, uh—" Frank looked uncomfortable. "No offense, but some of what you were asking was objectionable. We could keep out the answers."

"But you can't stop him from asking the questions. I sure as hell would." I let them stew on that for a few seconds. When Frank seemed on the verge of speaking up again, I said, "You know your other problem, don't you? You've got a second degree felony here."

"What? No, first. Burglary of a habitation. It's—" Frank looked embarrassed at having to explain the simplest facts of criminal law to me.

"Yes. And what's the definition of a habitation, Frank?"

"It's—I don't know, I don't have my penal code with me, but it's a place designed for humans to live in, overnight or some—"

"Right. But this was an office. The habitation part was upstairs. Your star witness there never said he and the other Joe Citizen even went upstairs."

"But they did. We'll bring that out. That's where they got the stereo and stuff."

"All right. But is that the crime Clyde Malish aided, encouraged, directed, and whatever the parties' language is? No. All he cared about was the papers. That's what Jesse said. And the papers were in the office. That sounds like a building to me. Second degree burglary."

"I saw that potential problem," Marilyn said. Frank looked

at her as if she'd just accused him of molesting a child. A boy child. "You did? Then why the hell didn't—"

"And suppose this," I cut in. "Suppose they only find him guilty of soliciting burglary? That lowers it a degree. Now you're talking third degree. Two to ten. And if you don't think Clyde Malish will have character witnesses out the ass, calling him the saint of the south side and saying he deserves a second chance— You know how much money he gave to churches and orphanages last year? You look forward to cross-examining nuns, Frank? Hell, if he only gets convicted of a third degree, I'd give him probation, especially after relying on the word of Jesse the burglar slash reformed junkie to convict."

"What are you telling us to do?" Marilyn asked. Frank was just sitting there stunned. An hour ago he'd been comfortably trying a simple little burglary. Suddenly it had become the most important case of his career.

"I'm not telling you to do anything. I don't interfere in cases. Have I ever? I'm just telling you what we need. I don't want you to be working in the dark.

"Look." I lowered my voice confidentially. "You know all about Clyde Malish, don't you?" They nodded. "You know we're trying to put together about eight other cases on him. You know he's behind half the burglaries and car thefts and God knows what else in this town. What we've got to have from this first case is a hammer. It's got to be a strong conviction. Probation won't cut it. If he gets probation, he's still sitting there fat and sassy running everything but being that much more careful about getting his own hands dirty. We might never get him again.

"He has got to go to prison. Understand? Prison." I was preaching, and I was sincere. They were leaning forward in their chairs. My hand shook a little as I slowly closed it on an imaginary Clyde Malish. "If he goes to prison, the whole thing falls apart. Nobody else can run that organization like he can.

And more important than that, they'll see he's not invulnerable. Other people will think about testifying against him, especially if we have something on them. You see? Set fire to his house and spear the rats as they come running out.

"That's what we've got to have from you two. Better to dismiss the case now than to try it and get him probation. Or, God forbid, an acquittal. He goes free, that's death to all our cases. Next case we bring against him, it'll look like we're just trying to harass him out of vindictiveness. We might not even get an indictment. Dismissal'd be a hell of a lot better than that. Dismissing it might even make him cocky. Careless."

I leaned back, tired. They stirred a little, but they both still pressed toward me, hungry for direction. "Our first case against him has to be rock solid," I concluded.

"So," Marilyn began uneasily.

I held my hands up. "What you do is entirely up to you. I don't know the case as well as you two do. It's for you to decide. I just want you to know what's riding on it."

They looked at each other. Frank started to speak, stopped. Marilyn did the same. They looked like partners for the first time since they'd come into my office. They looked like husband and wife.

I didn't say another word. Neither did Frank or Marilyn. They glanced askance at me and held silence. When they reached the outer office I heard their voices, jostling each other, climbing.

Left alone in the office, I didn't smile. I felt like a spider sitting behind my desk. There was no feeling of triumph in that.

It wasn't a tough decision. I was in the courtroom the next morning when Judge Marroquin told Frank to call his next witness and instead Frank rose to his feet and said, "Your Honor, the State of Texas moves to dismiss this prosecution."

The startled faces were comical, if you enjoy that sort of

thing. Clyde Malish's was one of them. What a cool customer. He didn't even glance at me. And looked as confused as anyone else at the turn of events. His lawyer had to lean over and tell him more than once that he was free to go. Jeopardy had attached when the trial began, which meant this charge could never be brought against him again. The state had had its one chance.

Malish rose slowly to his feet. For a moment it looked as if he were going to shake hands with Frank, but Frank was the first person out of the room. Malish joined the melee of jurors shuffling toward the door. He spoke to a couple of them and shrugged his shoulders clownishly. I don't know, pal, I'm just a rube here myself. I watched him all the way out of the room and he never looked at me. I had a motion to dismiss in my own pocket. I would have done it myself if Frank hadn't. But this way was better. Less traceable to me. Besides, I had denied Malish at least that much triumph. It wasn't quite clear he was pulling the D.A.'s strings.

That was a completely hollow and bitter triumph.

"What are you going to do?" Linda asked. I don't know when she'd appeared beside me. "I mean to him," she said.

She had to read my eyes for answer.

We discussed more immediate matters, though. I told Linda I wanted her to start preparing for the motion for new trial hearing. "I don't want anyone else in on this, not even Henry. Nobody else can know what we have. Do you think Mandy Jackson will testify for us? Admit she perjured herself?"

"I suppose," Linda said slowly. "Clyde Malish can probably make her. He'll still have over her whatever he already had. But I would rather—"

"You talk to her when we find her," I said. "She seemed to trust you. Tell her—"

Linda nodded. I was instructing her to do what she'd already intended. Linda had a client again. She had left the rest of the case behind momentarily while she decided what would be best for Mandy Jackson. "I will tell her we know what caused her to lie before. She should be relieved to have the district attorney's office on her side this time. We do not want to be in a position of forcing her to tell the new story. We are only removing the threat that caused her to lie, so now she is able to tell the truth. She'll be scared, Mark. We should—"

"We should not let Malish or any of his thugs near her again. And let her know—"

"—that we are preparing cases against them because of what they made her do. She will testify for us, Mark. You saw her strength. And once the new trial is granted, with that testimony of hers on record the case against David will have to be dismissed."

Yes. Very pat. Very easy to accomplish. Twenty minutes of testimony from the principal witness. Even an affidavit would be good enough just for the motion hearing. Clyde Malish could have that done himself. He wouldn't waste time as we did deciding how to proceed and what would be best for everyone. He would have acted already.

Linda cleared her throat. We were walking, a couple of blocks from the courthouse. It was lunchtime. She stopped a few paces short of the door of the restaurant.

"Will he really let us have her?" she said. She was being the voice of gloom and she didn't like it. "Mark, I don't want to— But why should he carry through now? He's gotten what he wanted."

She knew the question had occurred to me, but neither of us had voiced it before. I had an answer, the one I'd told myself. "He'd be stupid not to, wouldn't he? There's no risk for him in carrying through on the deal. If he doesn't, he risks what I might do."

"Such as?"

I turned away. She followed me into the restaurant. At the table she cleared her throat again. "Something else occurred to me. If the case against him was as weak as you made out, why did he go to such trouble to get it dismissed?"

"It wasn't that bad a case," I said. I had told Linda about the scene with Frank and Marilyn. "I made it look bad there in my office, but you can do that to any case. Jesse the burglar, for example, probably would have looked a lot better on the stand than he did in front of my desk. I crept up on him, pretending to be on his side. He would have been a lot warier with Joe White, he wouldn't have said such stupid things. I imagine."

"But still—"

"Why? Because Clyde Malish isn't a risk taker. He wasn't going to leave himself in the hands of a jury. Besides, you said why did he go to so much trouble, but this was no trouble for him. He set David up like you'd mail a letter. Easier. Just order it done. Find somebody like Mandy Jackson to put the screws on . . ."

I was still wondering about her. What was the leverage Malish had used on her? Her children, probably. Maybe something in her late husband's past that put them at risk. The dead husband, killed in a drug deal, was probably the link to Malish. After she came forward we'd have to protect Mandy as well. She might be the lever I could use to get back at Malish. David's release wasn't going to be the end of this. Not by a long stretch.

"You take it easy," Linda said. I looked at her, framed by a poster on the restaurant wall behind her. She was studying me. Why? crossed my mind. You know exactly what's in my thoughts, don't you, Linda?

"Don't take things at face value," she said. I didn't think I had been.

There was nothing to do but wait. As the little man had said, it would be automatic. I had done my part, I could only wait for Clyde Malish to fulfill his. At least David was back in the local jail. He seemed to be relieved to be "home." Strange: six months ago jail would have terrified him. Now it was such an improvement over the state prison it seemed little to endure. From my perspective, at least. I saw David every day, but he wasn't very forthcoming. He had settled back into that protective shell of apparent indifference.

Lois saw him daily, too, though not at the same times I did. The day after Malish's trial was aborted I left work early to pick up Dinah from school because Lois was at the jail. When I pulled up to the school I saw Dinah standing with a group of other girls. A boy walking by said something and she turned her head slightly to speak to him offhandedly over her shoulder. It was a very adult posture. A moment later she saw me and came running, skirt flying, face lit up like a five-year-old's. But when she was sitting beside me I noticed how high her head came and that the once-perpetual scabs on her knees were gone. Everyone says time flies, but if you want to see it happen before your eyes, have a child. I still thought of Dinah as a baby. She was in fifth grade and I was just getting used to the idea that she wasn't at home during the day if I dropped by the house. David had grown up behind my back. I'd thought I was keeping an eye on Dinah.

"Did they find Mandy Jackson?" she asked. That was as much as Dinah knew—it was as much as Lois knew—that I had some kind of new evidence and wanted to confront Mandy with it.

"Not yet." I wondered how much Dinah understood about rape. At first I'd thought her certainty of David's innocence was her way of not thinking about the crime he was accused of. Did she understand the news stories? I'm sure she did. She was no longer a little girl. How long would it be before she knew the whole David saga? When she did, what would she think of my part in it?

"What did you learn in school today?" I asked.

She rolled her eyes at me and we both laughed. "Surely you don't know everything yet."

"Pretty much," she said.

"Oh yeah? What are the principal exports of Brazil?"

She looked at me with a touch of exasperation. "When's the last time you had to know that?"

She had really taken me by surprise. "You know, when I was learning the principal exports of Brazil, it never occurred to me to ask when I'd need the information."

"You grew up in a less sophisticated age," she said, and I had to tickle her until she giggled.

"Seriously," she said, re-donning her composure. "When can I see David?"

"When he gets out."

"No, I mean—"

"You're not going to the jail."

It wasn't often I said something to her so steeped in parental authority. She sat brooding darkly for a minute. "Maybe I'll arrange a field trip," she finally said.

"Dinah."

"Yes?"

Silence stretched tautly between us. I waited until it grew slack. I put my arm around her shoulders and she moved closer to me. Such narrow shoulders still. My arm felt heavy on her.

"What year was the Battle of New Orleans?" I asked.

The best thing that could be said for him was that he didn't keep me in suspense long. The next morning about six I brought the paper in off the front sidewalk and dropped onto the couch with it. Strange that I learned the news from a newspaper. But the story had broken in the middle of the night and no one had reached me with it. The story was on the front page, below the fold. It wouldn't have gotten that much play except for the principal character's recent notoriety. Her name was Mandy Jackson. Recently, she was the state's chief witness against David Blackwell, now serving sixteen years in the Texas Department of Corrections. Mandy Jackson was worse off than that. Two preteen brothers playing in a culvert near their east side residence had found her very early that morning. The syringe was lying next to her, fallen from her hand. The overdose had killed her so fast she barely had time to pull the needle out of her arm.

PART II

A conspiracy is not finally terminated until everything has been done that was contemplated to be done by the conspirators.

—Robins v. State, 117 S.W.2d 82 (1938).

CHAPTER

11

'm here to see Myron Stahl."

"He's not in right now. Did you have an appointment?"

"No, but he'll see me anyway. I'll just see if he's in."

She got between me and the office door. "Sir, without an appointment I won't be able to fit you into Mr. Stahl's schedule today. If you'd care to leave a message—"

I laughed and went past her, careless of whether she got out of my way or I pushed her aside.

"Stop!" she shouted in the tone of a cop, the same expectation of obedience. It worked as well as a whisper would have. She turned to threats: "If you don't leave right now, I'll have to—"

"Call the police?" I turned on her. "Call them. We'll wait together." I flashed ID at her. "I am the district attorney. And Mr. Stahl will see me today. He can't be far. You call him back from wherever he is and tell him the faster he gets here, the less damage I'll do him. I'll wait in here."

I did not pause for an answer. The receptionist was having trouble changing gears and might not have been able to provide me with response for some time. I proceeded into the inner office and closed the door behind me. After a few moments a button on the phone on the desk lit up. I watched it until it went off. I had no inclination to rifle the desk. No lawyer would leave incriminating evidence in an unlocked desk. Besides, this was Clyde Malish's lawyer's office, not Malish's. Myron Stahl probably had nothing to do with the Mandy Jackson scheme, except as an adviser. I didn't know how crooked Stahl was. I didn't know if he was crooked at all. I only knew he had an evil client.

I paced. The office had an old-style gentlemanly charm. The wooden desk was antique without being spindly. Leather wing chairs stood in front of it. The two filing cabinets were oak—with sturdy locks. The walls were paneled. There were two windows behind the desk. The opposite wall was covered with framed certificates and photos. When I grew tired of pacing, I came up short in front of them. There were the obligatory law license and law school diploma. Stahl's was from the University of Virginia, I was surprised to see. The other certificates were standard issues from bar associations and civic organizations, nothing outstanding, the sort of tokens one is awarded for paying one's dues for a certain number of years and showing up at a certain number of functions. One of the photographs, the most blurred one, was of John F. Kennedy shaking hands with Myron Stahl. Both of them looked very young. I searched for a photo of Clyde Malish on the wall of honor.

Stahl must have been in this office a long time. Sunlight had faded the paneling slightly. A darker rectangle of panel wasn't completely covered by the photo and plaque hanging over it. After I noticed that, I saw other signs that the mementoes had been shifted around recently. He had more initiative than I did. The things I'd gotten up on my office walls stayed where they were first put. Some were still down on the floor, leaning against the walls.

I resumed pacing. One of those wing chairs blundered into my path and I kicked it aside. That was satisfying. I kicked it again, this time knocking it into the desk. I hoped Miss Pipe-up-the-Ass in the outer office thought I was wrecking the joint. That would make as much sense as my being there in the first place.

Myron Stahl had a bad sense of timing. If he'd been true to his last name another ten minutes, I would have reached the point of slamming out of the office, snarling at the receptionist for him to call me, and going on my way. As it was, he came in just as I'd worked my way into that pre-exit rage.

He looked affable as hell. The smile he gave me was much sunnier than a trespasser deserved. Professional courtesy. "Mr. Blackwell," he said. "This is unexpected. I hope in the future—"

He stopped talking in order to duck out of my way. But in that lunge it was the door I was going for, not him. The photos and certificates vibrated as it slammed. Myron Stahl retreated to a lawyer's barricade, his desk. In his three-piece pinstripe suit he fit that desk, this office, but what he really needed was a derby and spats. He would have worn them well. Stahl was a thin man of medium height and fastidious hands. He was well past forty, at least. Probably before today he'd thought he'd left threatening bullies years behind.

"I have a message for your client."

"Which cli—?"

"Shut up. Clyde Malish. The message is that he thinks this is over, but he's far wrong. The ball's back in his court now. He has to fix things to get my son out of prison. I'll tell you what his messenger told me: how he does it doesn't matter. Come up with some kind of new evidence, produce a witness who heard Mandy Jackson plotting the whole thing, a written statement from her, anything. It won't be examined too closely, he can fake it. He *has* to. Because if he doesn't, I'll get him. The next time he makes a move I'll be waiting. If I have to manufacture evidence to make a case against him, I will. Whatever I have to do I—"

When Stahl opened his mouth our teeth almost clicked

together. I was that far into his face. He had retreated but his desk chair had blocked him long enough for me to grab his lapels. I stopped talking because I was about to choke. The rage that had built up in me for weeks was spilling out, soaking my thoughts. As I spoke of doing anything I had to to get Clyde Malish, I suddenly thought, Maybe it would be better to kill Myron Stahl. Right here, with my hands. That would send the better message. Why just tell Malish I would do anything when I could show him instead? My hands were already close to the lawyer's throat, and clenching as if with a seizure.

I might as well have spoken aloud. The exasperation disappeared from Stahl's eyes, replaced by fear. He pulled away from me and glanced at the desktop—for a weapon of attack or defense, I knew. Both our gazes fell on the brass letter opener.

Stahl straightened his vest. "I suppose this refers to your son's difficulties. All right, all right!" He held out both hands against my renewed step and I stopped. "I'll tell him. That's all I can do. If you think Mr. Malish bows his head at my advice or anyone else's, you do not know him. But I shall certainly pass on your message."

He turned and went around the corner of the desk as if lost in thought. Maybe he was, but he was also putting the desk between us. I suddenly felt ludicrous. Attacking Myron Stahl. Like they taught us in school about bullies, I was a coward. If I were really so blind with rage, why hadn't I gone after Clyde Malish himself?

"All right," I growled. "Tell him he doesn't have much time. Every day David spends in jail is a year he owes me." It was sincere bluster, but it was bluster nonetheless. Stahl nodded.

"But you realize," he added, "this is not an admission of anything. Not on my part and certainly not on behalf of my client." I glared at him and he held up his hands, but they no longer trembled. He realized the moment of my doing anything to him had passed. In fact, I thought he gave me a small smile. Not a sneer, a look of camaraderie. We are lawyers, he seemed to say, we are not supposed to take these things seriously.

I gave him no smile in return, and I was glad to see him back away as I came around the desk. But once again it was only his door that was my target. If another melodramatic threat had sprung to mind, I would have stood in the doorway and made it. As it was, I only slammed the door back against the wall, making the receptionist jump, and went out with long strides, as if I had an urgent destination.

When the courthouse loomed in my windshield I had a sudden desire to turn away, but I knew nowhere else to go. I was seething, but I was also directionless. Returning to the courthouse was going to ground like a wounded animal, skulking.

It was still the same morning I'd read of Mandy Jackson's death in the newspaper. No one at the office had heard from me yet. There was the slim chance they had news.

Linda was at my desk again, but this time she wasn't making lists. She was just staring. A newspaper lay on the desk. When she saw me, Linda levitated to her feet and was against me. She held me for a long, long moment. There wasn't much strength in my arms; the dregs of rage had left me feeling hollow. After a while I felt some of Linda's life flowing into me, filling me up again. I could hold her more tightly. I had lost my hope of David's immediate release, but Linda had lost her "client," Mrs. Jackson. I wasn't forgetting that murder was now added to Malish's account. "I'm sorry," I said.

"We should have moved faster." Her voice was muffled against me.

"If we start making a list of how I've fucked up this case, we'll never get to anything else."

Her cheeks were wet when she let me go. But she looked more determined than when I'd walked in. "Where've you been?" she asked, and I told her as briefly as possible. I wanted to hear what she had to say. I wanted Linda to supply the ideas.

We began to talk slowly. Linda did start making a list. We would never have Mandy Jackson's testimony. What evidence did we have? Talk gave the illusion of productivity. We had to wait for so much. The autopsy report from the medical examiner's office. Investigators were prying into Mandy Jackson's past, looking for any link to Clyde Malish. And I waited with the vain hope of hearing from Malish in one way or another, the hope that my outburst in his lawyer's office would produce some result.

I fell into a despair so total it became a physical pain, a small burrowing animal trapped in my flesh, trying to gnaw its way out. I now knew without any doubt that David had been set up, I knew roughly how it had been done, and there was nothing I could do about it. In the days after Mandy Jackson's death I became a ghostly presence in the courthouse. I picked up a file, signed letters, but then I turned and passed through people and walls like vapor. I was not the ghost, though. I remained too solid flesh. It was the building that had become insubstantial. I could walk straight through it without experiencing any tugs of sight or memory. The battle was no longer in the courthouse, it was in the streets. There was nothing more to be done in the old stone building.

I discovered the truth of that when I responded to a growing stack of messages from Judge Watlin. As soon as I stepped into his courtroom he recessed the trial he was hearing, shot a look at me, and left the bench. I went around through his clerks' offices and John was waiting at the door of his chambers. He closed it behind me. He looked as if we'd already been caught in some conspiracy.

"Damn it, Blackie! Dead." He gripped my arm. "Tell me fast, don't take time to make something up. Did you have anything to do with it?"

"With killing Mandy Jackson? Are you crazy? She was going to be my witness. I needed her, that's why she's dead."

Watlin let me go and seemed to grow calmer. Logic was his

mistress. He believed me not implicitly but because I'd given him a good reason.

"But now your proof on the motion for new trial is as dead as she is. *Damn* it. Didn't you have the sense to—"

"I couldn't find her. Don't you think I looked? Maybe they had her all along, before they even threatened me. But look, don't you see? This *is* the proof. They killed her to keep her from recanting. That proves she was going to. Don't you—"

The judge gave me a look. "Easy to put words in a dead witness's mouth," he said. "But it's just speculation. Why would anybody believe it? Why would they even think she was murdered? It was just an overdose like happens every day."

"Not this one, John. She was no junkie. A junkie doesn't hold down the same job for however many years. And while going to school at night. When would she have—"

"Pull yourself together, Blackie. Character isn't evidence. You've got to do better than that."

I stopped talking long enough for him to see that I wasn't frantic. When his attention was centered on me I asked, "Do I, John? What if there isn't any more, ever? Would you grant the motion just on my testimony?"

He leaned toward me earnestly. "Don't ask me to do that, Blackie. You know I'd have to turn you down. Look, the only witness is dead now. Granting a new trial would be tantamount to dismissing the case just on your say-so, after a jury's already found him guilty."

"They'd still have her testimony from the first trial. They could retry him."

He made a face. "You know as well as I do how useless cold testimony is, read into the record by some assistant D.A. trying to be dramatic and flubbing half the lines. I couldn't do it. It smacks to high heaven of a deal. It would ruin us both." I didn't care about *my* political future. The judge and I had that much in common. "Besides," he was continuing, "even if I believed you, which of course I do, all we have is some stranger telling you she'd change her testimony. You can't even prove any connection between him and her. Maybe he was just trying to take advantage of your situation. You can't get a new trial based on double hearsay."

"But I dismissed the case against Clyde Malish. That's some proof."

"It's only proof of something you did. Maybe you went nuts and made up the whole thing, and dismissed the case to buttress your own story. Sorry, Blackie, but that's what people would say. Besides, you didn't dismiss the case."

He was right. Frank had dismissed the case against Clyde Malish, and for reasons having nothing to do with the dapper little man with the gun. I had covered myself too well.

That's what Watlin was demanding now, coverage. A month ago I would have understood his point of view. He wasn't opposing me. He was asking for my help. He was almost pleading.

"You've got the story, Blackie, now get the proof. You've got a staff, you've got investigators. Bring me some evidence. It won't take much. Give me a halfway good reason to grant your motion and you'll have it. Bring me the proof."

I was trying to do just that. Mandy Jackson's autopsy hadn't provided any help. I had told the medical examiner I suspected homicide, but he couldn't offer me any proof. "There's some bruising, but that could have come in the throes of the overdose itself. Or anything. I'll tell you this. She wasn't a drug user. Not a shooter, anyway. No needle tracks. 'Course, there's always a first time."

"If she had been an addict, would this amount have killed her? If she was used to it?"

"This would have killed anybody," he said. "Any three people. This wasn't some stepped-on street smack in her veins. It was very pure. There was enough left in the needle to test. It was the purest I've ever seen. Uncut."

"So it was murder. Whoever gave it to her knew it would kill."

"Or amateur's enthusiasm," the M.E. said. "If it was her first time, she just didn't know how much to fix."

I barely listened. I was on another track. Pure, uncut heroin. The kind a junkie, even a low-level dealer, never saw. But Clyde Malish could get it by the barrel. That wasn't enough, though.

Three investigators could find no link between Mandy Jackson and Clyde Malish. He had created the route to her and then destroyed it. There was no trace. Her late husband was the obvious connection, but no one had made that source yield anything. It was too old a trail.

Three or four days after her death I was walking through the reception area, hand lifted for the buzzing door, in my usual fog, hardly noticing the old man leaning in the half window to talk to the receptionist. Even his saying my name barely registered. But then he said the magic words: her name. Amanda, he said.

I was already inside, safe. I stopped behind the receptionist and listened to him. She glanced up at me and her eyes dismissed him. Part of her job was protecting me.

The old man was black, too. And when I looked at him I saw he wasn't so old. He was of Mandy Jackson's tribe, bowed by a life of hard work. Heavy veins in his forearms ran down to hands turning slightly clawlike, fingers melding together. He was mostly bald, had a strong jaw and a thin neck, and was somewhere between fifty and a thousand. His manner was not belligerent. He was entreating the receptionist to see me, obviously not recognizing me. After a minute I pushed the door back open and told him to come in.

"I won't take much of his time," he said as we started down the hall. I told him who I was. He was taken aback. He didn't stop walking and stand back from me, but he fell silent and gave me sidelong glances. When I closed the door of my office behind him he looked decidedly uneasy. "You knew Mandy Jackson," I prompted him.

"I always called her Amanda," he said apologetically. "Such a pretty name, it seemed a shame not to use it."

"You're a relative," I realized.

"She was my niece. Gregory Stillwell's my name. I— We been talkin' and I finally thought I's the one best come. Nobody sent me. Her mama—her mama just can't see no way— Some of the others . . . Look here. We know what happened with Amanda and your boy and all, but now she's dead and it seems like nobody's doing nothin'. And we thought maybe you—"

"Maybe I told people not to bother about her?"

He looked extremely uncomfortable. I understood how much courage it had taken for him to come here. "Police say they investigating," he went on, looking down, "but we figure it's not at the top of their list, you know? The girl that sent the D.A.'s boy to prison, maybe they figure—"

It was cruel to let him go on. "Mandy didn't send my son to prison," I said. "I know who was behind that. And I know the way she died—"

Mention of her death stiffened his back. He raised his eyes to mine for the first time. "Amanda didn't shoot herself up with that heroin. She hated drugs. After that fool husband of hers got himself killed the way he did, she hated them more. She was so scared her kids would get started. She would never, never in a million years—"

"I believe you. She didn't do that to herself."

When he closed his eyes a tear leaked out from under one eyelid. "I wish you had known Amanda. We so afraid you think she got what was comin' to her. But Amanda, she was something special. Her daddy shined shoes for a livin'. Sixty years old, still shinin' shoes, sayin' Thank you sir, for a quarter. Me, I digs ditches. I've taken enough dirt out of holes to bury this city. The whole family that way, work but never get nowhere. But Amanda—she was the fust person in the family to finish high school. Then college. It took her years but she made it. She was finally on the edge of makin' somethin' of herself. She wouldn't give that up for no heroin.

"Seems like this family never could get ahead. In a hundred years, since slave days, nobody ever got two steps ahead of bein' a slave, until Amanda. And now it's like somebody said, 'No, you come too far. I'm gonna knock this one down to nothin'.' Fust the . . . the rape, then she's dead in a ditch and nobody's gonna do nothin' about it 'cause of what she had to testify about your boy. But she never—"

I was sitting beside him in front of my desk. Both of us were bowed as if at a prayer meeting. I could speak very softly and he still heard. "Mandy lied when she testified against my son," I said.

He looked up at me so sharply, I thought one of those clawlike hands would clench and smash into my face. "She never—" he began.

"She did. But only because someone made her. She couldn't help herself."

Gregory Stillwell was staring at me. He had forgotten deference. He stared as if the truth were buried deep in my eyes and he could pry it out with his own. I told him about the dapper little man who had accosted me under the bridge, about the case I'd dismissed. I told him how desperately I'd needed to talk to Mandy, which was why she was killed.

"Who?" he said. He seemed to have accepted my story. I had told him everything but the name of the man whose case I'd dismissed.

"If I tell you, you have to promise not to do anything about it. I need your help to get him. If you go after him yourself, you won't get him, he's too well protected. And you might ruin my chance of getting him."

He didn't give the promise lightly. He stared at me awhile longer, then across the room. "It didn't have nothin' to do with Amanda," he muttered. "She just happen to be there, and once he got what he wanted he threw her away like a paper doll. And did it so's she look like a lowdown junkie, what she hated most in the world."

"Maybe it would be too hard for you to know and do nothing. Maybe I shouldn't tell you the name."

He looked at me. In his eyes years had fallen away. "I already know the hard part," he said. "Name don't make it worse. But what you gonna do to him?"

"My son is still in jail. In order to free him, I have to prove what this man did. I have the best incentive in the world."

He nodded. "And you'll prove he killed Amanda just because it's part of that."

I shrugged. I didn't try to bullshit him.

"This man as bad as you say, he wouldn't stop at killin' some poor black gal. And he's got to know you come after him." He was appraising me. "Maybe you bettah tell me the name, case you miss your shot."

You couldn't fault his logic. But, "Promise," I said.

"I promise."

"His name is Clyde Malish. I need your family to find out something nobody else has been able to."

"How this Clyde Malish got to Amanda."

"Yes."

"I can tell you that right now. Her kids. Nothin' else could make Amanda lie. She wasn't afraid of nothin' else. Only thing scared her was that her kids might turn out like their daddy. And her boy Paulie was gettin' to the age for her to worry 'bout who he ran with."

"I figured her children. But maybe you can find out who approached her."

He nodded. "I'll do what I can. It'll be good to have somethin' to do for Amanda. And if your way don't work—"

We stood up. I said, "I knew what kind of person Mandy was before you came. My investigator already checked her out from grade school on and didn't find one bad thing to say about her. I would try to bring Clyde Malish to justice for what he did to her even if it didn't involve my son."

He looked at me long enough to lend force to what he finally said. "I believe you. Just the same, it don't hurt that you have to do it for your boy's sake." At the doorway he shook hands. There was strength in that claw of his, but he didn't make the handshake into a contest. "I'm glad I came," he said, and was gone.

I found some of my own tension relieved. I had handed off part of the responsibility. If justice weren't done—and it was too late for justice—retribution would be exacted.

But that didn't solve my problem: how to prove what had happened. I had no clues. As the days passed, every thread I had ran down to nothing. September came, seemingly without Labor Day. I had no holidays, no workdays. I sat at my desk and shriveled. I stopped going to see David. I couldn't, not without some hope to offer him; and I had none.

CHAPTER

12

I returned to my study of the thickest file in the file center: the one on Clyde Malish. Our Special Crimes section had it because of the complexity of the case, or cases. They had subpoenaed bank records, taken statements from witnesses, secured copies of deeds and contracts. It was a great mass of paper and it mostly said nothing. You could put together the same kind of file on any successful businessman, or unsuccessful one for that matter. I had about given up on it, but when no other investigation produced a lead I burrowed back into the paperwork.

The bank records showed him with a large monthly income but not a huge one—not, that is, the income he actually had. Notes in the file indicated the obvious, that much of his revenues were hidden. For example, many of the men always at Malish's house passed themselves off as friends of his with outside jobs of their own. In fact, we theorized, Malish paid them well in cash.

On a hunch I looked through the file to see if we had a record of what Malish paid his lawyer, Myron Stahl. How much a man pays for legal work is usually an indication of how much he's doing crooked. We did have the figure: Malish had claimed it as a business expense. The year before he had paid Stahl fifty-five thousand dollars. That was on paper. I assumed it was at least double that under the table. Fifty-five thousand was about what new associates were paid in the largest law firms. My first-chair prosecutors made almost that much.

There were properties Malish had bought dirt cheap that now appeared to be producing healthy incomes. Contracts gave him percentages of distributions. And he wasn't going to go down the way Al Capone went down: he paid taxes on all of it.

I grew bemused among the figures. The numbers had a dreadful symmetry of their own that excluded human considerations. It looked reasonable that a man would protect this structure. How didn't matter. The numbers were clean of crime, of pain. In these equations David's imprisonment, Mandy Jackson's death, appeared only as arrows on a flow chart. I could see how a man could look only at the figures and give the orders that would produce those results.

But there were still things that didn't make sense. Linda was the first to point them out. "Why did he come after you?" she asked. "Why not Frank or Marilyn? They must be just as vulnerable somehow. Why blackmail the district attorney himself?"

"I had announced I was going to prosecute him myself."

"But you hadn't even started looking at the case yet. Frank could have convinced you to dismiss it the same way you convinced him. So why you?"

The file was spread out all over my desk. I indicated it as if it were Clyde Malish himself laid out there, smiling up at me.

"This is a guy who doesn't care about consequences. He goes after what he wants the surest way possible and thinks he'll fade the heat from it later. Think how he did this. He could have approached me as soon as David was arrested to say the witness would drop the charges if I cooperated. But no, he let it go to trial, he let David go to prison. This bastard doesn't care who—"

"Maybe if he'd given you that much warning you could have found the connection between him and Mandy Jackson before the case came to trial. He'd lose his hammer."

"I couldn't then. I can't now."

Linda shrugged. In a lengthening silence she looked at the file and I looked at her. Her cheekbones were more prominent than ever. The meals we'd had together lately she had only toyed with. She looked up, took two stabs at starting a sentence, then shook her head and gave up. She looked like a woman torn. I thought I knew why. She wanted to help me through this morass and at the same time she wanted to pull me back out of it, make things as they'd been. Linda knew that wasn't possible. It was beginning to look as if the case would never end. We would always have that wedge between us: my son, the lost cause.

And if she tried to comfort me, it would look as if she was trying to come between me and my family, when they needed me more than they ever had. Linda used to ask me about Lois occasionally and obligatorily and about Dinah with real interest. The casual mentions of my family showed her lack of jealousy of them. But in the last few weeks Linda had stopped mentioning them. The tension in that part of my life was obvious to her. But she wouldn't play the other woman, using this crisis to pull me away. She had seen me holding Lois, she knew crises sometimes draw a family together. Once that wouldn't have mattered. Linda and I used to occupy a separate compartment of my life. I had made clear she wasn't disrupting whatever I had at home to disrupt. Now my life had no compartments. It had been torn open from end to end. My loyalties and losses were spilled out for everyone to see.

One night I just didn't go home. I called Lois but didn't have to give her much of an excuse. It seemed so natural just to leave the office early in the evening, drive Linda to a grocery store, and then to her house. I hadn't been to the house in a couple of years, but I relaxed into it easily. When I opened the closet there was a hanger for my suit. An old pair of my jeans in the bottom of a drawer.

Linda set the table and poured wine while I cooked. She had lived alone so long she seldom cooked a whole meal. I did it often. I was the family man. The sparsity of her utensils scattered in a drawer made me sad. At the table I said, "Why did you never marry, Linda?"

"Never? Am I dead?" I kept looking at her as if she hadn't spoken, and after a moment her mouth twitched with wry humor and she said, "Who would I marry? A lawyer?"

"A criminal maybe."

"That is the same choice. You know the people I know. Who would I marry? You were lucky to meet someone before law school, Mark, and stay with her. Now, what would I bring to a marriage? An obsession with my work? Or a burned-out exhaustion so my husband could fill my emptiness?"

"You're not old, Linda. What are we, football players, thirty-five you retire and start selling insurance?"

"Maybe so." But after she said it she smiled and looked like a kid in the candlelight. "What is this?" she asked of her vegetable.

"Cauliflower. Very disguised."

"Cauliflower. You white people think the strangest things are food."

Later, after I'd taken the plates away, she frowned into her wineglass and said, "I've been thinking about Clyde Malish again. Some things still don't make sense. He is a businessman, whatever else. He should behave—"

I shook my head at her and refilled her glass. "This is not a business dinner."

"It's not?" She smiled again. "What is it?"

I didn't answer because I didn't know how. We clinked glasses and gazed out the window at a back yard as unfamiliar to her as it was to me, I felt sure.

After dinner it began to feel strange. To relax into the couch instead of beginning to think of the right time and remark to make my exit. It had been years since Linda and I had had a whole night together. Those had been out of town, on business. Now having the whole evening stretch before us made us slow and sleepy. We sipped more wine, we talked about our pasts, mutual and separate. I asked her no more important questions.

I don't know what time it was when I put on a record and remained standing by the stereo until Linda joined me, smiling at my silliness. We danced. For a long time it was just dancing. We had stepped out of our shoes. After long minutes we began slowly to undress each other. Clothes fell away easily until we were dancing nude. Even then for the longest time we just held each other, just swaying, no longer moving our feet. We were holding hands. Her cheek rested against my shoulder. I felt strangely youthful. It wasn't like a date, even less like an affair. It was like the beginning of a young married life, still a little strange but backed by a long commitment.

The next time I saw Lois it was immediately obvious she was ready for a confrontation. In the moment before she spoke I tried to set a limit on myself, on how much I would say, but she took me by surprise.

"I'm on my way to see David," she said. "What do I tell him when he asks?"

"Tell him—tell him I'm still working, I've talked to Mandy Jackson's family, I have three investigators—"

She was shaking her head. "What should I tell him about why you haven't been to see him?"

"I have been to see him. I don't tell you every—"

"Not in a week you haven't. *He* tells me. Have you been too busy?"

A peculiar emphasis on the last word made me think the conversation was going to veer aside. I spoke slowly, keeping to the subject. "Frankly, Lois, there is very little happening in

David's case. I am nearing the end of several leads without producing anything. I'm starting to think it would be best just to have the motion for a new trial now. My testimony would be some evidence, after all. I'm hoping there might be a public outcry that would convince Watlin the right thing to do politically would be to grant the motion. What I'm starting to think about now is how to handle the press coverage rather than the hearing itself. I think I can make David a sympathetic enough figure that . . ." I ran down. She was nodding her head in a way that meant she was no longer paying attention. Lois looked all business today, in a suit and heels. Her face was set in an expression nothing I could say would change. I tried to appease her anyway. "I'll go see him this afternoon," I said.

"It's probably best you don't."

That threw me completely off guard. She went on. "When you don't come it makes him worry, but seeing you probably depresses him more. At least he knows I believe in him. He can talk freely to me."

"What do you mean, believe in him? I believe in him, too. Christ, I *know* he's innocent. It was me the little man waved the gun at, remember?"

"Yes." I couldn't say she was glaring at me; there was too much disappointment in her steady gaze for that. But her eyes affixed me in place. "But until that happened you *weren't* sure," she said. "It took evidence to convince you. For me it only took faith."

I felt suddenly weary. "I'm sorry. I did have doubts. If it hadn't been David telling the story, I wouldn't have believed it for a second. Even knowing David it was hard. How do you have no doubts, Lois? Tell me. How do you banish them once you do have them? Tell me how to do that. Please, I want to know."

"You can't," she said. "You should never have had them to begin with."

"Well, it's too late to change that."

"But even that doesn't matter. It's that you didn't *do*

anything, after you promised. Remember, Mark? When you came to me, after the man under the bridge held the gun on you and told you what had happened, your eyes were shining. You were happy. You expected me to be happy, too. You said, of course there are things to do now. Remember? Don't you understand what that told me, Mark? It told me there was more you could have done for David already, if you'd believed him."

"No. That is absolutely not true. I did everything I could."

"Did you? Everything you told me you'd do? Lie, cheat, invent evidence? You could have told this same story about the man with the gun whether it happened or not." I rolled my eyes. "No," Lois said. "It never would have occurred to you. But if you'd been sure your son was innocent, you would have done *anything*. I would have done anything. But I didn't have your power."

I laughed at that. "Power. If you only realized—"

She leaned toward me. "If *I* had been district attorney for one day, the case would never have gone to trial."

I just shook my head. There's no way to convince someone who is arguing from ignorance.

Lois saw it was hopeless, too. "I shouldn't even have started this," she said. "I just meant to make you see that you *have* to do something now. You have to. Before the sun goes down. Before he has another bologna sandwich in jail. Mark. You know now."

She was crying. Not demonstratively, not with sobs. The two tears coursing down her face were as sober as her suit. If I hadn't known it would repulse her, I would have stood and put my arms around her. But that moment was long past. I did my best to comfort her from five feet away. "I am, Lois. I'm that close to having everything I need. I'm almost there. Believe me, I am."

Believe me, I wasn't. But I didn't need Lois to goad me into action. Maybe it was the feeling of youthfulness I'd been infused with from my evening with Linda. I remembered that

I did have power. I was not some hapless victim off the streets. Malish had made a mistake in coming at me. I'd make him know it.

He came to the phone when I called. That was a victory in itself. How many people could have pulled him through his intermediaries to talk directly? "This is Malish," he growled.

For a moment I doubted it. Not just that he would speak to me himself. I doubted that the evil cloud I'd felt surrounding me for months could really condense into one man, one palpable human being at the end of a phone line, sweating and impatient.

"This is Mark Blackwell. I'd like to see you."

"What about?"

He had gall. If he could have made me madder than I already was, that reply would have done it. "Let's say about Mandy Jackson."

"Who?"

"This is not the way to go about it, Malish. I'm giving you a chance to work your way out of this. Will you come?"

He hesitated. "Where?"

"My office. It'll be private enough."

In the long pause that followed I could hear him breathing. I wondered if his thinking was as labored. Then, "Lemme call you back," he said abruptly, and hung up.

I stared at the phone in my hand. He couldn't really be as dumb as he'd sounded. Not the man whose life was spread out on my desk. There was something I should do quickly, I thought. Dispatch someone to his house to make sure he didn't run? Or did I want him to run? More proof . . .

I had people outside his place half an hour later and was waiting for a call from them when instead I got a call from Clyde Malish. He hadn't left his house. He had no intention of leaving his house.

"I talked to my lawyer," he grunted. "He tells me what I don't have to do so now I'm telling you: you can stuff your request. I don't do this voluntarily coming in bit. You got enough on me to get a warrant, you get one. I don't know nothing about what you're askin' about and I don't see why I should help you fish for something. So good day to you."

"This is stupid. You don't really want—"

"That's me, I'm a stupid guy. That's why I pay people to tell me what to do. Adios."

And I was holding a dead phone again. I almost wanted to laugh. I'd been seething before. I was dumbfounded now.

I took his advice. I got a warrant. I didn't have nearly enough for one, but I knew what to put in an affidavit and I knew judges. Within an hour I had an arrest warrant.

My investigators didn't jostle each other aside in their haste to volunteer to serve it. I had really thought they would, those cowboys. The two or three who were eager I rejected, and gave the assignment to three of the more thoughtful, including Jack Pfister, who had the misfortune of having enough imagination to envision where he was going.

"Don't shoot anybody and don't handcuff him and drag him downstairs on his face. Just act like you're inviting him to tea, but you've got this to back you up if you need it."

"Right," Jack said. He was still looking at the warrant with pursed lips. I added:

"Have a police car sitting out at the front gate while y'all go in."

"Oh, that won't be necessary," Jack said, but he looked more cheerful when I insisted.

"Come on, Jack, he's just a damned dope dealer," one of the others said. Jack gave me a look indicating his opinion of the quality of his backups and off they went, Sargeant Fury and his Sober Commandos. If things went wrong at Malish's, I'd be chief mourner at the funerals. I wondered if I was abusing my newly rediscovered power. After the two seconds' consideration I gave to that, I went on to other matters.

There was no trouble. When the intercom buzzed, Patty said, "Jack and Mr. Malish are here," just as if it were the next in a series of appointments. I waited at the desk as they came in. Malish wasn't handcuffed and Jack wasn't laying hands on him. He stayed a respectful step or two behind. He could have been my butler.

I just stared. Clyde Malish looked amused. "Well, I told you to do it," he said.

Jack said, "He's okay," meaning unarmed. I nodded, moved my eyebrows fractionally toward the door, and Jack withdrew. Malish stayed on his feet. The speeches I'd prepared depended more on reaction than initiation. I just sat. Finally he said, not hostilely:

"Suppose you just tell me what this is all about and I'll see what I can do to help you."

"I already told you exactly what you have to do. Give me the fuel to burn down the house you built." Obviously metaphor was not his game. I specified. "You have to produce some evidence that Mandy Jackson lied. A witness, a statement. Somebody who says he overheard her planning it. You can get somebody. We know people'll lie for you. It won't take much to get my son a new trial. You don't have to implicate yourself. I'll deal with you later."

He plucked one word out of what I'd said. "Your son. Oh. Now I get it." He noticed the chair next to him and sat down in it. He looked around the office. "Am I in custody?" he asked with more curiosity than querulousness. "Can I get something to drink? I'd just got out of the pool when your boys came."

"What do you want?" I was thinking of the bar the investigators didn't know I knew they had in the office. "Diet Coke?" Malish said. "Tab, something like that?"

I ordered him a Diet Coke. Patty asked if I wanted anything. It was too open-ended a question. When his drink came Malish downed half of it. You'd expect him to drink like that. "What's the hold-up been?" I asked. "I thought I made myself real clear."

"Hey, I just got here," Malish said. He made a pacifying motion with his hand. He looked deep in thought. "Why d'you come to me for something like this? I mean, I'm not sayin' I won't help, but this is something you could do yourself."

I couldn't think of an answer. I felt as if I'd walked into someone else's conversation; there was a missing connection. I wondered if Malish thought this office was bugged.

"Now I see what we're talkin' about, I can sympathize. Listen, I've got a boy of my own. He's out in California, bein' a beach bum. Says he's gonna be a movie producer, but beach bum is what he looks like. I know how you feel when your kids get in trouble. You're mad at 'em but you'd do anything to help 'em out. I understand."

Of course he understood. He'd counted on it, not just with me but with Mandy Jackson. I said, "Just like when you're in trouble yourself and you'd do anything to get out of it. Right?"

"You mean that case of mine?" he said, and waved it away. "That was nothin'. You guys never had a case. No offense. I was surprised it went as far as it did."

"Stop it!" He'd driven me to my feet. "You son of a bitch. Don't tell me how trivial it was. Don't tell me you were just taking precautions. After what you did—"

He rose to meet me. I reached for him, but it wasn't like grabbing Myron Stahl's lapels and seeing the satisfying look of fear on his face. Malish stood his ground and knocked my hands away, so I almost fell into him. He was ten years older than I am but maybe an inch taller, and not as soft as his crumpled flowered sports shirt made him look. His face turned to granite. He looked like what he was, a man who'd built a criminal empire out of nothing because he wouldn't let anything stop him.

He held me off long enough to remind me that knocking him down wouldn't accomplish anything even if I could do it. I ended up standing toe to toe with him, trying to look menacing.

"You fixed up this scheme, Malish. You can unfix it."

"Fuck you. I ain't fetchin' and totin' for you. This shit is worth about as much as that lousy warrant of yours. How stupid you think I am? If I—"

When the door opened he turned toward it, so I couldn't see his expression, but I saw Linda's as she saw him. She was startled. When she looked back and forth between us she looked scared.

"What the hell is this?" Malish growled before she could think of something to say. He pulled away from me. "You blow the case so you dream up this stupid plan to get me to tamper with evidence? This is on a par with settin' fire to a bag of dogshit on my doorstep and expectin' me to step in it. Learn to take your lumps, sonny. You lost. And there's nothin' you can do about it."

"You're wrong about that. You're dead wrong."

"Yeah? Well, let's just see. You do your worst, ace. And the next time you wanna see me, don't bother with some trick warrant. Just come knock on my door. I'll see you get all the way in."

He stalked away, bumping off a chair. Linda got out of his way. I started after him. I don't know what I was going to do. Hurl one more playground threat, maybe. I had so little momentum, Linda stopped me with one hand on my arm.

"Mark?"

I heard the door of the outer office slam. Let him go. I felt as if his spittle were dripping off my face.

"What was he doing here, Mark? Mark? That man is dangerous. What are you trying to goad him into?"

That was a good question.

What did you expect him to do, confess? I asked myself. It had been a stupid idea, dragging Malish in. I'd made sure he was unarmed, but I had been without ammunition myself. I returned to my study of his file. It led me to other cases, supposed associates of his, some of them junkies long since sentenced and, no doubt, released. I picked up an itch somewhere in that mass of paperwork, as if an old flea had awakened from hibernation and lighted on my skin.

Myron Stahl returned to my thoughts. If I couldn't cow Malish, I could Stahl, but would it do me any good? It might. Stahl had represented Clyde Malish for years. If he was any kind of lawyer, he would have something on his client. Of course, that street ran both directions. Malish was more than just a client to Myron Stahl. Malish paid for everything from Stahl's nice little Victorian suite of offices to his shoeshine. A man could get addicted to that flow of cash, until it amounted to something more than representing a client. After this long their relationship would be more like a partnership, or a marriage.

I didn't have the plot pieced together, but I did realize something else, alone in my office one night musing about attorney-client relationships. I was thinking of the ways we serve our clients. Henry and me for David, Nora and Linda for Mandy Jackson, Myron Stahl for Malish. Thinking about the lengths to which we'd go. When I realized I'd been neglecting one of the players, the one I should never have forgotten, because he'd pointed a gun at me. When I thought about his part in the scheme he suddenly fell into place in the legion.

Of course, I thought. The dapper little man was a lawyer.

CHAPTER

13

It was in his manner of speech and half a dozen specific phrases he'd used. "I represent a client." "Jeopardy considerations are suggested." That was a lawyer talking. I had noted it without realizing it, because I was used to hearing people talk that way. That's why lawyers end up talking like each other; it's all we ever hear.

There was also one thing the dapper little man had stopped himself from saying. The sentence he'd begun in mild exasperation as he'd pulled the gun. "You—" was all he'd said. I'd thought he was going to say something about me, but it made sense that he was going to say something more general. That's why he'd stopped, because the contrast would have been a clue to his own identity. "You" what? Criminal lawyers? Texans?

Close on the heels of my revelation into my accoster's profession came a hunch, suggested by that profession, his age, and the frames that had been rearranged on Myron Stahl's office wall.

I didn't remember the date, but I remembered the school. I

made the phone calls myself. A day later—I'd insisted they use express mail, C.O.D.—I had the photo spread on my desk. Using the magnifying glass made me feel like a fake Sherlock Holmes, but it was necessary. The faces of the men in the picture—they were men only then—were not very distinct, and I was looking for two who had aged nearly thirty years since the photo. The school had been kind enough to send along a key to the picture, so I found Myron Stahl without having to search. He looked impossibly young, hair so full he could hardly comb it flat, a smile so engaging it peeked through his solemn mask. He hadn't used up a day of the future yet. I stared at young Myron a long time before moving on with the magnifying glass.

On the row in front of him was the dapper little man. He looked neither dapper nor little there in the middle rank of his law school class, but he had the little mustache even then, in the unadorned Eisenhower era. I found his name in the key. Simon Hawthorne. A name destined for dapperness. Him, too, I stared at for a long time before calling Jack Pfister into my office and handing the picture over to him.

Myron Stahl was the kind of man who would have a picture of his law school graduating class on his office wall. It had hung there, no doubt, until he'd hired one of those classmates to do a job for him Stahl wouldn't want traced back to him or his employer. Why not just use a local thug, one of Malish's cohorts, to threaten me into dismissing the case? Because there was the chance I'd recognize one of them, or find his face in a mug book. Maybe Stahl even liked the idea of having a lawyer explain the legalities to me.

And his old classmate Simon Hawthorne could use the work. Jack put together a file on Hawthorne easily and quickly. The attorney general's office in Virginia had known his name. They'd helped have him disbarred back in the early seventies. Income tax fraud had been his major indiscretion, though they suspected others. He'd avoided prison, but stripped of his livelihood he'd had a hard time of it the last decade. I remembered his frayed cuffs. The dapper little man would have been glad for the job from his old schoolmate.

"Is this enough? Is it? It's so hard to read the mind of a man who's trying to guess what everyone else thinks."

Linda just sat there, staring past me, thinking as furiously as I was.

"I mean, this is it, the link to Clyde Malish we needed. Will that be enough for Watlin? It will be if he thinks everyone in the county thinks he should grant the new trial. If we make the scheme look evil enough and obvious enough. What do you think?"

"I'm not sure," Linda said slowly. "Maybe if you talked to him, made him think he was the first one finding out about the big conspiracy. . . ."

"There's no point in talking to him again. He's made very clear what he wants, hard enough proof to cover his ass. The next time I see Judge Waddle, it's going to be with the bench between us."

She was nodding. "Maybe I . . ." she began, but trailed off. I was watching her. Linda still hadn't looked at me, not directly, since I'd told her I'd found out who the dapper little man was. She looked distracted, uneasy. It appeared the news had sent her mind in too many directions for her to be aware of her surroundings. I bounced another idea off her.

"Maybe I should go to the press first. It's a good story. If it's already the talk of the town before—"

"No," Linda said, and she was right. "If you use it that way and it doesn't work, you'll have lost the advantage of knowing without anyone knowing you know. Don't turn to the press until you're sure there's no other way. If you decide later the information is best used privately, it would be too late."

She looked at me until I nodded. "But that brings us back to the original question. How do we use it?"

We kicked the question around until it was thoroughly abused but had yielded no answers. Before Linda left she took

my hands and said, "Mark, don't do anything without talking
to me first. Promise."

"Don't you trust my judgment?"

She opened her mouth in what I knew was denial but
changed course before she even spoke. "In this, no. You
shouldn't trust it either. If it were me, you know you would
tell me the same."

"All right. I won't go off half cocked."

She put her arms around me briefly, as if bidding me a hasty
good-bye. As if she knew what my promise was worth. It
would take only one more nudge to send me over the edge,
and that was waiting for me at home.

"I'm home," I called. There was no answer. I hadn't
expected any, except maybe Dinah running to me. Then
Lois's voice came, raised for distance. "We're in the den,
darling."

It seemed like a long time since we'd had company at home.
I wondered who it was, and hoped they wouldn't stay long.
Maybe that's why I kept my briefcase in hand, to give the
impression I had work to do.

That thought must have taken only an instant, because
Lois's voice was continuing: ". . . just Dinah and me." She was
very good, Lois. She had just told me everything I needed to
know, but I wasn't alert enough to pick it up.

So I was worse than startled when I walked into the den and
saw the man in the ski mask. I stopped dead just a step inside
the doorway. I felt as if I'd instantly been stripped naked. My
skin felt that exposed. It tingled the length of my spine. Guns
sometimes have that effect on people. His was lying across his
lap. He picked it up when I appeared in the room.

The gunman was sitting in a chair at right angles to the
couch and three feet from it. Dinah and Lois were huddled
together in the center of the couch. There was a low coffee
table in front of them. Lois had her arm around Dinah's
shoulders. She had managed to put herself between Dinah

and the man in the ski mask. Lois looked at me with a moment's hope that died when she saw my stunned expression.

"We've been waiting for you," the gunman said almost jovially. It was a young man's voice, unconcerned, sure of himself. The kind of jolly young sociopath who kept our courtrooms crowded. "You sure do work late," he continued.

"Well, I'm here now." I walked farther into the room, which made his gun hand move to follow me. I wished I hadn't stopped so cold inside the doorway when I'd first seen him. It left me all the way across the room from Dinah and Lois. I was trying to get close enough to dive between them and the gunman, over the low coffee table. I was thinking of my briefcase as a shield. But even if I stopped his first couple of shots, what would Lois do then? She still wouldn't be able to get out of the room.

This was completely unlike my encounter with the dapper little man, when I'd been strangely confident in the face of his gun. This time I was scared to death. My hands trembled.

"What do you want from me?" I made as if to move in front of him to the sofa. He stood up.

"The first thing I want you to do is put down that briefcase." I did, bending over, setting it gently upright.

"Good. Now we can talk." He stepped in very close to me, the gun's barrel nudging my stomach. He was almost as tall as I am. Our heads were within a foot of each other. The clarity of his brown eyes and the square inch of skin around them was startling in the anonymity of the black ski mask: two holes punched into another, malevolent dimension.

I tried to back off, hoping he would follow. Instead, he grabbed my arm and held me in place, punching the gun into me more emphatically. He pulled me close as a lover and delivered his message in a throaty whisper.

"Lay off Clyde Malish. Stop looking for trouble. You dropped the case, now drop the investigation, too. Unnerstand?"

I exhaled and took a deep breath. It may have been the first time I'd breathed since I walked into the room. Suddenly I felt shaky from relief rather than from fear. He had a message for me. He had just come to scare me. There was no point in shooting any of us now. Malish would want me alive—and scared—so I could follow his dictates.

"Yes," I said. "Tell Mr. Malish—"

But he wasn't here for two-way communication. He interrupted me: "I'm takin' the kid to make sure you do."

"No!" Lois and I said together. The eyes in the flatness of the ski mask changed. He was smiling.

"Yes," he said softly. He held out his right hand, the one not holding the gun, toward the couch, over the coffee table. "Come on, girl. It won't be long. Into the car."

He was still looking at me, still pressing the gun into my stomach. His other hand hung suspended out there in space, waiting confidently for Dinah to take it. Dinah was shrunk back into the couch. Her eyes seemed to shrink back even deeper. She looked nothing like a little adult. She was a frightened child. A baby.

"Come on, come on," the gunman said, wiggling his fingers impatiently. He turned to look at Dinah. This is my chance, I thought, but before I could move, his head swiveled back to me. He grinned again. He could read my mind. "Want me to have to shoot one of your folks?" he said over his shoulder.

Dinah drew a deep breath. It made her swell out into flesh and blood from the flattened cartoon she had been. She pushed off the back of the couch.

But her mother moved much faster. Lois leaned forward and took the gunman's hand—he smiled more broadly, eyes crinkling; he thought it was Dinah—leaned forward even farther, and bit his fingers.

He screamed. I could see Lois's jaws clenched. She was straining as if she would bite his fingers off. Ski-Mask forgot me entirely. He pulled hard enough to lift Lois off the couch and he turned toward her, lifting the gun to slam it into her head. This time I did move. I drew back and punched him as hard as I could in the side of the head.

I hit bone. My knuckles might have been broken. The gunman staggered. His knees hit the edge of the coffee table and he fell onto it. "Move!" I screamed at Dinah, but she just sat there, paralyzed.

We all seemed frozen for a moment. I didn't know where the gun was or where it was pointing. The gunman rolled off the coffee table, onto the floor on my side of it. He was faceup. And he still had the gun. He pointed it straight at me. I moved to kick it out of his hand, but he didn't have nearly so great a distance to move. He fired.

I fell back. He had missed, but he leveled the gun at me again, and this time I wasn't even close enough to try to kick him. I jumped aside, the gun barrel following me, so close I could see the bullet in the cylinder as it turned.

But he had made a worse mistake than I had. He had forgotten Lois. She hardly had to move at all. Just reached under the edge of the coffee table and tipped it over. The top fell across him, cutting off his view like a closing coffin lid, and the edge hit his forearm, knocking the gun aside. He fired and missed again.

The table wasn't heavy enough to cripple him. I helped it. I stepped down hard on his gun. My heel crunched the small bones of his hand. The gunman screamed again. And then he was a gunman no longer. He yanked his hand free of my heel, but he left the gun behind. I bent to pick it up but his scrabbling hand got there first. Before he could get a good grip on it I kicked it aside, far out of his reach.

He threw the coffee table off him and bolted to his feet. He was a burly young man. I saw him thinking for an instant that he could still take on all three of us. But instead he broke for the doorway. Lois dived for his feet and missed. I swung at him as he passed me and missed almost as badly, just thumping his shoulder. But that was unexpectedly effective. It threw him off stride and his shin hit my briefcase, still standing placidly in the middle of the floor. He went down on his face and I landed on top of him. I lifted his head in both hands and slammed his forehead down on the floor. If that damned den hadn't been carpeted, I might have killed him. That was my intention. As it was, he shook off the blow and shook me off as well, just crawling out from under me. He was a very strong young man.

And fast. He staggered up and was out the doorway before I could regain my feet. I heard movement behind me as I scrambled up. For a long minute in the den the world had seemed deadly quiet, as if we were its last inhabitants. Now it was full of noise. I pounded after the man in the ski mask. Fear had turned to rage. I wanted my fingers in his throat. In my mind I still saw Dinah shrunk back into the couch, and his hand reaching for her. His grin behind the mask.

The front door slowed him down and I caught up. I punched him again, this time under the ribs. He grunted harshly but didn't fall. Completely to my surprise he threw his elbow back and caught my cheekbone. I fell back. He got the door open and slammed it against me as I slumped to the floor. By the time I got to my feet again he was halfway across the front yard. I was exhausted.

My short-lived rage couldn't touch Lois's. Suddenly she was beside me in the doorway. What had slowed her down was that she'd stopped to retrieve his pistol. She stood on the porch, both arms extended, and fired. The former gunman ducked his head and ran harder, toward the hedge that separated our yard from the neighbors'. Lois fired again. The recoil threw her hands upward and she lowered them and fired again and again and again, until the gun was empty. Her teeth were clenched and tears were streaming down her face. Her arms stayed rigid but her face was alive with fury. She hated him worse than I could ever hate. He should have fallen over dead just from the power of her emotion.

I went back inside. Dinah was just coming through the doorway from the den. She was shaking as if with a chill. I grabbed her, wrapped my arms around her thin body, and held her so close I could have pulled her inside me. "My baby," I was saying. My baby, my baby.

I don't think I had any more thoughts that night, but later I remembered that scene, holding Dinah so close, both of us crying, and I had a small revelation: This was how Lois had felt all along, about David.

CHAPTER

14

Police didn't find a trace of the guy, of course. There was a stolen car parked a couple of houses down, which meant the gunman had had to walk home. To Clyde Malish's home, I mean. We spent that night with a cop parked in front and another one parked in the den. Dinah slept between Lois and me, if any of us slept.

We didn't even bother to look at mug books. How could we identify the gunman from a pair of eyes and his height? I was convinced I'd know him if I saw those eyes in person again, but I didn't expect that to happen. Especially since he'd blown his assignment. His boss wouldn't reward failure.

It wasn't the guy in the ski mask I cared about. The next morning I was back in the office, trying to figure out how to get at Clyde Malish. It was hard to think when I was barely rational. I wanted him dead, dead and in the ground, along with all his men, no threat to my family ever again. But still I had to think of the way. I had him as a party to attempted aggravated kidnapping if nothing else. The gunman had tried to shoot me, so maybe it was attempted capital murder. But the only evidence was the gunman's whisper to "lay off Clyde Malish." Lois hadn't even heard it, though she would testify she had. But I wasn't willing to leave this to testimony. The courtroom was not where I wanted Clyde Malish. I had tried that with David.

I could have him arrested, legitimately this time. But then what? He could make any bond I could have set for him. The only witnesses to the offense he'd be charged with were Dinah, Lois, and me. Dinah and Lois wouldn't be safe even if Malish stayed in jail. Alternatively, I could have his house searched, but for what? We had the gunman's gun.

When Lois arrived I was starting to turn over the possibilities of Myron Stahl. It started with thinking of getting a warrant to search his office instead. But he wouldn't have anything incriminating there. What about the lawyer himself? He was threatenable, I remembered that. If I convinced him Malish's world was about to cave in, would Stahl do the same? Betray a client? Why not? But how to arrange it? What charge could I bring against Stahl himself?

The intercom buzzed as the office door opened. Patty blurted out, "It's your wife," and I saw that it was. Lois didn't look businesslike now. Not real estate business. She wore lightweight corduroy pants, tennis shoes, and a casual short-sleeved yellow blouse. She looked like a fashionable lady dressed to supervise others at manual labor, heavy house-cleaning, for example.

"Where's your escort?" I asked.

"I sent him on his way. I didn't want him following me all day today."

"What about Dinah?"

"She's safe. Reluctantly, she agreed not to go to school." Lois smiled ever so slightly, the only way I'd seen her smile in recent years. She had her perpetual air of restraint. Lois hadn't gone dead with the years. All that emotion she hid from me was spent somewhere, I was sure. After seeing her fury at the gunman, I knew it was still alive.

She closed the office door behind her. And said, "When—if —you come home tonight, Dinah and I won't be there."

"Maybe that's a good idea, until all this blows over. You'll be better off—"

"Don't try not to understand, Mark. We'll never be there. Not while you have a key. I'm leaving you, and I'm taking Dinah."

She was prepared to deliver a speech, and I said something, anything, that let her continue.

"I haven't been unhappy, even the last couple of years," she said. "We could have gone on like this forever. I thought at least you provided for us and kept us all safe. Last night I saw that isn't even true."

"Last night is something that is not ever going to happen again," I said levelly.

"How can I be sure of that? Where's David, Mark? Is it all over yet?

"What if last night had been another of those nights you decided not to come home at all, eh, Mark? I sat there in that den with that hulking boy with his gun listening to the minutes pass and wondering if I even wanted you to walk in the door. But wondering, too, what he was going to start doing if another minute passed without you appearing. Wondering if Dinah could get out of the room if I stayed between him and her when he started shooting. There's no reason I should ever have to worry about something like that again, Mark. It had nothing to do with me or Dinah. Why should—"

"Lois, you can't leave over something like this. Do you really believe that will ever happen again? This is an extraordinary business, not even a once in a lifetime—"

"We've had our lifetime, Mark. You know it's not just this. This is just what finally got me on my feet and moving. Something much smaller than this could have overcome my inertia."

"Lois, if you'll just wait a few—"

"We've waited too long already, Mark. Maybe if I'd said

something the first time you stayed late at the office, or the first time you'd missed a family occasion because you had work instead—I'm not here to assign blame. I found other interests, too. It's not surprising people who married at twenty don't have much in common at forty-five. I thought Dinah and the home were enough, but they're not, Mark. We're not so old we have to settle into this accommodation for the sake of ease or appearances. . . ."

She went on for another minute or so. She wasn't convincing me, she wasn't convincing herself. We'd been convinced long ago. I thought we'd reached an accord, but we had only put off acting.

While she talked I felt a flare of longing for her, an urge to hold her and tell her we could go back, we could start over. Scenes flitted past. It wasn't just Lois I was losing, it was myself. She was the girlfriend of my youth, the wife of my adulthood. If Lois left, I would feel old all at once. But holding her one way or another would be a sham. We'd cry and cling and have a good dinner and make love and by next week we'd once again be sitting in that silent den, turned away from each other, thinking of different worlds.

Every time you make a choice you divide the world in half, then half again with the next choice, and again, and again, until it narrows down to nothing. Comes time for the big decision and you find it's already made for you. The first time I'd chosen work over home it hadn't seemed an important decision, but there are precedents in life as well as in the law. By the time Lois finished talking I had resigned myself to her leaving. But that left the much harder question. I had to make it clear before she walked out. "I won't let you take Dinah from me," I said.

That snapped her restraint. She kept her voice low, but her eyes burst into venomous life. She walked toward me, pointing a finger low from her hip, like a gun. "Don't even think of fighting me on that," she snapped.

I said a word or two, but she rolled over me. "So you're going to be her parent now? When have you ever been there for her? Where were you last night? Who stays home with her when she's sick? When was the last time you took a day off work, or even came home early, because of Dinah? I didn't think you'd have the gall—"

She closed her eyes. When she spoke again her voice was lower, but it wasn't for me. "I promised myself I wouldn't be melodramatic," she said.

Her eyes opened. "They need someone who believes in them, Mark. When the crisis comes in Dinah's life, will you even believe what she tells you? Or will you cross-examine her to try to get at the truth? You know David so little you didn't even—"

"How long are you going to keep throwing that up at me? I can't help that I didn't have your faith in David. Belief is something you either have or you don't. You can't grow it. Listen. If you'd had the career I've had, if you'd heard all the denials, seen the implausible things people do in a moment of, of . . ."

Lois was shaking her head. She would have let me finish, but I suddenly had nothing more to say. I was thinking of Dinah. Of picking her up after school, her face when she saw me at a distance. Would she ever again have the same unalloyed delight in seeing me?

When I didn't speak for several seconds Lois said, "I don't believe what you do turns everyone cynical, Mark. It hasn't Linda." It was strange to hear Lois invoke Linda's name, as if they were both arrayed against me. She went on. "Sometime you made the decision to be the kind of man your career made you."

My baby. It was the doom of my training to see both sides of every issue. Last night I'd been suffused with love of Dinah, consumed by it. But even so Lois was right. I didn't know what Dinah had for a snack when she came home from school, or

even if she had one. I didn't know when she did her homework. My moments of epiphany couldn't stand up beside
Lois's quotidian devotion. Not in a divorce court and not in
the truer justice of everyday life.

"All right. You keep her for now. And stay away from the
house for the next day or two. I won't be there either. When
this is all over, if you still feel the same way, we'll talk."

"I want this settled today. Don't fight me, Mark. She's the
only person I have in the world. I think David is lost to both of
us."

That was the saddest moment in my office, the realization
that I'd conceded and Lois didn't even recognize it. That was
how far apart we'd grown. She couldn't see into my mind any
more. I had to say it plainly: "I won't fight you."

She drew back her head to stare hard at me, wondering
what new tack I was taking. After a moment she nodded.
Maybe there was enough left for her to read defeat in me, if
not sincerity. But resolving the main issue made her think of
something else.

"What do you mean, a day or two? What's going to happen
that soon?"

"I don't know yet. But I'm sure you'll hear about it when it
happens."

"Mark—"

We were standing five feet apart. She didn't know what to
say, or realized there was no point. I nodded at her. When she
did move Lois didn't hesitate, didn't take a step toward me
before turning. As fast as she'd entered she was gone.

The room felt very empty. It encompassed that empty
house, all those quiet rooms with furniture standing as empty
as the house itself. I thought of someone prowling through it,
looking for a clue to when we would return, finding a good
hiding place to wait. The joke on him.

We could have gone along comfortably, Lois and I, at least
until Dinah was grown, maybe forever. There must be lots of

marriages like ours that do just that, flow placidly along, undisrupted by the extraordinary events that had overtaken us. But one man had intervened in our lives and wiped them out. I stopped thinking about the subtleties, the legalities. Now I was just waiting for darkness.

I still had the gunman's gun. Somehow we hadn't mentioned to the police that he'd left it behind. I hadn't wanted an inquiry into Lois's firing after him. Maybe I'd had something else in mind all along, too, because on the way to work this morning I'd bought more bullets for the gun.

I went relatively undisturbed during the day. You'd think more people would have wanted to question me about the events at my house the night before, but hardly anyone did. Patty must have overheard some of Lois's scene. Maybe she steered people away from me. It wasn't necessary; I could have handled them. My facade was intact. I was no longer home.

For dinner I had the leftover half of the sandwich I'd had sent up for lunch. I fancied I could feel the hum of the building downshifting as people left and lights were turned off. At five there'd been such an outsurge you *could* hear it, people laughing as they left. It was long past five before I stirred from the desk. Something kept scratching at my mind and I finally realized it was the idea I should call home to tell them I'd be late. Even after I realized what the itch was, it persisted.

I had just finished my preparations when Linda came in. I knew she was still around. She saw the gun on the desk. She saw that I had changed into jeans and tennis shoes and a light jacket. Her hand stayed on the doorknob.

"Is it windy out?" I asked.

"You were supposed to tell me before you did anything," Linda said.

"I haven't done anything."

The jacket had an inside pocket low on the left side. I stuck the gun into it barrel-first. The length of the barrel made it awkward, but I'd pinned an extra strip of cloth above the pocket to support the handle. The jacket hung funny, but when I zipped it it didn't look bad.

"Who are you, James Bond?" Linda said. She failed at the light tone. "You need police, Mark, not this."

"It's gone way beyond police, Linda. He held a gun to my daughter's head. What would you do?"

She kept staring at me. I turned away to study the look of the jacket in the mirror inside my closet door. "I'm coming with you," Linda said.

"No."

"Yes. Or I'll call the police and have them stop you."

"No you wouldn't. You wouldn't stop me from this."

"Think. Would I? When is the last time you knew me threaten to do something I would not really do?"

I tried to think for a moment how to stop her, but my mind wouldn't turn that way. I was too hellbent in one direction.

"Put your suit back on," Linda said. I looked at her quizzically. She continued impatiently. "Going over the fence in your sneakers with black paint on your face is not the way. If you want to reach him, you must look official. Come, Mark, use your best weapons."

Her way made as much sense as mine, maybe more. I didn't know, I couldn't think. So I did as she said. I took the gun out of its makeshift holster, laid the light jacket beside it on the desk, and slipped off the tennis shoes. Linda waited until I was well started in my changing, then ran out. She was back in three minutes, now wearing slacks herself, and flat shoes.

"Can you run in those?" I asked critically.

"If I don't keep up, you leave me behind." A trace of her familiar heat.

"All right. Come on."

"Wait. Give me the gun." It was now in the inside pocket of my suit. I hugged it close against my side. Linda waved her hand impatiently. "In my purse. They will search you. They may not search a woman. I will stay very close to you."

"I'm still not sure I'm going to walk right in his front door." I gave her the gunman's gun as I spoke. She stowed it in her purse.

"That is the only sensible way," she said. "If they find you skulking around the grounds peering in windows—and they would, they have dogs as well as men—you would not get within three rooms of Clyde Malish. They would probably shoot you where they found you. But if you knock on his front door with me at your side, wearing your suit and looking official, you may get to see him. At least you won't be dead until they know who knows you came to see him."

"You sound as if you've been thinking about this."

"I am thinking better than you, I think" was all she said.

It *was* windy outside. It was mid-September in San Antonio, the sun had been down for two hours, and the temperature had plummeted below ninety. It was a hot wind that blew in our faces. There was no moon. Malish lived outside the city limits, beyond the streetlights. When we left them behind the night was very dark beyond our headlights. Linda drove, leaning forward so that the dashboard lights cast her face into shadows and planes. She looked pre-Columbian in that light.

"What will we do when we get there?" I asked, to forestall the same question from her. She answered obliquely.

"This still doesn't make sense. The part about David—"

"It makes sense if you think the way he does. If you've gotten your way so long you think everyone's scared to death of you."

"The part about David," she persisted, "at least had some subtlety. It took—"

"And when that failed he reverted to type."

"But it didn't fail. How could it have succeeded any better?"

"It failed because it didn't end things entirely," I said. "He knew I'd keep coming after him."

"Exactly. He knew you wouldn't quit with David still in jail. . . ."

I thought ahead to the man in the five-thousand-square-foot house. How many men would he have there? I expected an army, but maybe not. Malish wasn't at war, not that kind of war. Linda was right, it would be easier to get in with her along. She'd be a problem later though.

"Wait a minute," I said to her as we got close to the address, but she drove straight up to the gatehouse. An ornamental iron gate blocked our path. The house was barely visible through trees a hundred yards farther on. A private security guard in uniform emerged from the gatehouse. I recognized the insignia of his company. He was not what I'd expected.

"The district attorney to see Mr. Malish," Linda told him. That seemed to relax the guard. He went back into the gatehouse and a minute later the gates opened without the guard's reappearing. Linda drove up the stately lane of trees. I wondered if we could crash that gate from the inside. I hadn't given any thought to escape. That would have to take care of itself.

We were met at the front door by a man not obviously armed. He was Mexican, wearing black pants and a loose guayabera shirt. While he was not particularly thuggish-looking, his nose gave the appearance of having been in a few boxing matches or football games, and his overall look backed up the impression. I looked closely at his eyes. Linda said something to him in Spanish which I recognized as meaning literally, "We are here already," but three-word messages that pass between native Spanish speakers often seem freighted with implications I don't catch. "We're here to see Clyde Malish," I said, more to shift the conversation into English than anything else.

He nodded. "I must search you," he said.

"Do you know who I am?"

He managed to contain his terror. "I know who I work for," he said, and patted me down. I held my arms out to the sides to accommodate him.

Linda was right. He didn't search her purse. He took it from her entirely. "When you leave," he said, and put it on the top shelf of a closet. The closet door locked when he closed it. Linda glanced at me.

We found Clyde Malish in his study. The young man ushered us in and left us. It was a big room for a study, big enough to hold a desk, a sofa, and two wing chairs without crowding. It was a sportsman's study, not a scholar's. Only one wall held a bookshelf. On the other walls stuffed things were mounted: a pheasant, two ducks, a deer. The birds were mounted to simulate flight. The deer looked lost in thought, carrying its antlers as lightly as a cap.

Malish wore a guayabera shirt, too. His was baby blue. He looked healthy in a sixtyish way. Gray hairs showed against tanned skin at the open neck of his shirt. His desk was a rolltop, its back against the far wall of the room. He swiveled from it to greet us. "You have another warrant?" he asked me. He didn't acknowledge Linda.

The study was an outer room of the house. There were two windows in the wall opposite the door. To my surprise the grounds were unlighted. It was pitch-black night outside the uncurtained windows.

"I came to respond to your message," I said. He just looked at me. He was still sitting, his hands on his knees. "The man in the ski mask at my house last night mentioned your name," I elaborated.

"I read about that. Crazy business. And he told you to lay off me?"

"That part wasn't reported."

He looked modest. "I don't get all my news from the papers. Listen, it's good you came straight to me on this deal. I wanta find out what's going on, too. I'm lookin' for the jerk. I don't like people tossin' my name around. You know what I mean."

"What do you plan to do to ensure the safety of Mr. Blackwell's family?" Linda asked, as if she were my agent. I was looking at those windows. At first I'd been glad to see them—they meant I didn't have to go all the way back through the house to get out—but they were no friends of mine. It was too dark outside, while the room was well lighted. Someone could have been standing out there right then, watching us. I looked for curtains I could draw, but that would probably send a bad signal, too.

It didn't matter. I just had to do what I'd come to do and worry about the consequences later.

Linda was right, I was no James Bond. I had to say, "Excuse me," and take off my suit jacket.

"Sure, make yourself comfortable," Malish said. I took my arm out of the right sleeve carefully, then reached into the sleeve and pulled out the gun. I'd planned for it to slide out into the palm of my hand, but this not being a movie it hadn't worked that way; it had gotten caught in the sleeve.

"Hey!" Malish shouted, jumping to his feet. "I thought—"

"This is Texas," I told him. "Did you think I'd only have one gun?"

"Mark." Linda stepped close to me.

"And your man didn't search me very carefully because I came looking like a lawyer. You were right, Linda."

"Mark," she said again. She was right in front of me. I stepped to the side to keep Malish in sight.

"Don't interfere, Linda. I didn't want you here but you insisted. If you move your hands again, I'll have to shoot you now," I said to Malish. He raised his hands palms outward.

"I should have called the police," Linda said. She had gotten between Malish and me again. I had to step past her. That put her beside me, barely in my peripheral vision.

"That's why you're here, because I couldn't let you do that. Now, just stay out of the way."

"Mark, don't be crazy. What are you going to do, shoot him?"

Yes. I hadn't told Linda about Lois. She didn't know I had nothing left to lose. After I pulled the trigger I didn't much care what happened. Dinah would be safe. And I'd left a letter for Lois that explained enough to free David, too, probably, given the added evidence of my murdering Clyde Malish.

"Listen," Malish said, stretching out his hands toward me, toward the gun. He didn't look tanned any more. Linda was talking, too; they ran over each other. She kept looking back and forth between my face and my hand. I could see the hand myself, the whiteness of it, like marble. The room was stifling. Why didn't the air kick on? Was healthy-looking Malish one of those old guys who could never get warm?

Linda said my name sharply and waved Malish to silence. He submitted like a meek client. "Listen, Mark," Linda said again. "He is not the one."

"No, of course not. Someone *else* arranged David's arrest to get the case against *him* dismissed." I pointed with the gun. "And last night someone pushed a gun into my stomach and told me to lay off *him*. Who else would have that done?"

"But it's idiotic. Why would he do such a stupid thing?"

"Because that's the way he operates. Brute force."

"No. Is that how he built what he built, by being stupid? Look, did it work, sending someone to your house with a gun? No, it made you furious. It brought you here. He would know that. He would not—"

"Listen, pal, I don't work that way," Malish said. "Hire someone to tell you to lay off *investigating*? That's stupid. Would anybody really think you'd lay off after somebody did that to your family? I sure as hell wouldn't."

"You wouldn't try to stop an investigation, but you're not above having the case you'd actually been charged with fixed. Is that right?"

Malish was warm enough, all right. There was a line of sweat all the way down the side of his face. You'd think in his career people would have pointed guns at him often. You'd think he'd get used to it. But maybe it hadn't happened in a long time.

"Oh, man, I had that fixed all right, but not the way you

think. I had it a lot surer than that. You really think your crummy burglar was gonna get on the stand and testify against me? You think he had the balls for that?"

"When his other option was a life sentence, yes."

"Don't joke around. Life. What would he do, maybe eight? You really think instead of that he was gonna rat on me and then go plead for ten to do in TDC, where I'd know right where he was? Don't kid a kidder. I had little Jesse in my pocket before that indictment ever came down. He sat right in this room and said, 'Yes, Mr. Malish. Don't worry about a thing, Mr. Malish.' He woulda hopped up on that witness stand and slid your case right out from under you. I figured you knew that, that's why you dismissed it. Now, doesn't that make more sense than this cockamamie business of havin' your son arrested and this black gal I never seen before lie him off to prison? I'm gonna trust some maid I don't even know to do that? And trust a jury to convict him on her word? I'm not that trusting a guy, pal."

Well, that was a good line, but he'd had a long time to think it up. Linda chimed in in support.

"Remember the things we talked about that didn't ring true, Mark? Why would anybody do it such a roundabout way, why would they go out of their way to infuriate the district attorney when they could have worked the same scheme against an assistant who wouldn't have the same power to retaliate? We talked about the ways it didn't make sense."

Yes, we'd talked. I had talked far too long, when I should have acted. Lois had been right. I barely listened as Linda kept talking.

She was no longer speaking as swiftly, and Malish had lowered his hands. The frantic edge was off both of them. I'd stood there long enough without firing so that the tension had diminished. What they didn't know was that I'd been trying to kill Malish for the last five minutes. Linda had gotten careless in her advocacy and was no longer directly between us. I had a clear shot at Malish and I was trying to take it. If the gun had had a hair trigger, he would have been dead already. It was my gun, but I hadn't fired it in a long time. I couldn't remember how much pressure was required. I had already pulled the trigger back a fraction of an inch and was trying to force it back farther but I couldn't. I was convinced of Malish's guilt but my finger wasn't.

What was stopping me was the irrevocableness of squeezing the trigger. There would be no appeal, no chance for new evidence. It violated my career to end an argument by shooting someone. That would be a failure of logic on my part. I waited to hear what they had to say, to hear one argument that would convince me I was wrong. I hadn't heard it. I squeezed harder on the trigger.

"And the way it was done," Linda was saying. "Letting David actually go to prison before they contacted you. We talked about that, remember? As if it were designed to infuriate you."

"Or to make me frantic. To make me do what I was told unquestioningly. If they'd put this to me while David was out on bond, would I have acted as fast as I did? It worked, Linda, that's what you keep forgetting. It worked out just fine for him. Just like it was planned."

"I would've stopped it if I'd known," Malish said. He was trying to appeal to me man to man, father to father, as he'd done in my office. He was operating from a mistaken premise that I regarded him as a fellow human being. "I wouldn't let your boy go through that," he was saying.

It was a mistake to mention David. It made me remember his face through bars, his voice breaking as he told me about his first days in prison. I raised the gun. I wanted to hear Malish's voice break like that. He cringed satisfyingly.

"You don't know much, do you?" I told him. "For somebody who's supposed to have such good sources, you're amazingly ignorant." Like that day in my office when he'd claimed not even to know why I'd had him brought there. Ignorance is not only no excuse, it's a lousy defense. It's infuriating. "You slug," I almost screamed. "Don't you—"

"Mark!" Linda threw herself between us again. She put her hand on my arm. The gun was almost touching her chest. I could see Malish over her shoulder, wondering if he could bolt for the door. I wanted him to try.

"Mark," Linda said again. She pulled the gun hard against her.

I looked into her face for a moment. "This is why I didn't want you to come," I told her. "This is why I didn't let you know I had the second gun. Because you don't ever think anyone's guilty. You want proof I don't need. You'll keep insisting on affording him the presumption of innocence and all his rights no matter what it's clear he's done. This isn't a damned case, Linda, it's not theoretical. It's my son. You don't have any part of this. Stay out of it."

She stood her ground. "That's why we have to know the truth, because of David."

I didn't want to argue. "Just get out of the way, Linda." When she didn't move I tried to push her aside. It wasn't easy. She resisted. She was talking to me. Malish was talking. The world was full of talk. I was trying to push Linda out of the way and she was resisting, leaning into me. I said her name and she talked over it. Her hand was on the gun. "No!" I screamed at her. My finger was still tight on the trigger. Her hand closed over it.

I drew back my other hand. It was a fist. When Linda saw what I was about to do she let go of the gun and stepped back. Not in fear. There wasn't a trace of fear in her face.

"You think I care about him?" she said, pointing at Malish. "His rights? Damn his rights." She stepped out of the way. "Do it. Shoot. Now, do it!"

A little space of silence fell. They had both run out of steam at the same time. And I realized the room was cooler. The air-conditioning had finally come on. I stood very still, eyes locked on Linda's.

"You just said it," she said. "He doesn't know enough. You don't believe it, do you? If you believed it, you would have killed him already."

No, I believed it. I believed but I didn't understand. There was one thing I didn't understand, one reaction that didn't make sense. That's why I hadn't pulled the trigger, because if I did I couldn't learn the answer to that one small question.

Against my will Linda had engaged my mind. She had that knack.

And in the next moment I realized what was wrong.

"Just take your time," Malish said suddenly. "You two are the good thinkers. Think this one out."

He was a funny guy, Clyde Malish. Even sweating and pale-handed, he couldn't help getting off good ones.

He and Linda were too preoccupied to get the joke. When I spoke they both looked at me as if I were crazy, as if I'd been replaced by someone they'd never met.

I had eased off the pressure on the trigger. I took my finger off it entirely.

"I don't need to think anymore," I said. "I know just what to do. You'd better call your lawyer."

CHAPTER

15

Myron Stahl came in looking very professional. It was almost midnight but he was wearing a three-piece suit. His face showed grave concern but gave nothing away.

We were still in the study. I had allowed Malish to use the house phone, but I hadn't let him out of my sight and I hadn't let any of his staff in the room. Curtains were drawn across the windows now. The room felt smaller.

"I must say this is not what I expected," Stahl said. "Is the gun really necessary?"

"It is. I am taking a very dangerous man into custody. Your client asked to speak to an attorney and I allowed you to be called. It is a criminal matter. Do you wish to represent him yourself or would you like to call someone else?"

"I'll handle it," Stahl said.

Click.

He shot a look of concern at Malish but didn't approach him. "What is the charge?"

"Attempted aggravated kidnapping, for the time being."

In a low voice, but not low enough, Stahl said to Malish, "I told you not to touch his daughter."

Malish started up from his chair. Stahl backed off a step.

"I'd call that proof," I said to Linda. "Wouldn't you call that proof?"

"I would."

"No," Myron Stahl said, looking flustered for the first time, fluttering his hands. "You weren't supposed to hear that. That . . . that was a privileged communication."

Linda shook her head. "Not when others are present, it isn't. As you very well knew when you said it."

"What?"

"It isn't that kind of proof," I said. "Not against Clyde Malish. It's proof against you, Myron."

That hot wind was blowing dirt against the windows, making a sound like insects scrabbling to get in, or out. "Me?" Stahl said, but after much too long a pause. "I wasn't part of any conspiracy," he went on. "I heard them considering options, and I advised them against anything illegal. That's all."

"It was so stupidly done," Linda interrupted him. "Every step of the way the plot worked out for Mr. Malish, but in such a way that it would infuriate Mark. Drive him insane with hatred. And a man in his position could retaliate."

"But who would want to help Clyde Malish and set him up for revenge at the same time?" I asked. Malish didn't say a word. He had subsided back into his chair and sat there staring at his lawyer. Stahl wouldn't look at him.

"This is silly," he said. "He's talked you out of his own guilt and given you me as a sacrifice. But it will never work. You have no proof. There is no proof."

"So far only logical proof," Linda said. "Such as when you came in just now and we gave you the choice of representing Mr. Malish yourself in a serious criminal matter or seeking an experienced criminal lawyer to do it, as you did for his trial. A cautious man such as you should have done the same again.

But you wanted to do it yourself. You wanted to stay close so you could betray him, as you tried to do with your pretended indiscretion."

"This is silly," Stahl said again. "Do you really think you can obtain a conviction on something as thin as a startled outburst?"

I almost laughed. It wasn't a conviction I cared about. I'd thought Stahl was smart enough to realize that, to see that everything was changed, changed utterly.

"I should have thought of you some time ago," I told him, to draw his attention from another sidelong glance at his employer. "When I had Malish brought into my office. After, by the way, he had consulted his lawyer—you—and decided not to come in voluntarily, further pissing me off. But forget that. When I did bring him in he didn't know what in the world was going on. He didn't even know what I wanted to see him about. I discounted that at the time, of course, but it was something that stuck with me, because it seemed so real. He had no reason to feign ignorance. He should have known what I wanted; there was no reason for him to pretend not to. Because I had already told his lawyer. Told you, Myron. I had already come into your office and grabbed you by the throat and told you I was going to get him any way I could.

"Now, why on earth would a lawyer keep information like that from his client, that the district attorney was out to get him? Unless he didn't have his client's best interests at heart."

I let it stop there, and the silence grew. "Well, of course I did tell him," Stahl said, but that hardly disturbed the silence. I could have told Stahl about the discrepancies that were no longer discrepancies once we'd realized he was behind the Mandy Jackson scheme rather than Malish himself, but instead I let the silence do its work. It seemed to emanate from Clyde Malish, who sat unmoving, staring at his lawyer. The two of them knew the truth, of course, of whether Stahl had warned Malish that I was out to get him.

Linda broke the silence. "We had many indications that Mr.

Malish was behind David's imprisonment and the rest. But many of those indications were clues to you as well, Mr. Stahl, such as the man with the gun who was a classmate of yours. Once we stopped thinking of you and Mr. Malish as the same entity, everything fit. Once we had the thought that a lawyer might betray his client."

"Why would I do such a thing?" Stahl said quietly. He had taken his glasses off and was cleaning them with his handkerchief. "You know what he is. Why would I take such a risk?"

"For money, of course." That was me, joining back in. "That huge illegal income of Malish's, that you only got a pittance of. We know how much he paid you. I figured there was more under the table. There was more, but not enough for you, was it? He says you asked for more not long ago and he turned you down. And I believe him. Why should he have to pay you more? Where could you go? After twenty years of working for no one but Clyde Malish your résumé wasn't too impressive. So you had to be content with what you were getting from him. But you weren't content. You devised a plan. If Clyde Malish got killed or sent to prison, there was only one logical successor to his business interests. You're not the tough guy he is, but you're the only one who knows the business. Something else Mr. Malish tells me."

Again Stahl and Malish were the only two in the room who knew the truth of that.

"It was an elegant scheme." It was. I almost admired it, in the abstract, as a problem in logic. It had looked overelaborate when we'd thought Clyde Malish was behind it. As he'd said, it was too risky, depending on David getting convicted on Mandy Jackson's testimony. He wouldn't have counted on her unexpected acting ability. But for Myron Stahl it didn't matter. Even if David had been acquitted, he could have leaked to me the information that Malish had been behind the attempt. Even that would have set me against Malish. That was all Stahl wanted—for the most powerful law enforcement official in the county to be after his client.

Mandy Jackson on the stand had been an unexpected marvel. Her passion, the depth of her pain. Stahl must have threatened her children with something terrible. I remembered that look of hatred she'd turned on David. But it hadn't been David she was seeing. It had been Myron Stahl or Clyde Malish or whatever implacable manipulator she'd thought had put her there on that witness stand. David was just the innocent recipient of her hatred.

"There's just one thing I wonder," I said. "Was killing Mandy Jackson part of the plan all along? Or was that improvisation? The way it was done makes me think it was planned out. The overdose one more lead to Clyde Malish. That was your worst mistake, Myron. What you did to David doesn't compare with that. Aside from everything else, it was capital murder. It's not the kind of thing you'd do yourself; you must have hired someone. That makes it capital. And I'll bet the killer didn't find her in that drainage ditch. He took her there. That makes it murder in the course of kidnapping. That's capital. Any other way?" I asked Linda.

"You couldn't prove I had anything to do with that," Stahl said.

I laughed. "You don't know criminal law, do you, Myron? You don't have to be the triggerman to get the death penalty. I can tell you three men on death row in this state who weren't even in the same city when the murder went down. But they'll die for it all the same. Just like you will, Myron. I can promise you. When I put those two orphaned children on the stand to identify their mother's picture—"

"Your way is too slow."

We all looked startled, as if the stuffed deer head had spoken. It was Clyde Malish who had, for the first time in half an hour. We all turned to him, but he was talking only to me.

"You say he'll die for it, but you can't be sure. How long have some of those people been on death row? How many of 'em've been reversed two or three times? Even if everything goes right, it takes five years for 'em to get the needle. You really want to wait that long?"

Now everyone was looking at me. I was still the only one with a gun, but I'd been holding it carelessly, pointing at the floor. That wasn't what held their attention. "What's your suggestion?" I asked.

"Just leave. Just walk on out. And everything'll take care of itself."

I thought about it. I wasn't shocked the way I should have been. I'd come here with murder in mind. When it came right down to it, I'd balked at doing it, but that was because I wasn't convinced of Malish's guilt. I was of Stahl's.

Myron saw me thinking about it. "I'll come with you," he said hastily.

I put the gun in my pocket and stood up. So did Malish. "I don't have any authority to take you," I said. "No warrant."

Linda joined me. Stahl tried to follow us to the door but Clyde Malish stopped him with one hand on his shoulder. As I walked away I heard the lawyer making his last appeal.

When I opened the door the ex-boxer was standing there. One hand was behind his back. He glanced at my empty hands, then looked flatly into my eyes. Myron Stahl must have been able to see him, too. There was desperation in his voice when he played his trump card.

"What about your son?" he called.

I stopped. "What about him?" I said without turning.

"Are you just going to leave him in prison? I'm the only one who can free him. I'll testify that Mandy Jackson lied. I'll testify to the whole scheme."

Slowly I closed the study door in the ex-boxer's face, leaving the four of us alone again. When I turned around, Clyde Malish was shaking his head. "I can fix that, too. Anybody can confess. Even if we don't get him out right away I can make things right for your boy in TDC. It'll be easy time for him. I can do that. And when he gets out I'll give him a job."

"Is that what you want?" Stahl said. "Your son working for a gangster, becoming trapped the way I was? Because nobody else'll hire him if his conviction stands up. You know that."

"You shut up," Malish said. He slapped Stahl in the side of the head, staggering him. It was the first violence of the evening; it was strange that it seemed inappropriate.

"He's right," I told Stahl. "Anybody can confess."

"Not convincingly. Are you going to rely on some inarticulate thug of his? When your son's life is at stake?"

He was speaking rapidly but not frantically. He had a good answer for everything. His eyes appealed to me.

Linda was no longer at my side. She was at Stahl's. From Malish's desk she had found paper and a pen. She handed them to the lawyer and said, "Write."

He didn't have to be told twice. He dropped to the couch, pulled the coffee table close, and began writing. "Begin this way," Linda instructed. "'My name is Myron Stahl. I am an attorney, and know my rights. I have the right to remain silent . . .'"

"This ain't the way," Clyde Malish growled. Stahl wrote faster. We were good-cop-bad-copping him, but I didn't know if Malish was playing along or sincere. It didn't matter to me.

Linda continued her dictation. Her eyes stayed on me, and I nodded occasionally. Stahl balked at some of it. We quibbled over words as if negotiating a contract. We wanted details from him that would demonstrate his guilt. He wanted it worded so it could be interpreted to mean that Clyde Malish had been the driving force behind the scheme. And he absolutely refused to admit the murder. Even Malish wasn't a big enough club to make him confess to that. But for my purposes it didn't matter. He gave us details, facts that could be checked out and support the story. How and where he'd met Mandy Jackson. Her mother had seen him without knowing at the time who he was. She would remember.

Reduced to words, it began to sound unreal again. I couldn't quite conjure up Mandy Jackson's image, or even David's. How unconnected he was from it all! And Lois and Dinah were even less involved. There was no need for it even to have touched them. The gunman in our house had been Stahl's last ploy, when he'd thought I wasn't moving fast enough to pin the Jackson scheme on Clyde Malish. And it had worked: it had brought me to this house with a gun.

It was very late when the confession was finished, though it was only two handwritten pages. And Stahl refused to sign it.

"No. Then you walk out and leave me anyway." The little man's voice had firmed up wonderfully.

"Think about it," I said to him. "This is no good to us until we describe the circumstances under which it was given. You think I want to take the stand and say, 'And then we left him there and he's never been seen again'? Don't you think that'll destroy some of the force of the statement?"

But he wouldn't sign. "Once we're out of here," he said.

Linda nodded ever so slightly. I gave in. "Come on."

"What makes you think you're in charge?" Clyde Malish said.

I could have displayed the gun again. Instead, I motioned to Stahl and he scrambled up beside me. The butler with the nose was still there in the hall when I opened the door. Stahl edged past him ahead of me. I guided Linda out next. She might have murmured something to the ex-boxer, but I wasn't sure and his face didn't show it.

It was strange what we worried about walking down that long hall to the front door. I could read our minds. It wasn't bullets in the back we were worried about. We were thinking about that confession in my pocket. I was thinking about how to buttress it with the evidence I had and how to remove the taint of coercion from it. Myron Stahl was thinking that he could make it right once the facts of how the confession was given came out in court. But how to explain away those details he'd known? We were both—no, all three—rehearsing for the courtroom, knowing that what had happened could sound any number of ways when it was played out again, reduced to cold testimony. As we walked out of Clyde Malish's house we were constructing those various realities. We were lawyers again.

CHAPTER
16

The courtroom was abuzz, but I had expected a bigger audience. There were plenty of reporters, of course, and lawyers, but a big trial will draw a lot of civilian spectators as well, just come to see the show. David's trial had. But I guess the aftermath doesn't.

It was Monday morning. Watlin had already called his docket, but none of those cases had been resolved yet. We had first priority. So the jury box was still full of prisoners; lawyers were still conferring with prosecutors. We conducted our hearing amid the rubble of a normal courtroom Monday, as if soldiers took time out from a war to conduct a court-martial on the battlefield.

David was not among the prisoners, though he'd come with them. He was wearing a suit and sitting at counsel table. Lois was beside him, holding his hand. But it was the prisoners David watched. His expression was as if he didn't like being singled out from the other men in gray. David had changed so much in the weeks since his trial, he seemed no longer of our world. He did not look hopeful. His face was a prisoner's shield against hope.

A door opened, the stir rose and then fell in tone, and Judge Watlin resumed the bench. Lois slipped away to rejoin Dinah and Victoria in the front row of the audience, touching my arm as she passed. Lois and Dinah were back living in our house. I'd been there for lunch yesterday and spent the afternoon. While Dinah pretended to do homework at the dining room table after lunch—and listened to every word— I'd explained what would happen today.

"And what if he still doesn't grant it?" Lois had asked. I hadn't decided that yet. Accept Clyde Malish's offer of making things easy for David in prison, break him out, kill Watlin so a different judge would hear the re-urged motion: those were my options. I hadn't considered legal remedies. This was the last chance I was giving the legal system.

"This is the State of Texas versus David Blackwell," Watlin said, reading from the case file as if it were just another case. "Announcements?"

"The state is ready," said Nora Brown. She was still representing the state. Javier was nowhere in sight. I'd heard they'd quarreled over what course to take at this hearing. Nora had obviously won.

"Defense is ready," Linda said. You'd think someone so recently of the D.A.'s office might stumble and say "the state" by accident, but the words rolled off her tongue quite naturally.

Henry was in the audience, no doubt disgruntled at being off the case. I couldn't explain to him the reason, which was that this hearing was going to require some real tiptoeing through the evidence. Only someone who knew all the facts could avoid the danger spots, and I wasn't willing to share those facts with anyone else. I trusted only Linda.

"This is the defendant's motion for new trial," Watlin said blandly. "Defendant has the burden of persuasion. Call your first witness, counselor."

"The defense calls Mark Blackwell," Linda said.

I took the oath as solemnly as if I intended not to violate it, and took my seat. I looked only at Linda. The other faces inside the bar, including the judge's, were too disturbing: David with his hopeless gaze, Nora waiting her turn at me.

"Please state your name and profession."

The witness chair is always hard and uncomfortable. Anyone who sits at ease in it is a fool. It is an act of supreme faith to put yourself in the hands of an expert questioner like Linda. I settled back as she led me through the preliminaries.

"I'm going to ask you about the events of last Wednesday night, September sixteenth. Where were you that night?"

"I went from my office to the home of a man named Clyde Malish."

"Why?"

"The night before my wife and daughter and I had been threatened in our home by a man in a ski mask holding a gun who told me to stop my investigation of Mr. Malish. I went to confront Clyde Malish about that."

"Was that the only reason?"

"No. I also had reason to believe Clyde Malish was behind the prosecution of my son and other events related to that prosecution, such as another armed threat made to me."

"When was that?"

I explained the encounter with the dapper little man. I testified that yes indeed, I had caused the case against Clyde Malish to be dismissed as a result of that encounter. Nora was making notes at a mad pace while I talked, not even looking at me.

We returned to the events of last Wednesday night. "Who was there?" Linda asked.

"Clyde Malish and I and you, Linda Alaniz. Then his attorney Myron Stahl arrived in response to a call from Mr. Malish."

There were murmurs from lawyers in the audience, who knew Linda's status as a potential witness should have made her ineligible to represent David. But we had resolved that in the judge's chambers before the hearing. David wanted Linda and no one else. And Nora did not object. Pass up the chance to go head to head with Linda? No, Nora had had no objection.

Linda approached me. "I'm handing you what's been marked defendant's exhibit one. Do you recognize that?"

"Yes, this is the statement Myron Stahl made and signed that night."

"What were the circumstances?"

"Clyde Malish denied any involvement in the case against my son, David, and the other threats that followed that case. After we discussed the matter for a while we realized that certain things pointed not at Mr. Malish as the culprit but at his lawyer, Myron Stahl. Mr. Malish called Mr. Stahl, he came over, and after we confronted him with some of this evidence he confessed that he had been behind events leading to David's arrest and prosecution."

There was a rising stir in the courtroom. All I could see were the tops of reporters' heads as they bent over their notepads. The buzz must have gotten louder because Watlin called for quiet, but I was oblivious to the noise. My eyes were fixed on Linda's, as if I would be lost if I lost sight of her.

"Whose suggestion was it that he put this statement in writing?"

"Mine."

"Why?"

"For this hearing. What he was saying proved my son was not guilty of the offense he'd been convicted of. I wanted that evidence in writing."

"Were you also thinking of using the written statement to prosecute Myron Stahl?"

"That wasn't what I was thinking. I was just thinking about David."

"Was Myron Stahl under arrest when he made the statement?"

"No. I've never arrested anyone in my life."

"Was he coerced in any way?"

"No."

"Threatened?"

"No."

"Promised leniency or anything else of value to make the statement?"

"No."

"Your Honor, we offer defendant's exhibit number one into evidence and tender it to counsel for the state for any possible objections."

"Which I certainly have," Nora said from her feet, taking the confession from Linda without looking at her. "Your Honor, this statement is false. It was taken under the most coercive possible conditions, when the man who made it feared for his life if he didn't—"

"I object to counsel for the state testifying, Your Honor. If she wants to take the stand and claim personal knowledge of this—"

"I am only informing the Court of what the state intends to prove during our presentation of evidence," Nora said as if instructing a law student. Finally she shot a look at Linda, a look of contempt.

"Let's have the statement up here," Watlin said. "I will delay ruling on its admissibility until all the facts are in." He took the statement from Linda and blandly began skimming it. Judges can do that. If he ruled later that the statement would not be admitted, he would be presumed to disregard its contents. Another legal fiction. I saw Watlin's eyebrows go up slightly as he got to the bottom of the first page of the statement. "Proceed," he said suddenly, almost angrily, as if afraid he'd been moving his lips.

All too soon I was handed over to Nora. I turned my steady gaze from Linda to her. But Nora didn't look at me at first. She read her notes until she found one she liked.

"This Clyde Malish, what business is he in?"

"He owns a couple of appliance stores, I know."

"Those his only businesses?"

"That we've been able to prove."

"You mean he's under investigation by the district attorney's office?" She looked at me. She looked friendly.

"Yes."

"What's he suspected of?"

"Drugs, mostly."

"Mostly? What else?"

"Various kinds of thefts, burglaries, frauds."

"You've mentioned only nonviolent crimes," Nora said. "Hasn't he ever been suspected of any violent ones?"

"I'm sure."

"Armed robberies?"

"Yes."

"Assaults?"

"Probably."

"Murder?"

"One or two."

"Really," she said. "Clyde Malish has been a suspect in murder cases?"

"Yes. None that I know of where they thought he pulled the trigger personally, but—"

"Having people rubbed out?" Nora said wryly. Her famous sense of humor crept into her cross-examination only when she was trying to lull a witness.

"Yes," I said.

"In fact Clyde Malish has been a suspect in scores of crimes. He was under investigation by your predecessors in the district attorney's office, he's under investigation by your administration, and he'll undoubtedly be investigated by your successor, wouldn't you imagine?"

There were little gasps of appreciation from the audience at the word *successor*. Watlin didn't quiet them.

"You know as well as I do, Ms. Brown. You probably would've prosecuted him yourself if Hugh could have ever put together a case against him."

She smiled at me.

"And this is the man in whose house you had your cozy

little chat with Myron Stahl that resulted in this 'confession' you're trying to offer now."

I shrugged.

"No other employee of Malish's was there?" Nora continued, giving Linda a sidelong glance.

"Not in the room with us," I said.

"But there were other people in the house?"

"I assume. At least one other, who let me in."

"Was he armed?"

"Not that I saw."

"It's a big house, isn't it?"

"A lot bigger than mine."

"Myron Stahl had a long way to go to the front door if he didn't confess, didn't he?"

"It was a pretty long way no matter what he did."

"But no one told him overtly that he wouldn't make that walk if he didn't sign this confession?"

"No one told him that overtly or any other way."

Nora paused, calmed down, asked the question flatly.

"Did he seem afraid?"

I hesitated. "He certainly appeared unsettled. Whether he was afraid—"

"—would call for speculation, Your Honor," Linda chimed in smoothly. It was her first objection. There'd been nothing to save me from yet.

"Sustained," Watlin said.

"Would you have been afraid in his place?" asked Nora.

"Objection. Irrelevant."

"Sure is," Watlin agreed. "You can do better than that," he told Nora.

"I'm not sure I can with this witness, Your Honor." She turned back to me. "You knew the circumstances surrounding this statement would be questioned, didn't you?"

"I imagined."

"Then why did you let it happen where it did? Why did you keep Mr. Stahl in this suspected murderer's, gang lord's house, trapped there, while he made the statement? Was it because you realized he wouldn't make this false confession under any other circumstances?"

Linda stirred, but I made a small movement of my hand and she refrained from objecting. "First of all," I said calmly, "I didn't keep Mr. Stahl anywhere. That's just where we were when he started talking, where he came of his own free will. And anyone who's ever taken a confession knows that when the suspect starts talking, you don't call a time-out and take him somewhere else. You let him talk.

"But in answer to your main question, I *did* do something about the potentially coercive circumstances. After he'd finished the statement I didn't have him sign it there. I took him away with me, in my car, and it was only after we were miles away from Clyde Malish's house and sure we hadn't been followed that I had him sign the statement. That's why mine is the only witness signature on the statement. And he did sign it then, far away from any possible fear."

He had tried to renege, of course, but Stahl knew he had to repudiate the document in its entirety. Whether it was signed was of little moment.

Nora looked at me as if I'd just smeared the record with shit. *Come on,* her expression said. I looked back at her innocently. The spectators could see only my face.

"How far do you have to get from Clyde Malish to stop being afraid of him?" Nora asked. Linda didn't even bother to object, or I to answer.

At the end Nora went into the line of questioning we'd known would come, that had to come. She dropped her voice and sounded sympathetic.

"This whole thing, your trip to Clyde Malish's house and obtaining the statement from Myron Stahl, stemmed from your concern for your son, didn't it?"

I didn't deny it.

"David had been convicted of sexual assault and sentenced to a prison term, is that right?"

"Yes."

"Did you go see him in prison?"

"Yes."

"More than once?"

"Yes."

"Were you afraid for him there?"

"Of course I was." I didn't look at David. I glared at Nora. Asking for it. Put it across the plate, Nora.

"In fact, you had him transferred back to Bexar County Jail awaiting this hearing."

"I helped get him brought back."

"Did you see him in jail?"

"Yes. Several times."

"It wasn't much better there, was it?"

"That's a hard judgment to make."

"At any rate, you wanted him out," Nora said. Anyone would, her tone said.

"Of course I did."

"You would do just about anything to get him out, wouldn't you?"

It was a rhetorical question. She didn't care what my answer was. But she wasn't expecting the one I had for her.

"Not anything," I said. "For example, I could have had you yanked off this case and put one of my own prosecutors on it, someone who would've joined in the motion for new trial. Then it would've been easy."

"I'd like to have seen you try that," she said unprofessionally.

"Oh, I could've," I told her.

You could see it on the tip of her tongue. You could also see her looking at me, trying to read me. But she did it anyway. She asked a question to which she didn't know the answer. I think it was simply because she wanted to know. "Why didn't you?" she said.

"Because I wanted you to oppose it, Nora. Because everyone knows you're the best there is. And after this motion is

granted over your opposition everyone will know it's because
David is really innocent, not because of any back-room deal.
Because everyone also knows that you're such a hard, cold,
unfeeling bitch that you care more about winning a case than
anything else, so you'd never make a deal like that if it meant
having one of your convictions wiped off the books."

The courtroom erupted, is the way it's usually put. The
main sound was that intake of breath people perform when
they've seen a near accident or heard a blunt insult. There was
also laughter, mutters not too whispered, and at least one call
of "True, true." Watlin didn't try too hard to regain control. I
just kept looking at Nora. She had the strangest expression,
rueful but not unflattered. She had the expression a pitcher
might have watching a batter give him a long look and then go
back and select a bigger bat.

I flatter myself that my testimony was the most dramatic of
the hearing. We had other witnesses, including Lois. I'd
coached her in the art of perjury. "Keep it simple. Everything
happened just the way it did, except you heard him say 'Lay
off Clyde Malish' there at the end, just before the fight." She
did admirably, straight and pure and absolutely sure of
herself. I don't think anyone could have questioned her
sincerity. Nora didn't. Lois was David's mother; what she said
didn't count. Nora made that point by asking her no questions
at all.

Came the terrible moment we ran out of witnesses and had
to rest. You always think you've forgotten something. Watlin
still hadn't ruled on the admission of the confession, and
without that we had nothing. Nora called one witness: Myron
Stahl.

I knew she must have him, but I hadn't seen him in the
building. He came into the courtroom from a side door,
accompanied by two police officers. The officers took seats in
the audience, coincidentally near Clyde Malish, who had two
men of his own near the back door. Stahl took the stand.

He looked to me like a weasel in a suit. I tried to see him as he appeared to everyone else, particularly as he must have looked through that peculiar binocular vision of Waddle's; he'd try to see not only what the witness looked like but what he looked like to everyone else, the vast majority of whom were not even present. But I couldn't divorce what I saw of Myron Stahl from all I knew he'd done. I saw the moral cavity he was. Watching him take the stand, I was surprised I hadn't left him to Clyde Malish's care that dark night last week.

He did look professional. His clothes were neat and he appeared well rested. If he looked worried at all, it was only the worry of a busy man whose schedule has been disrupted.

"Please state your name and profession."

"Myron Stahl. That's S-T-A-H-L. I'm an attorney."

"Do you practice here in Bexar County?" He was her witness, but Nora didn't sound very friendly toward him. She had dropped into her just-the-facts-ma'am mode.

"Yes."

"Do you know a man named Clyde Malish?"

"Yes. He is a client of mine."

"How long have you represented him?"

"Oh, goodness. Sixteen, seventeen years." Stahl glanced at Linda. She was leaning forward, arms resting on the table, watching him. David was watching him as well. I couldn't imagine David's feelings. Stahl cleared his throat and looked back at Nora.

She cut right to the chase. "May I approach the witness, Your Honor? Mr. Stahl, I'm handing you a document marked defendant's exhibit one. Do you recognize it?"

"Yes."

"What is it?"

"It is a statement I wrote out at Mr. Malish's house last Wednesday night, September sixteenth."

"Was that your own idea?"

"Definitely not."

"Why did you do it?"

"My life was threatened if I didn't."

"Who threatened you?"

"Mr. Malish. Mark Blackwell, the district attorney. She was there, too," he said suddenly, pointing at Linda.

Nora could have done without the outburst. She didn't pursue it. "How did they threaten you?"

"Mr. Malish said, 'We need a confession. You're giving it.'"

"That's it?" Nora asked. Her tone made clear she could have resisted such pressure.

"I said that I wasn't and I rose to leave, but when I reached the door there was a man in the hall who wouldn't let me pass. He had a gun in the waistband of his slacks. I turned back and said something like 'What is this?' and Mr. Malish said, 'I told you you're signing it.' It was very clear what he meant, believe me."

"How did you take it?"

"That I would be murdered if I didn't do what he said."

"What was Mr. Blackwell's part in all this?"

"He just sat there, looking at me—the same way he's looking now. It was obvious he wouldn't intervene."

Nora returned his attention to the confession. "Would you look that over, please, Mr. Stahl?"

He did, then dismissed it. "I've read it before. I wrote it."

"How much of that statement is true?"

"Very little of it." He looked back down at the paper. "It's true my name is Myron Stahl and that I'm an attorney. From there on it passes into fiction."

"Let's be specific, Mr. Stahl. Did you hire Amanda Jackson to give false testimony against David Blackwell?"

"No. I don't know either Mrs. Jackson or David Blackwell."

"Did you then murder Mandy Jackson or have her murdered?"

"Certainly not. I read it in the newspaper like everyone else. I was sorry for her, of course, but it didn't have much—"

"Did you hire a man named Simon Hawthorne to threaten Mark Blackwell to dismiss a case against Clyde Malish?"

"No. No."

The denials and accusations went on for a while. Stahl began sounding more outraged. More perplexed as well. He looked at the judge and shook his head. I couldn't tell what impression he was making. But in truth, Myron Stahl did not look like a murderer and plotter. He looked too hapless. As he squirmed on the witness stand it looked as if the whole world was arrayed against him. We had made a mistake, I thought. We had made him look like a victim.

Don't hit him too hard, I thought when Nora passed the witness to Linda. Linda's first question was innocuous enough, but there was a hard edge to her voice. She wasn't going to try to get on his good side. Stahl knew she was nothing but his adversary. He settled himself into the chair and stared at her. He was going to give her nothing.

"Mr. Stahl, what business is Clyde Malish in?"

"Appliances originally. And investments."

"Does he pay you a retainer annually?"

"Yes. Monthly, actually."

"How much?"

Stahl looked haughty. "That would require me to divulge a privileged communication."

"No, it wouldn't. And as we all know, the attorney-client privilege belongs to the client. Clyde Malish is here to object for himself. Your Honor—"

"Answer the question," Watlin said.

Stahl glanced at the judge resentfully. His mouth went prissy. My God, I thought, he just doesn't want to say how much he makes in front of this roomful of strangers. What an ambitious little man. Could anyone else see that?

"It comes to roughly sixty thousand dollars a year," Stahl finally said.

"Thank you. And is Clyde Malish your only client?"

"No."

"Who are some of the others?"

"They might not want their names revealed. And they are

not here to assert their privilege. I may do so on their behalf, as I'm sure we all know."

"Telling us their names won't violate any privilege. Just tell us the name of one other person you've represented in the past year."

Nora stood. "I don't see the relevance of this, Your Honor."

"All right, if you can't answer that question, I'll ask another one," Linda said. She rode right over Nora's "sidebar remark" objection, and Watlin let her. "Why does an appliance dealer need to pay sixty thousand dollars a year for legal services?"

Stahl was ready for her. "He is also an investor, as I said. I help him acquire and sell properties, advise him on investments, write contracts of employment and purchase. All sorts of things."

"And for that he pays sixty thousand a year? Writing contracts?"

"For all I've said and more."

"You mentioned a criminal case against Mr. Malish that was dismissed. Did—"

"I didn't concern myself with that. He hired a criminal lawyer for that."

"But you were in the courtroom sometimes, weren't you?"

Stahl couldn't deny that, and didn't. "That doesn't mean I was involved in the case," he said testily. "There are people in this courtroom who aren't involved in this case."

"So you didn't involve yourself in Clyde Malish's criminal activities?"

"No."

"But you knew about them."

He hesitated. "No. Well—that one case I knew about. And of course I heard rumors."

"But you had no part in that."

"No."

"He paid you sixty thousand dollars a year only to write contracts for him. Did he have any other attorneys on retainer?"

"Not that I know of."

"But you had nothing to do with his criminal activities."

"Your Honor—" Nora began again.

"Let's go on to something else," Linda said. "You testified that you didn't know Mandy Jackson."

"True."

"Are you aware that Violet Wentworth, Mandy Jackson's mother, has already testified here today that—"

"Objection, Your Honor, this is a violation of the rule, to comment on another witness's testimony."

"Suppose, then," Linda said, as if showing a law student how to formulate a question, "suppose—hypothetically— someone had seen you with Mrs. Jackson two months before David Blackwell's arrest. Would you have an explanation for that?"

"Yes." Stahl was pleased with himself. "I said I didn't know the lady. I didn't say I'd never met her. I did go to her home once. I don't remember her mother being there, but perhaps she was."

I turned and looked a few rows back at Gregory Stillwell, sitting beside Mandy's mother. He was wearing, I was sure, his only suit, black for funerals. His arm was around his sister, but his attention was focused on the front of the courtroom. He didn't look back at me, as if keeping secret the fact we knew each other. Or he was just so intent on Myron Stahl he saw no one else.

"Why were you there?" Linda asked Stahl.

"I went at Mr. Malish's direction, to offer Mrs. Jackson a job."

"A job. As a maid?"

"No, as an accountant. She was a college student, I believe. Mr. Malish told me he thought he might be able to use her."

"Did she accept the job?"

"No. In fact, she became rather hostile when I mentioned Mr. Malish's name. When I left, it struck me as rather a fool's errand."

"Not only that, it is also a rather remarkable coincidence, wouldn't you say, that two months before she accused David Blackwell of raping her you were at the home of this woman who was central to the conspiracy you deny initiating?"

Stahl looked unperturbed. "If it is coincidence, it is nothing more than that."

"If—?"

His tone grew confidential. He was sharing with us. "It occurred to me later that the purpose of sending me there might have been simply to make sure that I was seen with Mrs. Jackson. In case later Mr. Malish needed to falsely accuse me of being the instigator of this scheme, just as he's doing now."

Linda sat there for a moment. It's lovely when a witness theorizes. "Then you think there *was* a plot to have David Blackwell arrested and tried for a rape he didn't commit?"

"I know nothing about that."

"But why should Clyde Malish frame you for it, Mr. Stahl? Couldn't someone of less value to him have taken your place in the frame? Someone worth less to him than sixty thousand dollars a year?"

"I don't know." Stahl hadn't thought far enough ahead when he offered his explanation for being seen at Mandy Jackson's house. He was regretting it.

"So we are left either with the fact that there *was* a plot to convict David unjustly, or the remarkable coincidence of your contact with the woman who accused him—before that accusation was made."

"Objection, Your Honor," Nora said. "First of all, I don't think that was even a question. If it was, it calls for speculation."

"Leave it unanswered, then," Linda said. "Let's go to the fact that Mark Blackwell was accosted under a bridge by a law school classmate of yours, Mr. Stahl. In your confession you admitted hiring Simon Hawthorne for that job. Is that true?"

"No."

"Would you call it another remarkable coincidence?"

"No. I'd call it a lie." The courtroom stirred again. I could feel the back of my neck growing warm. "I've seen no evidence that really happened," Stahl continued. "That was just something they put in my statement to further incriminate me. You'll notice there were no witnesses to the incident other than Mr. Blackwell himself."

Stahl looked satisfied with himself again. I looked at the judge to see if he caught Stahl's expression, that of a man who'd come up with a great explanation. But Watlin wasn't looking at the witness. Or at me. He was staring off across the courtroom, head cocked to show he was listening. Making a great show of impartiality.

Linda did Stahl no more damage. I thought she'd done plenty. I didn't see how anyone could believe him. If only he didn't look like such a schlump. He looked much more like the victim of such a scheme rather than the mastermind.

Linda had convinced one person. David's eyes hadn't left Stahl's face. And I noticed Stahl couldn't look at him. The bailiffs were watching David. And one person hadn't needed convincing. Clyde Malish, too, didn't take his eyes from his lawyer. Stahl was meat. No matter the outcome of this hearing. No matter the police protection. Clyde Malish and I had no agreement about Stahl's fate. I couldn't have stopped him if I'd wanted. And I doubted I'd be able to convict him after the fact. He would be careful. More careful than Myron Stahl had been.

That didn't even take into account Mandy's uncle, Gregory Stillwell. I wouldn't have been Myron Stahl, not for all Clyde Malish's income.

Nora mopped up a little on redirect. On recross Linda asked Stahl only one short series of questions. "You didn't know Mandy Jackson?" she began.

"Not really. That one brief meeting . . ."

"She meant nothing to you?"

"Not really," Stahl said again. "As I said, I sympathized—"

"Did you murder her yourself?"

"No. I—"

"Then you had it done? You hired someone to inject her full of lethal heroin—"

"No!"

"—which killed her as it was meant to do, and then dump her body in a sewer ditch? A woman who meant nothing to you, who only happened to have access to David Blackwell?"

"No, no, no. I never—"

"But someone did, didn't they, Mr. Stahl?"

"Not necessarily. She might have done it herself. Maybe she didn't measure right, and she—"

"If you were going to shoot up heroin for the first time in your life, Mr. Stahl, wouldn't you choose someplace other than a drainage ditch to do it?"

"I—I would never," Stahl began, stumbling. He was leaning forward, almost falling out of the chair. "Maybe whoever she was with panicked—"

"I have no more questions."

"Panicked and took her there, dumped the body—"

Stahl was holding out his arms as if in supplication, or as if he were carrying a body himself. His voice broke on the last word and he stopped. He looked down, as if finally seeing Mandy Jackson's body. He seemed on the verge of tears. More likely it was his own body he saw.

"You are excused," Judge Watlin told him, and before he could rise Nora added, "The state rests."

It was so abrupt I found myself on my feet. My hand was rising as if I were in a classroom, wanting to be called on. I wanted to prolong the hearing, keep it going indefinitely. Watlin gave me a hard, dead look. I remembered all there was between us. I'd almost had to threaten him even to bring David back from prison early for this hearing. I didn't want this left in Watlin's hands. When he retired to his chambers I would follow, I thought. I would tell him whatever he wanted. My resignation, my support—

"Counsel may be seated," Watlin said. "I do not need to hear arguments. The facts are simple and the legal arguments are well set out in the briefs by both sides."

Myron Stahl had left the stand and taken a seat in the audience near his police escort. Watlin was alone at the front of the courtroom, high above us behind the bench. His expression was stern but somehow placid. He knew what he was going to do.

"I expected this decision to be very difficult," he said. "It has turned out to be remarkably easy. I had thought I would have to take the matter under advisement for some time. That turns out not to be the case.

"The law concerning granting a new trial because of newly discovered evidence is clear. The evidence must be such that the defendant could not have discovered it through due diligence prior to trial. The defendant in this case has met this prong of the test. Next, the evidence must be such that the court is of the opinion that if the jury had heard the evidence at trial their verdict might have been different."

Watlin moved his hands on the bench in front of him slightly. My God, I thought, he's reading a prepared speech. Everything we'd just done was meaningless. He'd made up his mind before he heard a word of testimony.

"But there is a prerequisite to this requirement," Watlin went on solemnly. "The evidence must, of course, be credible. The trial court is the sole judge of the believability of the evidence at the motion for new trial hearing.

"The evidence adduced in this hearing could literally be called incredible, in its nonlegal sense. This Court in twenty years of practicing law has never heard of a conspiracy remotely approaching the one alleged by the defense in this case. The state has rightly pointed out that the defendant bears a heavy burden of proving his allegations before a new trial is granted. In this hearing that has been an even heavier burden because of the remarkable nature of the alleged newly discovered evidence.''

John, John. I would have done anything. Give me more time. Bring me proof, he'd begged, and I saw now I hadn't brought him enough. But there was no more. *John,* I thought. *If you only had a son.*

"The evidentiary conflict between the state and the defense is clear. There are no subtle distinctions of perception. The defense says this conspiracy occurred. The state says nonsense. The crux of the dispute is between two witnesses, both of whom have good reason to lie. Mark Blackwell's son has been convicted of a serious crime and sentenced to prison. Myron Stahl is accused of orchestrating that conviction, a serious offense in itself. Both are officers of the court. If they were not at such loggerheads, I would be almost professionally obliged to believe both. But in this instance I cannot. They are diametrically opposed. This is the only difficulty the case presents. There is corroborating and impeaching evidence on both sides, but it is thin or explainable.''

Watlin still hadn't looked at me. He didn't have the balls for that. But then, to my surprise, he did. He had been looking out magisterially, addressing the audience behind me. The reporters. Now he lowered his gaze to me. He didn't change his expression.

"So the only question is credibility. That is the difficulty, yet that is what makes my decision surprisingly easy.''

He wasn't going to go my way. He was going to protect himself. But it wasn't me. It was David. David's freedom was the stake here, not my reputation, or Watlin's.

"I have known Mark Blackwell for twenty years,'' Watlin continued. "I have never heard his integrity questioned. I daresay he has never before had such incentive to lie as he had today. But I do not believe that incentive was the force behind his testimony. I have spent ten years as a trial judge sifting

truth from lies. No doubt I have made mistakes. But I have
never before had the benefit of personal knowledge I have in
this case. I believe Mr. Blackwell's testimony. I believe he was
told that his son had been falsely accused. I believe he tried to
uncover the roots of that accusation. And I believe he succeeded.

"That leaves the second prong of the test equally simple. If
the evidence I have heard today had been heard by the jury, is
there a significant chance their verdict would have been
different? Undoubtedly so. I do not in any way impugn the
verdict reached by those twelve jurors. Knowing only what
they knew, hearing only what they heard, their verdict was
absolutely appropriate. But they did not have all the facts.

"The motion for new trial is granted. Bond is reset in the
pretrial amount. And as a final matter, I would urge the state
to consider carefully whether this prosecution should be
brought again. I cannot say what a jury would decide, but I
know how I would rule in a bench trial.

"That is all. The parties are excused."

My heart flipflopped. Suddenly I thought I understood. All
my worry had been needless. Watlin had intended to grant the
new trial all along. As long as I took the stand. *Bring me proof*,
he'd begged me, but that was only to cover him, to make his
decision look right. As long as I was the one who testified,
David would win. It was still political with the judge. I was an
elected public official. That meant that at some time more
than half the voters in the county had approved of me. Maybe
they still did. If I put on a good enough show at the hearing, I'd
undoubtedly have the sympathy of that magic fifty-one percent. Who was Myron Stahl against that? A nobody. No
political clout at all. It *had* been an easy decision for Judge
Watlin.

Maybe I was wrong. Maybe Watlin had decided based on
the evidence, disregarding other considerations. I would never
know.

I was the closest to David. I was the first to grab him. I was shouting, I think, but I wasn't the only one. I held David against me and hugged him as hard as I could. It was as if he had just become substantial again, after months of ghostliness. He hugged me back.

"I don't know how you managed this," he said in my ear. "I don't know whether to be happy or furious. I don't—"

"Just feel whatever you want," I said. "Just feel. You can do anything. You're free now.

"You can stick those up your ass," I added. This was to the bailiff who was standing beside David with handcuffs. He looked embarrassed.

"I guess we can do without the cuffs. But we gotta go back."

"Like hell. You heard the judge. He reinstated the bond. I've already made that bond."

"He's still gotta come back to the jail to be booked out. It'll only take an hour or so." The other bailiff was beside him now, looking equally embarrassed and equally adamant.

"You're not taking him," I said.

And then the sheriff was there. Their boss. He shook hands with me. I had lots of friends. The sheriff shook his head at the bailiffs and they remembered business elsewhere. "Screw the paperwork," the sheriff said to me, and winked, and drifted off. Another favor.

David looked relieved. He turned away, looking for Lois, I imagined, but the first person he saw was Vicky. She was standing there calmly in the chaos. David didn't sweep his wife into his arms. He looked at her as if trying to remember who she was. I realized I'd never heard anything about Vicky visiting David in jail. I'd assumed she had.

Lois appeared. She gathered David to her. "We're getting out of here," she said. Then she left David to Vicky and slipped close to me.

"Don't come with us, Mark," she said softly enough that only I could hear. Her voice was not unkind. "I'm going to take him miles away from here and try to pretend it never happened. We'll have the best lunch he's had in his life. Someplace so unlike jail he'll think he just woke up from a long, bad sleep. If you're there, he won't be able to forget."

"You think he ever will?"

"I think I can help him. Let him walk out without anyone from this place with him, Mark. I don't mean to hurt you. But you were there when it started and when it finished. Maybe if you're not there now it'll be easier—"

"All right."

She beamed at me. "Thank you. Come to dinner tonight. At home." She remembered: *her* home. "At—you know. Mark—"

I thought she was going to tell me what or who to bring or not to bring. "Yes?"

"You were wonderful on the stand," she said.

She managed to get David out into the audience and moving toward the door. He didn't look back for me. Maybe he assumed I was with them. Reporters lit on him like flies. Forget, I thought wryly. Lois was still touchingly naive at times. Time hadn't changed her. She had Dinah by the hand. Dinah did look back. She smiled and waved at me and gestured for me to join them. I shook my head and smiled back. The little group—the nonlawyers—made it to the door and out.

I was still inside the bar. I turned around and saw that Watlin had left the bench. But he'd be back. My eyes fell on the prisoners in the jury box. I looked at them more closely than I had in years. The only one who stared back had hooded eyes and armfuls of tattoos. There were no scared kids among the gray men, no one who looked as if he didn't belong.

There had been only one unusual element to David's case: David himself, an innocent. Anyone could have sat in his chair, plucked at random from the general population. The facts were unusual but the elements of the game that had sent

David up were the usual ones: an ambitious prosecutor accustomed to winning; a judge with more on his mind than the case itself; a witness with an ugly story to tell.

People swept by, congratulating me, but the greetings grew hastier. It was Monday morning, the day wasn't through. Lawyers were talking to prisoners. The prosecutors in the court had already spread the day's files out on the counsel table again. The courtroom was producing its familiar hum.

Linda was beside me, as always. Just once, when no one could see, she took my hand and squeezed it.

Her resignation was still warm on my desk.

"Better enjoy this triumph," I told her. "Defense lawyers don't get many."

She had been studying me—looking, I knew, for a wound left by Lois. After I spoke she smiled.

"Too early for lunch?" she said.

No one was watching us. Everyone was bent over files or arguing with each other. As effortlessly as if there'd been no interruption, the court had resumed its normal business.

"Let's get out of this Goddamned courthouse," I said.

POCKET BOOKS
Proudly Presents
Jay Brandon's New Courtroom
Thriller

RULES
OF EVIDENCE

■

A Pocket Books Hardcover
March 1992

The following is an exciting preview of
Rules of Evidence. . . .

San Antonio's most prominent black attorney, Raymond Boudro, has his first encounter with Detective Mike Stennett, SAPD, on the witness stand.

"Would you agree with me that the east side of San Antonio is the area with the greatest concentration of black citizens?"

Stennett appeared to think about it. "Yeah," he said.

"And in fact, the five men you saw on this street corner on this day last July were black."

"Yes, they were."

"Well, it's a black neighborhood, so that wasn't unusual, was it?"

"No."

"Then why did you note that in your report, Officer? That the men were black."

Stennett grew a little exasperated. "The report's written on a form. You have to identify all the suspects by race, sex, height, all that. Even the witnesses, you have to say what race they are."

"Yes," Raymond agreed. "In the space at the top of the form where you list people, you have to fill out all that information. But you also included it in the body of the report, in your written summary of the events leading up to the arrest." Out of the corner of his eye Raymond saw Rebecca looking at the offense report, frowning a little. "Do you have a copy of your report in front of you?" he asked Stennett.

"I think I left it on the table over there."

"Let me show you." Raymond approached the witness stand with long strides and stood beside the cop, pointing at the page he was holding. Judge Marroquin was looking down on them with some interest. It would have been nice if the witness had flinched from contact with the black defense lawyer, but Stennett only squinted at the report.

"You see?" Raymond pointed. " 'Drove to the location, saw five black males on the corner.' That is what 'BMs' stands for, isn't it, Officer? Black males?"

"Yes."

"Why did you note that? Did you think it added something to your probable cause that the men were black?"

"No."

"But you already said that when you drove by and saw them your suspicion increased. So seeing five black men together increased your suspicion that a crime was in progress. Would it still have looked suspicious if they'd had a basketball?"

The cop laughed and shook his head. He didn't look concerned, he looked like a man mired in silliness. When the elongated silence inflicted itself on his attention he glanced at the defense lawyer, who was staring at him. "I'll wait as long as it takes you to think of an answer," Raymond said charitably.

"I didn't think that was worth answering. It wasn't them being black that made me suspicious. It was five able-bodied young men standing on the street on a workday afternoon with nothing else to do. That made me think maybe they earned their living illegally."

Raymond looked at him seriously. "Do you know how many unemployed people there are on the east side of San Antonio, Officer?"

"I know how many drug dealers there are."

"Perhaps you can regale us with that information

if someone asks you a question that requires it. *My* question is whether you know how many unemployed people there are on the east side of town, how many young black men who can't find a job worth having because they don't have the education or qualifications or opportunity to find such a job."

Stennett held up his hands in a gesture of surrender. "We're way outside my field of expertise now, Counselor."

"But you'd agree that the percentage of unemployment is higher on the east side than in San Antonio generally?"

"I don't know."

"I thought you were rather expert on the east side," Raymond said. He resumed his seat. For the first time he opened the file beside him. Becky looked at him. The thickness of the file made her suspicious that Raymond hadn't been kidding when he'd announced he was ready to proceed on this motion. The defense lawyer riffled through several pages before he found the one he wanted.

"We've established, Officer, that the east side of town, where you're assigned, is the area with the largest black population in town, but in fact it's not exclusively black by any means, is it?"

"No." The detective sat alertly in his chair.

"No more than fifty percent black, would you estimate?"

"I wouldn't know that," Stennett said carefully. He had some vague idea where this was leading and he wasn't going to help.

"You see a lot of people over there, don't you, Officer? Would you say more than half of them are black? Or don't you make those distinctions?"

"I'm not a census taker," the cop said.

Rebecca Schirhart stood up. "I'll object to any

more of these statistical questions, Your Honor. The witness has already said he doesn't know, and I don't see the relevance anyway."

"Okay," the judge said noncommittally. That was the kind of ruling you got from Judge Marroquin unless you pressed him. The appellate court couldn't reverse his rulings if he didn't make any. Maybe he was sustaining the prosecutor's objection. It didn't matter. The judge would know the answer to Raymond's question. Even on the "heavily black" east side, less than half the population was black. The judge knew that. And this was all aimed at the judge. It didn't matter what the evidence showed, all that mattered was how the judge felt about what he'd heard.

"Let's say half then," Raymond said to Stennett. "Now, I assume you do have personal knowledge about how many people you've arrested. How many would you say it's been in the last five years?"

Stennett rolled his eyes. "I have no idea. Hundreds. Maybe thousands."

"Let's make it easier. How about just in the past year?"

Stennett was silent, calculating. He was intrigued. "Not that many anymore," he speculated. "When I'm undercover I don't arrest every drunk or speeder I see. Maybe one a week, maybe fifty the whole year?"

Raymond nodded. He had a piece of paper in his hand. Pieces of paper lent weight to questioning. "Very good, Officer. Would you disagree with the figure sixty-two?"

"Sixty-two arrests in the last year? No, I wouldn't disagree with that." Stennett was no longer casual on the witness stand. He was in a sort of stance, preparing himself.

"And what percentage of those arrestees would

you estimate were black?" Raymond asked. He put down his piece of paper, picked up another. He looked over its top at the witness.

Becky was poised to object again, but she saw the relevance of the question; so would the judge. The judge was watching the witness with interest. It was okay, Becky could clean all this up on redirect.

"I guess that would be about fifty percent too," the detective said.

"Would it surprise you to learn the figure is more like eighty percent?"

"Yes, it would."

Raymond approached the witness again. "Do you recognize this as a computer printout of the names of people you've arrested in the past year? And do you see this column that identifies the race of the suspect, as taken from your reports?"

"I object to defense counsel testifying," Becky said. The judge didn't even look at her. He was leaning over to look down at the list. Stennett was studying it too.

"I can't vouch for the accuracy of this," the detective said slowly. "But I wouldn't be surprised if the percentage is a little higher than the percentage of black population."

"Because the sight of a black man makes you more suspicious than the sight of someone non-black? Because you're more likely to investigate a black suspect?"

Stennett appeared to be keeping a rein on his temper. "If this is true I think it's because statistics will show—"

Becky didn't let him finish. "Your Honor. This is not only unfounded—the only testimony about the accuracy of these statistics comes from defense counsel himself—it's also irrelevant. The witness has testified to specific facts that gave him reasonable suspicion to conduct a frisk of this particular suspect. What's happened in other cases is irrelevant."

The judge didn't rule on the objection, but his expression as he looked at Raymond clearly said, "She's right." Raymond had taken the point as far as he could anyway. He returned to his seat. "Let's talk about the specific facts then, Detective Stennett. What was it that made you think you had to frisk Claymore Johnson?"

"As I said, fear for my own safety. I was afraid he might be armed."

"In fact, what you said was there's always the possibility a criminal suspect is armed and you're always concerned for your safety when conducting an investigation. Under that rationale, you'd be justified in searching everyone you see any time. What was it made you fear this particular"—the word was aimed at the prosecutor—"suspect was armed?"

Stennett looked sure of himself again. "The bulge in his pocket."

Raymond stood up. He was wearing his best suit, a midnight-blue pinstripe he had bought after his last major triumph in court. Three years later the suit still fit well, though maybe a little tight in the waist and thighs. Raymond put his hands on his hips, flaring the wings of the jacket back like a gunfighter. "A bulge about this size?" he said.

Stennett glanced at Raymond's pants. So did Rebecca. So did the judge. "Could be," Stennett said. "I didn't study the size of it."

Raymond reached into his pocket and pulled out a roll of bills, folded once and held by a money clip. "Did it occur to you, Detective, that it might be cultural, for a black man to carry a lot of cash on him? Maybe because he doesn't have credit cards, because he can't *get* credit?"

"As a matter of fact, I thought it might *be* cash," Stennett said. "That would fit the profile. Guy on the street corner, gathering a crowd, showing something, big wad of cash in his pocket—"

"So you thought it was cash, not a weapon."

"Possibly."

"And a black man with a lot of money just has to be a drug dealer, doesn't he, Officer?"

Stennett wanted to say it. You could see the words in his mouth. Becky was tense on the edge of her chair, willing her witness to keep quiet, but the cop wasn't looking at her, he was looking at Raymond, at the taunting look in his eyes. And Stennett said it.

"Not necessarily. He could be a pimp."

The silence was beautiful. Raymond held it, staying on his feet, not asking another question, the conductor of silence. Judge Marroquin was staring at the witness. It was the kind of joke the judge might have laughed at in another context, even have told himself, but in his courtroom, coming from a white cop, it was appalling. Judge Marroquin had been a well-respected member of the community for many years, but a Mexican-American man in his fifties would remember prejudice, remember the personal effects of it. As a matter of fact, Raymond knew that as a teenager the judge had been arrested and held in jail for a day just because he happened to be the only Mexican in the vicinity of a grocery store robbery in an Anglo neighborhood. The judge always referred to the incident in talks to juries. He didn't laugh about it.

"Or a lawyer," Stennett said weakly.

"I pass the witness," Raymond said.

Some months later, Mike Stennett is identified as chief suspect in the murder of a black man. A surprised Raymond Boudro hears that Stennett wants to see him.

Raymond's first impulse was to jump up and run out and see if it was true. Instead he kept his seat and told the intercom to send him in. And it was true. Mike Stennett walked into the office. Raymond still didn't rise. Stennett looked around the room someone had turned into a large office twenty years ago by knocking out a wall between two bedrooms. The office now comprised most of the back of the old stone house.

The desk would have been too large for a smaller office. It was walnut, with a glass-covered top. If Stennett had taken his best leap and stretched full-length across the desk he might have been able to touch the lawyer's chest with his outstretched hand. Behind Raymond were windows. To his left and right, against the far side walls, were floor-to-ceiling bookshelves. There were a couple of chairs in front of the desk and a large leather couch against the wall behind them. Raymond had taken the desk and the couch in lieu of a fee years ago. They weren't quite to his taste but they were as sturdy as old trees. His son used that couch for a trampoline sometimes.

"Usually at this point I say 'How may I help you?' In your case I'm really curious about the answer."

Stennett didn't like standing like a supplicant in front of that ambassadorial desk, so he sat, which wasn't an improvement. "You may have heard, I need a lawyer."

"I'd like to take your money, but you know you have a lawyer. A good lawyer." The Police Association, the cops' union, kept a defense lawyer on retainer to represent its members in criminal cases and disciplinary proceedings before the Civil Service Commission.

"Yeah, I know. A good lawyer very interested in staying in tight with the union. And I don't know what the union's position on me is gonna be. No thanks. I don't plan to have to watch my back all through this thing."

Raymond was intrigued. Why would Stennett think the cops might not support him? But that's not what he said. What he said was, "And I was the first lawyer you thought of."

"I've seen your work, remember? You're good."

"Very impartial of you. Let's cut the crap, Stennett. You think hiring a black lawyer to defend you'll make some jury think you're not a racist after all?"

"Maybe." Stennett leaned forward earnestly. "You want me to deny it? I won't. If that helps, swell. But you think that's my main consideration? You don't see me trying to hire Lawrence Preston, do you? I want you because you're as good as there is in this town. And you know the territory; I won't have to lead you by the hand every step of the way. And if you being black helps me out the least little bit in front of a jury I want that too. Because I'm not taking the fall for this. I didn't do it and I'm not going down for it."

At least he wasn't going to admit he did it and expect Raymond to defend him anyway. The lawyer studied the cop. Stennett had cleaned up a little, at least he'd shaved this morning, but he'd need more work to be presentable. Sweat veiled his forehead.

" 'Fraid it'll cost you business?" Stennett asked. "Or do you have a policy against white clients?"

Raymond's voice stayed cool, as if he were framing a hypothetical problem. "Tell me why I should try to get you off the hook for murdering a black man."

Stennett came around the desk. Raymond swiveled to face him but didn't rise, which finally gave the cop the chance to lean down over him. "I'll tell you why. Because you can win this case. Because this is gonna be a big public trial and the publicity of winning it'll do you as much good as it does me. Because I didn't do it, and you can prove I didn't."

Raymond was intrigued again by the repeated denial. His face didn't show it. "There's nothing worse than a confident client," he said.

"I'm no optimist. I know you can do it because I've seen you do it. Remember Abner Moses?"

"Nah, Stennett, doesn't ring a bell. Abner who?" The sarcastic tone was because Abner Moses had been Raymond's biggest case, a capital murder trial that had generated a lot of publicity at the time. Abner had been a small-time thief elevated to the big time when he was charged with killing a cop during a flight from a bungled burglary. The State had had an eyewitness and Abner had had the kind of record that would make the jury's choice on punishment between life and death easy. Death row was crowded with guys like Abner; everyone had expected him to fulfill his destiny by joining them.

"You weren't a witness in that case."

"I watched some of it," Stennett said. "Of course there were a lot of cops in and out of the audience. Muttering things like he never should've got to the station after the arrest. I think I was the only one who wasn't convinced. I could picture Abner going in an open window, but I couldn't see him pulling the trigger on anybody."

He hadn't. And the jury had reached the same conclusion. If Raymond closed his eyes he could still call up with textured clarity that moment of the foreman saying, "Not guilty"; Abner looking at Raymond puzzled, his life not having prepared him for those two words; Raymond's palm indented with four tiny slashes where he'd dug his fingernails in so hard he cut himself; the prosecutor, that son of a bitch Frank Mendiola, turning to Raymond with that look of loathing that made the moment even sweeter.

He didn't close his eyes. "Yeah, luckily the jury saw it that way too," Raymond said casually.

"And nobody was even bitter about it, 'cause by the end of that trial they knew they'd had the wrong guy. You didn't just poke holes in the State's case, you *proved* he didn't do it."

Stennett was looking at him appraisingly, wondering if Raymond still had what he'd had then. Raymond wanted to disabuse him of hope. "That was three years ago," he said. "Damn few miracles since then. You can't hope for them. Not too many innocent people get charged with capital murder. Or murder."

Stennett was untouched. He stared flatly. "I have to be innocent? I haven't noticed you require that in clients."

Raymond tried to read him. Was this a murderer two feet in front of him? Stennett looked capable of it. Those hands could do it. Those eyes wouldn't weep over it.

"This case'll do something for you Abner Moses' didn't," Stennett continued. "Where are you? You should be one of the busiest criminal lawyers in

San Antonio. Everybody saw what you can do, and what'd it get you?"

"I do all right."

""You get your share of pushers and junkies, that's true. But where're the big cases? When some rich boy gets arrested, your phone don't ring."

"Where do you live, Stennett, comic books? There aren't that many big cases."

"But there's some, and you don't get any. Why didn't Abner put you over the top? You know why. Because he was a nigger."

Raymond came out of his chair. Stennett didn't back up, so they ended up standing almost nose to nose, except that Stennett had to look up. He did so calmly, not watching Raymond's hands. "Thought I'd go ahead and drop the big one so we didn't have to live in suspense," he said. "Abner Moses didn't make you a star 'cause he was black and he was a crook. He didn't do that one, but that didn't make him innocent. But you get a cop acquitted, put him back on the force working for truth and justice, that's something people won't forget."

Raymond pushed him away. Stennett wasn't caught by surprise or off balance, so it took effort, but Raymond managed it. Their eye contact didn't break. Raymond almost wished he'd taken a swing at him instead, when Stennett had dropped the word. But Raymond had been too slow to react, the occasion had passed. It's the things you don't do you come to regret.

"You're not innocent either."

Stennett looked surprised. "What do you mean?"

"What happened to Claymore Johnson?"

Stennett made a face as if Raymond had changed the subject to something trivial. "Claymore? Claymore's in Atlanta." Raymond, startled, made a mental note to call Claymore's mother. But Stennett was going on. "Or Kansas City. Vancouver, British Columbia. Wherever he ran into a big city or an ocean in whatever direction he took off in. He's not dead, I'm pretty sure of that. The guys that had it in for Claymore, they're not subtle. They're not ones to do a Jimmy Hoffa with the body. They'd want it layin' in the street. Object lesson, you know?"

Raymond looked unpersuaded. Stennett waved a hand at him. "I know. You mean me. I didn't do nothin' to Claymore. Except run a scheme on 'im that worked out damn better than I expected. That's the truth."

He sounded sincere. Raymond pictured him using the same tone of voice in court. He could picture jurors nodding along.

"Sit down," Raymond said. After a moment's hesitation Stennett returned to the client chair. Raymond took the one next to it, leaning close. "Now in a minute, I'm going to tell you to tell me what happened. Before I do that you think about it. You know it'll never go beyond me. You know how lawyer-client privilege works. But let me tell you how *I* work. I don't work for somebody who lies to me. You can lie to everybody else on this planet, you can lie to God and your mama, but if you lie to me I'm gonna find it out. I'm gonna investigate the hell out of this thing, and I'll know what happened. If I find out you lied to me I'll get you for it. And I don't just mean withdraw from the case. I mean I'll ruin you. Y'understand? Now if that condition's all right with you, you sit there and collect your thoughts for a minute and then start talking. But if it even crosses your mind to lie to me, you get up and walk out now. Now."

Stennett looked at him levelly. He nodded. "That your standard speech?"

"Mouthing off is not one of the choices I gave you. Talk or walk."

"Jesus, don't go Jesse Jackson on me. All right. So you're taking the case?"

Raymond pointed at the door. "I've had every kind of low-life scum, degenerate, reprobate, human sewage in this town walk in that door and I haven't turned one away yet. If I've lowered my standards that far I can lower them a little farther." He held up a finger. "On my conditions. I mean it. The truth or I ruin you."

Or maybe both, he thought.

Stennett took his time, pursing his lips. "All right," he finally said. "Now? You're my lawyer, starting now?"

"Starting now. So take your time, think about what you're going to say. I'll know if you're lying. You better believe that."

Stennett took a long breath and looked away for the first time in minutes, out the windows where the day was turning crystalline, presaging summer.

"I didn't do it," he began. "I had no idea who it was gonna be on the slab when I went to the M.E.'s office. I wasn't on duty that night but I was cruisin' anyway. . . ."

Raymond's eyes narrowed. It would have been too easy if Stennett had confessed. But Raymond would know the truth before this thing was over.

"Back up," he said. "Let's get the details straight. What time was it when you got the call and what street were you on? Picture it. Tell me everything. . . ."

Look for Jay Brandon's
RULES OF EVIDENCE
Available in Hardcover
from Pocket Books
February 15, 1992
Wherever Hardcover Books are Sold